# UNDER GOD'S ROCK

UNDER GOD'S ROCK

Cover Art by Reina Marie Urban

Printed in the United States of America

ISBN: 978-1-09839-623-7

ISBN: 978-1-09839-624-4 (ebook)

*For Cindy, forever my rock in the storm*

# UNDER GOD'S ROCK

—— *A Novel* ——

## TIM URBAN

# Contents

# HISTORICAL PREFACE

Although overshadowed in history by the Battle of Hastings, fought on 14 October 1066, another clash that took place just nineteen days earlier in the north of England was crucial to Normandy's subsequent conquest of the ancient Anglo-Saxon kingdom: the Battle of Stamford Bridge.

In 1066, the most immediate threat to Harold Godwinson, the newly crowned—albeit disputed—King of England, was not from Duke William (the Bastard) of Normandy but another equally ruthless rival for the throne, King Harald Hardrada of Norway. In an often bloody challenge to his southern neighbor, Hardrada also claimed that he, not King Svein II, was the rightful ruler of Denmark. And as Denmark had long claimed sovereignty over much of England, Hardrada held that he was the true successor to the recently deceased King Edward the Confessor. Another combatant for the English crown, Tostig Godwinson—Harold's recently exiled younger brother whom had been stripped of his lofty, and lucrative, position as Earl of Northumbria, seeking revenge, gained an audience with Hardrada in Nitharos, Norway, and urged him to press his claim by force.

While hardly naïve of Tostig's intent to seize the crown for himself, Hardrada needed no prodding and quickly assembled an invasion fleet of 300 ships; with his vast treasure loaded aboard his kingship, the *Great Dragon*, he then set sail across the North Sea with 8,000 men in September 1066. Recruiting more men to his cause during brief stops at Shetland and Orkney, Hardrada then rendezvoused with Tostig's waiting fleet of twelve ships in Scotland and, with an army swelled to nearly 12,000 warriors, began marauding along England's east coast. Adopting Tostig's suggested invasion plan,

i

the Norsemen entered the Humber estuary and rowed their longships up the River Ouse toward the wealthy Northumbrian city of York. Forced to moor his fleet near the village of Riccall where the river narrowed such to make them vulnerable to an ambush, Hardrada—anxious to seize what he believed to be rightfully his—ordered his trusted marshal Styrkar to prepare his warriors for battle.

On 20 September, with their boar-head helmets and chainmail byrnies glistening in the sun, the heavily armed Norsemen began marching northward along the banks of the Ouse. Near the deserted village of Fulford, they easily shattered a shield-wall of Saxon thanes and fyrdmen sent out by the teenaged brother-earls Edwin and Morcar in their foolhardy attempt to slow the invader's advance upon York. Hardrada wanted to sack the city and strip it of its riches but was convinced by Tostig—who was secretly guarding his future wealth—that it made no sense to start laying waste to his soon-to-be new kingdom of England. It was unnatural to Hardrada and his men not to plunder after a victory but, quashing his barbarian urges, he agreed with Tostig and, instead, sent a third of his warriors back to help guard the ships at Riccall.

Still, Hardrada did not trust that Edwin and Morcar fully appreciated his uncharacteristic restraint and so demanded that they deliver 500 hostages to him to ensure there would be no skullduggery. The time and place of the hand-over were agreed upon. And, on 25 September 1066, after a long, hot march, the great warrior-king of Norway and 8,000 of his best men arrived at the place where the roads from all the four corners of Yorkshire met at the crossing of the River Derwent: Stamford Bridge. Expecting no fight this day, the lightly armed warriors were surprised by Harold Godwinson's hard-riding Saxons as they rested beside the river; by nightfall dead and dying Norsemen laid scattered over the field. A blood-dripping Styrkar—Hardrada's fearless front-center sword—was among them. Alive.

*How much more grievous are the consequences of anger than the causes of it.*
Marcus Aurelius, *Meditations*

# PROLOGUE

## NORTHERN ENGLAND, 25 SEPTEMBER 1066

I killed the man not because I was cold and wanted his coat, but because he was mocking me. His head landed between his horse's back hooves. Turned up to me, his face was still laughing even. So I kicked it as hard as I could. It bounced once on the dirt track, then rolled off so far into the high grass beyond I couldn't even find it. And that was too bad because I wanted to kick it again.

Fat and filthy and stinking of mead, with rings on every finger but no thumb on either hand, he was a thief. A thug. And with his broken old cart pulled by his broken old horse more a scavenger than the ravens I left picking him apart.

None dimmed in my mind's eye, I can still see the Saxon's headless body humped like a dead ox on the muddy ground of that dark English forest as clearly as when I shut his rot-stinking mouth that long-ago day. Just another fly-infested corpse lying amidst the countless battlefield dead he'd stripped of every glimmer of their worldly worth, he got what he deserved.

Lice-ridden and crusted with blood, the Saxon's coat was a shabby thing. More hide than leather. Soot-soaked. The lining coarse wool pricked with straw. And an ill-fit for a fat man, at that. One dead ugly beast wrapped in the skin of another, it was bare worth an acorn's weight of pitted slag. Only, I was a warrior, not some purple-born prince or preening peacock, and couldn't care less about wearing the stench of another man's filth. Slogging through the numbness of a battle's end. Cold. Wind. Rain. Half-naked and shivering. More of my blood on the ground than in my veins. My pride had no answer for that. So my generous offer to the Saxon: a trade of my hard-earned arm rings for that rat-skin he called a coat—three well-turned serpents all thick with the purest silver.

But for the look he gave me, I might as well have struck him square between the eyes with a rock. A look bewildered. Angered even. His snarl the same as if a fresh pile of mule shit just squished up between his toes. Pushing back his hood to expose his dark, brutish face and red-rimmed eyes, the Saxon opened his mouth like to shout. Yet the absurdity of my thinking a man with a convict's large blackened **C** branded on his brow might trade for anything only made him laugh.

"What farce!" the Saxon howled. "Give my coat? Look at you—like puked up with the pig's breakfast. Nothing but shit and blood. Why, not a stone's throw farther you'll fall over dead and I'll pluck your parts for free. Pocket all your bits of bead and bone and shine. Then I'll pick that teary little glint right off the black of your cold, staring eyes on the chance there's a fleck of silver in them, besides!"

Mocking me as a whore-suckled swine not worthy of the air I breathed—a lacy-waist—a silk-slippered eunuch—of running like a little girl—cowering in the shadows, yellow as the piss running down my leg—"No courage to die like the rest of those pagan brutes now rotting on the river's edge"—the Saxon then boasted that had he a weapon at hand he would split me wide and rip out my quivering rabbit-heart. "Go home, old woman," he shouted, "and attend to your loom and spindle, for you are but a pitiful failure in the test that proves a man." Then, feigning like to hit me with his whip, he spit in my face and laughed.

I didn't bother to wipe my cheek, but his insult was like to burn my flesh.

On any other day, I would have ripped out his tongue with my bare hands and rammed a sword so far up inside him that its gleaming blade would have come wagging out of his mouth instead. Only, I said nothing. Did nothing. For there was truth in the man's charge—my monstrous shame—my skull feeling like to split apart under the weight of dead men strewn into every crevice of my brain.

Unarmed and wearied by the daylong fight at the river, I turned away from the man, his loudmouthed taunts, and continued along the forest track. Only, in my slow, hobbled step, his slop-sided little horse quickly drew even, then passed, the old cart's creaking wood wheels throwing up mud nigh to my waist as they rolled close beside me. Not to be ignored or robbed of his fun, spitting his Saxon filth—"Fish-stinking son of a whore! I've seen more fight in a man strung between two trees with his bloody balls stuffed in his mouth!"—suddenly, the air hissed and I felt the sting of his thick braided whip across my naked back.

Hard-bitten and tearing my skin, for several heartbeats I could not breathe or even see.

Tripping over rocks and roots and tangled brush with my footfalls landing I knew not where, I stumbled in a deep rut in the road and fell hard to my knees.

Another harsh crack. Once. Twice. Ten times. More.

Spooked by the sound, the Saxon's whip-scarred little roan whinnied and reared up in panic, lurching forward in short, jarring hops. Casks and crates began spilling the cart, cheap birch wine drenching the ground. Out from under a ragged burlap cover, a jumble of steel the mudfoot Saxon had scavenged from the battlefield clanged over the sideboard in a heap: bloodied greaves, gauntlets, helms, and swords splashing down in the mud around me. With blue eyes wide and blond beard streaked red, the helmeted head of a Norse warrior tumbled to the ground besides.

"Calm, you bastard! Calm!" the Saxon shouted as he whipped the frightened cart-horse with red-faced savagery. Studded with sharp slivers of stone that tore into the roan's flesh like fangs on bare bone, feral dogs could not have done the work of that whip any bloodier. Mad with pain, thrashing this way then that, the screaming animal suddenly wrenched half around and crashed its flailing, iron-shod hooves against my spine. Knocking me to the ground face-first, the wild-eyed horse then trampled me into the thick, black mud.

All the breath went out of me. Pain came. Then laughter.

Broken in every way, I was ready to die. Wanted to die.

Only, as the Fates, those three old spinners of every man's destiny, had crossed my threads with those of such a simple-minded beast—all blood and mud and fists and fury without a thought of consequence—the easy kill wasn't enough for the Saxon. He wanted to have fun doing it. He wanted me to suffer, to beg for mercy. And, like a cruel joke played well, he wanted to laugh long and hard about it.

Just so, bounding down from his upturned cart and whooping out how "no finer coat could such a swine of a man ever hope to wear than a slop of shit-stinking mud!" that foul-mouthed Saxon never really had any choice but to end up with his head splashed down in a puddle of horse piss with a big, dumb smile on his face.

Ignorant. Arrogant. A fool. He didn't know not to mock a dying man. Not to torture him just to hear his mewing cries. Or that a man so bloodied and beaten could fast make him a ghost.

For Fate! Strange Fate! Like a rock-fall on my head—as I laid clawing at the ground amidst the detritus of battered helms, hammers, and blood-spattered shields spilled from the scavenger's cart and scattering the track—impossibly, my hand raked over the distinct downward-pointing quillons of a sword hilt stomped deep into the muck.

Bare trusting but with a heart twice quickened, I squeezed the hilt full round.

Imagining that at any moment its faint, metallic glimmer would be turned into but a cold gray stone by some trick of the gods, I then slowly slid my off-hand along the endless length of the unseen blade pointed straight ahead of me. Shining up out of the murk with an almost ghostlike iridescence—broad and beveled with a deep groove at the centerline, its face serpent-marked and meticulously etched with elaborate filigree closest to the hilt—in every detail it seemed more art than weapon.

That is, until the moment I curled my fingers over its preposterously thin edge.

A sword like no other, a terrifying jag of iron-twisted steel that had been wielded in battle only hours before by my king—a man like no other—my eyes needed not see the sword to know that it was a merciless killer every inch.

Another crack of the whip. Insults. Laughter.

Whirling around, the Saxon's head was on the ground even before the surprise could show in his eyes. I took his coat. I took his horse. I took his whip. And shoved it up his ass.

Two bends down the river, I heard voices, laughter. Three men on a high stone bridge making a raucous game of dropping large rocks on the dead, bloated bodies of my Norse brothers as they floated slowly past.

They never saw me coming.

So began a long night of dogged butchery.

For while I had lost all else that day, I still had my pride—and the bloody sword in my hand. Harald's sword. King Harald. My king. The king of all Norway. The bravest, most ruthless warrior I have ever known. A man I swore to serve. To fight for. To die for.

And a man I failed like no other.

I am Styrkar. The Wolf. Born in the valley of Thorsardalur. Iceland. The son of Kvendulf Skullsplitter. The father of Kalf and Thjodulf. Slayer of the Nord Wood ogre. And while I expect nothing of my life will be remembered to this world, I was King Harald Hardrada's field marshal at the grievous battle of Stamford Bridge. Fought along the banks of a dark Northumbrian river near the English stronghold of York on a cold September day in the year 1066, it was the day my world went black.

Ambushed, outnumbered, and poorly armed, we were whipped and the memory is bitter—a thousand shapes of death haunting me like the shrill echoes of a scream. Mutilated bodies floating the river, bloodless and naked and jagged bone jutting. An arm, a leg, a headless torso—an ax-head impaled—being shunted this way then that by the rippling red eddies. Men squirming in piles, crawling on their bellies, desperate for cover like maggots fleeing the light of day. The spattering strikes of broadsword on bone and spear-thrusts to kill. Ghost white hulks slopped in gore. Screams of agony growing faint, then no more. Norwegians, Danes, Icelanders, Greenlanders, Shetlanders, Orknians, Faeroes, Swedes, and Scots—so great was the feast of Norse flesh spread upon the banks of that unhumble stream as to feed the ravens the land over.

So it was, in the dead of a moonless night, I rode that headless Saxon's old cart-horse down the river's wooded bank and, killing anyone foolish enough to try to knock me off its back, returned to the massive fleet of warships I'd left anchored under guard near an abandoned village far to the south. First, I saw the bright orange glow in the sky. Then the tall fires raging on the water. Hearing the enemy before seeing them, rooting around like wild pigs along the swampy edge of the little village, I watched in horror as the ships were being burned by giddy, torch-bearing Saxons determined to kill every Norse-man they could find.

No matter. For, I would gladly die to be rid of the burden of my soul-crushing dishonor. So did I unsheathe my bloody sword, put my spurs to the screaming little roan, and charge straight at the stunned Saxons. Galloping through a gauntlet of spearmen, swordsmen, ax-men, and archers amidst a volley of vulgar threats to make my gruesome end, I shouted back at them that "no true son of the mighty Thor will ever have his skull hung from a gatepost without a fight!" And what a gruesome end it was, as all those Saxons who dared to close within the arc of my massive scything blade left their heads rolling in my wake.

Beating a fast path to the *Great Dragon*—my king's ship, a thirty-five bench beast with a belly filled with treasure won in battles the world over—I rode that half-dead cart-horse straight out into the middle of the river before clambering off its sinking body, grabbing hold of a halyard dangling from the warship's bow, and pulling myself up over the gunwale.

A much smaller ship—a river raider—was roped to the *Great Dragon's* sternpost. It would slow my escape, but it was too late to do anything about it. For, knees high and splashing through the shallow water, the Saxons were closing on me fast.

Putting the *Great Dragon*'s small surviving crew to oars amidst a rain of spears and flaming arrows, I promised those English bastards that I would be back—and that there would be a massacre. I shouted at them that I had ten good men with me and that I would be returning with ten thousand more. "Mark my words," I said. "Led by the Lord of Hosts himself, Odin's legions of undead warriors will march down on you out of the great hero's hall in the sky in such numbers as to feel their footfalls shake the very Earth!"

And I meant it, every word.

Only, not two hours into our undermanned attempt to sail King Harald's huge dragon-ship back across the rough waters of the North Sea to our beloved Norwegian homeland, the sea goddess Ran held us to account for our battlefield failure, loosing a storm upon us like none before or since. With our sail shredded and our masthead snapped in half and fallen into the sea, we were at the mercy of the voracious water. So it was, in the black of night being driven by the howling winds we knew not where, the Fates delivered us into the jaws of pure evil.

Wrecked on the rocks of an enemy shore far opposite that from which we sailed and immediately attacked by a hard-charging army of horse-born men across a wide, stony beach, we were in a fight for our lives. Amidst a rain of flaming arrows, a man of seemingly great self-importance pulled up his massive black stallion at the water's stony edge, stood in his saddle, and began shouting threats at us. Tall and round with a blunt nose, and wearing a bright blue tunic under his steel jerkin, he had a long-sword in his hand, and fire in his eyes. Speaking a crude Norse dialect mixed with bits of French, I could hear only snatches of the endless insults he was bellowing at us between the roaring gusts of wind.

"Norse scourge! ... Pestilent dogs! ... As claimed by ... the Comte de ... lord of the sovereign state of ... Your ships and their contents ... now the property of Ponthieu ... and so demand ... lay down your weapons or suffer—"

In the next moment, any notion of our surrender to these little fops dancing around on the shore with their fancy head feathers blowing in the wind was emphatically quelled when my iron-tipped spear ripped into their fearless leader's throat and shut his mouth forever.

Truth be told, putting bravado aside, the situation was desperate. Kill or be killed. With our massive sea-dragon floundering on the rocks amidst a vicious hand-to-hand fight against the dead man's bloodthirsty minions, I would not give up my king's ship or the gods-bequeathed riches aboard to the sea or any number of men. Fighting with a murderer's zeal, I was determined to redeem myself for my battlefield loss, to restore my lost honor upon those bloody gunwales, to be victorious, or die a death the world would long remember.

I accomplished none.

Broken and burning, the *Great Dragon* was doomed. With my men grabbing up one ponderous oak chest after another filled with King Harald's treasure from below-decks as fast as they could and piling them in the hold of the sleek, little river-raider lashed to the warship's sternpost amidst a crash of waves, we'd moved hardly half of the vast hoard when the smaller boat's beam began to sag badly and its hull to creak; riding low in water now splashing over its top-strakes, it could bear no more weight. Shouting "Abandon ship!" whilst slashing my sword at the swarming Ponthievins, determined to leave nothing aboard the *Great Dragon* but their severed heads, I watched as my men struggled to load the last of seven identical wooden chests marked with the runic symbols for *Gydingaland*—Norse for the "Land of the Jews." I knew them to be much heavier than all of the other treasure chests, for I had helped to carry them out of a cavernous vault carved in the rock beneath King Harald's hilltop palace in Nitharos just hours before we set sail from Norway in our ill-fated attempt to conquer England. There was no thought whatsoever that I would leave the chests behind as I knew them to be filled with enough pure gold looted in the Holy Land to buy the city of Jerusalem itself.

With my brave warriors being cut down one after, I ordered the men "To oars!" as one last, small chest was heaved over the *Great Dragon*'s gunwale and dropped on the deck of the overburdened river raider. A simple stone box seemingly of great antiquity radiating a strange, golden glow through the squall's swirling mists, the chest was like no other salvaged from the *Great Dragon* that day; the treasure it held within seeming to be not of this world.

With a great shout to the raging sky, the last man alive on the savaged king-ship, suffering a whirlwind of slashing Ponthievin steel, then selflessly cut the thick hemp rope lashed to the smaller boat lest we all sink to the seafloor together. With its hull moaning, weighted down by the remainder of Harald's hard-won treasure, the *Great Dragon* then disappeared in a froth of whitewater and blood.

Ordering my seven remaining men to push off with their oars against the huge boulders littering the Ponthievin shore, with a loud cracking of beach stones under the raider's dragging hull, we then began rowing out to sea with an arm-burning fury. Shunted this way then that by rocks unseen as the violent, up-and-down hogging over the crashing waves threatened to break the boat apart amidships, at last, the seafloor fell away, and the incessant banging against our keel stopped when the last rock was breached.

The rain dwindled to a drizzle. The wind diminished. My stroke count slowed.

When far removed from the perilous shore, I gave the order to raise the oars.

The men fell back off their benches, gasping for breath, exhausted. One brave warrior, his guts running out so fast you would think a pit of vipers nested inside him, was slumped dead over his oar. Quick-slipped into the water with his sword tied to his hand, he was fast on his way to Valhalla even before the circling vultures of the sea took their first bite.

Slumped down with my head rocked back against the gunwale, I too was tasting blood. A tooth was missing. My jaw ached. And my throat was gashed nigh to the windpipe. Just so, I was their *Styramathr*—their captain—and I would betray no weakness to my men. With the ship rising and falling on the heavy chop, we sat in silence, not a moan, not a prayer.

Suddenly, off our stern, voices shouting in the darkness.

The unnerving sound of oar blades slapping on the water.

The Ponthievins were coming.

In a voice as harsh as ever, I ordered the men back to their oars.

They did so without a moment's delay.

I felt for a small iron key deep in the pocket of my tattered britches. One by one, I approached my hacked, bloodied men at their benches. Showed them the key. Asked them if they were ready to go to Valhalla. To sit at the long table in the great Heroes Hall in the sky. To eat and drink with the greatest warriors that ever called the Northland home.

Six times I heard a deeply convicted "Yes."

"There will be no capture of our king's treasure," I said in a rising voice as I shackled each man to his oar. "Even if we have to row this ship to the bottom of the sea."

"Fight. Die. And then fight again!" they cried out in unison.

And, O! How those six brave men earned the skald's eternal glory-shout in those next murderous hours!

# I

## THE PHANTOM DESTROYER
*UPPER NORMANDY, 26 SEPTEMBER 1066*

The wind laughed. And the boy on the rock laughed back.

Wild-eyed and turning circles atop a massive boulder lodged in the face of a towering sea cliff, the smoke, smolder, and arrogant noise of the onrushing storm was just the thing to liven up an endlessly boring life lived on the thin edge of nowhere.

Demanding the boy's immediate return to the safety of their shack, his mother's shout that he was stupid—"A brain like a hoof!"—was nothing new to six-year-old Wido. Nor was ignoring any attempt to interrupt his fun. Pointing at his ears and feigning confusion at her too many, too fast words, with a big smile and a wave he, instead, dropped onto his belly and began inching across the rock's rain-slickened surface much as a larval bug just washed up out of the dirt. Indeed, taking malicious pleasure in turning his mother's tremendous love for her only child into utter anguish, with his arms thrown wide and pretending to glide like a falcon in flight, Wido then dropped his head over the edge of the rock as if ready to swoop upon whatever fantastic beast might come crawling out of the turbid water below.

Mother could scream all she wanted. Her threat of whipping his backside didn't scare Wido a whit. The sky sizzling above him. The earth crumbling around him. None of it scared Wido.

God didn't scare Wido.

Only, as many times before, Wido had already crossed that fine line between thrill and terror, and no full-throated squeal of death-defying joy could disguise it. Telling himself that the little flinching of his muscles, that twisting of his gut was not fear, he was determined to not turn back up the steep-sided gully. Flee into his mother's arms. She would win. Scream. Call him stupid for doing such a dangerous thing. Punish him.

So ... no.

Rubbing down the gooseflesh on his arms, Wido again stood on the rock; glanced back at his mother; and then stepped a little closer to the edge.

Mother screamed.

Wido laughed.

And the thunder rolled.

"God's Rock," the cliff-dwellers called it. Huge. Black. Its smooth, glassy face bulging toward the sea. With deep fingerlike depressions grooving its sides as if grasped by a massive hand, the local legend was that God had flung the otherworldly rock through the stars and crashed it down on Earth in warning of the brutal end awaiting all who denied His existence and power.

But as a rock is a rock in the light of day, it was during the darkest and stormiest of nights—a night like tonight—that the beauty of the brute black stone came to shine: a yellow-green olivine glow as if encased in hot crystals. Resplendent atop the towering white limestone cliff, a beacon for sailors upon the sea, the rock burned through the night's dark mists like a massive jewel in the crown on a massive god's head. A guard of Heaven for time eternal.

Only, now—with a prideful planting of his little flag—Wido claimed God's Rock as his own. For Wido, not God, was the supreme ruler of his life—God's big, black book of laws be damned. And Mother? What with Wido always out playing on the rock in defiance of her loudly forbidding it, she called it the "Devil's Throne." That the name was meant to shame him to a better behavior proved a miserable failure.

Wido would do what he wanted to do, when and where he wanted to do it.

Although clouded in his memory by the smoke of his ongoing rebellion, there was a time when Wido believed his mother to be the most beautiful, pure, and innocent creature God ever put on the Earth. Her smile gentle and voice sweet, her every movement light as a butterfly in flight, he lived for those times when she would grasp his hands, swing his feet up off the ground, and twirl him around and around in circles, flattening "angel rings" in the tall grass fringing the cliff-top before drawing him back against her breast in a kiss-smothered hug. Her laugh loud and playful and her big green eyes alight with the joy of their spirited adventures in the forest, in the fields, and down on the beach, those days now seemed so long ago to Wido—that short time in his life when the rampant violence of the world was yet unknown to him. Before his father, a humble woodcutter—a man he had loved, followed everywhere, and mimicked his every action—walked off one summer day, ax in hand to fight for the glory of some heavenly king named God—or some earthly god named King. It hardly mattered which one to the blubbering three-year-old boy the woodcutter left standing at his wife's side. A fortnight later—with Wido's face buried in his mother's skirt as she tearfully picked over a cart piled full of bloodied weapons and dead men in the village square—the splintered old ax made the trip back to the shack on the cliff. His father did not.

Lying amidst the faded yellow windrows of late September leaves and staring up at the stars on a cloudless night, Wido snuggled against his mother's side and asked: "Is God here with us right now, Mother? Like your big storybook says—in every rock, every tree, and every cloud in the sky? Even in the air we breathe?"

3

"Yes, Wido," his mother answered as she stared into his keened green eyes and traced a light finger over the curve of his spine. "He is everywhere."

"And if I talk really loud, can He hear me say how much I hate Him for killing Father? How much I hate Him for making you cry?"

Adelvia of Arques, barely twenty years old and already three months a widow, jerked her head up off the ground as if struck by a knife. Shocked by the sudden blasphemy spewed from her son's mouth like the Devil's own venom, she smacked a hand across Wido's wan, guileless face, then grabbed him by the shoulders and, shaking him hard, admonished him for his hateful words. "We do not speak such words, Wido! We do not think such words! We do not question God! He is our Lord. Our God. Our Savior. Ruler over the highest mountain in Heaven down to the deepest cavern in Hell. He sees all, knows all, and is all. Everything to come in our lives is by His command. And His every act has a purpose beyond our understanding."

With Adelvia's voice breaking and her heart in tumult—never before having struck Wido—she then pulled her trembling son close and, telling him how sorry she was, smoothed a hand over his reddened cheek. Kissing his forehead and gently hushing his loud sobs, she spoke to him in words now soft and slow. "I fear for you. Fear for your soul. You must believe that God is a good and loving God. For to believe in Him with your whole heart will keep the Devil's head pinned under your heel forever."

Her eyes glistening with tears, Adelvia then picked up her son's chin and looked into his red, swollen face. "Only, sometimes it's hard. Serving God blindly and without question, following where He leads you, trusting His plan. Our place among the angels must be earned. The climb to Heaven is steep. And we will not pass through its gates without a struggle—the struggle of faith." Adelvia's voice again rose. "Bow down to Him, Wido. Praise His Holy Name. Honor Him as King of kings, Creator of every creature of the Earth. God must be loved! He must be feared! Do you understand me, Wido?"

Wrapping the bewildered boy in a crushing embrace and kissing him all over his downcast face, Adelvia let out a sudden sob and started to cry. Wiping his mother's big, scalding tears from her cheeks with his little fingers, Wido quietly asked her through a sob of his own: "But why, Mother? Why does God do bad things to people? Why does God make us sad?"

Trying to force a faint smile through her tears, Adelvia answered, "God will test us. Test our faith in Him. Test our love for Him. Test our worthiness for the life He has given us. And through these trials, He will reveal His plan for our lives, make us understand how much He loves us, and make us love Him even more with the promise of our eternal lives to come."

Running her fingers through his dark, wavy hair, Adelvia pulled Wido close and whispered in his ear, "Ours is a big, powerful God, Wido." She opened her hand under his thoughtful gaze. "He can hold the whole world in the palm of his hand. And, remember—like Father always told you—the bigger our God, the smaller our Devil."

Walking hand-in-hand with his mother back toward their little one-room shack on the edge of the cliff, Wido looked up to the sky and mumbled under his breath, "Maybe our god is too big if we always have to be scared of Him squashing us like bugs anytime He feels like it."

Adelvia jerked Wido toward her and asked him to repeat what he said.

He responded, "Nothing."

The slap across his face hardly hurt at all.

As defiance ignited an excitement that obedience did not, Wido—who lived so close to Heaven—seemed destined to burn in Hell. A sinner from the day he was born—lo, a victim of Adam's original sin—rebellion was in his blood. And he would eat as many apples off that forbidden tree as he pleased.

Of an age when peace and innocence flourish in the hearts of most young boys, Wido's core had become uncommonly hard since his father's death. No longer the kind little boy anxious to help his widowed mother do her countless household tasks—feeding the chickens and cleaning their coop, carrying water from the creek, and gathering kindling wood in the forest— he had developed a thorough contempt of anyone telling him what to do:

God, Mother, and, especially, priests. They were mean like Satan, and Wido hated going to church—the nearby ringing of Saint-Aubin's bells making him cringe more than any thunder-boom in the sky. Refusing to worship this cloud-bound phantom who kills on a whim, he would not bend to the will of any of these self-righteous God-mongers; right and wrong were what Wido judged them to be in his own mind—ever-changing and unique to a specific moment in time.

Worse still, there was an increasingly malicious boil in Wido's blood—malevolent thoughts creeping out of the recesses of his brain, daring him to do dastardly things just for the fun of it. Tearing the wings off butterflies. Whipping birds' eggs against rocks. Twisting the mane and tail of their new little mule into painful knots.

God? Wido believed God to be as much a figment of imagination as Satan. Fantastic beasts written onto the pages of a big storybook and preying on the ignorant of the Earth.

And Mother? Her screaming never stopped. Her slaps turned to spankings turned to beating his backside with that same walking stick she had so meticulously peeled and rubbed smooth for him while out exploring the forest on a happier day. Reading to her son every night from the gospels, struggling to imbue him with the basic Christian traits of goodness, humility, and restraint, to guide him onto the path of eternal light, Adelvia hoped that Wido would become so miserable from the painful punishment of his sinful ways that he would soon end his youthful rebellion and flee back into the arms of God.

Only, Wido had just begun the fight. In fact, he thought it preposterous that his mother—night after night kneeling before the little silver man hanging on a cross above her bed—was so naïve to think that her troubles could be turned into joy just by whispering a few prayers.

And, oh, the power that little man had over her.

"When has He ever done anything you want?" Wido ridiculed his mother's nightly ritual of adulating the crucified Lord, rubbing her little beads, whispering prayer after prayer to God, Jesus, Mary, Joseph—and ten thousand Saints! So too, it angered Wido to hear his name in every one of her prayers. Father's name, too. "A waste of time, Mother. Does God even listen? Does he care? All's the same before and after your prayers. Tell Him to send a sign. Make a miracle! Turn water into wine! Rock into bread! Raise Father from the dead!"

"Testing God is a fool's game, Wido," Adelvia snapped at him. "You must have faith."

"Faith! God has done nothing but make you his slave, Mother. Praying your fingers to the bone day after day, feeding on the scraps He throws you, hoping someday He will make good on His promise to set you free—only that you should die still chained to that little silver cross."

"Enough, Wido," Adelvia shouted through sudden tears. "You will live by God's rules, not your own. Not a single creature of the earth who crosses the Creator can win. So, please, Wido—take Jesus into your heart. Embrace Him as your Lord and Savior before it's too late. For to die in the arms of Satan is to be tortured for all eternity."

*Die in the arms of Satan!* Wido thought. *How dramatic. But no more a warning I will heed than the time she told me not to play close to the fire. Yes, I did fall into the flames. I did get burned. But, so too, I proved my point: Fire hurts— but it doesn't always kill.*

And God? This ghost? No more substance than air? He is more destroyer than savior.

Worming into the mind of this phantom of the sky who maims and kills simply because He has the power to do so, Wido concluded that God— hiding behind His many masks of wind, fire, and ice—was driven by fear. A fear of the day He must answer the challenge of an oppressed and angry human tribe to reveal Himself. And the only way He can maintain his power over them is to claim to be in and of everything that exists. So the monstrous lie by which He has long deceived the world was written into the outrageous myth as gospel—the black-robes preaching just so much drivel and Mother believing that God is all and all is God. In every rock, tree, and cloud in the sky.

Fools! Wido would not be shackled by God's chains. Not now. Not ever.

Again, the wind laughed. Staggered by a rain-spitting gust sweeping over God's Rock, Wido again dropped down onto his belly. A thunder-boom. A shaking of the cliff. Then, with a low rumbling sound rising in the steep-sided gully behind him, without a clue of what was coming, a torrent of storm-water exploded against the half-buried back of the massive boulder. Gutting the gully's soft chalk walls and nearly washing Wido off the top of the root-fast rock—in a matter of seconds, a few muddy rills had turned into a roaring whitewater fall dumping off the cliff into the sea below. With huge chunks of the sheer white wall now falling away under God's Rock, Wido was forced to consider the possibility that his mother was right: this was the stupidest thing he'd done in his six years of life.

Still lying to himself that he was not scared, Wido's stubbornness persisted. *What's to worry? Just hold on tight. This rock has been here for millions of years: it's not going anywhere now.*

Absorbing the worst of a rain now blowing in flat sheets off the sea, Wido's clouded eyes were suddenly drawn by something bright down on the water—whale-sized and floating as if an island of fire. Captivated by its violent rise and fall on the mountainous sea-swells—maybe it was just a trick of the mist—but the closer the inferno got to the shore, the more it looked to Wido like a dragon swimming. Fully ablaze on the dark sea with its fearsome head held high and its mouth spewing flames—its tail coiled and thrashing about—Wido stared, stunned, as the tormented beast suddenly dropped down the face of a huge, curling wall of murky-gray water and was swept toward the crumbling cliff.

Narrowing his eyes in a scrutiny that was already intense, Wido could see through the flames engulfing the dragon's massive head a bold, white-gold glow radiating out of its broad, scaly breast. At first glance, the flames seemed to be burning across the full breadth of the monstrous wave. It was only when the swell started to break and litter with foam that he realized that the light was, in fact, of the dragon itself—kindled in its beastly heart and the obvious source of its mouth's fiery expulsion.

Never imagining such a creature existed, Wido watched spellbound as the dragon continued its fiery rush toward the cliff. With his heart beating faster and faster against his ribs as it swam straight toward him—directly below God's Rock—the childish look of wonder on his face vanished at the very instant the burning dragon slammed onto the stony shore and quickly disappeared beneath the whitewater pounding down from the cliff. As the deluge instantly extinguished the fire and mercifully drowned the flailing beast, Wido stared, mouth agape, as once again the phantom destroyer demonstrated the brutality with which He had ruled over the world from the beginning of creation.

With fear now pulsing in every nerve of his being as the whole world shook around him, Wido was no longer able to make himself believe that he wasn't going to die. Rocked by a sizzling whip of white-hot fire striking the cliff just beneath him, Wido could barely hear his mother's anguished screams over his own when—amidst a terrible cracking sound and an angry rumbling of the Earth—God's Rock suddenly tipped toward the frenzied sea. With great chunks of the gully's soft chalk walls breaking away on both sides of him, Wido desperately tried to grab a hold of even the smallest crag marring the rock's glassy face. On his belly and with his legs dangling over the rock's seaward edge, he cried out for God—his mother—anybody—to save him. Another massive thunder-boom. The towering white wall quaking and crumbling into the sea. God's Rock, again, shunting forward. Wido and the rock slipping ... slipping ... slipping. Hanging on the edge for a moment. Swept off the cliff by the seething whitewater fall. Hurtling through dark mist. Then crashing down on the dead dragon below.

Adelvia screamed. Lucifer laughed. God reaped His righteous retribution.

Wido entombed in the dismal world of the dead ... yet still wretchedly alive.

Crashed down like a hammerhead's strike, never had a god unleashed such vengeance on his own creation as the massive black boulder Odin pounded down on those six fearless Norsemen that dark and roaring night. Spewed off a towering white sea-cliff by a thunderous floodwater's fall. Demolishing their ship. Pulverizing their bones. Pulping their flesh. Beaten on the field of battle by just so many dogs of a lesser god, they'd shamed Odin's name and had to die. Six screaming shades cast into the fiery lake of Hel.

Lo, that one man still lived beneath the mountainous rubble heaped on the obliterated dragon-ship was not a miracle, but a punishment far worse than any cold-blooded slaughter. Exploding on the rough stone beach in an aureate flash, Odin—the great god and rider of heaven's brute light—then dragged his most odious creation out from under the fallen cliff and back into the glare of the storm-thrashed night.

Made of the same fire and ice as the gods, Styrkar Kvendulfsson was a warrior like no other. Savage and strong with a *berserker's* fury. Widow-maker to women the world over. A true son of the mighty Thor. And for that, he was to do Odin's will. Slaughter and blood are what he lived for. Conquering lands and piling treasure to the sky. Only, beaten on a far-off battleground by a bunch of horse-faced warriors fighting for this new Christian God— Styrkar had failed him.

Wild in his howl, Odin grabbed up Styrkar's broken and bloodied body off the beach and watched him twist in the wind—limp—puny—worthless— before tossing him aside like a half-dead fish. Flipping him once, twice—he then kicked him back into the sea. Glaring down at the wretched Norseman as he floundered in the surf and his mouth fast-filled with sand and shell— so then did Odin boom out over Thor's hammer-shocks of ground-shaking thunder: *"You writhing sack of worms! You will not die this night. Or the next. Or the next. Your life to be spared only to give Me the pleasure of hanging you on Hel's gallows ten thousand times more!"*

His structure gigantic and eyes ablaze under dreadful brows, Odin's angry words began raining down on the disgraced warrior like a pelt of icy stones: *"Oh, the blood-dripping swords that have devoured the North's cherished sons! Our mighty warrior-king struck down and his body desecrated. His banner burned and stomped into the ground! And you, for all your fearsome pride, only lying here in your impotence with the blood of five thousand brothers on your hands. How reckless! How stupid! No mind to discipline! A leader of men, yet acting no different from a boy-soldier in his first combat. Blindly marching those brave warriors off to a certain slaughter. That you, the most foolhardy of men, should have survived that storm of Saxon steel, I cringe! But know this: that which mere mortals could not exact on the field of battle, the gods now will. For I am blood and I am vengeance! All power is in my hands. I am your doom. I alone will decide your fate. And so my decree of the infinite deaths you will suffer before ever Valhalla's threshold you shall cross. Now, stand to me at once, you quivering dog! Dry your girlish tears and get back in the fight! For your king, for his honor, and for the return of his hard-won treasure upon the shores of his beloved Northland! Fight! Die! Then fight again!"*

Turning his blazing eyes upon the massive boulder with which he obliterated Styrkar's crew and ship, Odin then pounded his fist on the piled rubble to put an instant end to the incessant moaning of that loudmouthed little bastard that had been standing on a huge rock atop the cliff ridiculing the notion that any otherworldly power would rule his life. Odin cared not a whit about the boy's pain. The shame of another god—he could rot where he laid.

Whipped by an icy air seething with accusations of foul treason and blood oaths broken, Styrkar Kvendulfsson—the blood-dripping front-center sword of the fiercest fighting force the Northland ever knew—laid, naked and shivering on the rough stone beach, stripped of his dignity, his honor, fighting for something as trivial as one more breath. Beaten on the field of battle. His army destroyed. His king dead. Styrkar would suffer Odin's wrath without complaint. Nor would he make any argument that his exclusion from Valhalla, the great heroes' Hall of the Chosen Slain, was not just. But, oh, if only to crawl inside his veins and witness the blood-boiling rage stirred within him by that army of immortals stomping on the sky, shouting his name with derision—the butt of all their jokes—woe to any fool of the Earth who dared speak the same to Styrkar's face.

For Pride's beast lived inside Styrkar Kvendulfsson. As much a part of him as his heart and soul. And, oh, how the beast loathed his weakness—lingering on the beach, sprawled on the rocks, meek as a clubbed baby seal awaiting the killing blow. With his pride demanding that he rejoin the fight no matter the agony of his wounds, Styrkar slowly struggled to his feet and, with a low feral growl, thrust his words into the wind-howling face of the god who threatened to destroy him: "In Your image I was made, Great One. And in Your image I have lived. A murderer's heart and a mind of war. I have defended your honor. Killed in your name. Poured out my blood for you like barnyard slop the world over. And although I know not a single star of hope shines above me and grim fate to be hard in my face, be warned, Lord of All Lords, that you come after no cowering dog."

Staggering on his weak legs before finally steadying to a posture straight and proud, Styrkar then turned his black, burning eyes to the sizzling sky and—goading Hel's swarming demons into proving their utter depravity, to do their worst to him—bellowed at a seething Odin: "Ney, god of all gods! Hardly will I just sit here in your hollow hand waiting to be crushed! I will fight! I will die! And then I will fight again! The ravening hand of Death having not the weapon to maul my warrior soul!"

With his mouth twisted and filled with blood, Styrkar then spit into the wind.

The wind blew it back in his face.

Buried under the rubble of the fallen cliff and barely breathing, Wido laid all night on the rough stone beach, an endless *God is the Devil* scream inside his head marking the malingering hours as if time had stopped at the height of his pain. In a mind dark and raging, wordlessly challenging God to prove that He cares more about human pain and suffering than gathering gold and glory to His name—to prove He is the merciful God the Bible says He is—lo, that He even exists—with a tongue thick as a reptile's tail, his incessant calls for help crept over his parched lips as the barest of whispers.

At the time, the pious young widow Adelvia, the youngest daughter of Albert of Arques—an affable, God-fearing tenant farmer who was carelessly trampled to death by a nobleman's horse as he carried a crate of chickens across the road—was a mother still learning her trade. A fresh-faced beauty with her mother's jade-green eyes and long, dark hair, Adelvia's contours were every bit a woman twenty-two years matured, but who, in many ways, was still a girl unable to help her only child in even the smallest way. Dropped down on her knees, convulsed and wailing at the edge of the rubble piled beneath the fallen cliff, she did nothing but cry out over and again to her God and buried son. "Oh, no destiny so cruel! To be so young and full of life, and yet your days already run out! And I the nagging bitch that drove you to this horrid end! Oh, God, I beseech You—fix my broken heart! Save Wido—my only child! Raise him up from this rocky tomb so that I might do better for him. That I might do better for You. That together we may serve You forevermore."

Miraculously, God, in all the goodness born of His tremendous love of the stricken woman, answered Adelvia's impassioned plea before another cry crossed her trembling lips. Stunned by the power of her prayer, she sat staring in wide-eyed disbelief as a man whom she did not know suddenly appeared out of the pre-dawn mist and, without speaking a word to her, climbed onto the debris pile and began tossing the huge rocks aside. Tall. Muscular. Corn-silk hair streaked with blood. The same as Jesus, there was no rock he could not move. Driven by the sound of a faint and weakening groan deep within the rubble, the man stayed at the backbreaking work for hours. No matter that his hands were ripped raw by the sharp fragments of flint littering the marl, and pausing not a moment for the pain, with a quiet fury he tore apart the huge pile as if digging for a son of his own.

Finally, the narrowest sliver of mid-morning light found its way into Wido's blood-crusted eyes. A few agonizing minutes more, and the tremendous weight of a single kettle-sized stone was lifted off the boy's chest. Picked from the pile by the man's large, strong hands, Wido was then laid gently on the beach as Adelvia's rough, trembling lips smothered every inch of her son's brutalized face. Bones were sticking through his skin. Blood bubbled from his mouth. He couldn't see. He couldn't breathe. And his legs. There should have been so much pain. But it was as if they weren't even there anymore.

Standing back from the devastated woman and her barely breathing son, Styrkar stared as if in disbelief of the immense size of the boulder Odin had crashed down on his ship. Unbroken despite the impact of its fall from high on the cliff, it was of such vast dimensions that it covered the vessel nearly bow to stern.

And, shackled to their oars, six of the bravest warriors upon which the sun ever shined.

As he dropped to a knee and put his face in his hands, Styrkar's every faculty was nigh paralyzed by the horrid scene replaying in his mind. His burning ship being flung onto this rocky shore by a monstrous wave. The cracking sound of beach stones breaking under its hull as it skidded across the rough shingle beach. Gouging the ground. The bow suddenly dropping into a deep hole under a towering waterfall. His men—chained in place and unable to escape their rowing benches—shouting, cursing, groaning, trapped beneath the relentless whitewater pounding down on them from the cliff. A seething bolt of lightning suddenly striking high on the cliff, shearing off huge chunks into the sea. The huge glowing rock on the cliff that had guided them into the shore as if the Norse god of light himself, Heimdall, breaking loose. Crashing down on his ship. Chunks of rock and rubble raining down, burying him where he stood in the ship's stern with his hand still grasped to its dragon's-head rudder. The massive black rock coming to rest only inches from his face. On the rowing benches. Crushing his men alive.

Slumped back on his haunches and staring at the boulder, Styrkar felt the sudden fire-like burn of big, blurring tears filling his eyes—and a tremendous pride surging in his heart. For, being pursued by a bloodthirsty enemy along the storm-ravaged coast, his men would have rowed that ship over the edge of the world if they had to, even to the bottom of the sea. Chained to their oars in a do-or-die fight to prevent the capture of their fallen king's hard-won treasure—no matter pierced by arrows, engulfed in flames, or their blistered, bloodied hands peeled of flesh by the oars—they had not surrendered.

Withdrawing a small iron key from the thigh-pocket of his tattered britches and staring at it on his open palm, after expelling another hard, grief-burdened breath, he softly tossed it onto the rubble. Closing his eyes and listening to the key tink and clink through the dark, slivered gaps between the high-piled rocks, he thought, *So that those six brave men will have it to free themselves from their shackles, rise from the gravemound's darkness, and fight again.*

"Kalf … Thjodulf," he said softly. "Goodbye, my cherished sons. Your dauntless spirits forever to endure. Go now to your mother in her place amidst the brightest stars of the heaven so that she will weep for you no more.

"Ivar, Thormod, Asmund, and Finn. The best of men. Fiercely loyal to the end. Until that glorious hour when we all stand again with our swords, shields, and spear-points gleaming and raise the charred black hulk of King Harald's once-fearsome dragon back into the light of day—Fight, my brothers! Fight! And die! Then fight again!"

Kissing his lips to the small silver Hammer of Thor amulet hanging between two matched glass beads at his throat and whispering, "Godspeed to Valhalla," Styrkar then took up the broken little boy in his arms and carried him to the top of the cliff.

On the water. Voices. A ship. Square-sailed. Sleek. Turning the headland. Swords. Spears. Helmets. Gleaming in the sun.

Angry men. The Ponthievins looking to kill those thieving pagans who stole their treasure.

# II

## THE PRISONER

*Afternoon*

### 9 SEPTEMBER 1100

**N**igh thirty-four summers have turned on winter since Styrkar's ship last saw the light of day. Vanished from the face of the Earth with enough precious metals and jewels piled in its hold to fill a king's grave, the shackled Norseman is the only man alive who can answer the riddle of its sudden disappearance.

Hunted for months before being captured and thrown in a dark hole in the ground by the most brutal warlord who ever prowled the Channel coast, not a day has passed that the old warrior has not been whipped, beaten, or burned trying to make him give up its hiding place. Yet, even as Styrkar is as fierce in holding on to his prize as Count Guy of Ponthieu is in trying to take it from him, neither can remotely fathom the true treasure buried in the belly of that long-dead dragon.

Before the next sunrise, it will come to light.

And there will be fear.

Sitting atop his huge black horse with his face turned as brilliant a red as the sweat-sopped samite kersche tied to his utterly bald, overlarge, and misshapen head, in a voice more like a roar, the big Ponthievin *gard-sarjent*—a beast of a man named Odo—bellowed at his prisoner, "Nay, wretch! Enough! A plague on my ears you are! A dog's barking or a goat's bleating I could better understand than your gibberish!"

Then he smashed a rock-hard fist against the side of the old man's head.

It had been a miserable day. Hot and sticky. And then cold and wet. And windy. All goddamned day it had been windy. Only now, there was none. Not a wisp. And then the water. Flat and low. No way to get his goddamned boat off the goddamned beach and away from this cretin gurgling spit in his throat all day.

Glowering down at the desiccated old man flopping around in his lice-eaten brown burlap tunic on this, the ninth day of his dubious "escape" from the dungeon at Beaurain, Odo thought him grotesque. Everything about him suggested a dead man wakened. Haggard and hollow-eyed in his wrist-worn shackles, his face was sunken, skull-like, and the thick plaited scar streaking down from behind his left ear onto his collarbone so inflamed by the sun as to appear to be bleeding. His breathing was strained, gusty. And he smelled worse than last night's whore. With Odo's rage rising as the man continued to spew forth some cryptic tale in nothing but spits and slurs and raving howls for hours on end, finally smacking an open hand against the back of his prisoner's head, he wanted the wretch to shut his goddamned mouth. Quit his yammering. Or, better yet—Odo flashed a hand to his hip and crushed it around the hilt of his sword—just kill him. It would be so easy. And, orders be damned, he probably would.

Mocking the whip-scarred old man as a "no-count, pissed-pants, boy-lover," Odo then told him to shut his "windy hole right goddamned now—or I'll shut it for you!"

His eyes the color of fire—indifferent to the pain, but not the mockery—Styrkar Kvendulfsson had killed more men than the god of war. He wanted to kill one more. This foulmouthed guardsman was just begging to die. So it worked out well.

Glaring into Odo's red, snarling face and promising him such pain in death as befalls only the worst of men if one more filthy word came out of his mouth, Styrkar left no ambiguity as to the wreckage he would make of the man. Recalling a murderous day in his far-off past, with the simplest of words he drew a vivid picture of the brutal end Odo could expect: "He was a fat man, like you. A mud-foot Saxon. Old cart, ugly horse. Deep in an English forest. Wind. Rain. I was cold. Bloody. And wanted his coat. Told him I'd pay for it, even. That I killed him wasn't because he said no—but because every word that came out of his shit-stinking mouth was mocking me."

Styrkar's look was dark as nightfall. Spitting out his words in gritty, garbled chunks, as if with a mouth full of gravel, he growled at Odo: "I am The Wolf. Son of the Skullsplitter. Slayer of the Nord Wood ogre. Then as now, I dole out death to those who desire it. So my fair warning: hold your tongue and mock me none. For, just as that loudmouthed Saxon learned that long-ago day: a man laughs too long, too loud about a thing, sometimes his head falls off."

Odo didn't have a clue as to what his prisoner said to him—but he damned sure didn't like the way he said it. So he hit him again.

Even that the brain-wrecked wretch should think to have actually escaped the torture pit in which he'd been held captive for God knows how many years at Beaurain Odo found comical: the only way a man gets out of that vermin-infested hole is when his limp, beaten body is dragged up by the chain around his neck, loaded on a cart, and dumped in the swamp with all the other prisoners' corpses.

So too, Odo thought, how absurd it was that his notoriously brutal lord, Count Guy of Ponthieu, had baited the prisoner's escape. Allowing him to slip into the night as if a cat chasing a mouse through the crack of a slow-closing door, the count had not a glimmer of a doubt that the old man would lead them straight to that singularly stunning treasure the count claimed the barbarian and his horde had wrested from his rightful grasp one dark, stormy night many years ago.

While outwardly mocking the old man as he shadowed his every stumbling step over and around Normandy's hills, bogs, rivers, and ravines, and then his slipping, sliding descent of a steep gully gouged into the face of a towering white sea-cliff before, at last, his comedic tumble onto the beach below—Odo could not deny that he showed grit like few men possess. Even did he think: *Not so different from one of those hard-backed beetles that won't be squished the first time you step on them, this little dung-eater might just have some fight in him before I kill him.*

Odo had tracked the flesh-starved wretch for days. Leading a contingent of Count Guy's personal houseguard—ten men on horseback and another twenty men aboard a ship just off the Channel shore—it was a mindless waste of his time and talents. Slow and plodding—a task that any ten-year-old who could keep his fidgety ass in a saddle could accomplish—Odo had the old man in his sights every step of his pathetically slow flight to freedom.

Only, when Odo could no longer rein in the raging boredom of watching the man do absolutely nothing but stand next to some big black rock on the beach staring up at a ramshackle shack perched on the edge of the cliff above him—growling, "I'd sooner watch turds pile under a dog's ass"—with a curt wave of his hand, he signaled for the men waiting on the water to weigh anchor and row their ship into shore.

*Maybe another good bashing of his head will help this pig-ignorant wretch remember where he hid this big treasure of his, Odo thought. End this fucking charade.*

Struggling to regain his footing on the shifting beach stones after Odo's latest strike, with a horrible eagerness to salvage a vestige of the ruthless warrior he once was, Styrkar resumed his telling of "that rot-stinking Saxon whose worm-filled skull I would joyfully crush underfoot this very day"—none aware that not a single word he spoke the big Ponthievin could understand.

"Mocking me as a coward. An old woman. Vermin. Spitting in my face. Laughing. The Saxon was as stupid as he looked. Rejecting my lavish offer to trade for that dead cow he called a coat, even the smallest of my hard-earned arm-rings was worth more than his life."

Again, Styrkar glared into Odo's dark, contemptible eyes.

"Squeezed out the hole in a jackal's ass—he was a man a lot like you."

Odo shifted in his saddle some, an ursine growl seething through his gritted teeth. Again, he demanded the man's immediate silence. His language was French, his words indecent.

"Goddammit, you gob-slobbering shoat, I said shut it, and shut it now!"

Only, the old Norseman didn't understand a word of French.

Ignored, a frustrated Odo then reached out a large, open hand and cuffed the shackled wretch about his mangled ear. Punched him. Kicked him. Then, drawing out his sword's long, double-edged blade from its scabbard with a hiss, he pressed it against the man's wriggling throat bone with the vow that he would be taking his head back in a bloody sack if he did not.

Styrkar's overwrought pride crackled on the air like chained lightning.

White-fanged and snarling and hungering for the guard's heart on a stick, the proud old warrior growled, "Deathblows declare victories, not some blow-hard threat!" Then, whirling around, Styrkar made like to cut off Odo's head with an invisible sword and kick it into the sea.

# THE GUARD

*Late Afternoon*

## 9 SEPTEMBER 1100

"**I**diot!" Odo snarled from atop his horse. "A grim, fucking idiot, you are!" Gnashed in anger, his uneven rows of yellow, corn-like teeth seemed to buck forward and nigh explode out of his mouth as his prisoner—suddenly, inexplicably—wrenched around and got his wrist-chains tangled with the horse's reins. Reaching out a rough hand and twisting up a fistful of the few coarse hairs scattering the old man's head, Odo again put his sword to the imbecile's throat. In words sharp and cutting as a scythe through a winter's field, he threatened that there would be no further warnings: the old man would shut his mouth "right goddamned now—or die."

Blowing out a hard breath, Odo then turned his eyes to the sundown light, grimacing as the lapping surf washed up around his horse's hooves, barely, and then retreated. The rain had finally stopped, but so too the robust southerly wind that had swept it up the coast. A canvas-bellying gale typical of early September in the Channel, it would have driven his ship swiftly north toward Ponthieu and into the mouth of the Somme River with nary an oar-blade touched to the water.

That is, had the goddamned thing even been in the water.

Odo's gaze cut sharp across the rough pebbled beach to where the clunky, high-sided cog laid, its keel dug in and heeled to one side. Less a ship than a barn floated off its foundation, he'd had his men run it into shore at midday when the tide was at its height, beaching it far-high upon the steep shingle where the white-chalk cliff met the sea. Clinker-built with heavy oak planks and stout crossbeams to accommodate a weighty cargo—Count Guy's long-sought treasure—Odo's men heaved and heaved on its broad hull through the worst of the squalling rain, but it would not budge.

The beach was nothing but rocks and bigger rocks. Above them, a forest of beech, oak, and ash trees rose up just beyond a fringe of tall grass along the cliff's edge. Odo glanced around him. Sea-birds—gulls, sanderlings, and waders—were seen everywhere among the countless kelp piles, but not even the smallest fallen tree to use as a rolling log. He would have to wait to refloat the hulking vessel on the tide's return. That would be long after dark.

A dozen heavily armed men were at Odo's back. He had them scraping the ship's strakes with stones for nothing better to do.

*Christ! I am a sword-warrior! A falcon, not a duck! A scion of kings! On the scorched stone of my father's grave, I swear nevermore will a handful of coins command my following such a fool's course!*

With Count Guy's big blue *léopard* insignia glittering on his chest under the late-day sun, Odo of Montreuil thought rather much of himself; yet, save for the few drops of Charlemagne's blood rumored to run through his veins, there was not a hint of prestige attached to his name. Odo had not a hide of land to call his own. A lowly swine-herder in the service of Eustace of Boulogne—a man hailed as the "Hero of Hastings" and a direct descendant of the great Christian King Charlemagne—Odo was the son of a son born to one of his lord's numerous concubines.

And a bastard in every sense of the word.

Of course, that was but a trifle to a man who had tried to attach "the Great" to his name even before he could raise the tip of his wooden play sword off the ground. Always picking fights with the biggest, toughest boys around, and always losing, Odo was knocked down, bloodied, and pissed on so many times that the only name that ever stuck for long was "the Yellow."

That is, until the day Odo killed one of them. With a real sword.

Insomuch as Odo was by law his responsibility, Lord Eustace grudgingly paid the blood-price demanded by the dead boy's father—the eldest brother of three prominent nobles in the realm—and further agreed to the family's demand that Odo depart the duchy at once, forbidden to return. Thus, "gifted" by Eustace to his longtime ally to the south—the aging Count Guy of Ponthieu—the prideful young swine-herder was summarily deposited on that far, rocky shore without so much as a pitying look backward.

Count Guy liked Odo immediately. The strapping stable-rat was a fighter. His talk crude and his fists ever striking out in fits of wild temper, a humorless thug who detested being told what to do, Odo had all the trappings of the young man Guy had once been: fearless and fiery with something to prove. Busting the teeth and blackening the eyes of all those pitiful, yowling whelps lucky enough to be born to their noble titles, Odo made no pretense to alliances. He always stood alone.

Now, at a mere twenty years of age, having served out the last of his days in the ranks of all those bootlicking squires, Odo was the unchallenged—if unofficial—leader of Count Guy's personal houseguard, both feared and despised to a man.

Only Odo craved real power. The power to make men die for him. And as his every thought and action was singularly focused on expediting that end, he had recently acquired a wife. Plain-faced and fleshy, she was the only child of a sickly, middle-aged *vicomte* of modest holdings who had not a single invitation to sit at Count Guy's high table for so much as a swig of ale in the past ten years. Nevertheless, as Odo allowed the girl was not as bad as others he had considered to spur his social climb, he had petitioned the count to arrange the marriage in return for his assuming an old debt owed his liegelord, a sum substantially more than the girl's struggling merchant father had the purse to pay.

Although a bare sixteen years of age and yet untwined from her many childish fears and emotions, Odo's new wife had the competence to manage a household of a woman twice her age. The girl had been doing it for years, her mother having died scant hours after her first drawn breath.

Her name was Annalie. Or Amelie. Or something close. Not that it mattered to Odo; she was nothing to him but a hole to rut while passing the time. A lamb slowly turning on a spit that he would eventually devour. For soon enough the girl's ailing father—the same as her mother—would fill a six-foot hole on some far back hill and, by right of matrimony, those fair-few hides of remote forestland he had inherited in the Pas de Calais would become Odo's own. Upon the formal transfer of titles and settlement of the *vicomte's* debts, Odo's feudal investiture would be complete. Never again would he be another man's servant. Count Guy had even promised to make him a knight. As such, humped belly to back in exhaustion atop another no-name Ponthievin whore at the end of another drunken night, Odo's head would swim with dreamy visions of the vast *demesne*—an immense estate—soon to be rolling out over the surrounding hills under a banner of his own colors. He would have a castle. Ships. A stable of mounts. Squires, oarsman, cooks, and concubines. Vassals by the thousands. And a new wife—one considerably more worthy of his lofty status. Smaller here. Bigger there. And very pretty.

The *vicomte's* daughter? Odo would have little use for her then, her only remaining worth that which was to be found in that over-tight space between her legs. His wife was young, Odo reasoned, with many childbearing years ahead. Surely one of those barbarian slavers in the north would pay him much to have her ample belly turning out tens more strong-backed men in irons to row his ships. Odo laughed at the thought: his prudish, kicking, scratching, and shrieking wife a *breeder*. Oh, only to imagine the horde of filthy, pagan thieves she could suckle with those big, floppy breasts! Nor did he have any worry of masking such devilry, for to anyone who had ever seen Amelie's bruised, beaten face, it would be easily believed that she had run off during the night.

A woman of great piety, Amelie had begged Odo for a release from their hateful marriage so that she might enter a convent and embark on a life of service to her one true Lord, Jesus Christ. Only Odo couldn't care less about her craving to save souls, her wanting to "spread God's word." He possessed her as legally as a milk-can or a mule, and she would serve his purpose or by his hand fast become one of those "imperishable spirits" she cried out to through her fat, bloodied lips. *To Hell with this Jesus Christ!* He, Odo of Montreuil, here on Earth, in all his pounding flesh, was her one true lord! Voracious—a monster—Odo's power over her was as complete as he imagined it would someday be over all the land from the River Canche southward to the Talou Forest.

Only, Odo, this son of a swine-herder, would realize nothing of the sort. He would be dead before the next day's sun climbed over the cliff. Rammed down headfirst into a grave of his own digging with an ax buried between his shoulder blades, more than nine hundred years would pass before anybody cared in the least to know what had happened to him.

Anyone could have killed him. Many wanted to. A few had tried. For there was an arrogant, bullying violence about Odo in everything he did. Even in issuing the simplest command.

"There, boy, enough! Fetch me the biggest," Odo ordered of a small, skinny-armed bond-slave knelt down by a burgeoning flame and turning gulls on a spit. Odo had demanded meat tonight—bear, boar, deer—thick brown slabs dripping juices and steaming with scent, not another bite of that stewed fish-and-roots rot to be suffered by his tortured innards. Only, the hunt had gone poorly. He would eat gull instead.

"And bring me ale. My horn is dry."

"But the gull, it is not quite—"

"Now!"

The task-man did as he was told, and quickly.

Odo took up the gull with his thick fingers and tore into its charred flesh with his large, yellow teeth. Chewing around its half-cooked grayness a few turns, his overstuffed mouth reigned over but a few moments of glutted satisfaction before his face turned bitter-screwed.

"Wretched bird!" Odo shouted, spewing it from his mouth in a gust. "It is fouled!"

"But, beg sir." The slave bowed deeply, fearing. "Again, it is not quite—"

"It is poison!" Odo swallowed hard on the bile rising in his throat, balled a fist, and then cowed the cook with a deadly look. "Incompetent dung-raker!"

Odo cursed the bird. The boat. The bugs. The beach. The flux in his bowels from last night's drink. The stench on his skin from last night's whore. Stranded on some godforsaken, rock-strewn edge of nowhere countless rowing-spells from home, he longed for his well-spread table, his ale board, his hunting dogs. Even his priggish new wife. For, while hardly fulfilling the needs of a man in bed, at least she could cook.

Hot and sticky under the late-day sun, Odo pulled his red silk kersche down over his face and rubbed it into his eyes. None disguised by its utter baldness, his head's deformity—a deep cleave in his skull caused by the poorly fused fractures of the cranial bones on one side—ran with a rivulet of sweat over a large, venous bulge that started above his right ear and down onto his cheek. Rough to the touch, like a thin layer of skin stretched over an accretion of pebble and shell—it was grotesque. They said Odo's mother had stumbled and dropped him when he was a baby. That he hit his head on a rock. Others said she never wanted him. That she had been raped. Smashed his head with a rock. And left him to die. When he was a boy in Montreuil, just the sight of Odo made people shudder and turn away. They called him ugly. A beast. A monster.

So he became.

Odo let the kersche slip, catching it over his mouth and chin, a few loose gold threads from its tattered embroidery clinging to the ragged red whiskers of his recent beard. Clean-shaved in his normal routine—Count Guy allowed no beard, side-whiskers, or mustache worn by any member of his personal houseguard—neither did Odo ever permit a single hair to mar his fearsome head. For if Odo learned one thing well from living a life of violence and intimidation, it was that mean is good, but mean and ugly is better.

Only, violence and intimidation did not seem to faze this prisoner. Again, from atop his horse on the beach, Odo's anger seethed toward the babbling halfwit standing at his mount's left flank. Count Guy had been right about him: he had the heart of a lion. Yet, Odo decided—being much amused by the old man's facial antics and wild gesticulations in punctuation of the telling of some fantastic tale long-lived in his maddened mind—that the midget *jongleur* at court wasn't half as funny. A crooked smile slowly creased Odo's haughty look and, hopeless to defeat it, he began to laugh.

Quick, as if a knife slashed through his vocal cords, the old man fell stone silent.

Thus it was, at that very moment, quite unbeknownst to Odo, the tide began to turn.

Styrkar's slight, tortured muscles began to twitch, his fists to clench, and his mouth to pull sideways in a rabid snarl. Bile seeped over his lips. Blood streamed off his brow. Then, slowly … slowly … like the waters drawing back from a shore before a mounting wave, with a distant reflection of arrant brutality burning in his eyes, he turned on Odo with murderous intent.

Only Styrkar saw Odo not at all. For, with the clarity only enduring hatred could provide, it was that fat Saxon's dark, ugly face laughing down at him instead.

Running his fingers over the thick, rope-like scars criss-crossing his arms, face, and chest, tracing them every ragged inch, hot and hard to the touch, the rivers of venomous blood coursing within them could barely hold all of Styrkar's rage. His body full-aquiver like a snake boldly hissing and ready to strike as once again he saw himself bloodied and beaten on that cold English ground, with all the ferocity of the merciless *berserker* he once was, the old warrior again whirled around and, with his bound hands clasped together, made like to slash a sword across Odo's throat.

Stunned into silence, Odo stared a moment in wide-eyed disbelief—*The strangeness of this man,* he thought—before he exploded into outright mirth.

Turning up a dark, fearless eye into Odo's laughing face, in his spitting, grunting speech Styrkar slowly repeated: "I killed the Saxon because he was mocking me." Growling, he then drew a fast finger across his throat and spit on the ground.

Odo struggled to hold back his urge to kill like a mad dog on a short rope.

His reddened face a web of strained, contorted lines and his body full shaking like in a temblor, Odo raised his sword as if to strike. Stammering out, "Tis but a fool craving death to be governed by such pride!" he then brought the blade back down in a sharp, whirring arc nigh to cutting Styrkar's throat before viciously stabbing it back into its metal scabbard.

Obedience to orders was a hard, forced act for Odo, and patience not a trait he possessed or valued. "A waste of my time, nine days tracking this worthless drooling pig!" he growled. "Brain-dead dreg! Stolen treasure! *Puh!*" Odo had waited quite long enough for the monkey who'd swallowed the key to the golden chest to shit it out. Now the big dog inside him was breaking loose. And the big dog hated nothing more than a chattering monkey.

# THE COUNT

*Late Afternoon*

## 9 SEPTEMBER 1100

O do wasn't sure who was nearer to death: the old man he tracked or the old man who ordered it. Secreted in the bejeweled death-box that was his bedchamber high above the River Somme at Abbeville, Count Guy of Ponthieu was nearing the end of his eighth decade of life and had not risen off his bed in over a month. His head bald and blotchy, and his gray-skinned face wrinkled in a most violent manner, he did not sleep nights, but only quivered in the dark under his soft velvet cover in fear for his immortal soul. His sins were many, and unforgiven. The recovery of this thieving pagan's hidden hoard was to be his salvation.

Long walking a twisting side-path that only occasionally crossed truth's hard road, the count considered the barbarian to have stolen the vast treasure out of the very hands of his Lord God King and Savior, Jesus Christ. From the Mother Church. From *his* church. And while long guilty of the same himself, Count Guy now fancied himself some sort of avenging angel for years of vicious Viking plundering of Christian churches and monasteries the world over.

Whether Guy truly believed he could buy his place in Heaven with the recovery of the massive trove he dismissed as moot. It's what he *needed* to believe. His grave-hole was already open under the floor of the old chapel at Saint-Riquier, and soon he must lie in it. How ironic that the fervent prayers he now so often recited were from a large, gilded Bible he had lifted years before from its very altar.

Contriving the circumstances to make possible the "escape" of this certain "nameless, stupidly stubborn, prideful prisoner" rotting in a pit dug eight ells deep into the rock beneath the dungeon at Beaurain, Count Guy had assured Odo that, "Like a hound bounding off through the reeds to retrieve a downed quail, he will lead you straight to the prize. He clings to his life only to reclaim it. Find it," the count had said, "and one in ten pieces you may keep in payment of your service. The rest is to be delivered into my hands, as on the jagged rocks of our turbulent shore it was wrested from my rightful grasp one dark night so very long ago. … That is, of course, so I may return it to our sweet Lord."

Crossing himself—the Father, the Son, and the Holy Ghost—Count Guy then kissed his lips to the large silver crucifix hanging around his neck before fighting on against his strangled thought.

"But be no such fool, brave Odo, to think that your ruthlessness and cunning will work against this man. For, in my younger day, I was you twofold. Relentless. Summer upon winter, my best and my worst visited upon the barbarian in his hole. Threats, torture, beatings. Starved and blinded. Chained to the wall. A plaything for snakes and vermin. Yet, all was as nothing to defeat the monster inside him: his heart. Possessed of the courage of a lion, he would growl but would not roar, absorbing every horrid pain with his jaws clamped shut. I only wish I'd had a thousand more like him to carry the Ponthievin shield. That fat turd William the Conqueror? Oh, that today I would be king over all his lands!"

Still, Count Guy vowed a final triumph over the godless brute. With his gaunt face sharpened almost to a point by pain as he raised his head off his pillow, he growled that he would not be beaten by any creation of the Devil. "He is a thief and a murderer. The foulest sort of heathen rot. He will answer for his sins. And he will tell all that he knows."

"His brain is mush, my lord," Odo responded to the count with the direct-ness of a father stating a simple fact to a child. "You have beaten him senseless. He can no longer speak. Why, were you to run a sword blade in one ear and out the other and pick the bloody matter off the tip, you would have a better chance of disgorging his secret than through his mouth."

"Aye, there is no twisting the truth," Count Guy replied, drenched in sweat and his voice weakened to a whisper. "My overdoing has proven a bit unwise. Yet, as long as he still lives—"

Odo, louder, unsparing: "As long as he still lives, he will have his revenge on you for what you have done. For your treasure is buried *in his head*. And should he die," Odo added, quite relishing holding the count's feet to the fires of Hell, "his revenge will be for all time, as your treasure will be buried *in his grave!*"

"Grave, you say, Odo? *Grave!* His body will be but two bloody bits among the rubble on a salt rock beach if you return to me empty-handed!" Count Guy's teeth gnashed hard together as blood quickly stole over his death-gray face to crimson his very temples. He raised a fist like to strike Odo. Only, suddenly, he fell back grabbing his chest, at a pain sharp like a stuck knife. For long moments, his mouth hung open like screaming underwater, making no sound. Not a breath went in nor out. He began to shake and to turn blue.

Odo was speechless. He had seen men die before—from wounds, from disease, even from poison—but never from abject fear. *Let him sink into that hot place*, Odo thought. *For to be the Devil's plaything serves such a coward right.*

Only, just as quickly as it had come on, the attack dwindled. Count Guy settled back stiffly, mumbling out some ill-spent prayer as the pain slowly passed out of his chest and his skin returned to its icy-gray pallor. After a time, he reached for Odo's hand and pulled him close.

"Never have I wanted to make this friendship honest between us more than I do right now," he whispered through shallow, rasping breaths. "For should you unearth the brute's hoard from its nefarious hiding place, brave Odo, with but a quill-stroke the debt you owe me will be discharged. More-over—as sure as if I had sworn it upon Our Holy Father's most sacred book—I will make good my promise to you: your lowborn dream of becoming a nobleman will no longer be a fantasy. At last, you will have the lands you desire, your vassals and their fealty. Find the treasure, Odo Swineherder of Montreuil, and no longer will you be just another stone on the heap."

"And you, my lord? What is treasure to a dying man?" Odo pressed.

"Why, it is rebirth to a dying man!" Count Guy suddenly boomed. "For I, with your success—newly light and unburdened—might then pass on to that far-greater place above, the eternal salvation of my soul assured and my every sin forgiven by our most merciful Lord upon my overflowing the coffers of His earthly domain at our blessed Saint-Riquier." In his delirium, the count's words began to flutter, singsong. "And so I go on, as I must, day after day suffering the calamity of my tribulation, laboring through this intolerable pain, His humble servant to the end. Even so, the possibility of years from now having my own bleached bones displayed upon its sacred altar … hallowed by the masses for my exceeding generosity … a saint at last."

Drawing in a great pinched-nose breath of dreamy resolve, Count Guy of Ponthieu then settled his head back onto his soft, rose-silk pillow, drew his velvet cover close, and closed his parchment-thin lids over his fading eyes, quite exhausted by a life lived much too long under God's thumb.

His eyes flat and burning like trying to see through smoke, Odo again stared down at the grimy wisp of a man standing beside him. Many details of the circumstances surrounding his imprisonment at Beaurain were known only to Count Guy and—unbeknownst even to the count —one grievously lame monk at Saint-Riquier, the monastic heart of Ponthieu. The monk's name was Wido. He had been only a boy at the time. All others who had ever shared this knowledge were now dead or unknown.

For his part, Odo could not have cared less of his prisoner's tale. Still, his curiosity was piqued by how such a mule of a man could have pulled off such a great heist. *Of what land is this man? How and when his arrival on this shore?*

*Where amassed this mountainous treasure? Did it even exist, or had it been quickly devised as a clever ruse to spare his life?*

In his five years squiring in the service of Count Guy, never had Odo even known of the existence of this prisoner secreted in the darkest depths of the dungeon at Beaurain. *How many others had we hauled out yet living from their rat-infested holes and drowned in the swamp for the need of the space for our winter stores of salt pork and wine? How absurd then that this one, nearly rotted in his skin, still lives.*

"Be wary of this man," Count Guy had warned Odo. *Wary of what? In his stumbling, mumbling step, he is less threatening than a housecat in repose. And bring him back alive? Why? Only to spare the carrion birds such a meager, gristled meal? Oh, no doubt, he has played the game well. Duped the count. Done what he has needed to do to keep living.*

Only, as far as Odo was concerned, the game was up. *We all do as we must, old knife. But I am in no way the fool Count Guy is. I think your trove is a lie, and I will sooner beat the fact of its fiction out of you and then gut you like a fish before I dig one more hole in a spot you stare at too long!*

With each day passed trailing the old man along the barren coast, Odo paid the dying count and his fanciful story of buried treasure less and less heed. Because he knew Guy all too well, his brutal history. He wasn't that gullible. He was guilty, his conscience black and burning.

Ascended to his position only by the luck of being next in line to inherit a title first bestowed on his great-grandfather Hugo Miles upon his marriage to a daughter of Hugh Capet— the future king of France—it was well known that Count Guy had plundered the abbey of Saint-Riquier for years. Ever a greedy man, he had harvested its abundant riches to add to his already considerable wealth with the fervor of a fat little squirrel stuffing its cheeks with nuts. Refusing to be shackled by social or religious moralities, he would go to any length to secure his power and comfort. He had no compunction about taking or selling off the church's many valuable artifacts—gold, silver, and gilt-bronze candelabras, chalices, bowls, icons, door knockers, and bells—even prying loose the ornamental mounts and embedded jewels from its founts and altars.

Then, too, more detestable, Count Guy had raided the reliquaries, the sacred shrines containing the varied remains of many esteemed Christian saints and martyrs. Once, being an avid admirer of horseflesh, he had even traded a dusty old arm bone for a fine Norman *destrier*. This was no small sin. Boundless faith was placed in the divine healing and protective powers of these holy relics. Carried into battle, sworn upon at the crowning of kings, and prayed over in times of plague, utter catastrophe was certain to befall any who desecrated them.

Only, Count Guy had never believed such witch tales: his piety was a lifelong lie. A show for the masses. In fact, for most of his life, the count had scorned "our most merciful God" for taking his mother away from him at a very young age, often crying at her side for hours on end as a tiny bug in her bowels slowly ate her alive. He had prayed for a miracle but gotten nothing. And Jesus?—the man he had often referred to as that "famous Jewish peasant"—Guy secretly believed that His death and resurrection were more myth than fact.

Despite this litany of moral and physical transgressions, the likelihood of burning in Hell for all eternity hardly occurred to the count until his heart's recent lapse. Having passed from this world for a few horrifying moments, he had gotten a glimpse of the other side, and it was a black, howling hole. Not so very different from the torture pit at Beaurain. The cleaving of bone and the flaying of skin, the bloodcurdling wails and the screams for mercy. Its dark theater had seemed almost caricature but for the fact that it had been so real. Returned to his un-anointed mass of flesh and bone amidst a tearless few members of his comital staff—gasping for air and crying out for forgiveness—now, more than ever, he needed to believe that there was a huge pile of precious metals buried out there to save his immortal soul. Or, at the very least, a Jesus as forgiving as that Guy long pretended to pray to every Sunday.

For his part, Odo could never pretend to be something he was not. Nor feign traits he did not possess. Loyal? Caring? Odo was as loyal to Count Guy as a dog is to the man who throws out the biggest bone. And as caring as the shepherd who will protect his flock from the wolf just long enough to deliver it for slaughter.

*I would suppose that there were certain oaths of obedience to Count Guy proclaimed by Lord Eustace in my youthful behalf,* Odo allowed. *But I will sooner take up this decrepit old man like a shovel, divine the location of his mystery hoard by the wag of his tongue, and dig it out of the Earth with his gaping mouth before I follow him one more step!*

Again, Odo fought the urge to cleave his prisoner in two as he stood. With his every fiber, he wanted to. But he wasn't that stupid. There was a sack of coins tied to the return of this pale-faced windbag that was going to get him a lot of cheap whores and ale. Bringing back a dead man would get him nothing. Bringing back a dead man with no treasure would get him his own dark hole in the dungeon at Beaurain.

# THE KING

## *Twilight*

### 9 SEPTEMBER 1100

Wall-eyed and with gnats dotting his face, Styrkar stared out over the calm waters of the Channel at the bright orange-pink clouds piled on the far-off horizon. Reliving the bloody day when all sense of honor and worth was lost on that dark English isle upon which the bleached bones of five thousand of his brothers-in-arms yet laid, guilt clawed at his conscience like a beast.

Snapping from his trance, Styrkar twisted his look back to the scowling guardsman. With a stream of incoherent gags and kecks spilling out of his mouth without intermission, and seemingly without end, Odo would hear his murderous tale whether he wanted to or not.

"Tormenting me like no pain I've ever known, I can still feel the dead stare of my great lord Harald's accusatory eyes boring straight through me as if through the floor of the great hero's hall of Valhalla itself.

"So haunting a defeat! The triumphant shouts of ten thousand Saxon warriors still swarming my brain: *'The barbarian is killed! An arrow in his throat! The great warrior-king. Harald Hardrada. God-like. Godless. A devil on Earth. Dead on the hill!'*

"Tall and broad with the strength to split a man skull to crux with one blow of that massive, god-made blade, Harald Sigurdsson of Nitharos was feared like no other warrior in the realm. Born of, and a survivor of, a land savage and cruel, wild and lawless, of arbitrary violence, murder, and vengeance, he was imbued with a savagery rare even for a man wielding Thor's hammer.

Often attacking like a wild beast without a weapon or shield and simply tearing men limb from limb with his bare hands, Harald's rage was such that he could defeat a foe by the weight of his reputation alone. Men would either submit to his will or pay with their lives.

"A voyager, a raider, and an audacious treasure-hunter in his younger day, Harald had sailed his ships into the farthest corners of the world—Rus, Byzantium, Bulgaria, Rumania, Grikia, Afrikka, Serkland, Sicily, Italia, Dalmatia, the land of the Moors, even the land of the White Krist—and amassed great riches. Putting to the sword holy men and laymen alike, an insatiable plunderer of anything silver or gold, silken or bejeweled, pagan or Christian, Harald's singular purpose was to finance his long-planned quest to bring the far-flung clans of the vast Northland under his yoke. A gregarious, open-handed man to those who served him faithfully and an ardent heathen worshipper, he achieved his goal with little bloodshed and ruled Norway for many years.

"Only Harald wanted more. More land. More treasure. More power.

"His two young sons were fast growing into men, and they would soon need kingdoms of their own. And the blind loyalty of the fiercest fighting men on Earth, sworn to deliver such, could not be paid for with anything less.

"So it was that my lord Harald—called *Hardrada*, 'Hard Ruler,' but never to his face—turned our awful war dragons toward the shore of that bountiful island kingdom far across the western water: England."

With Styrkar's view of the sun pouring down its last rays on the very land he spoke of blocked by Odo's massive silhouette, with a curt wave of his hand, he indicated for the guard and his horse to step aside. Styrkar then motioned for Odo to turn about, the better to enjoy the view—knowing that it was a sight neither of them would see again.

Odo glanced over his shoulder. Nothing more.

In a voice much softened, Styrkar then resumed the telling of King Harald's tale. "The sickly Edward the Confessor, the last king of the House of Cerdic, had finally died and the claimants to English throne were as many as the ravens on a rotting corpse. Yet, it rightly belonged to Harald. I do not pretend to know why that is true, for the trail to that end wound like a long, dark serpent through a field of thorns. Cnut. Emma. Harthacnut. Estrith. Svein. Magnus. William the Bastard. Harold Godwinson.

"No matter, any of them. Harald said he was the rightful king, and so Harald was.

"Always Harald would say to me: 'A man is given no eternal glory; it is but for him to seize when the gods give him the chance.' And as a favorable toss of the rune sticks indicated the time was right for him to make good his inheritance, Harald would not be denied.

"'The shaft shall sing, the shield shall ring, the ax shall fall on the target,' Harald recounted the Norns' foretelling. And as a great light streaking across the night sky all that spring of his fifty-first year of life further confirmed the gods' approval, we had no doubt of the outcome.

"Many famous victories had Harald Sigurdsson won for Norway, and never had he failed to return us to the fjords without our longships weighted down by the vast treasures of the vanquished. He was as the great thunderer Thor himself come down on Earth, and I, for one, convinced of his invincibility, had long followed wherever he led.

"Harald had appointed me just weeks before we sailed to England to fill the void left by the sudden death of his most trusted commander—a fellow Icelander and one of my own truest friends—Marshal Ulf Ospaksson. The three of us could not have been closer even if our veins ran with the same blood. Fast friends as young men, I loved them both like brothers, a bond further forged during our many years served together as Varangian Guards in defense of Emperor Michael IV and Empress Zoe in Constantinople before Harald returned home to claim Norway's throne.

"I had sworn to die for Harald Sigurdsson, and fully expected that I would be joining him in Valhalla with the legions of other heroes slain beside that English river that mournful day.

"Set out under a glorious morning sun over the parched land of our Northumbrian foes, a maundering mob, jostling, joking, and jabbering without a hint of formation, we were on our way to collect the spoils of a great victory won only days before outside the gates of York. We were maybe five thousand strong—barely a third of our available strength—as most of the men I had left behind to guard the ships at our anchorage downstream near a deserted little village named Riccall. My two sons, under the command of the brave-hearted Eystein Orri—King Harald's handpicked man to marry his precious daughter Maria—I tasked with guarding the king's longship, the *Great Dragon*, heavily laden with much of Harald's vast treasure. Looted from lands the world over, it included a single gold ingot the size of an ox's head that took six of us to load. Diamonds, rubies, emeralds, pearls. And old bones.

"Some of us had helms and swords. A few of us shields. But armor? Hauberks? Byrnies? Not a man. I had given the order for full battle-dress in contemplation of a possible ambush, only to be serenaded with as vociferous and profane a protest as ever my ears have endured. It was hot, the men argued. They were tired. Wounded. The gear was heavy. The trek was long. And so—for the first time in all my days making war—against my better judgment, I relented. The men were right: there was to be no fight this day, only eager anticipation.

"We had fought the battle. We had conquered. Now we were going to be rich.

"Only, as those pompous little Northumbrian lords Morcar and Edwin, holed up in York, had sent out a desperate cry for help to Harold Godwinson of Wessex—a man they'd sooner make dead than king—we were surprised by a hard-riding force of Saxons bent on denying us our prize.

"Slaughtered like pigs—the endless what-ifs and should-haves of hindsight are nothing more than an old man's useless self-excoriation for blatant foolishness. I failed my men. Utterly.

"The Saxons fell on us as we languished in the shade of some tall trees beside the River Derwent awaiting Morcar's delivery of the demanded hostages and loot; no one saw the great cloud of dust rising over a near crest in the road until it was too late. I had posted no sentries along the route, detailed no outriders, set no pickets. In fact, barefoot and wearing only my woolen britches after a swim, I was off chasing after some stray cows in a nearby field at the very moment that tall, mustachioed man on the jet-black horse at the head of the Saxon column first appeared. A man I had never even heard of until that very moment he came over the hill.

"Harold Godwinson. Earl of Wessex. Half-Anglo. Half-Dane. King Edward's named successor. Loathed by Northumbrians. By Normans. The Welsh. His own brother. A liar. A womanizer. A heretic. A cheat. A despoiler of the lives and lands of all those he tyrannized. Damned to Hell by the pope. And, for one day at least, the greatest Englishman who ever lived.

"An uncountable number of our men on the bank below the road, trapped with their backs to the river, were cut to pieces by Godwinson's long-axed housecarles before they even realized we were under attack. The few that managed to escape across the narrow footbridge or splash through the stream were thrown into the countless gaps in the thin defensive line we were forming on the opposite bank. Every man with a shield I ordered to take a step forward and close shoulder to shoulder. Those with any kind of weapon to fall in behind them. The unarmed I sent out onto the flanks. I then ordered the line bent back until the last man on each end met to close a ring around King Harald and his retinue of banner guards, standing within.

"Burying my spear's shaft in the ground in front of me and turning its iron tip toward the enemy lines, I took my place, as always, dead center of the front rank. Feeling a bit like a bully facing down some slavering brute hell-bent on avenging the beating I'd just given his little brother, I crouched behind my battered lime-wood shield, peered past the nosepiece of my boar-head helmet, and waited.

"Stacked up as far as the eye could see behind the high-flying banners of Godwinson's golden dragon, big men, ugly men in white byrnies—full-length chainmail coats—and burnished helms faced us in a formation three times wider than our own. Bright and shining as the midday sun, thousands of swords, spears, axes, and pikes gleamed across the full breadth of the Saxon line like the bared teeth of some fabulous beast inhabiting a skald's netherworld.

"Swords beat on shields. Mocks, oaths, and insults volleyed on the air.

"A thousand arrows, like falcons beaked in cruel attack, arced across a flawless blue sky.

"All along our line, men screamed as steel barbs buried in dirt and wood and flesh.

"A singular crash of metal rims on wooden faces as Saxon shields rose and overlapped. "Spears lowered and pointed straight at us.

"One long blast of a war-horn.

"A blood curdling yell of 'Kill them all!'

"Then, much as the sudden surge shoreward by a swollen sea, the Saxons came on in one massive, roaring wave.

"King Harald—the tallest man on the field and the biggest target in a thousand archers' eyes—sprinted back and forth behind our line furiously, proudly, waving his black, terror-inspiring, raven-emblazoned banner, the 'Land-Waster.' His basso voice booming above the din of battle like the gods' own thunder, he shouted at us to 'Close the gaps!' To 'Hold our position!' To 'Wait for them! Not one step forward! Not one step back!'

"Dug in with our feet spread wide and every man leaning hard into his shield against the full weight of the Saxon charge—'Backbone, men! Backbone!'—hacking at the closest enemy head, arm, or leg in a desperate, *berserker* rage, we gave as well as we got when the sword blades turned crimson. Spears jabbed. Battleaxes whirled. Shields splintered. Every thrust or scything blow meant to kill or maim. Only, in the end, our courage alone was no match for whetted steel.

"The greatest Norse fighting force ever assembled was wiped off the face of the Earth."

# THE DAMNED

## *Dusk*

---

## *9 SEPTEMBER 1100*

As a gentle wash of seawater swept over his feet, Styrkar fastened his pale, icy eyes on Odo's face only to encounter the guardsman's sullen stare. A look that said he didn't want to hear another sound out of Styrkar's mouth but was too exhausted to do anything about it. Short of killing him, the old man would not be silenced.

Odo looked away. And Styrkar continued with his dark tale, reliving slowly dying.

"Humped across a breakwater of corpses piled on the swampy edge of the river, wretched to the core with cold and pain, I was only waiting to die. King Harald, with fiery wounds gaping, laid on the slope just above me—his arms and legs splayed at grotesque angles and an arrow sticking straight up from his throat. He was completely naked as a horde of pitiless scavengers—mostly women and children from York who had fled before the battle with their beasts and chattels to the safety of the forest beyond—had returned and was already on the field stripping the dead.

"One, a boy of some twelve years of age, approached near me with a blood-dripping boar-spear in his hand. Barefoot and stepping lightly, a fast shadow caught by my bare-slit eyes, he bore his mischief over the rippling red water like a young lion preying on whatever he might find. Glancing here and there into the swampy underbrush while loudly cursing all those many men already dead and worth naught for fun, he had a wickedly wild devil's craving in his look to find one man even half-alive that froze me solid as a stone in a midwinter's stream.

"I dared not draw another breath.

"Kicking and poking at the piles of mutilated flesh for any sign of life, the boy was jabbing his spear at the man lying face down in the water beside me when with a sound of thunder, just above him, a flight of fierce Valkyries suddenly appeared. Swooping down like a vicious wind tearing through the dark, overarching trees, Odin's dread judges of a warrior's worth—women all—quickly fanned out over the ground and began gathering up the best and bravest of the hundreds of dead Norsemen littering the battlefield. Dark-eyed and dirty as tunneling shrews, they passed me by with nary a glance.

"Distracted for but a moment, the bloodthirsty little boy was now standing over me, his eyes like needles as he bent ever closer in suspicion of my deathly mask. Parting my lips with the tip of his stone-tipped spear and then pushing it into the back of my mouth, the dead air in my chest was about to burst from my lungs when, from my left, out of a clump of tall reeds growing at the edge of the swampy water, I heard a man groan.

"It was Ull, a one-eyed, flat-nosed giant of a man from Orkney whom I had met in the very hour of our great victory before the gates of York a day earlier. The noise he made was low, almost imperceptible. But in the dead silence of our dark, bloody surround, it called attention like the screech of an owl.

"My blood turned to slush in my veins.

"For as a groan meant life, and life meant a chance to make dead, no sooner had the sound escaped Ull's lips than, wind-swift, the boy sprung on him and plunged his spear hard into the warrior's riven flesh. Grunting as he drove it in as far as his strength allowed, the boy then leaned all his weight against the shaft and waited. Only, to his great dismay, there was no great gasp, no death rattle, no screaming end for the big Orknian. Nay, instead, as he bent close and listened for Ull's breath, just that fast, the proud warrior answered the boy's dastardly act, flashing up a hand to seize him by the throat before—with the last of his immense strength— ripping the wheezing cur to the ground and splitting his skull open on a rock.

"'So it is agreed,' I heard Ull then say to the boy, 'that you will never do that again.'

"With a thick, blackened froth now bubbling on his lips, Ull then let out a low, gurgling laugh at the small silver crucifix he discovered in his hand. Torn from around the boy's neck, he held it up close to his one good eye with his head cocked sideways like a bird. Seemingly contemplating the strange little man hanging on the cross—and what an incredible fool he must have been to die for a bastard like that—he then let it drop atop the rock into a creeping pool of the boy's brains and blood. In the next instant, wrenching himself forward and spitting on the curious thing, Ull's silent ridiculing of the Christian belief was etched in hard lines on his face: *Bald-headed black-robes! Spreading this White Krist like a plague! Man-God? Savior? What a fool believes! Gods don't die for the everlasting life of their people! People die for the everlasting life of their gods!*

"Turning his bloodied face up to the darkening sky, Ull then called out to Odin in a voice clear and strong as a war-hammer's strike: 'I have given my all, Great One, as no warrior's place in the mighty hero's Hall of the Slain can ever be bought with anything less. I am now at the border of Death, and ready to cross. The demon dog Garm is howling, ready to devour my soul. Yet, even as Ragnarok—the utter destruction of all we hold sacred—is now upon us, do not doubt, Great One, that I shall fast return to my appointed place in the line of battle before ever these ravenous Christian beasts—murderers of their own god—contrive to kill mine, too. So raise me up, Lord! Raise me up far-high above this mortal world, above the mountains, the seas, and the stars, to Valhalla, to the fiery battleground of Vigrid, so that I might once again stand shoulder to shoulder with my brave-hearted brothers-in-arms and fight for your everlasting glory!'

"Wracked by a violent cough and shaking uncontrollably, Ull then curled his massive hands inward against his chest like giant hooks, trying to grab hold of the last beats of his fading heart. Crying out, 'Take me, Lord! Take me!' over and again as he bit down hard on his pain, suddenly, his head lolled down onto his chest like pig-drunk, his one eye frozen and staring straight at the ground. 'Take me, Lord,' Ull again pleaded softly, tearfully. 'Take me now. Because I want to fight again.'

"In the next moments, a long, jagged streak of light lit up the wide smear of stormy gray, the thunder rolled, and the rain started pouring down. Drenching. Cleansing. A squall like none I had seen before.

"Slowly, so very slowly, Ull of Orkney lifted his face to the sky, a slight smile on his lips. His shivering calmed. His eye closed. A last shudder. Then he became perfectly still.

"Whirling like dervishes through the trees, the fire-eyed Valkyries again descended onto the field and took up the big warrior in their arms. Like hawks in flight, climbing back into the sky on a high, howling twist of wind, they rose higher and higher into the farthest reaches of the heavens' realm. A sudden, aureate flash. A rumbling of thunder. Then they were gone.

"They would not return. Because there were no more heroes left on the field.

"Far beyond the leaden thunderhead that masked the pale end of the day, massive, red-headed Thor—the mighty god of war—beat his war-hammer against the sky in a portent of the punishment I would suffer for shaming His name. Enduring the god's angry glare as I remained, but bare breathing, still-laid across a rock, no pith in me, no nerve, it was hard to admit my consuming dread of the inglorious end I had wrought. Indeed, having so often imposed my will on the meek-hearted of the world, I had walked life big and brazen, blatantly mocking those so easily plundered by fear of an uncertain end. Death was but a game, a craven game. And the rules were simple: Live with courage. Die with honor. Give no quarter. Beg no mercy. And if you ended up in Hel, well—that was your own damned fault.

"Only the dire retribution of a bloodied, rioting god awaited my grim descent into the fire."

# THE MOTHER

*Dusk*

---

## 9 SEPTEMBER 1100

Squirming in his saddle, Odo returned his look to the Channel. He scoured it for whitecaps, any hint of a rising tide, as if by wishfulness alone he could speed the water's turn.

The sea remained low, hushed, far off.

His prisoner had been unusually quiet for many minutes now, looking up with his eyes again fixed on the little wooden shack precariously perched on a big limestone slab jutting from the top of the cliff. An old woman now stood in its doorway. Raising a hand slowly, the shackled old wretch waved at her. Nothing in return. He raised his hand a little higher over his head, held it there a while, and then dropped it back to his side.

A few moments later, the woman waved back.

Odo thought nothing of it. Just two ugly old people spending their last useless breaths.

The big guardsman was bored.

Raising a hand, Odo swatted at a horsefly, missed, and then swatted it again. A hit. A crash onto the beach. Twisting in his saddle and bending low, he stared at the dazed bug awhile, watching it turn tight circles on the sharp gray stone. Finally, it stopped. Righted itself. Then flew away. Seconds later, it was back buzzing in his ears. Odo swatted it again.

Tracking the insect out of the corners of his eyes, a bemused smirk crept onto Odo's face as he considered not such a far-fetched comparison: the feisty green-headed fly and the old man at his side. Both were pests. Only the bug was less irritating. And harder to kill. Odo took a swipe at one, and then the other. The fly. The man. Over and again. A hit. A miss. A hit. An angry buzzing. The old man bloodied and on the ground. A rampant game. There were no winners. There were no losers. But at least it passed the time.

Standing in the open doorway of her shack atop the cliff, an aged and sickly-looking Adelvia stared down in confusion at the commotion on the beach. As if they had appeared out of nowhere, she saw soldiers, horses, and a large ship keeled over at the base of the cliff. Standing in the shadow of the massive, fallen God's Rock next to a big soldier on a big horse, a shackled old man was looking up at her with his hand raised in the air. Waving it, he then dropped it to his side, waited a moment, and then raised it again. Studying him in wonder of why any such man in chains should think to know her, Adelvia was about to turn back through the shack's doorway when—with a sudden gleam of recognition quickly turned to unconcealed amazement—she, too, slipped her hand into the air—and gasped. *My God. No. It can't be!*

Absorbing the cold despair traced by every ragged scar marring Styrkar's dead-pale face—stunned by the wounds wrought by her atrocious act—no matter how hard Adelvia crushed her hands against her ears, she could not muffle the sudden sound of all those snarling dogs tearing the man to pieces as she was forced to relive the most wretched day of her life.

The day she sinned. The day her spirit died.

Within hours of young Wido's great fall from the cliff, a large troop of heavily armed men surrounded "the Dead Woodcutter's hut" in search of a very dangerous man. Only, Styrkar—resting under the low roof of a rickety wood-shed built beside Adelvia's chicken coop near where the meadow met the forest—jumped up at the sudden sound of hoofs splashing through a nearby stream and escaped the Ponthievins' tightening noose into the depths of the vast Talou Wood.

With every road and beaten path for miles around blockaded by the swarming bounty-hunters, people were being interrogated and every house in every village searched. Styrkar, fleeing through the woods as fast as his injuries would allow, did not stop running until he suddenly tumbled, then half-slid into a deep, bowl-like depression masked by a dense thicket of hornbeam saplings covering the forest floor. Squirming on his belly in a struggle to extricate himself from the sticky, sucking, mush-bottomed gouge in the ground, when at last he wiped the mud from his eyes he was surprised to see a small patch of blue sky at the distant end of a narrow, rain-gutted tunnel eroded through the soft chalk-rock. Wriggling into the opening and then slipping along the tunnel's slight downward pitch, Styrkar would hide in this small blowout in the cliff face for days without food or water and little sleep, deciding that he'd rather die there than be captured. Upon its discovery early the following spring, the long, ragged tunnel quickly became known as Kark's Grave. Named after a young Ponthievin soldier gone missing during the frantic hunt for the elusive barbarian, Kark's smashed skull was found next to his outfitted corpse. A bag of silver coins—presumably his recent pay—remained on his person. Strangely, his cheap leather shoes were missing. And never found.

Flattened on his belly in the deep shadow of one of hundreds of holes pocking the towering chalk wall, Styrkar had a commanding view of the beach and Channel below. Losing track of how many days had passed, he knew not when the hunt would end as, hour after hour, an uncountable number of soldiers, ships, wagons, and horses set off this way and that with a bat-like whirl from a large central camp in search of a badly wanted man.

Yet, unbeknownst to the human bloodhounds, the capture of the murderous invaders was of little importance to Count Guy; for it was Styrkar's treasure-filled ship—seemingly vanished off the face of the earth—that the notorious relic-monger wanted far worse.

Searching the land over, Count Guy's men repeatedly returned to the shack on the edge of the cliff to question the woodcutter's young widow about any tall, bloody, yellow-haired men she had seen lurking in the area. Described as thieves of a sort never before seen on these shores, they told her that they had killed many good men in Ponthieu and, by order of the count, once captured would be beheaded in Abbeville's court square and have their corpses mounted on pikes above the Somme River.

Adelvia steadfastly repeated what she had told the Ponthievins from the first: "There is a rumor of many such men as you describe seen creeping across a farm field at the far western edge of the Talou Wood in the early hours of the yester-morn," she said. "Heading toward Fecamp. I heard some pigs were stolen. A horse. And a cart."

Adelvia was lying through her teeth and did not know why. She knew nothing of the man she had sheltered for those few hours after the storm. But he had selflessly rescued her son from the rubble despite his gruesome wounds, and she felt she owed him, at the very least, the protection of her deceit. As for all these sword-faced miscreants milling around, leering at her as if she was a piece of meat, eating all her eggs, bread, and vegetables, not a man among them would lift a finger to help her son. It was a waste of their time, the Ponthievins said, peeking in on the feverish Wido. The boy would be dead soon. And that was that.

After hiding in the cliff wall for more than a fortnight, the first light of a foggy morning revealed to Styrkar that the beach was being quickly abandoned. And while he knew nothing of the Ponthievin warlord who hunted him or his familial ties to the powerful Duke William of Normandy—the newly crowned king and conqueror of England whose army was still clearing the Hastings battlefield of hundreds of dead Saxons after winning a great victory days earlier—Styrkar benefited from the animosity between the Norman strongman and his troublesome cousin, Count Guy.

King William wanted his piss-ant cousin and his trespassing Ponthievins to get off his land. Out of his duchy. Now. Guy had no right to the treasure; and, as William had made quite clear to him in the past, anything buried anywhere in Normandy the Duke claimed by birthright. William had imprisoned Guy years ago for another of his arrogant challenges to his supreme rule, but—as his belligerent cousin had demonstrated time and again—not only was he pompous but a slow learner, too.

The last time, William had threatened to hang Guy. This time, he would cut off his head.

Guy scoffed, as usual. And then told his men, "Get your asses off that beach—now!"

Styrkar peered down from the blowout in the cliff-face as the last of the count's huntsmen rowed through the heavy morning mist in three small skiffs to a large ship waiting just off the shore. With his heart beating faster and faster against his aching ribs he watched as, one by one, the Ponthievins climbed up the ship's steep side and then dropped over the gunwale onto the crowded deck. After a time, the anchor was raised. The sail was unfurled. And the ship turned the east headland.

Toward Ponthieu.

Adelvia's eyes ignited at the unexpected sight—her jade-green stare burning in the half-light as she watched the last of the Ponthievin ships go under sail and turn the east headland. *Was the stranger aboard? Shackled like a filthy animal? A sword at his throat? Or was he already dead? His bloodied, beaten body stuffed into the tight space between an open barrel of mead and a bucket of fish?*

In the fitful half-sleep of her nights, Adelvia had visions of the wounded man running through the forest. Hunted like a wild boar. A thousand men in pursuit. Of him being trapped against the edge of the cliff. His body riddled with arrows. Of him roaring in pain. Then turning on the hunters with a hair-raising war-cry. Attacking. Of a spear point suddenly buried between his blazing eyes ... the blood-dripping man crashing face-first into the dirt ... made dead in the midst of his full-on charge.

With warm tears streaming down her cheeks, Adelvia's eyes fell wistfully to the ground.

Inasmuch as Count Guy's hunt for the man seemed driven by the same panicked zeal as King Herod's Biblical search for the Christ child, she supposed she had been lucky to survive her brief encounter with the purported criminal.

Still, doubts persisted—Adelvia's mind wrestling over the true nature of the man like two ravens picking at the same dead rabbit. On the one hand, it was not farfetched to believe that he was, as accused, an invader, a thief, a murderer set down upon the beach by the hand of a sorcerer. God knows he would not be the first of such barbarians to have fallen upon their shore. But, then too—given Count Guy's dastardly reputation—Adelvia's desperate hope was that the hunted man was guilty of nothing more sinister than being in possession of something the notoriously greedy Ponthievin lord wanted very much for himself.

Following a course dark and tangled and bent at hard angles to avoid detection, Styrkar emerged from the Talou Forest just before sundown, long hours after the count's ships had sailed.

Standing in the doorway of her little shack on the rock with her arms folded across her chest, balefully studying him as he approached ever closer, Adelvia was sure in her heart that she had never met a man like this before. Her hard-cut eyes softened into an expression of chastened delight as the bloodied, mud-covered stranger slowly raised a hand and waved at her. The voice in her head was almost hypnotic: *He is a good man ... He is a good man ... He is a good man ...*

Halted at the precipice on the far side of the gully, unsure if he was welcome, Styrkar again waved at the young woman. After a long, impressive pause, she waved back.

A few moments later, Styrkar was standing at Adelvia's side.

Staring him in the face with wondering eyes, trying to make sense of the bizarre chain of events that had allowed the man to take this strange hold of her heart, Adelvia had every intention of demanding the full truth of his tale. She would make it clear that this unspoken arrangement between them was very much temporary. But later. Her son was awake and calling for her help.

More often than not, Wido was sleeping, struggling to recover from his injuries. Lying flat on his back on the shack's cold stone floor, unconscious for hours on end, his awakenings were brief and blurry. Hours passed into days. Days into weeks. Day upon night, no talking, no eating, no laughing, no crying. More dead than alive.

Pray and pray as Adelvia did, the hand of Almighty God would no more heal Wido's broken body than any of the endless chants and foul-smelling poultices inflicted upon him by the wart-ridden old hag who rode in every full moon from the far eastern edge of the Talou Wood. There was no magic potion to drink. No wand to wave. Only pain and endless waiting as her son's bones slowly fused back together at all their gruesome angles. Never again would Wido walk upon the Earth but by the four short legs of a mule. His anger at God was extreme. And turning to hate.

Slowly recovering from his own gruesome wounds, Styrkar was very kind to Wido, often kneeling beside his sleeping pallet to keep watch over him whenever Adelvia was busy with such things as readying another change of his bandages or preparing a soft vegetable mash to slip over his lips.

Thinking to give the sullen boy hope for his future, even did Styrkar try to explain the rules of a ballgame he played as a boy in his native land so that Wido might be ready to try it when he was strong again. Only, closing his eyes and turning his head away, Wido could not understand the strange man beside him or had any interest in what he was saying.

Another time, Styrkar collected an assortment of small stones and sticks from the ground around the shack and set up a game of *bnefatafl*. Moving the pieces around, he tried to explain to Wido that the object was to capture the opponent's largest stone—the "king-piece." Only, again, Wido could not comprehend what he was describing and turned away from Styrkar as if annoyed by his constant pestering. Shrugging at a smiling Adelvia, Styrkar quickly regathered the game pieces in his large, gnarled hands and tossed them out the door.

Confused by the stranger's presence, Wido was jealous of his mother's subtle diversion from her sole attention on him, and was anxious for the man to be gone.

Still, Styrkar remained attentive to the suffering child. One morning, Styrkar—seeing how much Wido admired the silver Hammer of Thor amulet he was wearing about his neck—took it off for the first time in years and put it on the boy. And it seemed to have the desired effect of brightening his somber mood. Wido wore it for a time that day, often holding it close to his swollen eyes and staring through the glass beads flanking the small silver pendant. But, later in the day, when Styrkar noticed the amulet was no longer around the boy's neck and asked him where it was, Wido waved a hand around him to indicate that it had come loose and dropped into the deep straw covering the new sleeping pallet Styrkar had made for him. Pawing into the straw a time or two, with a shrug of his shoulders, Wido then turned his head away from Styrkar and stared at the wall.

Raking his hands through every inch of the straw surrounding the boy in search of his precious amulet, but not finding it, Styrkar burned inside.

He would not see the totem again until his last, dying day.

Styrkar spent his nights bedded down on a thin layer of bracken—fern fronds—piled in a corner of Adelvia's small chicken coop, about thirty ells removed from the shack near the edge of the woods. Never sleeping more than an hour at a time, his head was filled with thoughts of capture and his blood jumped at every noise of the forest. Mornings always seemed so far off.

But then, more and more often, Styrkar would see the door to the little half-timbered wattle-and-daub shack propped open just after sunrise. With his stomach made growly by the smell of Adelvia's truly remarkable pork hash wafting from within, he would peer through the coop's wire mesh in eager anticipation of the beautiful young widow stepping outside and then making her way through the tall grass toward him. Entranced by her look—so pure and innocent, almost angelic, in the soft morning light—at her light knock upon the coop's thin wooden frame, Styrkar would feign surprise at her warm gesture for him to follow her back to the shack and take his meal with her.

Sitting on opposite sides of a small, round, three-legged table—he in his filthy gray tunic and she in her sleeveless drab-white—Styrkar and Adelvia would attempt to communicate some. Gestures and shy smiles, mostly. With their faces often turned down toward their bowls, whatever talk they made was awkward, and long silences often filled the air. But they persisted and, little by little, they learned a few words of each other's language. With understanding, their smiles became more genuine. And a growing glimmer in each other's eyes often forced them to look away.

The sun had been up for almost an hour already, but, oddly, Adelvia had not yet appeared to invite Styrkar to eat with her. She was a magician with the simplest of ingredients, and he hungered for whatever she was making for the day's first meal. He could not deny that he desired her company even more. To hear her voice; her laughter music to his ears.

With wonder in his look, peeking out between the thin posts supporting the roof overhanging the front of the adjacent woodshed, Styrkar then crawled out of the chicken coop and into the morning light. Brushing away a smattering of fern leafs clinging to his recently mended britches, he stood staring toward the shack for long moments, hoping to see Adelvia's sunny face appear in the doorway. But no.

Maybe she was busy attending to Wido—the boy's pain particularly severe this day. Shirtless and walking barefoot across the meadow toward the shack, Styrkar would offer his help with whatever she needed done. It was the least he could do as he knew it was becoming increasingly difficult to settle Wido's anger since his realization that he would never walk again.

Arriving at the shack's open door, Styrkar knocked lightly and, with his heart quivering just the same as if charging into battle without a shield, peered inside.

Adelvia was on her knees, eyes closed, praying.

Wido was sleeping.

Styrkar's heart thumped in the silence.

At last, Adelvia's eyes opened; a rapid, oblique glance revealing a huge, black silhouette in her doorway. Showing alarm, her green-eyed gaze quickly softened when she realized that it was Styrkar. A gentle smile. Holding up a finger to him indicating that she needed a moment more, she then turned back to the little silver crucifix hanging on the wall above her sleeping pallet, closed her eyes, and finished her solemn prayer. Crossing herself—"In the name of the Father, the Son, and the Holy Spirit .... Amen"—she then stood up and, with her eyes sparkling with a light not of this world, motioned for Styrkar to come inside.

Pointing at the little silver man on the wall and nodding his head at Adelvia, Styrkar said in his fractured Norse-French: "It is right that you worship in this way. Believe in this man. Your Maker. I have not lost faith in my gods. Nor will I. But that does not mean that I deny your White Krist exists. Or that he is good, and powerful. I believe there are many, many gods. In the sky, on the earth, and in the sea, too. Now this Krist, this Lord Savior you worship—" Styrkar again pointed at the figure of the crucified Christ—"an argument can be made that He may be the greatest god of all, more powerful than Odin even, for the majesty of His Earthly creations are without compare. I have traveled to many places in my life and have seen the great cities of the world—Rome, Constantinople, Jerusalem, Alexandria—all raised by your God's mighty hand and gleaming with riches. The cathedrals, the palaces, the stadiums. Grand boulevards. Bridges. Colonnaded plazas studded with ornate sculptures and fountains. Market squares stocked with every kind of delicacy. Gifts of the White Krist to his children for their unshakable belief in Him and obedience to His laws. Despite them never having seen Him. Him never walking side-by-side with them. Never taking up a sword for them. Or speaking to their face."

Adelvia remained silent, entranced by the expression of sturdy honesty as Styrkar spoke.

"Upon the fell green sweeps of the northland the gods have bequeathed no such splendor to our far-flung tribes. Our fjords' glassy waters reflect no marbled cities carved into the winter white of the enveloping hills. No spires stretching into the sky. For Odin is not a builder. He does not sit on a bejeweled throne under the dome of a high-soaring stone church. He does not eat off a plate of gold. Nor wear a purple robe."

Never shy about stating his true beliefs, Styrkar was a straight-talker almost to a fault. Only now, after a brief pause, Styrkar's low, strong voice sounded almost apologetic as he indicated for Adelvia to take a seat at the small table she'd already set for their meal. With his face betraying not a hint of guile, again he spoke. "While I do not mean to disparage your God—a god who has proven to possess the power to crush all others—those things are not important to Odin. Nor does Odin allow any distractions from His singular focus of protecting His children from the myriad evils that seek to destroy us. Odin desires no grand cathedrals be raised in His honor or riches laid at His feet. Faith, service, and a blind willingness to die for Him are all He asks of us. And, while I admit that I know little more than what I've seen of this Krist-man's Heavenly Father—the grandiose proof of belief He demands, His preoccupation with building extravagant places of worship—" Styrkar glanced over at Wido wracked by fits of pain even as he laid sleeping on his pallet—"just maybe Odin is the more generous god—bestowing his love and compassion more freely upon His children than your God does on His."

Styrkar stopped speaking and stared at Adelvia. Struggling to interpret the utterly blank—even bewildered—expression on the widow's face, fearing that he had offended her, he shrugged his shoulders and let out a slight, almost sheepish, smile.

Dropping her eyes to the floor under Styrkar's questioning look, Adelvia nodded her head as if in uneasy agreement with his words—while pretending to understand them. His Norse-French was mostly Norse. Deciphering a semblance of the names Christ and Odin and maybe a city or two, she could only guess at what Styrkar had said to her. But, with each passing day, Adelvia realized that her initial instinct about this outwardly very rugged man of war having a good and gentle heart inside him was correct, and somehow she knew that his long, animated statement was thoughtful and sincere. However right or wrong it may be.

Living as if he was already dead during the earliest weeks of his convalescence, Wido paid little attention to the tall, yellow-haired man he'd so often see sitting beside him. Fevered and confused as he laid on his thick straw pallet tucked into a corner of the one-room shack, it was only with the passing of time and an increased clarity of mind that Wido's wonder began to grow. *Who was this stranger sitting in his father's chair across from his mother in even the earliest hour of the day? Eating their food? Where did he come from? Why did he not speak French? Why was he dressed in rags? And how did he get so many horrible cuts and bruises?*

What Wido noticed most about the man was that he was very tall and strong. His hands, shoulders, and chest were huge. His feet big like a bear's, and his toes always had mud caked between them as if he had just been out walking barefoot in the rain. The man had shoes of a sort—set near the door—very similar to those Wido had often seen horse-soldiers wear. Only the stranger never wore them much, as for some reason they didn't fit him very well, seeming to belong to a much smaller man. A bold-lettered KARK was burned under the tongue of the left shoe. Wido didn't know what it meant but, letting his imagination run wild, he considered that maybe the stranger had stolen the shoes. Or, maybe, given his barbarian look, even killed someone for them.

Appearing to be much older than Wido's mother—with his bruised, weather-beaten face, crooked nose, and a long, red scar slashed down onto his shoulder from behind one ear—the man was hardly handsome. Yet, Wido supposed some women might find him tolerable-looking nonetheless. At times, he was funny. Gross, even. He put butter on everything. Even his wounds. He prayed often. Asked for nothing. And got less.

So also, Wido thought the stranger was a very shallow man. His wits neither quick nor nimble. His talk more grunt than speech. And then there were all those little pictures he was always drawing in the dirt—apparently describing to Wido and his mother the many exciting things that had happened in his life. Military matters mostly: battles and formations, ships and shields, swords and the like. And truth be told, for a finger dragged in the dirt, his representations of dogs and sheep and hawks and hunting weren't half-bad.

Seeing his mother's face beaming with delight as her eyes traced over the stranger's artful lines, Wido sensed that she was quite fascinated by these tales of blood and battle and life in far-off places. Laughing in sweet tones from behind a muting hand as the man struggled to draw the pictures just right—to make those dragons' heads jutting up from all those ships' prows as fierce as possible—she imagined that in his native tongue he was a thoroughly mesmerizing storyteller and how popular he must be with children.

As such, being quite skilled at needlework, Wido's mother would often sit in a small wooden chair by the fire burning in a pit at the center of the shack and give life to the man's little finger-in-the-dirt sketches by the weaving of many bold-colored threads into elaborate pictures depicting his far-flung adventures. Many times Wido would see her shaking her head with a kind of cool disbelief at what were certainly wild exaggerations by the man—if not outright fabrications—and yet she would faithfully record them in her growing tapestry. His tales of gods in the sky. Of the Earth. And in the sea. Even had he drawn what he claimed was a god in a box. His mother's skilled hands weaving life into the ethereal scene the man described in bold yellow threads, such radiance that burst from the little box—loaded into the hold of what appeared to be a small Viking ship—stood out on her small tapestry, lighting up the surrounding blue-stitched water brighter than the light of day. Upon drawing a picture of a vast sea, the stranger then pointed a finger at its far eastern edge and indicated that the box was found in a cave on a hill in a faraway land. His subsequent glassy-eyed stare into the heavens told of his belief that there was something powerfully magic inside that box. Something to be revered—and feared.

*Oh, so many outrageous lies the man tells!* Wido thought.

Even so, years later, reflecting on his old life, Wido often wondered in whose hands that little roll of cheap canvas his mother had so richly adorned with images portraying the man's tales was now held. *Not that it had one stitch of truth,* Wido told himself. *Six strong men needed to carry one massive gold ingot? Ha! Precious gemstones and pearls buried in the rock-bottomed beds of a hundred forest streams? Silver coins piled waist-deep in a cave behind a great highland fall? All fable and wind!* Still, the possibility that the man's endlessly streaming saga—a swashbuckling life of unimaginable riches bracketed by war, storm, and strife—had been born out of even a kernel of truth made such tales maddeningly intriguing to Wido.

Stuck in his brain like a splinter just beneath his skin—irritating but impossible to remove—Wido would secretly search for the tattered little picture-cloth for the rest of his life.

# THE WIDOW

*Night*

## 9 SEPTEMBER 1100

Adelvia of Arques bore not even a faint semblance to the immodest, bosom-baring women so prevalent and provocatively displayed in the skin-tight tunics of the day. In every detail presenting herself in the plainest way, her sober demeanor was a purposefully dull reflection of her characteristic modesty and virtue. She was not silly. She told no jokes. Winked no eye. Wagged no tongue. Yet, she alone, poised in that wide space between beauty and divinity amongst a hundred other women, would draw the lustful stares of every man in the village square. Even that she might allow one to take hold of her delicate hand and help her down from her little ox-drawn cart equated to a conquest bragged about in local drinking halls for weeks. That was the effect Adelvia had on men. So too, it was the secret attraction building inside Styrkar that fired his yearning to take into his arms and hold the most thoroughly perfect creation of the gods he had ever known.

The weather was turning cold, and Styrkar had been wrestling with the fact that he must be leaving soon. Upper Normandy was crawling with armed men as for the past fortnight Duke William, recently returned from his conquest of England, had been sending troops into the area almost daily in search of a band of brazen outlaws rumored to have rowed into shore below the dead woodcutter's hut aboard a burning ship laden with stolen gold. So also, tens of bounty-hunters contracted by Count Guy of Ponthieu were still creeping about, desperate to capture the murderous scum and collect their reward. All of them thieves, thugs, and rapists. Crouched behind a downed tree at the edge of the forest and peering through the dense brush masking his hiding place, even did Styrkar see one slovenly man among them grab Adelvia about her waist and—offering her the protection of his sword—jerk up his tunic to reveal his small but stiffened penis. Red and repulsive, as if rubbed raw by his own rough hand, he then began grabbing at Adelvia's tunic and groping her breasts. Struggling to fight him off, a shaken Adelvia later told Styrkar that she feared the worst if not for Wido's murderous glare at the man—and his threatening hold on his father's ax.

Styrkar knew this to be true, as he'd witnessed the scoundrels' uproarious belly-laughter at the sight of the "ugly little cripple" worming over the ground in attack. With their cruel intent withered to red-faced mirth, the starch went out of their pants, and the bounty-hunters moved on.

What with all the lies Adelvia had told to protect him, Styrkar feared the consequences would be severe should she be caught harboring a man hunted by the most powerful lords in the realm. Dragged off in chains. Prison. The gallows, even. Her death would be a public spectacle. Many times Styrkar had decided that today was the day, the day he would start making his way north, but then he would find one more thing he wanted to do for the beautiful young widow in return for all she had done for him. He would not be remembered as a freeloader.

Day after day, honing the blade of her dead husband's old ax against the well-worn edge of a large flint stone jutting out near the top of the steep-sided gully, Styrkar would spend hours splitting dark hearts of beech, oak, and ash wood at the edge of the forest into fire-logs to help Adelvia meet the quota demanded by her unsympathetic liege-lord—a pompous little man living in a little fortress in the middle of the forest.

So also, gathering the materials and tools necessary to mend a section of the coop netting, Styrkar had replaced all the old floor rushes in the shack with fresh-cut straw; fashioned new hinges for the door; made new pegs to secure the crude mortise and tenon joinery where the wall supports met the roof trusses; and scraped out and replaced the decomposed gypsum daub in the gaps between the shrunken clapboards to keep out the coming winter winds.

Still, there was the problem of the rather flimsy connection of the one-room shack to the large stone slab it sat on. Little skilled in construction, Wido's woodcutter father had pinned the house to the outcrop by means of a few short, stout hearts of oak driven through the sill plate at the base of each wall into cracks he had widened in the rock and then filled with a small amount of a poor-man's concrete—heavily sanded chalk mixed with stone and shell fragments.

Only, over the years, battered by the constant winds blowing in off the Channel and the endless cycle of winter freeze and spring thaw, the inferior aggregate had crumbled to dust. Any bond between the wood stakes and the stone was destroyed. And, with the shack's half-timbered frame slanted to one side and the wattle infill rotting beneath its grayed clapboard siding, it was not uncommon for the structure to outright lift off the slab whenever a hard wind blew in through its open door.

Worse, the high chalk cliff the ledge rock sat on was, at best, temporary. Consisting of little more than the relentlessly stacked and packed parts of millions of tiny plant skeletons that floated in what was a warm tropical sea long ago, the towering cliff's soft marl base was fast eroding under the eternal attack of the now very cold Channel water. Massive sections of the chalk face would sheer off without warning. And that big black rock down on the beach—God's Rock, Adelvia called it—the rock that months earlier had fallen from the clifftop and crushed Styrkar's ship and crew—was the proof. Styrkar hung his head over the edge of the thin ledge rock and looked at its underside. Worry darkened his face like the shadow of a passing cloud. The undercutting of the shack was already apparent. It was a disaster waiting to happen.

Somehow, someway, he needed to shift the little shack away from the precipitous edge of the cliff and reattach it as far back on the stone as possible. Or, better yet, move the shack off the stone altogether, away from the cliff and the steep gully bordering one side into the grass meadow fronting the forest. Unmoor its base plates from the rock and—with help from the new little mule Adelvia had gotten for Wido before his crippling fall from the cliff—drag the wholly assembled shack to its new place. Adelvia thought it impossible that it could be done, but agreed to let Styrkar try.

Only it was raining this day. He would start on the morrow.

Pushing off her quilted cover and swinging her feet onto the floor, Adelvia lit the candle on the small trestle-table beside her raised bed pallet with an ember from the fading fire. With her long, dark hair falling over the shoulders of a heavy nightdress dappled with countless little tears and unmatched patches, it was obvious even to a sleepy Wido that his mother was endeavoring to attract no one with her look when she slipped on her dark woolen cloak and opened the door.

As a matter of routine, Adelvia had been bringing her new young mule inside the house every cold or stormy night. So also, her favorite goose, four goslings, and two chickens rescued from the crate her father was carrying at the moment of his death.

Only now there was a man out there. A man cold and wet and likely sleeping not a wink. A man Adelvia had come to care for very much. Thoughtful beyond anything she believed a man capable of, just the other day he had brought her three big armfuls of fresh-cut straw for her floor. Tossed with lavender, he said, to keep the bed bugs away. It was a wonderful surprise. And one that she would now return in kind.

Rocked back against the door frame by a gust of crying wind, she stepped out into the rain in her bare feet, stared up long and hard at the storming night sky, hesitated a moment, then ran across the meadow toward the chicken coop as fast as she could.

The door opened. The rain swept in. Then his mother. *Then the man.*

Glancing up from his pallet on the floor, a sleepy-eyed Wido could see by the light of the flickering candle that his mother was drenched from head to toe. Her feet as muddy as the man's. Pushing back her hood and slipping off her cloak, she stood in a shallow tub of water a few moments, watching it turn brown before quickly drying her feet on a coarse white cloth spread out next to it; she then climbed back into bed.

Dripping in the doorway, the man seemed not sure what to do. Glancing about, but not moving.

Wido saw his mother smile at the man, and then point to a spot on the floor on the opposite side of her pallet.

Slicking the rain water off of his face, the man nodded his head. Crossing a few steps to the other side of Adelvia's raised bed, he stared down at the thick, clean straw he'd laid on the floor and smiled at her. Picking up a few of the dried lavender blooms, he handed them to her in a neat little bundle and said, "*Merci.*" Startled by the warmth of the smile Adelvia gave him in return, he nearly choked as he quickly swallowed his tongue, and then backed away.

With the golden glow of the candlelight on her moist cheeks complementing her cheerful countenance, Adelvia then picked up the thin cotton gloves she had been wearing to bed every night for most of the past three years, and the smile slipped from her face. Dingy white and purposefully pricked with rose thorns—she studied them a moment with a glassy-eyed stare. Pressing a thumb against a thorn, she watched as a dot of blood quickly appeared. Then, matching the gloves palm to palm, finger to finger, and smoothing them flat, with a quick glance over at Styrkar, she replaced the gloves on the small table beside her. Behind the candle. Out of sight. With one last dark, sparkling look at the man and a smile for her son—she then blew out the flame.

Standing in the darkest corner of the shack, Styrkar quietly stripped off his wet clothes and piled them on the floor. His britches, although damp and uncomfortable, he left on. Lingering a moment to feel the warmth of the low fire burning in the central hearth, he patted the sleepy-eyed little mule on its muzzle, carefully stepped past the softly clucking hens, and then settled himself onto the fresh-cut straw. Surprised to find a thin gray blanket folded at his feet, he pulled it up over his shoulders and closed his eyes. He had not felt so peaceful and at home since his last night in Nitharos before sailing off to England with King Harald. And that seemed like a lifetime ago.

The rain had finally stopped and all was quiet … so quiet.

Still, Adelvia could not fall asleep.

Since her earliest childhood, the fear of God had been nurtured in the woman who was to become Wido's mother, so she was keenly aware of the peril her soul was in. No matter that she was three years a widow, she had sworn a forever obedience to her Lord-Savior's laws to never lie with any man but her legal husband. Still, at times, under the dark veil of night, there raised out of the crypt of her mind the rock-hard embodiment of the heinous crime she contemplated. Blessed with a lovely face and the curves of body many a man ached for, she so deeply lamented these middle-of-the-night fantasies as to start wearing those thin cotton gloves splintered with wild rose thorns every night to prevent her hands from responding to the hot, wet tinglings of her taut, lonely flesh. Tossing and turning this night, tortured by her adulterous imaginings, it was as if she was submerged in the fiery Lake of Hell with nothing but her own hot sweat to wash them away.

Slowly turning onto her side, Adelvia peeked over the edge of her pallet at the man lying on the floor below. Styrkar. An unusual name. Masculine. Strong. Perfect for this man. Stretching her neck forward with her head raised up off her pillow, listening to his shallow breaths, she then quickly pulled back for fear that he was staring at her, too.

With her senses suddenly awhirl with the imagining of Styrkar's hard, muscular body lying beside her, of his warmth seeping into her humid skin, Adelvia tried to convince herself that there was no real harm in fantasy. That one's conscience should demand no accountability for such meaningless thoughts. There was no treachery. No physical act. No sordid tale for a tattling tongue to tell. Still, with such pleasurable imaginings stirring her mind to the sharpest remembering of those long-ago nights spent under the slow, caressing hands of her adoring husband, a sudden and powerful wave of guilt forced her to flip onto her opposite side. Pulling her legs up hard against her chest and burying her face between her knees, Adelvia then let out a long, silent scream.

Such was the life of a widowed woman living under the glare of an all-seeing God. Her heart had been in tumult for years; yet, according to Him above, Adelvia had much more grief to suffer. She'd had a husband and could not have asked for a better one, she told herself. She did not want to be desired. Nor did she need the love of another man. Still, was it so wrong to want to be cared for, truly cared for, and to give as much in return to another lonely person? Was it really a sin to feel more alive than she had in years?

Out of the darkness below, Styrkar's long, restless breath gave Adelvia a hopeful answer. For, he, too, was wide awake. And thinking of her.

# THE VARANGIAN

*Night*

---

## 9 SEPTEMBER 1100

Staring away the hours as the night's brightest stars faded from the dawning sky, Styrkar had not felt his heart jump for a woman in many years. Not since his beloved Hild had passed in the winter of her twenty-sixth year after months of breathing in the air of a Norwegian sky blackened with volcanic ash. He wasn't at her side when her soiled lungs expelled their last breath, finding out only months later that she had died. A hurt in his heart that never went away.

Hild died in 1041. The year was easy to recall, for it was in those same months when Styrkar and his great friends—Harald Sigurdsson and fellow Icelander Halldor Snorrason—ran their warships up onto the shore of *Gydingaland*—the land of the famous White Krist—and then struck at the very heart of Palestine.

By the command of the powerful Byzantine Emperor Michael IV of Constantinople—Basileus of the East Roman Empire—self-proclaimed King of the World—120 hand-picked Varangian Guards—battle-tested Norse mercenaries employed to protect the Queen of All Cities—were tasked with manning two small, swift pirate-chasing ships in the escort of an enormous twin-masted Imperial dromon carrying a "most pious" royal princess and her ridiculously large retinue on a pilgrimage to the Holy Land.

Enabling his favorite niece to fulfil her desire to glorify her Savior Jesus Christ in the very land that He lived, so, too, did the avaricious Emperor Michael—often referred to as the Paphlagonian—have a much less righteous reason for raiding the imperial treasury to pay the trip's absurd cost: the nefarious looting of every crypt and cave his minions could sniff out between the Mediterranean Sea and the River Jordan.

Making it clear when appointing Harald *komes*—or captain, of his Palace Guard—to lead the expedition with Styrkar as his second-in-command *stallari*—that he wanted no less than a ten-fold return on his investment, the Emperor bellowed from his jewel-encrusted throne, "You're *Barbaroi*, goddammit. Godless pirates plundering what others have labored so hard to acquire. It's what you're good at."

Inasmuch as the Emperor was determined to raise Constantinople—already the foremost city of the Christian Empire in the East—to such heights as to challenge Rome's arrogant claim as the supreme city of the world, he wanted to add many more Holy relics to the city's already vast collection. Relics that would inspire the same awe—and subsequent emptying of pilgrims' pockets—as those he already possessed: Jesus' Crown of Thorns, the True Cross, John the Baptist's head, even a letter said to be written in the Lord's own hand. Day after day, year after year, such was the endless stream of the sick, the poor, and the penitent masses that poured into the cavernous space under the soaring silver dome of the Hagia Sofia to grovel before these spirit-infested scraps of bone and wood, praying—and paying—for their miracles, that the Emperor wanted more, and more, and more.

The Emperor Michael further explained to Harald that a team of expert stone masons had been sent ahead of the planned pilgrimage at the invitation of the new Caliph of Egypt—a Muslim holy man born to a Byzantine mother and ardent in his efforts to wipe prejudice and bigotry from the face of the Earth. After setting free fifty thousand Christian captives, the Caliph had granted permission for the rebuilding of the Church of the Holy Sepulchre in Jerusalem, which had been destroyed by fanatical Muslims three decades earlier. Having negotiated a thirty-year peace agreement with the new ruler, the Emperor assured Harald that every town along the pilgrimage route would throw their gates wide and warmly welcome the Christian travelers. "And there will be your opportunity," the Emperor quickly added. "Those old towns are filthy rich with spoils easy for the taking."

Harald and Styrkar were not two steps removed from the closure of His Imperial Majesty's big, bronze chamber doors when they shared a long, hearty laugh at his expense.

For, despite the Norsemen's unparalleled experience in stripping foreign lands of their worth, a raid on the decadent, treasure-rich Levant in the guise of escorting a royal pilgrimage to Jerusalem was no easy thing to accomplish. Months were spent in the planning. Weeks in the loading. Days more waiting for Her Highness to come down from her tower and get on the ship. The princess was still resting, they said, after her weeks-long carriage ride to Constantinople from her father's grand hall in Thessalonica. "She arrived a month ago," Harald grumbled to Styrkar. "I mean, it's not like she walked here. How tired can she be?" When at last they got underway, the gods rewarded Harald's atypical patience with day upon day of cloudless blue skies and calm waters, and the Imperial convoy completed the sea voyage leg of the journey without incident.

The easy part was over. Now they had to unload the ships.

Sweating like a plow-horse during a hard pull as he helped his men wrestle cask after cask of water, wine, and food stuffs out of the dromon's hold and onto its broad deck, Styrkar was oblivious to the hundreds of the town's inhabitants crowded along the shore in witness of the extraordinary sight: 150 Imperial Army cavalrymen; 240 foot soldiers; 100 oarsmen; 120 Varangian Guards; horses, mules, carts, carriages; casks, crates, chests; tents, tubs, tables, sofas; priests and poets; capons and chamberlains; coopers and farriers; servants and slaves; a princess—and her dull-witted, little-lord-fluffy-slippers brother, to boot. All disgorged from the massive dromon onto the dock at the great port city of Jaffa like so much flotsam washed in with the tide.

After days of restocking their spent provisions in the local markets and loading every last sack of grain, basket of bread, jar of olives, and velvet-covered footstool onto the wagons, carts, and mules—"Finally!" Harald shouted—the royal caravan began creaking down the long, dusty road toward Jerusalem.

Crossing the wide coastal plain on foot with their single-edged axes slung over a shoulder, bows and quivers hanging down their backs, and carrying shields emblazoned with the ancient double-headed eagle symbol of the Byzantine Emperor, the predominantly pagan Varangians remained ever vigilant in their protection of the Emperor's niece and her long baggage train as it rolled along the heavily travelled road. With their heads on a constant swivel and their eyes peeled for any sign of Saracens—or worse, Seljuk Turks—lying in wait of an ambush, Komes Harald would direct an occasional two- or three-man foray in search of whatever might be found of worth amidst the many ruins littering the surrounding hills.

Slowed by the rough, undulating road and frequent stops to water the pack animals, the city of Ramla—or what remained of it—was reached in the hour before sundown. Told it was a well-built and prosperous city with plentiful water and markets that offered anything and everything the never-ending procession of dusty, tired, cross-carrying pilgrims trudging along its main thoroughfare could want, the Varangians were dismayed to find that most of Ramla's buildings—including its beautiful, centuries-old White Mosque containing the shrine of a famous Islamic saint—had been reduced to rubble by a massive earthquake a few years earlier. Scooped up out of the debris heaped around the jagged, three-story remnant of the mosque's once-towering minaret—"The Tower of the Martyrs"—the whereabouts of the holy man's bones was now unknown.

Staring around at the shattered stone columns, ragged walls, and fallen towers flanking both sides of the road, Harald and Styrkar could not disguise their disappointment. Ramla had been identified by the Emperor as a particularly desirous target to plunder. They would have to tell Michael that an angry god had gotten to the city first.

Situated at the intersection of two major roads, the Via Maris—the "Way of the Sea"—linking Cairo to Damascus and the east-west road linking Jerusalem with the coast, Ramla was believed to be the Biblical Ramathaim—a village known as Arimathea in the time of Jesus.

Sorrowful at the destruction of the once beautiful city, it was the princess herself that declared to her pagan escorts that the original settlement of Arimathea was, in fact, the home of a wealthy Israelite named Joseph—the man said to have begged Pontius Pilate, the Roman prefect of Judea, to let him take the great Jewish prophet down after his crucifixion on a large wooden cross raised on a rock called *Golgotha*—"the place of the skull"—before carrying Him off to this place to give him a proper burial.

Reclining on a plush, velvet-cushioned sofa as she gazed out through the carriage's open flap at the huge, crumbled limestone blocks and vine-covered columns, the bejeweled, raven-haired princess was the very picture of Byzantine royalty. *"Most pious,"* maybe, Styrkar recalled thinking upon his first good look at her standing on the wharf at Constantinople. *But she's no nun.*

Stunning in her gauzy, crimson silk, gold-embroidered gown, the ruby-lipped princess watched with haughty disinterest as Styrkar and his Varangians worked to shoo away a murmuring swarm of street rabble trying to steal glances at her godly form through the carriage's gold-plated door. Fanned by an attendant to ensure her ultimate comfort in the insufferable heat and dripping with allure, so, too, had the full-bosomed, wasp-waisted beauty caused Harald—the cocksure future King of Norway—to become uncommonly awkward, almost comically obeisant, from the very moment she stepped off the dromon's gangway at Jaffa. Styrkar had seen that look on his friend's handsome face many times before. Seduced by her sultry look alone, it hardly mattered that Harald didn't even know the princess's proper Christian name. He was smitten. And that, as Styrkar knew all-too-well of his friend's fatuous fawning over beautiful women in the past, was a very dangerous thing.

What with the caravan arriving in Ramla late in the day, the princess declared to Harald that she'd been discomforted quite enough by her cramped, bumpy carriage ride from the sea, and ordered a stop for the night. At Harald's barked command, the princess's army of attendants began scurrying about, grabbing long wooden poles and twined ropes off the wagons and quickly raising her huge, bronze silk tent amidst the shade of an ancient olive grove flanking the road.

Some of the Imperial Army's shield- and spear-bearers were tasked with refilling the many water casks emptied during the day's journey from what was described by the local peasants as a large cistern still intact beneath the ruins of the White Mosque. They even showed the soldiers where a set of stairs led down to the hidden pool. Others fanned out over the surrounding hills in search of fresh fruit, grains, and vegetables for the troops, and fodder for the horses.

Styrkar—standing within a force of twenty Varangians who circled around the royal carriage as men bustled to and fro unloading wagon after wagon and arranging the many gilt furnishings the princess required within her private tent—was growing impatient: he wanted the princess to get out the carriage; into the light; the better to gawk at her in all her glory. When, at last, all was ready and every Varangian standing at rigid attention, Harald took a hold of the princess's proffered hand and helped her step down on to the road. With his broad, inner smile belied by an over-serious face, Harald then began slowly walking the gold-shimmered princess toward the grove and the silk tent raised within.

Walking between two lines of *tzakones*—Christianized Turks employed as local guards in Ramla—the silvered glints of sundown light that reflected off their curved-blade scimitars perfectly complemented the radiance of the princess's impossibly white skin. Upon reaching the tent's entrance, the princess turned her head and looked up at her escort—a man nearly two ells taller than her and the largest man she had ever seen. She spoke Greek to Harald, little of which he understood.

While hardly fluent in the Norse language, the Royal Chamberlain—a paunchy little eunuch with tiny eyes following closely behind them—did his best to translate her words.

Harald attempted to reply in Greek, prompting the princess and her chamberlain to exchange an amused look. Many of his words did not easily translate, as might be expected of a *Barbaroi*. But, then—surprising the chamberlain—Harald turned to the princess and asked her a question in perfectly articulated Latin. Jerking her head and eyebrows up, the ivory-skinned princess riveted her eyes on the Norseman's handsome face. Studied it a while. Intrigued. Hardly did she know that the mighty Saracen-Slayer, renowned for his physical prowess, also had a brain. With the barest wave of her hand, she then invited Harald—and Harald alone—into her tent. And closed the flaps.

Stunned by this breach of imperial protocol, the *Kortinarioi*—a specialized unit in the Byzantine Army responsible for guarding the royal camp—quickly formed a perimeter around a tent large enough to hold their entire sixty-man troop. They were then instructed by their captain—aptly named the Count of the Tents—that the princess and the *komes* should not be disturbed.

Standing outside the tent, Styrkar shook his head at the imagining of the nameless princess at this very moment unfastening that large silver brooch at her breast, unwrapping her sleek silk tunic, and letting it fall to the floor. He then rolled his eyes to the sky and walked away.

Pulling himself into the saddle of his waiting horse and reining it around in the direction of a cluster of overloaded wagons, Styrkar didn't even see the ragged little peasant in his path until the very moment his big stallion knocked him to the ground. In the act of carrying bales of hay to the horses, the man's loud, fast-spoken Greek was laced with red-faced epithets until, with a glance up, he realized how fortunate he was that the big Varangian Guard looming over him didn't understand a word he was saying.

Sloven, drunken, and his soiled tunic dark as burnt wood, the peasant scrambled to his feet, desperate to disappear amidst the milling crowd, just another sweat-stained rag floating in a sea of downtrodden humanity. Only, fleeing down the fastest lane of escape, he ran straight into another huge Varangian Guard. Bigger than the one on the horse. Bigger than the horse. Or so he seemed.

Halldor Snorrason. Harald's naval commander.

"So who's this pile of goat shit?" Halldor snarled in his hard Icelandic Norse. He examined the man lying at his feet. "He looks a lot like that no-cock Pecheneg we blood-eagled near the falls of the Dnieper that day."

Styrkar grinned at his old friend, fully regaled in his gilt leather kilt and chainmail shirt.

"No, I'd say he's more like the one we strung up and snapped in half between the trees."

Halldor disagreed. Halldor always disagreed. He turned a hard look back on the peasant. He liked to scare peasants. To toy with them. He pulled a long, filigreed dagger from his waist-belt. Ran a finger along its whetted blade. "So, what's your name, turd?"

With his voice rattling as if a pack of lies was lodged in his throat, the peasant coughed and finally spit out "Yitzhac!" It was a lie, of course. The first of the many he would tell.

"Hall—dor," Halldor said to the peasant. "It means large, loud, and ready to kill."

A long, boisterous laugh followed. Styrkar, too.

"So, tell me Yit-sack, where's all this treasure I'm hearing is around here? All these rich Jew's golden shits: where have all you little rodents stashed them?" Halldor put the point of his dagger under Yitzhac's chin. Lifted his head a little so that he could look him in the eyes. "Huh, Yit-sack? The pile of treasure that this dung-breathed Islamite pickpocket so suddenly remembered in the very moment before I cut off his nose? Saying it is buried under some grand palace here in Ramla. And then the cave he so graciously told of before I cut off his ears. Swearing it's crammed with enough gold bars and dinars to sink an Imperial dromon. Where, squirrel?" Halldor lowered the point of his dagger from the man's wheezing throat to his crotch. "Where are your nuts?"

With blood trickling down the front of his cheap linen tunic, Yitzhac waved a fast hand at some ruins littering a distant hill to the north.

Thrusting a look into the peasant's dark, watery eyes like a hot brand and finding only lies, Halldor then threatened to cut them out.

The man's face flushed, his words rushed, Greek, and vaguely understandable.

"παρακαλώ ... νούμερο ... αλήθεια ... Please! ... No! ... Truth! ...

"λόφος ... μονοπάτι ... σπηλιά ..." Hill ... Trail ... Cave...

"Plague-rotted rat-eater!" Halldor twisted his dagger blade between the man's lips, pressing it to the man's tongue, and threatening to fork it just the same as a serpent of the dust.

Frantic and flailing, the peasant quivered in his bones. Babbling as if brain-dead, few recognizable words studded his high-pitched chatter.

Still, enough for Styrkar to get the gist of it. Earthquake ... Palaces ... Rubble ... White Mosque ... Treasures ... Relics ... Peasants digging ... Loading carts ... Caves ... Near Lod.

Styrkar pulled a single copper *folleis* from the coin pouch hanging at his hip and held it out to the man. Roman-made and impressively large but coated with only the thinnest layer of silver—the peasant knew the coin was of little worth, and so declined to take it from Styrkar. Wearing his ragged poverty, Yitzhac shook his head and said in passable Greek, "No. Much danger, little reward. But for two handfuls of silver—big hands like yours—thirty Roman *miliaresia*—the same as the Christian lore says was paid to Jesus' evil apostle—I will lead you to the treasure."

Halldor loudly praised the man for his temerity, as if his brazen lying was in a way heroic. "Ah, Styrkar! These Jews. Such fabulous tales they have to tell! Playing us all for fools!"

Only Styrkar wasn't so sure there wasn't some truth buried beneath the dirty little man's mountain of exaggeration. *This dog has learned some tricks,* he thought. *And now thinks to turn them back on his master.* After a moment's hesitation, Styrkar again reached a hand into the coin pouch and this time pulled out two small pieces of silver. Offered on his open palm, the peasant quickly took them up. And smiled. For, little did Styrkar know that the literal Hebrew translation of the man's name, Yitzhac, was "He will laugh"—and that the barefooted wretch would have happily led him and his gold-grubbing Byzantines astray for even one *miliaresia*.

"It's a set-up, Styrkar," Halldor growled in objection. "The man's tale reeks of lies. Just look at him: a piss-spewing wine-bag. He will lead us into a trap and then vanish into the night. Let those Seljuk devils do the rest." So loud was Halldor's cursing of the peasant for his intended treachery as to call forth all of Hel's demons to devour him where he stood. "Lead us to the treasure, Styrkar? By the looks of him, he wouldn't know how to dump piss from a pot!"

*Just Halldor being Halldor,* Styrkar thought. An irascible sort, scaring men half out of their skin was fun to him. He meant no real harm. Most times.

Halldor ranted on: "That same lust Harald has for the female pelt, you have for gold, Styrkar. Like a poisoned arrow stuck in your brain. A madness in your head. And this time it's going to get you killed. All the men are assigned to their guard duties. We'll be on our own. That cave will be our tomb."

Styrkar knew Halldor was right, of course. He craved the yellow metal like a bear does honey. But that was hardly the matter. Halldor was not privy to the Emperor's directive to hunt down the land's hidden treasures and pirate them back to the Imperial Palace. Nor did he know of Harald's recent discovery of the rapid depletion of the Imperial gold reserves, which made it imperative that their mission succeed. Relics bring pilgrims; and pilgrims bring money.

Now minted with only a coloring of gold, the widely circulated Byzantine *nomismata* had lost much of its value, and the Empire lacked the means to acquire the gold needed to rescue it from its fall. What with the perfectly paired Emperor Michael and his wife Zoe—her a lascivious vixen and him a panting hound—continuing their irresponsible spending on pretty things to wear and impress while sending the Imperial armies here, there, and everywhere in an attempt to bring the world to its knees, the Empire's de-facto gold-standard was becoming more silver all the time. Foreign markets were rejecting the Byzantine currency out-of-hand, and the Empire's money-mongers were being crushed. Charges of treasonous malfeasance were hanging over the Emperor's head like an executioner's ax. Rebellion was in the air.

Such was of little concern to Styrkar. As long as he was being paid his fourteen *miliaresia* on time every month, the Empire's troubled finances affected him no differently than standing in the eye of a circling wind but feeling only the faintest breeze. A Varangian Guard, and proud to be one, Styrkar was sworn to serve the Imperial Eagle. Loyal to a fault, his decision was easy: he would do as the Emperor commanded and seek out the Holy Land's hidden riches. "I may be wrong," he said to Halldor, "but I am wont to believe that there is more than two *miliaresia* of truth in this peasant's outrageous claim, and I'm going into the hills with him tonight."

Grown only louder, Styrkar waited until Halldor was done with his vile soliloquy. For, despite his vociferous protest, the man was afraid of nothing and there was no better friend to have at his side.

When at last Halldor's rant steamed out, Styrkar's voice was calm. "So, are you with me?"

Halldor shook his head No! No! No! But his tight, white lips said, "Odin damn you to Hel if we're killed, Styrkar!"

Styrkar smiled at Halldor; patted his shoulder. "Oh, like you're not going to Hel, already."

Halldor scowled at the truth. "I'll go tell Harald we're going."

"No. Don't. I suspect he's buried a foot deep in his own royal treasure by now."

Clicking his tongue, Styrkar turned his horse onto the road. "Stay here and keep an eye on our little friend. I'll be back." Spurring the horse forward, he then disappeared into the crowd.

Yitzhac remained under Halldor's distrustful glare until Styrkar's return. Lifting the little man up onto the empty cart he'd dragged up behind him, Styrkar said to Halldor, "Try to think of Yit-sack as an ally, of sorts, the point man on our appointed mission of acquisition. No less important than this brainless mule." He indicated the stout little beast pulling the cart.

Oblivious to the insult, Yitzhac slipped the two shiny bits of silver into the hem of his tunic and laughed through his rotted teeth.

Following an old, overgrown cart track north toward the village of Lod, Yitzhac directed Styrkar to turn off across a wide, grassy field studded with half-dead cypress trees and scrub before arriving at the trailhead just past sundown. With a narrow shaft of rain sweeping through the twilight, Styrkar helped Yitzhac down from the cart and told him to take the point in their hike up the hill. "Let's go. A rain is coming."

Only, Yitzhac's ruse had played out to its end. His courage faltered.

"No. There are ghosts in every one of those caves. I will take you no farther."

Halldor and Styrkar exchanged wry looks.

With a low growl, Styrkar showed Yitzhac another piece of silver.

Yitzhac reached for the coin before pulling his hand back and shaking his head no.

Halldor threatened to kill him.

Ignoring the threat, Yitzhac pointed to the narrow path, overgrown with scrub-brush and grasses. "Follow it up the hill. Around to the backside. The cave is near the top. Overlooking Lod."

In a flash, bounding down from the cart, the aptly named "He Will Laugh" then took off across the field at a sprint. That damned Yit-sack is a lot faster than he looks, Halldor thought, and gave up the chase after only a hundred ells.

Red-faced and breathless, Halldor returned to Styrkar's side, fixed him with a hard look, but said nothing. Unhitching the mule from the cart, he then started up the rock-strewn hill.

Hating that Halldor was always right, Styrkar followed.

Even the sure-footed beast struggled with the steep and craggy ascent. Twisting past massive rock outcroppings and vine-covered ruins, the trail seemed to fork every ten steps—some across the hill, occasionally downward, but always returning straight up. The light was low; the wind shrieking one moment, then suddenly quiet. Too quiet. Like devils on the prowl.

With the twilight quickly dissolving to darkness, Styrkar was forced to light the small oil lantern he'd brought to give light in the cave. Only, when at last they reached a narrow shoulder of rock just a few ells from the summit of the hill, they could see nothing that even remotely resembled a cave entrance. Certainly nothing a man could stuff himself into with any expectation of getting out. Bloodied by an overgrowth of thick, thorny vines as he ran his hands along the broad, craggy face of the huge limestone boulders embedded just below the hill's crest, Styrkar followed Halldor in shuffling along the ever-narrowing limestone shoulder until it ran out over a sheer drop into the darkness below. As he shined the light into the deep fissures between the stone outcrops, no sizable void was detected. That is until, with one last sideways shuffle, the ground crumbled under Halldor's feet and he fell into one.

With his chest pressed against the rock face, Styrkar leaned his head down toward the seemingly bottomless hole and called in to a groaning Halldor. "See any gold?"

"Damn you, Styrkar! You're so hungry for gold that your farts stink of it! Now enough! I'm hurt! Get me out of here!"

As always, Halldor was right. Unable to deny his primal instinct for treasure hidden within, without hesitation, Styrkar dropped himself down the nearly vertical shaft into the cave to find it. Landing on Halldor's head before falling off to one side in a heap, Styrkar cringed at his friend's angry shout: "I think I busted my goddamned ankle!"

Again, the wind rose—not a howl, not a shriek—but of Yitzhac laughing.

Striking a flint and relighting the lantern, the two Norsemen sat staring at the rock cased around them. Holding the light close to the rough, in-pressing walls, the cave was much more colorful than first apparent. Red-orange-gold-green striations swirled across the low ceiling, and white-quartz veins streaked the walls.

Squatted on his haunches and shuffling his feet across the grit-covered floor, Styrkar reached the lantern forward upon spying what looked like the entrance to a dark tunnel beyond. Telling Halldor to wait, he then squeezed through the narrow opening between the walls and began dragging himself on his belly through a low, twisting passageway until the floor suddenly fell away and he tumbled into a large, craggy vault. Having dropped the lantern and its flame instantly extinguished, utter darkness reigned.

The air was heavy and hard to breathe as Styrkar—on his knees and crawling—swept his hands across the cave's gritty stone floor in search of the lost light. Banging the knuckles of his right hand against something hard—the cave wall, perhaps—he slid closer and pressed his open palm to it. Surprised to find it neither craggy nor smooth, but slightly rough like chiseled stone, Styrkar concluded that it was not *of* the cave, but *in* the cave. A box. A stone box. With a stone lid. No locks. No chains. No ruse of mind. His hard-hunted quarry finally found.

Thanking Odin for guiding him to the prize, Styrkar then slid the thick stone lid to one side, half-open, and reached a hand inside. Only, in that very instant, there shined into his eyes, aureate and blinding, a light as bright as the mid-day sun. An incandescence like to expose the very soul of a man. Even to make Styrkar, a warrior who knew no fear, fall back and shiver in his spine.

Closing his eyes against the light's brilliance, Styrkar rocked back against the cave's wall, alarmed by a strange, powerful presence stirring about him in the floating gold dust. Even as the otherworldly aura began to fade as if a heavy mist dissipating before the rising sun, the enveloping presence remained. Neither shadow, nor light. *Maybe it is a ghost*, Styrkar thought. *A god. A devil.*

Reaching for the dagger tucked in his boot, Styrkar crawled back toward the little stone box. Looked inside it. And smiled. For it was filled to the rim with Roman gold. Or so it seemed.

Styrkar slid the thick stone lid back into place. Fumbling in the dark, feeling for the tunnel entrance, he then hurried out of the cave like a thief in the night.

Styrkar and Halldor would return to Ramla before the cock's first crow. And carry the box away. To Constantinople. To Kiev. To Nitharos. To Stamford Bridge. Only for it to end up buried under a big black rock. On a beach. In Normandy.

The same as countless other chests filled with gold, the Emperor never knew the box existed. For, while it was true that to the Emperor and Empress belonged the spoils, as always, the Varangians took what they believed to be their fair share—an *ex gratia* payment, of sorts—compensating for the low pay they received for the dangerous service they performed. Enough treasure, in fact, for Harald to return to his Norwegian homeland and buy a kingdom of his own.

A few weeks after the princess's safe return to Constantinople—*Miklagard* to the Norsemen—Michael IV died. Wasting no time in seizing his power, the purple-born Empress Zoe—who was suspected of poisoning to death her first imperial husband—was married the same day to her handsome young lover—and adopted son—Michael Kalaphates, and proclaimed him joint ruler of the empire. Zoe couldn't care less about matters of state—defense, finances, and the like—and was now free to indulge in her true passion: spending money. Once described by a royal courtier as "the sort of woman who could exhaust a sea teeming with gold-dust in one day," such were the costs of her extravagances as to require the treasury to pay with coins stripped of their gold to meet Palace expenses.

Within five months, Michael Kalaphates, the teenaged son of a ship caulker—now Emperor Michael V—turned on Zoe. Dragging her before the Senate and accusing her of trying to poison him, he publicly stripped her of her imperial robes, chopped off her hair, and banished her to a far-off island. Only, when Zoe's loyal subjects in Constantinople realized his devious scheme to depose their "Little Mother," they rose in rebellion and toppled him, instead. Zoe was back on the throne in two days. Again dressed in her purple silk garb, a bejeweled Zoe stood watching from the high balcony of the Imperial Palace as the angry mob burned out the usurper's eyes with a hot iron poker and then hauled him off wailing like a baby to die a traitor's death.

So did the empowered Empress then turn her attention onto Komes Harald and his Varangians—her personal guards—questioning their loyalty and the part they played in her unceremonious ouster. As her suspicion that they had joined the insurrection was confirmed by a small color-changing metal icon of Christ that often dictated her rash actions, she had Harald, Styrkar, Halldor, and all the other officers of the Varangian troop imprisoned for hiding away the lion's share of the plunder they'd seized in far-flung places over the years, but which rightly belonged to the Empire.

In a savage act meant to instill fear in all others thinking to steal from the Imperial purse, Zoe ordered the *Barbaroi* thieves castrated to a man—"Cock. Balls. All!" Dragged off by the heavily armed Scythian slaves that had replaced them as palace guards, the Varangians were held in the dark, windowless cells of the infamous Numera Prison deep in the bowels of the Imperial Palace until such time that Zoe would have them marched out in chains for the public spectacle.

Bound hand and foot with heavy burlap sacks pulled over their heads, soon enough Harald and Styrkar would have their bloody manhood thrown in a bucket with twenty others and delivered to the Empress so that she might feed it to the pigs she'd be eating at future meals. In a nod to their *Barbaroi* custom, Zoe would then have all the Varangians' heads cut off and piled at her feet.

Only, such was Harald's and Styrkar's good fortune as to have those Varangians Zoe deemed to have stayed loyal to her and still freely roaming the Palace grounds overwhelm the Scythian guards, and free their Norse brothers in the dark hours before their eagerly anticipated dismembering.

With the Hagia Sophia's huge bronze bells sounding a call-to-arms throughout Constantinople, Harald, Styrkar, and the rest of the condemned Varangians grabbed up as much of their hidden plunder as they could cart, wheelbarrow, or carry away. Fighting their way out of the great walled city, they then spirited off the hoard aboard a stolen galley under a hail of Byzantine arrows. Nearly breaking the galley apart amidships as they rocked up and over the colossal iron chain that was stretched bank-to-bank across Constantinople's harbor entrance every night, amidst a barrage of liquid fireballs—the terrifying Greek Fire—the Varangians then made good their improbable escape into the Black Sea.

Ditching the galley and commandeering a small fleet of river raiders, they then rowed northward through the land of the fearsome Bulgars and up the hellish Dnieper where many men were killed in ghostlike nighttime attacks by the savage Pechenegs. What was left of the fugitive Varangians arrived outside the gates of Harald's great friend, Jaroslav of Kiev—the King of the

Rus—and Harald's soon-to-be father-in-law—with such riches as never before seen in the possession of one man.

Sharing out the treasure among their loyal fighters after years of relentless conquest, Harald and Styrkar—the Raven and the Wolf—then returned to Norway and piled the lion's share of the hard-earned trove into a huge vault carved into the rock beneath Harald's grand hall at Nitharos. Many years later, on the eve of Harald's fateful invasion of England, the uncountable number of Byzantine chests filled with treasures untold were brought forth and loaded onto the *Great Dragon*. Once Harald had conquered England, the so-called "Thunderbolt of the North" would then generously reward all the thousands of brave warriors who aided his ascension to the island kingdom's vacant throne.

Only, by then, Styrkar—once so driven to amass huge piles of glittering gold, silver, and jewels—no longer cared about increasing his personal fortune. For, being a rich man had lost all its importance the day he found out his wife, Hild, was dead.

Even so, in the very hour in which Styrkar learned of Hild's passing—standing on the bank of a bloody Bulgar river amidst a horde of sparkly trinkets taken from another vanquished foe—the grieving warrior turned his teary eyes to the sky and made a promise to give every ounce of his riches to the gods if only they returned his beloved wife to the land of the living.

Styrkar's fortune had grown twenty-fold since. He was still waiting.

# THE ADULTERESS

*Night*

---

## 9 SEPTEMBER 1100

Tossing and turning on the floor, Styrkar was restless like no other night in his life. Closing his eyes against a ghostly nimbus of light shining around an imagined image of Hild's face, never did he think it possible that any other woman of this world could stir such feelings in him as that beautiful, blue-eyed princess.

But, now, there was this new face. And Styrkar struggled against its green-eyed allure.

In a mind long bereft of matters of the heart, Styrkar was tormented by such confusion, such guilt. Staring into the darkness with a growing ache in his chest, with his heart kindled to the point of exploding, he could keep his emotions inside no longer.

Styrkar had fallen in love with Adelvia.

Thus did his heart make his decision for him: he would have to leave. Now. Right now.

In the low light of the new day, Styrkar rose up off the floor and stood beside Adelvia. As she laid on her side, her back was to him and, unsure of what to do, he gently touched her on the arm.

Startled, Adelvia rolled toward him. Sat straight up and stared at him. And he at her.

"*Merci, mon ami,*" Styrkar whispered in his fractured French before pointing a finger at his chest and then at the door.

Adelvia's eyes contracted with the inner anguish of instant understanding. With tears shining, heavy and ready to fall, she took his hand in hers—her grip soft, girlish, and moist.

A sudden weakness took Styrkar's knees. A cold sweat beaded on his brow. With his blood pulsing in a rigid response to Adelvia's gentle touch, he wanted to hold her. To love her. To know every inch of her. Not just as a bedmate, but in the depths of her soul where her true beauty was fully manifest.

*No! Don't! God no! Stop!* Adelvia's conscience screamed as she suddenly pulled Styrkar's head down toward her and gave him a kiss full on his lips. Her beautiful green eyes smoldering with intent, she then let her fingers trail down onto his bare chest as, once again, the Devil gained the upper hand.

Styrkar's body stiffened as Adelvia began tracing a line of mist-soft kisses down his belly, unlacing the waist of his linen britches, smoothing her hands over his naked hips and buttocks as she slid them to the floor. Dropping his head close to hers, running his fingers through her hair, and staring into her upturned face, Styrkar could feel the heat of her. Breathe in the smell of her. The possibility that she wanted him to make love to her was intoxicating.

Betraying no hidden doubt, Adelvia then slipped her fingers inside the sagging neckline of her old nightdress and peeled it off her shoulders to reveal the flawless contours of her full breasts. Putting her trembling lips just barely on his, Adelvia then clutched Styrkar's head to her bare flesh, her heart beating against his bearded cheek as fast as a sparrow in flight. Throwing her head back and arching hard, she was like to melt in his arms at the first touch of his hot tongue on her yearning nipples.

Showing no shame for the fervent desire he now so obviously displayed as Adelvia's small, delicate hands' slowly coaxed the full breadth of his passion, Styrkar then lowered himself onto the softly moaning beauty. Pressing his hardness against her soft, open thighs, she denied him nothing. Their hands, lips, and tongues roaming over each other in delightful exploration, all was as the magic conjured in an impossible dream. Only then, with a faint, tremulous gasp at Styrkar's first full thrust within her, Adelvia began to quietly weep.

Awakened by a sound like no other he had ever heard in the night, Wido's sleep-blurred eyes struggled to focus in the dim early light. Then, with sudden, shocking clarity did he see the tall, yellow-haired stranger standing beside his mother as she laid on her pallet. Naked in a way that he had never seen a man, Wido watched in horror as the man's huge hands, hungry eyes, and mouth then began roaming over every inch of her remarkable form.

Crushed under the man's tremendous weight, Adelvia uttered not a single word, only a low, airy sound like moaning in pain. Never had Wido heard his mother so vigorous of breath before. With a great, hollow scream stuck in the narrow of his throat as her moaning only got louder, he began to panic. Helpless to escape from under the huge man, but for an upward thrusting of her hips, his mother could barely move, her whole body at times going into a violent spasm as she struggled to break free.

With his teeth gnashed in half-cry, half-rage, Wido thought his mother might be dying. Only, in his pitiful, crippled state, he could do nothing to help her. He could not walk, nor even rise up off the floor.

*A weapon,* Wido thought. *A club. A knife. Or, better yet*—from flat on his back he stretched his arms over his head into the nearest corner of the shack and grasped hold of his father's old wood ax. Slowly, silently, he pulled it toward him and then dragged it over one shoulder. As he hugged its heavy blade to his chest, for long moments Wido listened to his mother's muffled sobs while steeling himself to the fact that he must kill the man to save her life. Pressing his quivering lips to the icy blade, he then slipped off his pallet, rolled onto his stomach, and, while pushing the ax ahead of him, began inching across the cold stone floor.

Undetected by the grunting beast, Wido then pulled himself up against the side of the bed's raised wooden frame. Half-sitting, half-leaning with his head pressed against the side-rail, he slowly dragged the ax onto his lap and looked up. All was but a squirming tangle of naked flesh. Legs, breasts, thighs, buttocks. Mashed together and slicked with sweat. Peering over the top of the bed's thick straw-tick mattress amidst the man's hard, rhythmic rise and fall upon his writhing mother, Wido then positioned his hands on the ax's thick wooden handle just the way his father had showed him and squeezed it tight. Straining under the weight of the gleaming steel, the boy struggled to lift the ax head barely higher than the man's exposed left flank and, nigh biting through his lip, held it poised to strike. With his arms shaking and his shoulders burning, unable to hold the ax overhead a moment longer, in one quick motion—more like dropping it—Wido then brought the heavy steel blade down on the man's back with all the force his broken little body could bring to bear. Alas, the sickly boy had not the strength to bury its wood-dulled edge the least bit into the man's thick animal hide before the ax suddenly twisted sideways in his hands, slipped from his grip, and clanged on the floor.

Startled by the sudden ruckus beside them, Styrkar and Adelvia froze where they laid. Feeling a strange, dull pain in his back and not knowing by whom or what he was attacked, Styrkar reached a fast hand toward the floor and grabbed hold of a shadow he saw moving in the half-light. Inclining his head for a closer look at what it was wriggling in his grasp, he then saw a trembly, teary-eyed Wido slumped by the side of the bed.

Sitting up, Adelvia saw Wido, too. Horrified at the realization that her young son had witnessed her shameful act—and desperate to cover her nakedness—so loud was her sudden cry it was as if some kind of beast had swallowed her whole.

Her breasts silvered by sweat and heaving with hard, wet sobs, Adelvia then thrust her hands at Styrkar's chest and shoved him away from her just the same as if he was a big, playful dog that had bitten her without warning. Recoiling at the sight of his glistening manhood, at his filth spread over every inch of her marital bed like a blackening burn, she cried out over and again for Styrkar to leave, to get out of her house at once.

Kneeling beside her on the bed, Styrkar tried to calm Adelvia, to put his arms around her, only to have her pummel her fists against his chest and slap him across his face. Yet, strangely—when, at last, Styrkar did stand to leave—Adelvia clambered off the disheveled bed and threw her fully naked body at him in a wild attempt to rejoin their adulterous embrace. She shouted out that she was sorry. That it was all her fault. "You owe me nothing," she shouted. "For it was a pleasure I sought!" Then—seeing a bewildered Wido staring up at her from the floor—she grabbed up the thin linen sheet off the bed and covered herself, yelling, "But you must leave! Now go!"

Picking up his damp britches off the floor, Styrkar turned a long look back at a sobbing Adelvia slumped beside Wido, her arms wrapped around the boy and hugging him tightly. Staring at her through tear-glazed eyes as he pulled on his britches and retied the rope at his waist, he then dropped his head on his chest and pushed out the door.

Not a minute later, naked and fraught with anguish, Adelvia too banged out the door, running across the wet, grassy meadow and calling Styrkar's name. Only he was already gone, disappeared into the dark shadows of hundreds of storm-bent trees beyond.

Hardly seeing the path through her tears and with briars raking her bare skin as she pursued him deep into the Talou Wood, at the sudden sound of bloodhounds barking and men shouting ahead—realizing what was happening—Adelvia threw herself flat on the ground, rolling, writhing, and beating her fists into the dirt, only wanting to die. Clutching her hands to her face, she then cried out as if her heart had burst in her chest, "What have I done? *What have I done?*"

So it was, at that very moment, deep in that dark forest amidst the horrible sound of rabid dogs and cursing men, an angry God did deem that Adelvia of Arques would never smile again.

Streaked with blood and mire as she stumbled back to the shack under the dappling light of an early-morning sun, Adelvia dropped at once onto her knees and began loudly confessing her depraved act to the image of the crucified Lord upon the wall. Bent half in supplication, beseeching God's forgiveness, she promised Him that for all the rest of her days her desires would burn for Him, and Him alone, only that He have mercy on her. So too, with a quiet vehemence, she begged the Lord's protection of her pagan lover. "Or, Heaven forbid, should his life be at an end," Adelvia prayed, "his soul's merciful deliverance into the hands of his own god."

Flushed from the forest and running just ahead of a pack of wild-eyed horses and snarling dogs through the tall, sun-coppered grasses fringing the edge of the cliff, the shouted threats and epithets of no less than ten red-faced bounty hunters filled the early morning air around Styrkar. Men excited by the chase. The impending capture. The promised reward.

One man, riding at the front and pointing this way then that with a long wooden bludgeon in his hand, shouted, "You two—go left! Cut off the bastard! Three others—get ahead of him! The rest of you—fan out! Step on that runny piece of squirrel shit if you have to! Trap him against the edge of the cliff! And have the net ready! Count Guy wants him taken alive!"

Suddenly tackled from behind as he ran barefoot across the field's rain-slickened ground, Styrkar twisted away from one dog tearing at his left leg and then another biting his back. "You are lost!" shouted the club-wielding leader, approaching near. "Give up!"

Yet another dog, attacking from Styrkar's right, slammed into his side and locked its jaws onto his forearm. Only Styrkar was a god-made *berserker* and the Norse battle-rage filled him. Sooner to die a violent death than surrender.

"By all the gods, man! It is done! Give up!" the club-man cried.

Ripping the snarling dog off his arm and flinging it into the chasing pack, knocking one attacking beast into another, Styrkar then jumped to his feet and began running toward the cliff. Closing within a few ells of its precipitous edge, with nowhere else to run, he suddenly cut hard to his right and made a mad dash between two hard-charging horses in an attempt to return under the cover of the dark forest beyond.

And then they were all running. Men, dogs, horses.

Jerking his horse's reins and wheeling around in pursuit of Styrkar, one of the riders yelled, "Son of a bitch is fast! Running like piss down a drunk's leg!"

"And all this way then that! Wilder than a flame of Hell!" the other shouted.

A third rider peeled off at a sharp angle, trying to get ahead of Styrkar. "Heard he killed twenty men in Ponthieu!" he shouted with his ax held high. "Cut off all their heads! Ruthless!"

"Damn it, you little pig-fuckers!" the lead hunter growled through a beard streaked white by age and foam. "Catch him! He's just a man! And without a weapon! Go straight at him!"

Styrkar could feel the pounding of iron-shod hooves on the ground behind him as the riders jabbed their heels into their sweat-shimmered horses, and chased him across the field.

Breaking from the pack, two of the bounty hunters streaked through the tall grass straight at Styrkar while the others passed him on both sides. Fanning out in a wide semicircle between him and the edge of the forest, with their swords drawn and spears held at the ready, they then drove him back toward the cliff, trapping him like a wild boar as he sprinted back and forth along the soft edge. Quickly dismounting, the hunters leveled their spears, and closed on Styrkar in wary steps.

Bare-chested and dripping sweat—exhausted—Styrkar stopped running. Bent at the waist with his hands on his knees and heaving hard breaths, he glanced around him and wondered if he had enough of the *berserker* rage of his youth still inside him to kill every last one of these peach-fuzzed shits with his bare hands. Wiping away the grit caking his forehead and blowing out a hot breath, he tossed another hasty look over the ragtag bunch. And laughed at them.

In the next instant, the rabble rushed him.

The first man to reach him—big and mean—lowered a massive shoulder and bull-rushed Styrkar with a roar. Easily sidestepping him, Styrkar seized the red-faced rogue by his throat, rammed a swift knee into his gut, and then twisted him to the ground in a heap. Wrenching the man's arm behind his back at a gruesome angle before snapping it at the elbow, he then grabbed the howling beast by the crotch of his piss-dripping britches and slung him over the cliff.

With the other hunters momentarily frozen in place, Styrkar baited another attack. Shouting out, "Who else wants to fly?"—two of the younger ones, both with faces prettier than most women, suddenly leapt at Styrkar. Yelling at him like little boys at play as they slashed their short swords at his head, neck, and arms, Styrkar ducked—once, twice, then again—before throwing himself down and rolling onto his back. Hardly a fair fight, after kicking the stockier man's legs from under him and smashing a fist into his face at the instant he hit the ground, the skinnier man jumped on top of Styrkar with his sword pointed at his chest like to run it through his heart. Howling in victory, little did the boy-warrior know that playtime was about to end. For—amidst his loud, self-glorying celebration of his single-handed capture of "this murderous thug!"—Styrkar suddenly reached up and—grasping the blow-hard's long, double-edged blade with his bare hands—smashed the sword's large, spherical pommel against his pretty little laughing face. With the man's good looks suffering further ruin when Styrkar's following, mule-like kick drove his formerly thin, graceful nose into his suddenly senseless brain, the self-proclaimed "King of the hill" then fell over backward, never to move again.

Outraged by the brutal murder of their longtime comrades, three more of the manhunters quickly piled on Styrkar's supine body, pummeling him with their fists and gouging at his eyes.

Again, it was hardly a fair fight, as all the attackers had only about a minute more to live.

Grabbing up a large, loose stone off the ground and smashing it into one man's face, shattering his teeth, Styrkar then whipped around and crashed it against the side of another's head before jumping up off the ground. With a desperately squirming little man draped over his massive shoulders—his little fists awhirl and kicking like a little girl—Styrkar then spun toward the cliff edge, grabbed the worthless, sniveling cur by his throat, and flung him to his screaming death.

But for one pretty-boy in a shiny blue silk tunic running off across the meadow—his fool's courage replaced by a cold dread of being the next to die—every last man among the howling horde then attacked Styrkar in a wild, animal rush.

With three beaten, bloodied men lying at his feet like limp, wet rags and two more reduced to dark red stains on the beach below, Styrkar was about to throw another of the hunters off the cliff when their white-whiskered leader— his lips streaming with slaver and his face brilliant with outrage—yelled at his remaining men: "Dammit, you imbeciles! Do I have to do everything myself?"

In the next instant, struck from behind by the old hunter's huge hardwood bludgeon, Styrkar sank to his knees … dropped the screaming man he held aloft off the cliff … and then fell flat on his face.

Dragged off to the torture pit at Beaurain, he was in Hel before nightfall.

Adelvia would wear a look of profound loss on her face for the rest of her life. The repercussions of the young widow's adulterous act led not only to a lifetime of misery but of utter wretchedness. Broken in spirit and consumed by anguish, she confessed the same sin to God every day. Her high-pitched chants of "*Pardonnez moi, Seigneur, car j'ai péché!*"—"Forgive me, Lord, for I have sinned!"—only interrupted by the most terrible sobs or another recitation of the Bible's seven penitential psalms. Sorrowful to the point of death, she beseeched God to "Stay here and keep watch over me. For even though my heart and my flesh have failed and the earth may someday open up beneath me, I know You love me in a way greater than I can understand. And that my prayed-for salvation will be worth every tear I cry."

Living a most frugal existence, Adelvia no longer had any worldly passions. Eating the simplest of foods and wearing the plainest of clothes, she had long ago thrown away her stained bridal mattress and tattered nightdress and spent her nights on the bare floor in a painful hair shirt without the cover of even the thinnest sheet. She felt lower than the lowest serf—a *villein*—and no amount of tears could wash away her filth. Sick at heart—her sin no less than the crimes of those unrepentant murderers, thieves, and rapists she'd seen flogged and gibbeted in the village square, their stinking, fly-infested bodies spit on by a hundred laughing children—never did she achieve the peace of mind that an angry God had forgiven her.

Fallen, a sinner, a victim of Satan's senseless evil—still Adelvia proclaimed her belief that God was good. "Though You slay me, Lord, yet shall I forever praise You."

Until his crippling fall from the cliff, Wido had slept within his mother's loving embrace from the very night his father went off ax in hand to fight in Duke William's stupid war. Feeling her arms wrapped around him, the warmth of her body and heavy breasts against his back as she nestled close from behind, was a comfort, something especially his, and it never occurred to him that he would share her with anyone ever again.

But, oh, how all had changed in that wretched hour of that wretched day when that huge, yellow-haired fiend with the mud caked between his toes had crawled on top of her. Wido would never look at his mother with the same eyes again. Despite witnessing all her years of wallowing in the debilitating guilt of that one willful act of fornication, she would always be as obscene a whore as any bare-assed woman bent over a bedstead for money has ever been.

Taking the Devil inside her, Adelvia lost her soul that day. And Wido's life went to Hell.

With each passing day, becoming more and more consumed by her relationship with her Lord King and Savior, Adelvia all but abandoned her young son as a hopeless sinner. Thus it was, with his newfound freedom, Wido began to break all of God's laws without restraint. *Have no other gods before me?* Wido had no god at all. *Take the name of the Lord God in vain?* He would speak it no other way. *Lie? Steal? Cheat?* Every day of the week and twice on Sunday.

*Kill?* In due time …

Despite her efforts to live a life holier than the Virgin Mary herself, Adelvia had broken her marriage bond, and in nine months' time, her adulterous act came to something worse.

So why his mother did not fall down on her knees and praise him for chopping the head off that crying heap of filth in the very moment when it came squirming out between her legs, Wido did not know. Oh, the shameful lamentations his mother bellowed while cradling that putrid mess in her arms! A stinking river of blood pouring out its neck-hole and forever staining the floor where she stood! Collapsing onto her knees with her murdered child's slimy blue head turned straight up to her face, Adelvia roared at the crucified Man on the wall with such hatred that had she been there that long-ago day outside the walls of Jerusalem she would have hammered those iron spikes into Him herself. Only, just then, amidst Adelvia's uncontrollable wailing against the pain and pressure of another intolerable mass pushing its way out from deep inside her, as if born of a crazed delusion, she heard a baby crying.

Unbeknownst to Wido, who pulled himself up onto his young mule's saddle and fled through the forest the same as a rampaging beast finally escaping his pen, the specter of the yellow-haired stranger's evil spawn he thought to have so swiftly killed in his jealous rage was already on the path and stalking him.

For—indistinguishable amidst the carnage spreading the floor of the shack—Wido didn't know that the dead baby shared his mother's womb with an identical twin. Nor that he would become a very powerful man. Vengeful. A killer.

# III

## THE PHANTOM CREATOR

*Midnight*

### 10 SEPTEMBER 1100

The early Norse settlers of Upper Normandy called the giant ash tree Yggdrasill, whose roots grew around the massive rock at the Earth's frozen core to emerge on the far side of the ocean at the world's end. At the base of the great tree, nestled within its immense root ridge, was the Well of Fate and Wisdom. Tended by the Norns, the three spirits who wove the threads of every man's destiny, they believed its depth was such that none of the thousands of precious stones tossed in with prayerful petitions for an exceptional life ever reached the bottom. And as the souls of all Odin's children were stored in Yggdrasill's seeds and every aspect of their lives revealed by the veining of its leaves, the tree was a metaphor for life itself. Rising into the sky like a giant pillar with its branches overarching the breadth of its sacred grove, the inevitable fall of each of the tree's leaves signified the death of someone in their tribe, the slow denuding of which could only diminish its strength and identity. So did Odin's servants fastidiously care for the tree, day after day, carrying buckets of water from a nearby stream to pour at its base, caking its roots in rich mud to keep its foliage vibrant and green, while ever vigilant to ward off the many rascals of the forest that came to feed on its thick peels of sugar-sweet bark.

But Normandy was no longer Odin's province, and the tree belonged to the White Krist now. The echoes of the old gods' last footfalls were fading as they trudged off into the distant northern mountains. This new deity from far to the south, a place called Palestine, watched over them now. Much as a long winter giving way to a greening spring, the White Krist offered hope of a better day, of life beginning again.

So, the birth of Jaune Faucon De La Foret—the Yellow Falcon of the Forest.

A gift from God.

The mirror image of his murdered twin.

Found wrapped in a lowly serf's cheap canvas cloth at the base of the biggest tree in all of Normandy amidst the rabble of barking dogs and birds taking flight, Jaune Faucon's greatness was foretold by the brightest star ever seen streaking across the sky on that very night.

Yet, even as this powerful new God blazed a wide, sun-lit swath through that dark pagan realm of superstition and doom, a vast army of witches and warlocks trailed in His wake. With every sort of unearthly demon consuming the fearful mind of the times, the dread of black magic infiltrated their new religion like a harrowing plague. Only Jaune Faucon De La Foret was a manifestation of white magic, which was much rarer than black; the newborn babe a true miracle worked by this mysterious cloud-bound God.

So also, in the early Christian belief, certain natural landmarks had a mystical or more hallowed relevance than just another shiny rock or limpid pool of water. The sacred "Saint's Tree"—in earlier, pagan times known as Yggdrasill—was such. A local legend held that the tree sprouted on the very spot the bones of some forgotten-named wonder-worker of a thousand miracles had returned to the dust of the earth. That a baby should be discovered nestled within the massive root tangle of this very tree by one of God's own keen-eyed creations of the forest was such an unfathomable occurrence that even the most cynical person had to rethink their lack of belief.

According to the story told from the earliest days of the Christian canon, the tree's care was entrusted to an unending succession of poor, penitent, bare-footed monks training for the priesthood. Attended to by teams of twelve brothers representing Jesus's first followers, often they would leave behind a cherished book of Gospels, a crucifix, or a small wooden rood upon the completion of their yearly clearing of the fallen leaves and twigs piled over its magnificent crest of far-reaching roots.

So also, many noblemen over the years had made claims of leaving vast deposits of gold and silver at the tree's gnarled base in appreciation of all God's most humble servants. And, while that may have been true, not an ounce of it was ever found by a certain Brother Wido of the monastery at Saint-Riquier in all the times he made the excruciating trek over the dark, bramble-pinched path to collect what he believed was his rightful due.

Tonight was no different. And he was beginning to wonder if it was just a matter of his poor timing—or those goddamned noblemen were lying.

Wido had stood in their churches. These grand cathedrals popping up on every hill top. Built by the finest craftsman with the finest materials the world had to offer. Sumptuous. Supernatural, even. Bejeweled walls. Pearl-white marble columns. Gold beams studded with silver medallions. Stone inlay bird-and-flower picture-work on the floors. Soaring stained glass windows and monumental statues. The Bishop's seat more like a king's throne, huge and gleaming like the sun.

"Paying mountains of gold for all their sinful pleasures, yet not even one piece of silver the size of a whore's pink-painted fingernail offered to the lowly monk that purges the demons from their souls."

Empty-handed and angry, Brother Wido rode on.

# THE MONK

*Darkest Night*

## 10 SEPTEMBER 1100

Atop the cliff, it was so dark that the path was hard to see. Yet the old gray mule faltered not a step, his short legs pounding up the steep side of a rock-strewn gully to reach the cusp of yet another grassy plateau. His trek was near its end. The muddy fields, waist-high brambles, and deep cold-water streams of an early day spent slogging through a driving rainstorm were far behind him now. One last descent of a short, yet terrifying path into a deep, U-shaped hollow carved in the soft white rock and he would be safely home.

The man on the mule's back was nearly asleep. And a little drunk. As usual.

With a hood on his head and his chin on his chest, Brother Wido of Saint-Riquier had no doubt his mule could find its way even backward and blind. Although separated by the wide, forested expanse of Duke William's Normandy, the path never changed—the same back-and-forth between the church on the hill and the house on the cliff they'd walked once every spring and fall for the past twenty years, precisely dated to Wido's twentieth birthday.

Lifting his groggy head at a sudden splattering of large raindrops on his face, Wido stared a moment through his sleep-heavy eyes at the growing commotion in the sky before dropping his chin back onto his chest. *A little rain. A little thunder. I have time … a little, anyway.*

Turning down the side of a steep, forested hill, the old mule then began plodding through the thick, sucking mud of a long, centuries-old gully cut into the soft, chalky earth. Pushing through a long, leafless tangle of thorny brush growing out its increasingly high sidewalls, he then entered a short tunnel eroded through the cliff face that offered a slick, but navigable, descent onto a small stone ledge. Skidding on the gravelly rubble beneath his worn iron shoes, the mule somehow came to a stop, as always, at the very edge of this thinnest of stones jutting out near the top of the towering rock wall. Full of his foolish courage, the shaggy little beast then stood softly braying over the vast body of water below. Home at last.

It was a habit of the old mule, but Wido didn't like standing so close to the edge of the cliff. Countless times in his younger days, Wido had stood on a huge black rock at a spot just above where he stood now watching thunderheads much like these collide over the Channel. As such, he was all too aware of the speed and ferocity with which such storms attacked the soft chalk wall. The rock was no longer there, having long ago crashed down onto the beach below. A monument to his monumental stupidity, it was a constant reminder that only a fool stands on a big rock sticking out the side of a cliff above a beach strewn with big rocks that *used* to stick out the side of a cliff while all the rainwater in Normandy gushes in rivers around him.

A fearless, fiercely independent boy, Wido never imagined the ghastly efficiency with which his arrogant challenge to both God and nature would be crushed that day. And although spared the ignominy of being left to rot in a wave-battered pile of rock and marl under some little driftwood cross with his name scratched onto it, he was right to think that no one would waste their time to save him ever again. People just didn't like Wido much. Thought him a bigger ass than his mule. He would die someday, and that would be that. Nobody would care. It was not his intention, however, for today to be that day. As such, he turned back through the blowout in the rock face and started back up the gully.

At a spot near the top of the cliff, Wido suddenly jerked his mule to a stop and glanced up at a dilapidated old shack set upon a big flat rock a few ells above him. The "Dead Woodcutter's Hut," as it had long been known in these parts. The pathetic wail of a sickly, old woman seeped through the gaps between its shrunken clapboards.

His mother. She wasn't dead yet. And that was a shame.

*We all shall die, yet we know not how soon.*

Wido was thinking of his mother. Her face. Her younger, better face.

And of his long-gone father. His big hands. His wood ax.

He was thinking about God. And Jesus. His brother monks. His mule.

About how they could all really piss him off sometimes.

Especially God.

He thought how funny it was—but not really—that if God—Almighty God!—was supposedly everywhere, why was He nowhere when you needed Him?

And if, according to his mother's deepest belief, all great events were caused by the will of God, why did He so often choose death and destruction over merciful acts of love to visit upon His helpless children?

"Oh, He has His reasons," his mother would say.

His reasons? Like there was a carefully thought-out plan or purpose for that massive surge of water to blow out that big, black rock her little boy was standing on during that monstrous rainstorm all those years ago? That there was a plan for hurtling him off a cliff and breaking his body into a million pieces? What kind of goddamned plan was that?

The wretched life he was forced to live from that day forward was the answer.

And that pissed him off, too.

Adelvia, who was always fearful, often to the point of hysterics, of any storm blowing in off the Channel, had forbidden Wido to be out that long-ago night. She'd told him she had a premonition ... no, a dream ... a nightmare! God was angry with him for his many sins. For his utter lack of contrition. And she feared his punishment would be severe. Seemingly born without morals, her six-year-old's behavior was beyond shameless. An unclean spirit riding fast to Hell on a raft of abominable vices, Wido had a thorough contempt of the world and so much filth streaming out his mouth that she oft referred to him as "the fount of Satan." The constant stinging slaps across his face were but a trifle, and no number of blows with that wicked walking stick she kept in a corner of the shack could deter him from anything he wanted to do.

And there was nothing Wido wanted more than to laugh into the face of an angry God.

Such a glorious night it was!—the passing of thirty-four years doing nothing to diminish Wido's memory. The lightning sizzling across the sky. The thunder shaking the huge chalk wall to its very base. The great white flumes of storm-water spewing off the cliff-top as if boiled out of the Earth's hellish core. There was even the very real illusion of fire burning on the Channel: a huge, dragon-like sea creature, fully ablaze, and swimming toward the shore, lighting up the surrounding water as if the day-end sun had literally fallen into the sea. It was all so fantastic.

Until that moment it turned all so cruel.

The night had already counted its first hour when the first large drops of rain began to fall. Down on the beach below Wido, many of Odo's fellow guardsmen were passing the time drinking, singing, and playing dice games around the blazing cook-fire while others dozed against the hull of the grounded ship. None aware of their prisoner's current whereabouts, nor caring to look for him, neither did the Ponthievins seem to notice the wind coming up, the growing chill.

But Odo knew: another storm was coming. With a fury. And soon.

From atop his horse, Odo stared out over the dark, churning Channel. Only moments before it had been a lazy, lolling calm, the flat slack water between the ebb and long-awaited flood tides. Now, as he watched it surge over the break-line where the shingle sloughed off into a strand of gravel and then washed far up the beach, not even his perpetually jutted lower jaw could deny the first flicker of fear in his eyes.

Hawking in his throat against the palpable smell of rotted kelp—aye, of death itself—and spitting it back into the sea in defiance of the gooseflesh now crawling across his back and shoulders, Odo's face was an utter grimace. He had never learned to swim. And as the seething whitewater was not a foe he could beat down with the weight of his fists or the violence of his voice, he would wear those emasculating bumps of a scared man's skin for the rest of his life.

Odo glanced back at the huge rocks scattering the beach; at the massive cliff jutting up from it like a looming gravestone; and then, again, at the high, white-capped walls of water churning up the shingle along the shore. *Such a fool I've been!* Odo silently berated himself. *In all these hours spent brooding over the creeping return of just enough water to refloat that barn of a ship not once did I consider the ramifications of its over-swift delivery by an attacking sea!*

There could be no escape on foot, he thought. At two hundred ells straight up, not even a squirrel with grappling hooks for legs could surmount that rock face. So too, the two gullies gouging the cliff top to bottom were not only too steep and slick but blocked by large chunks of fallen chalk besides. Still, Odo knew that to remain on the beach was to die. He and his men would be engulfed by the storm surge within minutes, dashed against the cliff and the fallen rocks.

There was no other choice but to board the ship.

Odo squinted into the swarming darkness, unsure of where he'd left his prisoner. Warned by Count Guy that if he returned to Abbeville with no treasure and no old man he would be thrown into his own dark hole at Beaurain, he had no choice but to take the wretch aboard. So he would. *Only*—Odo pulled his sword from his scabbard—*the man's head will remain here on the sand.*

The monk and his mule stood frozen in place at a spot about halfway up the gully, close to where God's Rock used to lay. Wido thought he'd heard something during a short interval between his mother's incessant wails. Wrenching his head around like fearing an attack from behind, he stared into the blackness, and the blackness stared silently back. Twisting his old mule toward the tunnel, he took a few quick steps back down the slope and, bent half against the beast's neck, craned his head forward to assist in his scrutiny. Seeing nothing, he leaned back in the saddle satisfied that the noise must have been a trick of the wind. Only, moments later, just as he had turned back up the gully, he heard it again. The clamor of what seemed to be many voices rising up from the beach below. Men shouting. And horses screaming.

Quickly pushing back through the tangled brush growing out the gully's sidewall, Wido again skidded his mule down through the short tunnel and onto the perilous ledge. All before him was impenetrable black. No moon. No stars. Nothing but the wind, crashing clouds, and the cold shiver up his back.

Yet, then, as revealed by a sudden bolt of lightning exploding high on the western headland, Wido caught a glimpse of an enormous, hulking mass, just to his left and lying close to the base of the great chalk wall. Another long, strobing flash of light and he could see it was a ship. Heeled over on one side. Ten men or more scurrying over it like rats on a trash heap. A large man on a big, black horse was galloping back and forth in half circles around them, shouting obscenities at everyone. Wido immediately recognized the ship. And the loudmouth, too.

The monk and his mule had made but few stops of any length as they followed the Abbeville road west from the monastery toward the sea before turning south along the Channel coast. Determined to cover the ground faster than ever before, Wido was anxious as the last he'd seen his mother in the spring she was writhing on the cold stone floor of her little shack, crying in fear of dying that very night. The same plague that had been attacking her for years. Only, this time there was a rumor of fevers; of bloodletting; of an imminent end. He wanted to be at her side. To make sure it was true. *Lo! The one person at the root of all that is ruin in my life—and she just won't die!*

Exiled by his pious young mother for his recalcitrance to any form of discipline, his propensity to lie and to steal, and, especially alarming for his tender age, his depraved enjoyment of mutilating or outright killing any and all of God's most delicate and defenseless creations—Wido hated the world and Adelvia simply didn't know what to do with him anymore. Day after day, kneeling before the little silver image of the crucified Lord on the wall—given to her by her God-fearing father on his deathbed—she would fervently pray for His help with her son. Yet, in what she deemed the truest test of her immense belief in Him, He did nothing. Eventually taking it upon herself to do her Savior's dirty work, Adelvia had tried to beat the Devil out of her wayward son: a daily deluge of hard open hands smacked across his smirking face and welt-raising strikes on his backside.

But then, Adelvia would feel guilty. Somehow, it didn't seem right to her. Not the Christian thing to do. To beat nearly to death a young boy who couldn't even walk.

She would let someone else do it.

So it was, a young and most belligerent Wido was scooped up from his sleeping pallet one gray winter morning barely a year after his great fall from the cliff and given to the monastery in Ponthieu to be trained as a monk. He was barely seven years old.

"I'm trusting you with my boy," Adelvia told the Abbot of Saint-Riquier. "Make a gentle, caring man out of him. Put him on a path of righteousness. A soldier for God, marching in lockstep with the Lord."

The opening lines of a miracle story of a sinner saved? Hardly. After thirty-three years of mindless chants and hair shirts and eating lukewarm gruel in a stone-cold cell, about the only thing Wido had in common with Jesus of Nazareth was his belief that both their mothers were completely insane.

Once described by none other than the Abbot Evreux himself as "a pop-skulled mean, fiery squirt of piss as ever spilled his poison across a cold church floor," Wido hated every minute of his life of forced servitude to the god that destroyed him. An oblate, they called him in those early days, with all the religious rigmarole that entailed, which, as he recalled it, was mostly beating him like a dog while forcing him to read aloud from the Bible ... in Latin ... in the dark ... while standing on his head. Taught to honor the strict vows of poverty, chastity, and obedience; to tend to the poor, the sick, the orphaned, and the immoral; and to devote every hour of every day of a quiet and peaceful life to loving and serving God—Wido hadn't thought about killing his mother for years.

The shouting down on the beach snapped Wido back into the present time, and to a recollection of when he first met these rogues two days earlier.

While not a man to waste time on saintly contemplations, Wido didn't want to be out on the trail any longer than God's supposed protection would allow, as it was rumored that a cutthroat of the most miserable sort had escaped from the dungeon at Beaurain during the past fortnight. Wido knew it made no difference whether he was a man of the cloth or a man of the dirt to any of these cave-dwelling barbarians along the way: they would steal the eyes out of the head of the Devil himself if they thought them pretty enough.

Detained by Evreux, his spiritual mentor from his earliest days at Saint-Riquier, for the purpose of another pointed, often brutal examination of his faltering faith, Wido didn't complete his assigned penance of shoveling copious amounts of shit out of the goat pens until the sun had fallen below its apex in the sky. The unplanned delay required that he take a shortcut through the forest to reach the town of Treport on the Channel before nightfall. As was his custom on these twice-yearly treks to see his mother, he would over-night at Saint Michael By-The-Sea, the monastery there, before setting off southward to his old home on the cliff in the morning.

Arriving just in time to catch the day's last ferry across the Somme River at Abbeville, Wido then turned his little mule off the Saint-Riquier road on to a narrow forest path. Dark and pinched by bramble—more of a deer track than an established trail—Wido groused to himself that it hardly seemed to be a shortcut, at all. *Such a liar that Evreux is! Telling me that it was the fastest route to the sea!* With all its twists and back-switches, by the time Wido emerged from the forest the daylight was nearly gone. Loudly cursing Evreux for the tremendous delay his self-righteous little sermon had caused and then sending him down a path no man had ever walked before, he was still far away from Treport—and standing on the wrong side of the storm-swollen Bresle River, besides.

With his stomach churning out one long, miserable whine after another, Wido was much worried that he would miss the last sitting for the monks' supper at Saint Michael's and decided, instead, to ride along the river's north bank and stop for the night at the old castle at Eu. Far short of Treport, Wido loathed having to eat that leftover fish-mash shit they always fed the peasants in the castle yard, but Eu was a good place to intercept the southbound trail in the morning, and would spare the mule some of the up and down crossings of the deep gullies cutting across the rugged trail above the sea.

Dropping down onto the mud flat below the trees bracketing the river, Wido could see a group of men in uniforms sitting at the water's edge eating, drinking, and raising a ruckus less than a swan's-hop downstream. There was a large, high-sided trader's ship anchored in the middle of the river just below them, and many horses milling in a high grass field dotted with heather and gorse beyond. Waving his arms at them from the opposite bank, Wido called out over and again, pleading for someone to take him over in one of the little fishing boats he could see pulled up on the shore beside them.

At last, during a brief pause of their incessant singing, shaking of rattles, and blowing on horns, someone heard Wido. Glanced his way. Then ignored him.

At a distance, in the fading light, and without his monk's telltale round cap on his head, Wido was sure he had the look of a shitty little peasant. A peasant they could care less to help. So he quickly identified himself: "I am Wido the Lame, a monk traveling on very important business at the behest of Evreux, the abbot of Saint-Riquier. If you please, I am in need of—"

"*Gyrouagi!*" they jeered back at him in unison without hearing another word he was saying. "Nothing but a worthless, wandering monk! Important business? My horse dropping a load of shit is more important business than anything you've got to do!"

Wido was in no way offended by the slur. There was much truth in the man's charge. With hardly anyone of worth joining the monks' ranks in recent years, when some administrative duty delegated by the Abbot to a seemingly trustworthy brother required travel beyond the monastery walls, invariably what little money given for his expenses would be spent on quite unrelated— and unholy—comforts along the road. A little chocolate. A rib of lamb. A shiny new ring. A big-breasted, back-alley whore in need of getting a little religion in her.

"You want food, *gyrouagi?* Is that what you're whining about?"

The guardsmen then told Wido they knew, for a fact, he would have a very meager meal at the castle—if anything at all—as Eu's entire supply of grain, wine, and lard had been recently carted off by a ruthless band of marauders.

Wido was sure they were lying. He had heard nothing of the sort. Still, he was wasting time. He turned his mule toward the southern hills, determined to cross the river and move on. He would forage for berries and nuts in the forest ahead.

A few of the uniformed men quickly mounted their horses and began trotting upstream toward the hobbled monk, calling out for him to wait. Stopping across from Wido, the big, ugly one on the coal-black horse urged him to cross the river. Assuring him they would give him food and drink for but a pittance of gratitude—and maybe a coin or two—he held out his hand to Wido and told him he would meet him halfway, the better to assist his crossing. The river was silted up from an afternoon storm and very shallow in the middle, he further assured the famished monk. "Easy footing for your little mule. Hardly any rock in the bed at all."

Wido's first and only thought was, *It's my legs that are lame, brigand! Not my brain!*

Wido knew well that members of the local clergy were often targets of playful humiliations in which neither their person nor their goods were spared. Moreover, these guardsmen were no different from a greasy band of death-mongering Scythians. A tribe without laws. More so, this big bald one, this Odo—their so-called leader—had such a reputation for lies and brutality as to be known even to a man living for years in utter solitude within the thick stone walls of a church.

Brother Wido had once met the man's unfortunate wife Amelie while she was in the care of the cleric Otmund, warden of the young women's monastery in Ponthieu. Black-eyed and trembling, she had shown up at the gate one dark rainy night begging the Benedictine nuns for protection from the monstrous man. Wido would not see her again until this past spring, walking on the road just outside the monastery wall. Her over-swollen belly seemed to indicate that she was many months pregnant. Bent to one side and lurching her body forward in a morbidly comic sidewinding gait, she could take no more than three consecutive steps without falling to the ground. Her hip was badly fractured. Her spirit irreparably broken. The last time Wido saw her was the day they buried her stillborn babe in the commoners' graveyard.

The mule-bound monk dismissed Odo's invitation to meet in the middle of the river out of hand. But, then too, he knew how risky it was to be out at night alone. The big *gard-sarjent* said as much, warning Wido that in just the last month alone a priest, a bishop and an archdeacon had been murdered in these parts. "And I must tell you, Brother Wido," Odo further admonished, "a thieving convict of the most horrible sort is now on the loose. Escaped, they say, from the deepest, darkest depths of the dungeon at Beaurain. There's a very good chance you will be robbed tonight, captured for ransom, or killed for fun." Again, Odo extended a large, open hand toward the nervous monk. "Please, the food is hot and the ale is flowing. Come join us."

Wido knew better. Knew that this cold, callous man and his armed band of ruffians would not hesitate to strip him of what little he had, and then toss him in the river weighted down by a bag of stones. He was no unsuspecting lamb in the midst of a pack of wolves. He had but one small silver coin in his shoe, and he would like to keep it. To that end, with a loud growling in his belly, he ignored the cacophony of jeers at his back and turned his mule back upstream to look for a more navigable river crossing.

Darkness drew its veil.

Wido didn't like being in the forest alone at night.

He wasn't.

Jumped from behind, the hungry monk would have nothing to eat but a mouthful of dirt that night—his precious coin tucked into the deep cleavage of another man's whore even before the first star was shining.

Peering down at the men on the beach, Wido's eyes showed fire from within their blackened, raccoon-like surround as he recalled the beating in the forest he had taken just two nights past. The sudden, hammer-like strike at the back of his head; his neck being crushed in the crook of a powerful arm; the knife at his throat; the blood gushing out his nose as he laid in the thorny underbrush bordering the path; dragging himself over the crusty earth; the struggle to remount his waiting mule. Left for dead, with no Good Samaritan coming to his aid. Or anyone at all.

"So much for God's prayed-for protection, Evreux," he remembered shouting at his longtime mentor through the dark tangle of ferns and oak saplings as he pulled himself back up onto the beast. "A priest, a bishop, and an archdeacon all killed in the last month? Men God might actually care about?

And you have the gall to talk about my faltering fate? The power of prayer? The power of the Lord?"

No matter that Evreux was not there to say it himself, Wido could hear his mentor's self-righteous retort—as loud and predictable as ever: *Your prayers are worthless, Brother Wido, but for the reason that you have no conviction in your belief. No purity in your soul. No love in your heart. Hollow inside, as a weed withered to its roots, you can't be cured of your affliction any more than a man can be raised from the dead ... unless you truly believe.*

Wido could care less of the old priest's opinion. He did not respect Evreux. Indeed, looking down on him as intellectually inferior, he did not think his hatchet-faced taskmaster had the competence to teach him anything at all. Neither did Wido subscribe to the ridiculous doctrine Evreux preached. Wido's common sense and utter disdain of superstition would not allow him to believe in spirits, angels, or resurrection as Evreux did, and he was always quick to condemn the hypocrisy and corruption of the Church they served.

Truth be told, Wido could give a rat's ass about swaying sinners off their paths of perdition. He pretended no righteousness. He hated God. His mother. The church. Day after day, staring out at the world through the only opening cut in his tiny cell's thick stone wall, reliving his crippling fall off the cliff, wishing he had died—longing for it, even—any kind of life worth living had ended long ago for Wido.

*All things according to His immutable plan.*

"Puh! What fools believe, Evreux!"

*Do not grieve the Holy Spirit of God, with whom you were sealed for the day of redemption. Get rid of all bitterness, rage and anger, brawling and slander, along with every form of malice. Be kind and compassionate to one another, forgiving each other, just as in Christ God forgave you ... 1 Corinthians 13:4-5.*

"The wisdom of Corinthians? The scions of Sisyphus? A man famously punished for his deceitfulness. The Corinthians were but Philistines masquerading with halos and harps, Evreux."

*Pray to God to help you defeat your anger, Wido. Furious and brutish, it grows like a devil in you. Either you must kill it—or it will kill you.*

Wido turned away from Evreux as if from a hot wind blowing into his face.

*Act with wisdom and a gentle spirit, Wido. Be a good witness for God. For God is good. God is loving. He keeps no record of wrongs. Take the Lord into your heart and have Him exorcise this perpetual wrath that lives within you and, in that very moment, you will emerge from the darkness and stand in the light of a joyous new day.*

Wido had been listening to Evreux's God-is-great tripe for thirty-four years now.

Even so, many years ago, an overhanging, stone-faced Evreux had laid a large crucifix on the scribing desk beside the young oblate Wido and asked him to render a spiritual portrait of himself in the form of a confession to God. To detail his own sense of what made him who he was; to reveal the framework that informed his moral thoughts and actions; what mattered to him, and why. Only Wido had no intention of showing himself naked before Evreux—or the dead man on his desk—and instead scrawled across the cheap, yellow parchment a stark revelation of why he believed the Catholic Church to be spiritually impure and at the root of all that was evil in the world.

Evreux was furious. The whipping severe.

Wido cried a little. Then laughed a lot.

Later, colored by the many deep-seated grievances and prejudices that, in fact, made Wido who he was, in the darkness of his cell the young apostate only shook his head in reflection of a beaten, bloodied Jesus hanging on a cross under the misguided notion that by His death He could redeem the sins of such an evil race. If Wido was only to consider the immensity of his own sins, the naiveté of the man was astounding.

So, too, that of those people who blindly believe Him to possess such power.

Recalling the words his mother had spoken to him with an impossibly straight face that very day she handed him over to that beady-eyed pack of bald-headed black-robes milling outside the door of their shack—"No matter a sinner or a saint, Jesus loves all God's children. But only to ask him, even your worst transgression will be forgiven"—caused Wido to burst into outright laughter.

"How ironic a statement that turned out to be, Mother," Wido shouted against the walls of his cell, loud enough for Evreux to hear. *Never has Jesus had a follower more devout in the belief of his saving grace than my mother,* he thought. *And yet my mother—as attested to by her white, calloused knees and haggard face, after a lifetime of begging his forgiveness for the only aberrant act in her entire life—remains utterly unforgiven. Jesus forgave a harlot ... but not my mother! Christ! I killed a baby! What chance have I for redemption?*

His mother's ascetic adherence to God's laws and Mary-like virtue was intimidating to a lifelong sinner, and Wido believed she would die of mortification if she ever looked into his blackened heart and realized how terrible a creature she had birthed. His soul would never be taken into Heaven. Not by his prayers, and not by hers. As such—with the demons of his mind shrieking that he was the worst kind of sinner—Wido found it infinitely easier to convince himself that there was no such place. No Heaven. No Hell.

So why then, Wido asked himself, had he, once again, lifted his eyes to the sky that night of his brutal beating in the Talou Forest and silently prayed to God for protection from all the evil that lurked along the long, winding path ahead? A child does not determine from whose womb he will be birthed, and despite his fiercest argument with himself he could not deny his mother had been especially chosen for him, and had loved him beyond life itself. Nor could he deny that she had instilled a semblance of belief in him. God existed. The risen Christ was watching over him. He drew strength from his belief in Jesus. Rooted inside him, Wido considered that belief to be his greatest weakness. And there was nothing more Wido hated about himself.

*Once again, I suffer the frustration of my intellect succumbing to some nebulous spiritual creation spawned by an ancient oral tale,* he silently lamented. *Even as the idea of this simple man's anthropomorphic divinity is virulently denied by my strongest sensibility, somehow I believe this Son of God incarnate nonsense to be true. And, while hardly one of them, like Evreux and all these other cloistered fools, I pray to the Jewish carpenter from Nazareth every day: "I will lead the blind on unfamiliar roads. I will lead them on unfamiliar paths. I will turn darkness into light in front of them. I will make rough places smooth. These are the things I will do for them, and I will never abandon them"* ...

So did Wido pray those very words two nights earlier while traversing the forest.

Recalling little else of the attack, Wido's last memory was of climbing back atop his waiting mule, gulping down a long draw from his wine flask, and then setting off for his mother's shack on the cliff. Closing his eyes against the darkness, against his fear, exhausted, Wido was soon asleep. And dreaming. Not of carnal pleasure or great wealth, but of the phantom beast that had long inhabited his mind. Conscience.

There was no more time to debate whether God was real or a mere illusion.

Judgement Day was upon him.

*Every man must conquer his own demons, Wido. But only to have faith—in God and in yourself—will you find the strength to escape Satan's grasp. Obey your conscience, its righteous council, and all things are possible. Even a miracle to save the worst of sinners.*

Shut up, Evreux.

Safely returned to the cliff and peering down into the darkness, Wido focused his attention on the life or death struggle playing out on the beach below. The huge walls of whitewater now battering the Ponthievin's hulking ship, spinning it this way then that; men shouting, bobbing helplessly in the spiraling surf. "Mother of Jesus," Wido whispered in shock as he stared down from his high perch, "Odo of Montreuil is going to die tonight. That stinking pile of human excrement finally washed off the face of the Earth! And, hard as it is to believe, maybe, just maybe—for the first time in my forty miserable years of life on this planet—God has the upper hand on the Devil."

With chaos overruling his every command, Odo visibly seethed as he watched his men scatter in a pell-mell flight from a surf now pounding on the grounded ship's massive hull. Barely audible over the howling wind, he called out to two Ponthievins struggling to calm their terrified horses in the lee of a large boulder, and then to another hurriedly filling skins from a fall of fresh water near the ship. "Goddammit, you buckets of goat piss! To hell with the water! To hell with the horses! Find the prisoner!" Then turning his face into the stinging salt-spray now blowing in flat sheets off the Channel, Odo spurred his horse into the crashing whitewater in desperate search of that shriveled little man rumored to have all that gold shoved up his ass.

Furiously dragging his sword blade back and forth through the churning waves in hope of snagging the shackled wretch, Odo again shouted toward the beach, ordering his men to ready the oars, to stow the sails. There could be no delay. For while he was duty-bound to search for this "scantling whey-faced woodcock"—and he would, for maybe a minute more—he would not die for him.

At his command, two of the guardsmen came up beside him bearing torchlights, one of them shouting that only moments before he had seen the Norseman standing at the water's edge but a stone's throw to their left. The other was pointing at something rolling in the water straight ahead of them. A huge wave carrying a call for help. Odo shouted at them to shut their windy holes so he could listen. He then turned an ear to the sea with one eye fixed on the surf like a gull spying crabs in the sand. Sure enough, though faintly at first, he did hear something like the desperate cry of a drowning man. Only, judging the sound to be much the same as the shrill, high-pitched whine of that skinny-armed bond-slave that had tried to poison him earlier, he ignored the plea and instead turned his look down the long line of beach stretching to his right.

Turning circles against the waves now breaking hard against his gelding's chest, finally, amidst another torrid flash lighting up the leaden sky, Odo caught a glimpse of the haggard old warrior about fifty ells off, standing amidst an outcrop of large, jagged boulders. Buffeted by the powerful swells with his arms outstretched and his head thrown back like beckoning the storm to kill him, but for a few links of broken chain dangling from each wrist, he was completely naked.

Wheeling his horse in the face of another breaking wave, Odo raced to the spot, slapped the flat of his sword blade against the man's sodden flesh, and corralled him against the beast's heaving flank. Blood was trickling down the man's back from between his shoulder blades where one of the many barnacle-encrusted rocks had gouged out a large chunk of his flesh. "Goddammit, you braying mule!" he shouted as he plunged into the waist-high water and seized the staggering wretch. "Haven't you sense enough to get out of the god—"

Only, just then, Odo's favorite word in all the world was suddenly broken off half in his mouth by the sight of another dark, shivering wave mounting to more than three times his height just off the shore. He stared at it with macabre fascination, as if some otherworldly beast risen from the deepest depths of the sea. When it was nigh upon him, with a crushing hold on his prisoner's bony upper arm, he finally turned to run. His knees pumping nearly to his chin while yelling at the old man to keep up, Odo sloshed through the water as fast as he could.

But not fast enough.

By the wildly flickering light of the booming sky, Brother Wido watched wide-eyed from high on the cliff as a tremendous wall of water seemed to stand straight up off the surface of the dark, wind-thrashed Channel and begin a mad rush toward the beach. His heart's echo pounding against his temples like the beat of a war drum, he hadn't wasted but the first two words of a prayer on Odo and his men before he realized God had already decided: every one of those foul-mouthed, whore-mongering, blackguards was going to die tonight.

Seemingly running in place, Odo could put no more distance between him and the great wave than a one-legged man crossing a freshly furrowed field on crutches. Stumbling, falling, and crawling on the shifting shingle, dragging the old man on his face, at last, he cast his prisoner aside. Rolling onto his back, Odo began shaking his fist as if in defiance of the seething black water now curling over him. The night suddenly falling deathly quiet just the same as a bloodthirsty Roman crowd at the very moment their champion raises his sword on high to strike off his opponent's head, in the next instant, amidst a massive ground-shaking crash, Odo the Swineherder—the most hated man Ponthieu ever knew—disappeared from sight.

In the dumbstruck silence that followed, the few guardsmen who had managed to cling to the gunwales of the battered ship strained for a glimpse of their leader's body floating in the bubbling maelstrom. With torchlights flickering, one by one they jumped down into the receding water and fanned out over the beach. Finally, one of them pointed to a spot about thirty ells away, at something humped up in the streaming backwash. The two men closest to it took off at a sprint to investigate. Stopping just short of the hulking, black mass, they stared at each other a moment and then walked a wide circle completely around it. To their great chagrin, it was only Odo's dead horse. Staring at each other, wide-eyed and wordless, they feared the worst: that swine-herding son of a peasant's whore was still alive!

High-stepping through the wave's crash and bound, their decision to flee for the relative safety of the ship was an easy one. Odo? The old man? They could both go straight to Hell.

Brother Wido didn't know much about Odo, but he didn't much like what he did know. So it was strange, in the aftermath of watching the big Ponthievin meet his brutal end, he should feel such a kinship with him. After years of forced self-scrutiny, the ill-fated monk knew all-too-well the horrible beast inside such men as Odo. Knew what it was like to have feelings of goodwill and decency toward his fellow man so often overruled by a heart blackened by anger and hatred. Indeed, at the height of his pride, Wido had been Odo. So full of himself that it seemed at any moment he would rip right through his skin. But, oh, how far Wido had sunk over the years of demeaning servitude to his present bottom-feeding nadir of self-loathing.

And how much farther down he still would go.

# THE VICOMTE

*Predawn*

## 10 SEPTEMBER 1100

Normandy forged its greatness as a Viking province, and Duke William—a direct descendant of the Norseman Rolf who was granted the land by the emperor Charles the Simple in exchange for halting his endless attacks on Paris—ruled over it with the same iron fist as had his exceptional forefather. Rising to power despite the stigma of his bastard birth, William staked his claim as the most outstanding of this remarkable family when he assumed the king's throne as conqueror of England in 1066. Seizing his vast new opportunities and resources with a brutality that was characteristically his own, William exercised his unprecedented authority by installing a cadre of handpicked magnates in strongholds throughout the whole of England and Norman Gaul, as the lethal threat to his hard-won dynasty swarmed from both inside and outside his borders. Raids from Brittany, Anjou, France, Scotland, Scandinavia; his own brother; his own son. Even that some of William's most-trusted magnates had seized some of his Norman fortresses in the past was still prominent in his mind.

Duke William's overtly ambitious uncle, William d'Arques, was such a man. Revolting against the fledgling ruler in 1052 with hopes of claiming the ducal title himself, in quick succession, he convinced every other lord of the Talou region to desert his bastard-born nephew. In fact, only one little-known family from the tiny hamlet of Auffay remained loyal to Duke

William's cause. Having settled the town years earlier, a man named Richard de Heugleville alone held his castle near the church at Saint-Aubin against the rebels, and steadfastly maintained his allegiance to the duke against any attack by the garrison occupying the Fortress Arques. Richard recruited to this enterprise his son-in-law Geoffrey and Hugh de Morimont, both sons of a faithful servant who had been killed while fighting off the young duke's intended murderers in 1041.

Alain De La Foret, while arriving late to the action, rode in from the Bois de Aunay to lend his sword to the cause. A young dandy in the fashion of the silk-slippered fops at court, dashing through the forest with his hair slicked back both sides of his head like the folded wings of a duck and a cluttered strand of cheap, shiny baubles jangling at the neck of his shimmering silk tunic, Alain had never been in a fight before. And, the chicken-shit that he was, he would not enter the fray this day either. For, at seeing Hugh de Morimont's little band of defenders cut off from Richard's main force and surrounded by the heavily armed men serving Duke William's traitorous uncle, Alain wheeled his horse in its tracks and ran off as fast as he could with his sword still in its sheath. Turning back nary a glance as the Morimont men were then cut to pieces in a storm of flashing steel, a subtle pang of guilt struck at his coward's heart for not remaining with them while they bravely fought to the last. But, true to Alain's self-preserving nature, it would not trouble him for long.

In a few months' time, with the rebellion quelled and Duke William's uncle expelled from the duchy, this little family of Auffay received a formal escort to the ducal court at Rouen, where they were greatly rewarded by the great Norman lord for their unwavering loyalty. The heroic Hugh Morimont was dead. Richard de Heugleville, too. Richard's son-law-Geoffrey, one of the few loyalists who survived the fight, was elevated to *vicomte*, and given command of a fortress on the border of Beauvais, charged with defending the important northeastern edge of the province.

As for Alain De La Foret, there was not a man alive who had witnessed his cowardly act. Nor a man who could swear that Alain had done anything at all. Still, Alain claimed he had ridden to the duke's defense, and as such, was subsequently installed in a significantly smaller stronghold in the area of Saint-Aubin. A simple wooden structure built on an artificial motte surrounded by a palisade in a large grassy glade of the vast Talou Wood, its western wall sat on the edge of a deep cut in the land called the Gorge du Petit Ailly. Cramped and comfortless with few rooms and fewer windows, it was accessed by a cleated drawbridge that descended to the far side of the gorge to give better footing to Alain's many horses, goats, and sheep. Everywhere there were ladders instead of stairways and a ridiculously large and ornate Paris-made iron lock on the little front door. Installed by the soft, delicate hands of Alain De La Foret himself.

The steep-sided gully, gouged into the earth by the eternally rushing storm-waters of northern Gaul, ran straight through the heart of the Talou Forest before making its sudden end high on the face of the great white-chalk wall above the Channel. A small wooden shack built atop a big flat rock sat precariously on its western prominence. The "Dead Woodcutter's Hut," they called it. It seemed to have been there forever.

Now—after last night's brutal storm—it was gone.

A *vicomte* of little distinction, Alain De La Foret considered himself more Duke William's protégé than his vassal. And nothing suited Alain better than living the life of a sycophant lord riding roughshod over a land and people forced to serve him. Much the same as having to warm your feet in a puddle of horse piss while trying to fight off frostbite on a fierce winter's night, men loathed serving Alain De La Foret but had no other choice. Characterized by arm-waving flamboyance and loud speech, the little lord imagined himself cast in much the same mold as the great Norman ruler and was voracious in pursuit of growing his name to similar renown. Yet, as he had neither the stomach to carry out the war-making required nor the physical presence to instill much fear, Alain's achievements greatly paled by comparison. He didn't have the stuff William had. And with each passing year while sitting upon the high seat in his modest little hall, he began to realize what a trivial little perch it was, indeed.

A man equal parts egotistic and arrogant and far from intelligent, Alain De La Foret often bragged that he was no Icarus—the Greek boy whose wings melted when he flew too close to the sun—his hubris such that he actually thought he could fly. Notorious for making a ready submission to any false prophet of the forest selling a dream, searching for the secret that would allow him to roll a seven with only one die, he was an unconscionable spendthrift, and his small inheritance was running out like water through his fingers.

Unfettered by marriage and lavishly spending on carnal delights and the empty splendor of big shiny things, Alain had a vulgar taste for worthless curiosities including his many portraits depicting him as myriad magnificent beasts of the jungle devouring prey. He wanted to be rich, only had yet to figure out the easy-money scheme that would turn his small economy into gains. Thus, the circumstances under which a woman as remarkable as Judith de Heugleville had become his wife became the talk in all the local shops and taverns from the very moment she appeared on his arm.

Many felt this accomplished and sharp-minded younger daughter of the heroic Richard de Heugleville had married Alain for much the same reason a she-wolf, wearied by the pursuit of so many hang-tongue, pink-pricked males, couples with the one she feels worked hardest to get her, hoping that he is exhausted to the point that he will make no unreasonable demands. Judith would give Alain the one thing he truly wanted from her—the buttered side of the bread, so to speak—in hopes that she might then go about living her life without his meddling too much. Only, everyone knew Alain was as much wolf as the animal itself. A craven coxcomb harboring such self-centered greed that he would always take his fill first, leaving nothing but the scraps of his time and attention to Judith and any future children.

And they were right. A man neither courteous nor courtly with a laughable lack of maturity, even after years of Judith's incessant, stern counseling, Alain did not, in even the smallest measure, draw back from his myopic ways. Someday he would have to answer for his self-serving petulance, Judith warned him. "God is watching you." And He was.

Despite his middling stature and juvenile behavior, Alain De La Foret had a way of looking down on everyone whether seated on his high horse or not. No matter the situation, he always sought to dominate. Playing the part of the hatchet-wielding fishmonger surrounded by a hundred smelly fish, he was often seen riding in the fields and forests surrounding his stronghold deriding the work of lesser men he had tasked with this or that. Everything was "godawful shit." And a serf's best effort was more likely to earn the sting of his whip than a pat on the back.

So too did Alain cherish pretensions of superiority in battle and sport. He was particularly proud of his horsemanship, which was good fiction, to be sure, as his mounts were far less fiery war-horses than stubby little hill ponies. Given to hunting and hawking and all the accouterments and fine garments that went along with the noble sports, Alain had an innate need to call attention to himself, and always set off with a rousing yell and a flourish of his tall, red-plumed hat. Like a jester at court, he played well the buffoon; everything about him was laughable. And, once well out of sight, he never failed to receive the loud, guffawed applause he so deserved.

For her part, Judith was a masterful rider.

So that she had been thrown from her horse while pregnant in the early days of her marriage to Alain was stunning in its consequence: the baby died in her womb and she had been unable to carry a child to term since.

While in no way typical of his character, Alain genuinely cared about the loss; for as the father of three illegitimate daughters during the years he had been waiting to marry Judith—and two more after—he had no sons, whore-born or otherwise. His older brother was a monk; the younger one was dead. On Alain alone rested the hope of continuing his father's line. And that was one of the few things in life truly important to him.

Nevertheless, when finally Alain did marry, it was not so much for the sake of offspring as much as for convenient carnal pleasure. Despite his always bragging on himself that he was the prized stud in the barn, he was laughably short on manliness, and numerous back-alley whores swore his hump-dog wiggling was over even before they'd drawn three breaths.

Judith would have him no other way.

Impressed by young Alain's creative telling of his heroic struggle to survive the massacre of the Morimont men, on his deathbed Richard de Heugleville promised him Judith's hand in marriage upon her seventeenth birthday. Only so slowly did the years pass before her coming of age that even as Alain stood at the altar and the priest at Saint-Aubin Church finally proclaimed Judith to be his wife, the little fop was so rigid in his pants that no blood remained to color his wide-smiling face. For, oh, how Judith de Heugleville could spark Alain's eye in her younger day! Her face absolutely beautiful and with golden hair falling to her waist, she had curves of body scarcely believed possible. But time was passing. Judith wasn't all that pretty anymore. Her tits not so well placed. And she still hadn't given him a son. Eager for fame, Alain wanted a boy to be proud of. To raise to a position of power. Real power. To make the name De La Foret known the land over. By God, the first name written onto the pages of all Norman history! But with all Judith's silly crying over that one dead baby in her belly long ago, she had hardly allowed Alain to touch her since.

Judith was eighteen years old in 1061, the year she buried her stillborn son. Prudent, fluid in speech, and exceedingly devoted to God, this second daughter of Richard de Heugleville, founder of Auffay, was, in fact, his niece. The only child of Richard's wife's older brother—who was killed in that same encounter with the Arques men near Morimont in 1053—Judith was just a young girl when Richard, setting her up on the back of his horse after the battle, took her home to raise as his own. Alas, Richard died of his wounds six days later. Judith's aunt followed him into the ground the following year. She was raised by their oldest daughter, Ada.

Soft-spoken and slight of smile, Judith had a queen-like elegance about her that made heads turn and eyes gleam with respect. She could seem quite aloof, untouchable even. Just the same, Judith sought no reward for her immense generosity and lived a life not so different from those bound by their oaths to monastic discipline. As she would often ride through the forest to share her bountiful inheritance with the widowed, the sick, and the poor, it was not uncommon to see a serf's young son or daughter sitting on the front of her saddle and handling the reins.

Neither cost nor care for priests and monks did Judith spare. Providing daily loads of firewood for their cooking and heating, and every Christmas morning having delivered all the wine needed for use in celebrating the next year's Masses, she would also pay for all the oil and wax needed for the hundreds of candles lighting the local church of Saint-Aubin. Often taking her meals at the abbey, Judith was beloved by the monks, and at her death, they honored their special friend by burying her near the church door. A large stone arch was placed over her grave, framing a view of the day-end skies she loved so much. On its face was etched in florid script: "Here lies Judith de Heugleville—a most blessed lady lost. May the God of Heaven bestow eternal life upon her unblemished soul."

So also, Alain De La Foret believed in God. Only, he was not so sure He was as powerful as He was made out to be. Or that all those biblical accounts of Jesus's works weren't maybe a bit over-colored. Regardless, as his wife would have it no other way—denying him even the smallest nibble of her "buttered bread" if he protested too much—considerable gifts did he confer on many small churches in the area. Preceded by great pomp and pageant in the presentation of all the shiny little things, he would swell with the pride of a peacock at the height of all its feathery glory as the priests then lined up to press their lips to his rings and make deep, sweeping bows before him in acknowledgment of his magnanimity. And it would make Alain feel good about himself for a while. But as giving things away was not in keeping with his assiduous struggle to amass great wealth, he would often demand them back, explaining the simple misunderstanding that they had only been on loan. If refused, under the cloak of darkness, Alain would steal them back. And, oh, how he would then brag about it to the tight-lipped serfs—the hilarity of the escapade: the frantic little monks running around like chickens without heads, shrieking at the golden Madonna having run off in the night to return to her chosen place of worship on the edge of the Gorge du Petit Ailly!

Again, Judith's stern warning. "Beware, Alain," she would say, quoting an old and favorite saying of her Norse ancestors: "A man laughs too long, too loud about a thing, sometimes his head falls off."

And so did it come to pass, with one too many gilded virgins walking off in the night, a dry-eyed Judith stood watching without a hint of despair as her husband was dragged off in chains behind a big Norman horse to become reacquainted with the king.

Alain was a man very much of the human race—often egregious in his acts, but not immune to bouts of guilt. As such, with his appointed death fast approaching, a most merciful God was quite perplexed over whether the man was sufficiently contrite to be spared spending all eternity burning in the fires of Hell. Was Alain's belief genuine enough to enter the Kingdom of Heaven? There was no purgatory. It was Heaven or Hell, and a decision needed to be made.

Only, as God sat His throne in the sky thoughtfully weighing His judgment, the reigning power on Earth suddenly rose up and decided Alain's fate for Him. William the Conqueror, King of England and Duke of Normandy, as pious a Christian monarch as the world had ever seen and suffering the full burden of the atrocities committed by his Viking forefathers, held that there was no sin more despicable than stealing from the Mother Church. The point needed to be made, and very clearly, that neither he nor God would be trifled with.

So it was, with his thieving hands deposited in a small wicker basket and his head lying upon the cobbles of the crowded court square in Rouen, in the year 1086, at the age of fifty-three years, Alain De La Foret was delivered into the waiting arms of the Devil. Expunged from all written records and quickly forgotten, his name was not spoken in the great province of Normandy ever again.

# THE PAGAN

*Predawn*

## 10 SEPTEMBER 1100

That the God of Heaven, bountiful in His gifts, had at last given the little lord of Auffay the namesake he so desired was not enough to turn Alain De La Foret from his sinful ways. But oh, in those last years before being cast into that hot, stinking cesspool of Hell, how Alain had relished basking in the light of his son's glorious life!

Often referred to by the only mother he ever knew as *Grand Don Des Dieux*—God's Great Gift—Alain De La Foret II was the baptismal name of the boy everyone else in Talou came to know as Jaune Faucon.

Found at the base of the huge Saint's Tree with a Hammer of Thor amulet hung around his neck, Jaune Faucon's future greatness was never doubted. Yet, as that greatness had been imbued by a god that was, undeniably, not their own, there was much wringing of hands by the black-robes at the highest levels of the Catholic Church over the true circumstances surrounding the pagan babe's sudden appearance in that sacred Christian place. An intense, questing search by these true lords of the Norman realm for the perpetrator of the travesty—this pollution of holy ground—persisted for months but amounted to nothing.

Still, someone had to know something.

And one woman did. Yet, Adelvia was never suspected, as the only clue she ever gave the inquisitors—the thousand pages of lies she'd torn from her Bible—that preening Prince of Heaven's evil book—and then scattered around her bloody cliff-top rock the day Jaune Faucon was born after hiding him in the forest—had long since blown away.

Trodden upon for centuries, the path to the great Saint's Tree was hard beaten dirt, the main spine upon which many smaller tracks—winding around bogs and downed trees, through fields and along circuitous streams—gathered before making an end on a wide loop around the tree's massive trunk. Rooted in a slightly sunken glade overgrown with a dusky green carpet of myrtle fringed with tall ferns, bluebells, and white anemones, the giant ash tree stood up with singular prominence out of a vast surround of beech, elm, alder, and oak.

So also, living in and amidst the leafy boughs of deep wood flora, the fauna was equally varied and plentiful. Hares, squirrels, weasels, and rabbits. Pine and beech martens. Roe, red, and fallow deer. Hart. Bear. Boar. Horses, hounds, and raptors too, as it was a common sight in the Talou Wood for a lord and his wife to ride about the forest with falcons and goshawks on their wrists—hunting hares, squirrels, weasels, rabbits, martens, and anything else that moved.

It was an opportunity to display wealth. A sign of gentility and status. So, it was no surprise when Alain, a man well practiced in creating illusions, bought a falcon for Judith, as he knew the bird would add splendor to his home, to his name.

The falcon had come from Scandinavia. By way of Flanders. A Brabantine dealer. Dashing, noble, and strong, trained to the wrist and ready to fly. When pressed for the price paid for the falcon by fellow enthusiasts, Alain boasted that he had paid whatever exorbitant sum necessary to acquire such a fine bird ... although he surely did not.

In truth, it was the most beautiful of the three falcons Alain owned. Gray-green in body with long, curled talons yellowed right to the spur, it was magnificent in every detail.

Yet, the widow Lisbeth—the fat-chested, pagan-turned-Christian wife of Alain's dead younger brother—was present at the unhooding. The oldest daughter of a dead barbarian warlord whose family fled to the Norman province from Denmark years ago, Lisbeth was Scandinavian through and through, and, as such, knew more about falcons than most. Knew that the female—almost without exception—was the larger, faster, better hunting bird. "So why this male?" she asked Alain.

"One hundred sous cheaper than the girl bird," Alain stated matter-of-factly. Then, caring less of the deep scar on Lisbeth's Danish heart—and with every intention of beating her back onto the blood-red shore of her Fyn Island home and a recalling of her father's brutal beheading by the famous Norwegian warrior-king Harald Hardrada—the little lord of Auffay loudly proclaimed he had named the falcon Hardrada—"Because he's a first-rate killer."

Alain did not like Lisbeth. Smart girl. Pretty enough. And, as was Alain's experience with any of these Norse wenches, the only thing she was more eager to display than her big, fat tits was her knowledge of falcons. In fact, so much so that he often referred to Lisbeth as "the Peregrine." Little did she know how derogatory the name was meant to be as it literally meant "the Outsider." Lisbeth's family was nothing. And she was even less. Perhaps good enough to use that big mouth of hers to dissipate his brother's carnal appetites, but certainly not good enough to be his wife. Why, the gall of her to question his decision to buy the most voracious raptor he had ever seen!

While Alain was loathe to admit it, his wife Judith was far superior to most men in most things and was a master falconer. Even she had made no argument against the bird.

Nor would she. Hardrada could flat-out hunt. Judith had been introducing Lisbeth's young daughter Sille to the basic release and recall aspects of falconry with a pretty little finch—a superb aerialist, but harmless; more a toy than a bird. Now, Alain's new falcon: he was a wolf in the air. Looking down on the world from above before descending in a brilliant stoop to either kill with a blow of his scythe-like talons or bind to his prey until the dogs arrived, Hardrada brought instant death to his quarry like no bear or boar she had ever seen. So too—as Alain quickly learned, what with that big, gaudy feather he loved so much sticking up from his hat—to wear something red around Hardrada was at your own risk. For, like the blood on the fur of a wounded animal, it was a call to attack where you stood.

Therefore, the part the color red played the day Judith first laid eyes on her newborn son.

Hard in the saddle with Hardrada on her wrist, two young handlers and four spaniels were walking at Judith's side through a light morning mist. Passing in and out of the shadows under the high-arching boughs of a verdant summer forest, there was no breeze, no noise, nor anything worth hunting anywhere spied. It was a lazy day. A peaceful day. A time for reflection. Silent. Pleasurable. Away from Alain. Only just then, rounding a bend ahead of Judith where the stream forked into two, the dogs' heads suddenly lifted as something came into view.

Judith, now standing in her stirrups with her head in the leaves, put up a hand, whispered "Don't move," to the handlers, then stretched her look over the stream and into the trees. She could see it, but didn't know what it was: barely visible through the bramble, about ten *toises* off—fifty feet—something red—nameless, shapeless—peeking up out of the root tangle of the great Saint's Tree. *Maybe a fox; maybe a squirrel,* Judith thought. *No matter. It's not fare for the table, but food for the dogs.*

The spaniels, whelps all—baying, barking, and turning tight circles—strained at their leashes, desperate to run and get the first bite.

The falcon Hardrada—hood off, eyes keened and wings tensed at his sides—dug his talons into Judith's thick-gloved hand, sensing imminent flight.

A squeak or a cry. Judith was not sure. Yet, at the young handlers' wild halloo, she quick-slipped the knot tied to the raptor's feet and Hardrada fast flew. A green blur streaking straight to his quarry, his leg-bells chiming, and feathered lure trailing, with a sudden dip of his wing, the falcon dove down hard, and then disappeared from sight.

Snarling, snapping, and breaking every rule of the hunt, the young dogs then crashed through the brush, a flight of startled thrush flushed upward in a whoosh.

Judith, weaving her horse through the trees, ducking under branches as she rode through the stream, then slid from her saddle and bent low for a look. So did she see—unblinking of eye and talons dug in, the falcon Hardrada— the avian King of Norway—proudly perched on his throne ... and ready to kill.

Streaks of red. Flesh in his beak. A bloody head. Then Judith's sudden shriek.

Streaming hot tears, Judith saw her hawk, her hounds, and a baby most fair. Green-eyed, golden-haired, and wrapped in a bloody cloth. *Grand Don Des Dieu*, she whispered to herself—God's Great Gift at last bequeathed to Judith de Heugleville, the son she had asked for in prayer.

Unconquerable as a mid-summer sun's climb to the highest point in the sky, a young Jaune Faucon De La Foret—The Yellow Falcon of the Forest— displayed an uncommon tenacity and depth of courage that would be his distinguishing trait for the rest of his life. Spending many of his days at the Fortress Arques, he would rally with friends and cousins outside the massive stone walls of the grand castle on the hill and lead them on great "Viking expeditions," returning in the dying light with mounds of "treasure" unearthed in the surrounding forest. Often making incursions into the local farm-fields to harry and plunder and burn villages far and wide, Jaune Faucon would report "killing" many people, and taking many "hostages." One memorable day, he and his Viking horde fought fourteen separate battles and emerged victorious in all—without losing a single man. Another time, Jaune Faucon gained access to a tall timber blockhouse in the guise of a dead man borne on the overlapped faces of six upturned shields. Solemnly laid on the ground, in the next moment he jumped up, as planned, and led a rush upon the stronghold's stunned guardians. Their surrender was quick, complete, and with little bloodshed.

Blunt-swords and play-shields notwithstanding, Jaune Faucon's cunning and bravery were proved time and again, and many of Duke William's future fighting men flocked to the Yellow Falcon from every corner of the Talou Wood. Caring less of whose god created him, they followed Jaune Faucon everywhere. And always would.

Nor did the starry-eyed boys' hero escape the notice of their Norman fathers. As Jaune Faucon grew ever taller in stature and strength in the fast-passing years, his increasingly bloody exploits in "battle" only served to accentuate his pagan birth. And while it was true that little more than a century separated the establishment in Gaul of the Norwegian Rolf from the birth of his most illustrious descendant, Duke William, Normandy was Christian now. A soldier of Christ was to be civilized rather than barbarous. Wars had rules. The *berserker* fury of their Norse ancestors had been outlawed. And as any such warrior was regarded as an ungodly fiend, there was considerable angst at a young man of so obviously barbarian stock rising among them. Seeming to relish the thought of wading into a sea of blood and squirming guts and cutting off heads, carnage suited a young Jaune Faucon. And he made no apology for it. "So the pagan boy," the elders said. "So his pagan god."

Raised under the tutelage of his authoritative mother, Judith—a woman secretly proud of her own Norse heritage, but relentless in orienting her son's every thought and action to the service of the Christian Lord above—she often fretted about never having taken that Hammer of Thor amulet from around Jaune Faucon's neck. Believing that he would need the protection of his creator against all baleful influences when he was young, it was not lost on Judith that its similarity in shape to the crucifix had helped ease the conversion of her own Scandinavian ancestors to the Christian faith. The Norse Valhalla—or "Hall of the Slain"—in time, became "Heaven," and the gentle Christ the Redeemer eventually eclipsed their pagan pantheon of war.

So also, a lowborn rising to a position of power was hardly unique in the Norman realm. Duke William himself was a bastard of pagan lineage, and Judith could teach Jaune Faucon to walk and talk and act like a proper Christian just the same. Only, as he quickly became his own man, she could almost hear that voice deep inside him screaming: *"Odin! Heimdall! Frey! And Thor!"*

Even as Robert Curthose—the oldest son of Duke William who had been in open rebellion against his despotic father for many years—was building a massive army on the backs of the young firebrand sons of the duke's most loyal magnates, there was fear among the elders that Jaune Faucon would be recruited to their cause. This was not a man any battle-scarred, middle-aged warrior of the day wanted to face in a fight.

Already they had witnessed how fearsome Jaune Faucon had become. His minority had ended, and in the summer of 1087, he demonstrated in a whir of merciless scything steel that playtime was, indeed, over. Turned twenty years old only days before he fought in his first battle of any consequence, Jaune Faucon was in the vanguard of Duke William's force that made a quick-strike, retaliatory invasion of the French Vexin following King Philip's raid into eastern Normandy. Spurring his horse forward in a reckless charge, Jaune Faucon almost single-handedly cut to pieces the Capetian monarch's *conrois* of better than twenty mounted knights who had sallied forth to meet the Norman charge, and then—rushing on torch in hand—started the fire that by nightfall burned the town of Mantes to the ground. Roaring in victory, yet stunned by the *berserker* rage inside him that made it so easy to kill, such was the number of lives the Yellow Falcon of the Forest cut short in the ensuing years that much of the legend quickly gathered about him, while fabulous, bore little exaggeration.

Still, the Norman lords whispered, "It is more a trait of race than religion. And we should bind the pagan tight and feed him to the wolves of the court in Rouen for the laws that he has broken." Only others, their voices hushed further still, answered in Jaune Faucon's defense: "But our coffers are so much fuller with him than without him. He is a barbarian, yes. But he's our barbarian."

In fact, never was a man with such a ruthless fighting spirit seen on the continent before. Possessed of a heroic, almost supernatural quality, even as Jaune Faucon was laid in the ground more than fifty years later with all the pomp of a Christian saint, old warriors on bended knee hallowed the glorious victories this true pagan had gained for their God and their Church in words last spoken of the fabled Christian King Charlemagne himself.

# THE CHRISTIAN

*Predawn*

## 10 SEPTEMBER 1100

For his part, there came a time in Jaune Faucon's life when his passion for making war no longer burned as brightly as in his younger day. Judged by his own conscience, he was not so proud of all the killing he had done in the name of God. Not so proud to have worn the Christian *croise* on a tunic spattered with the blood, flesh, and brains of old men, women, and children. Thus, the day Jaune Faucon infamously tore from his chest that evil, red-silk symbol of Catholic fanaticism and ripped it to pieces.

For more than a thousand years, the sword more than the cross led the Christian climb to religion's mountaintop as soldiers of the Lord, following in the footsteps of God's most passionate warriors—Constantine the Great, Charlemagne, Charles Martel, Marcus Aurelius and his Thundering Legion—sloshed through rivers of blood to spread Jesus's precious name. That anyone would scorn coming to baptism, daring to worship their own gods, brought instant death.

Awakening that same bellicose spirit from its long sleep at Clermont, France, in late November 1095, Pope Urban II's declaration of war on "those vile blasphemers trampling on Christ and the Holy Land with impunity" unleashed almost unhuman carnage on the non-believers of the world. Carrying the Pope's call to arms into every corner of Western Europe, firebrand preachers rousing cries of *"Dieu le volt!"*—"God wills it!"—inspired the sons of Christendom to "take up the cross" and purge the Muslim scourge once and for all.

Neither did Jaune Faucon have any doubts about the righteousness of the action. A base, bastard, repugnant race, this insolent tribe of Seljuk Turks roaming the streets of Jerusalem had been profaning sacred Christian sites and relics for years. Starving, torturing, and butchering like beasts those who dared apostatize from the Lord's sacred Gospels, so also did the pollutions of these psychopathic warmongers include forcing the faithful to sacrifice to idols and demons— even selling thousands of worshippers into slavery. They deserved to be killed.

Jaune Faucon had been a warrior his whole life and excelled at his craft like no other of God's soldiers. Having the further advantage of possessing a pagan's animal rage, killing was what he knew most about living and he was soon being sought out to fight under the banner of every lord in the Christian realm.

The Pope deemed the Holy Land to be the rightful property of the Church and the recapture of Jerusalem—the city Jesus, the Lord Protector of the Pious, "made illustrious by His advent, beautified by His residence, consecrated by His suffering, redeemed by His death, and glorified by His burial"—was a moral obligation. Cleverly playing upon the European nobleman's characteristic piety, greed, and lust for power, the Pope promised the faithful not only a cancellation of their debts, exemption from taxes, and vast new estates in the reconquered Holy Land, but a complete forgiveness of their sins and the most direct path to the imperishable glory of the Kingdom of Heaven.

"The Holy Land must be cleansed of this abhorrent race," Urban II proclaimed whilst standing before a large silk banner bearing the red Christian *croise*—the words *"In Hoc Signo Vinces"*—"With this sign, you will conquer"—written in bold letters above his head. Pointing at it, the Pope said, "It is imperative that all true and spiritual soldiers of God take up the sign of the Lord's cross—the stigma of His Passion—and smite the enemy wherever he may be found. Not only is the action honorable and virtuous, the future of all Christendom is at stake. Heed my warning: all your sons and daughters will be condemned to lives in bondage, suffering under the yoke of a burgeoning evil if you do not act."

Urban II envisioned an army the likes of which had never before marched upon the Earth. Frenchman, Normans, Flemings, Englishman, Angevins, and Lotharingians no longer fighting and killing each other, but united as one to destroy a common enemy. Long, rigid columns of skilled, professional fighters led by princes, barons, and shining knights on big white horses. Banners flying. Armed to the teeth. Fearless and strong.

What the Pope got instead was the offal of the Earth.

A rabble of shoeless farmers, their filthy wives, and disease-ridden children.

Peasants. Beggars. Outlaws. Prostitutes.

Dirty. Barefoot. Covered in open sores and sackcloth.

Armed with clubs, sticks, and rocks.

Anyone and anybody willing to take up the cross and leave their sorry lives behind.

A mandate of God, Jaune Faucon would be undertaking his own spirit-journey, fighting his way into Heaven, and so found himself sitting his high horse in the midst of this foul-smelling peasant horde as it swarmed over the French countryside out of every shack and shit-hole from hundreds of miles around. Never had he known that so many of these human cockroaches even existed. And neither would he much care when they started dropping dead by the hundreds on the side of the road. Fewer mouths to feed. Less stink in the air. More glory to God's chosen few.

Most peasants of Western Europe feared they were living at the end of days in the spring of 1096. That the Antichrist was walking the Earth. Despite their devout belief—nigh to a blood-boiling fervor—the peasants' faith was shaken. They were beaten down by drought, famine, and deadly diseases

141

for years on end long before the Pope's dire revelation of the imperiled Holy Land. Even the most common occurrences now told of an evil force at work. A recent spate of lightning strikes, meteor showers, an eclipse of the sun, and strange cloud formations were indisputable signs that the end was near, with every birth defect or sudden death of a child taking on a prophetic meaning.

Added to that—as if life on Earth wasn't bad enough—a peasant's path to Heaven was an infinitely hard climb. Strewn with rocks and pocked with craters, one bad step, they feared, would send them hurtling into Hell. Even for those few who successfully negotiated the perilous ascent, there was the very real chance of being turned away outside those glorious golden gates as inferior, unworthy, unredeemed penitents. As such, some peasants chose to brand their bodies with the crusader cross, flog themselves for unconfessed sins, or bang spikes through their hands and feet so to experience the intolerable pain their Savior had suffered. Desperate acts by desperate people trying to prove to God their ardent belief in His divine Son, Jesus Christ.

It had been over a thousand years since the Redeemer's crucifixion, and the peasants believed, as written by the prophets, Jesus would soon return upon the Earth to reward those who served His messianic cause. The righteous would be saved; all others cast into the fiery abyss. The peasants were anxious. Ready to fight. To shed their blood. Many even asking excitedly at every town they came to if it might be Jerusalem. And when would the killing start?

That hardly a one of the ten thousand ragtag avengers came within two thousand miles of Jerusalem or killing a Turk diminished their enthusiasm not a bit. For after countless days dragging along the rain-drenched Palestine road behind their notorious, cruelly lawless and brutally anti-Semitic leader Emicho of Leiningen, the maundering mob was easily swayed by the Swabian count's argument that they need not pursue the Lord's enemies in such ridiculously far and distant lands. There were plenty of non-believers to kill, he told them—right now, right here in the German Rhineland. "Throngs of vile blasphemers far worse than any Muslims, the god-killing Jews are not far away from us, even living in our midst," Emicho shouted as he stood in his stirrups high above his army and within a sword-stroke of an enthusiastic and heavily armed Jaune Faucon. "These infinitely despicable people murdered the gentle Jesus of Nazareth, hanging Him on a cross, and it is God's will that they pay with their lives. Even the Lord Himself did say, 'There will come a day when My children will avenge My blood.' And, as sure as the Redeemer's glorious light is, at last, shining down on us out of this majestic blue sky, rejoice—for today is that day!"

So did it come to pass, hours later, cresting a hill and pointing his sword forward, with a full-throated shout of "God wills it!" a crazy-eyed Emicho led a charge upon the little riverside village of Speyer under the graying light of the early eve. Murdering with sanctified glee, the slaughter of the settlement's unsuspecting Jewish population was ruthlessly complete. The bestial behavior of the bloodthirsty peasants was almost subhuman. Houses burned. Women raped. Children gored. All along the Jerusalem road, boisterous hallelujahs raised as thousands of the faithful rejoiced at being one step closer to Heaven.

Acting by his own will, Jaune Faucon was no less an executioner in the fulfillment of his God-sworn duty. Yet, inasmuch as his morals had always dictated whom he could engage in warfare—any enemy of his homeland and those who abetted such devils—he found himself struggling with the notion that these unarmed Jews were neither. He felt strangely dirty wearing the blood of innocents even as he hacked his vicious scything blade through another old man trying to shield his screaming wife; another mother huddled over her wailing children; two old women hiding behind a chair. Moving from house to house with his victims' last desperate appeals for mercy still burning in his ears, Jaune Faucon found himself less and less inspired by Count Emicho's wild exhortations to "Kill those thieving usurers!"

God was not answering every question in his mind, so when faced with yet another man choosing to die a martyr's death, Jaune Faucon suddenly checked his blood-dripping sword mid-strike. He could not help but consider that what happened in Jesus's passion a thousand years ago could not be rightly charged against all Jews without distinction, then alive, or dying all around him today. Staring down at the quivering yet defiant old man, and then at his own bloodied hands, unable to resolve his problems of conscience within his own head—*A God-ordained slaughter of unarmed innocents?*—Jaune Faucon suddenly sheathed his sword and walked out the door.

Still, the hundred thousand Seljuk Turks awaiting him on the walls of the Holy City demanded that he not lose sight of the fact that he was a Christian soldier sworn to smite God's enemies. To shirk his duty was to deliver his soul straight to Hell.

So it was, in the following days and weeks, riding high above the peasant rabble through the pristine lands of the lower Rhine Valley, Jaune Faucon loosed God's fury on the next village ... the next ... and the next. Trier. Metz. Worms. Cologne. All was death. All was despair. Orchards and fields blackened by fire. Animal carcasses littering the hillsides. Churches, homes, and public halls burned to the ground. The Jews, unrecognizable as men or women, slaughtered like pigs and piled along every roadside and river. Oh, such joy among the bloodstained crusaders! A prideful vindication of the Holy Roman Catholic Church! All the glory went to God.

Yet, Jaune Faucon could boast of no such pride. For viewed through the prism of his blood-splattered eyes, he increasingly saw himself not as a heroic son fighting for God's good and glory, for the future freedom of kith and kin, but as a zealot spearheading the extermination of an entire race.

God would not release Jaune Faucon from his duty. The strength to do what was right and good had to come from within. Driven by a pure and honest soul. Washed of the sins now staining it black.

A farmstead was burning. Just a few outbuildings in a clearing of the forest. A dog howled from somewhere within. A roof fell in. The howling stopped. Jaune Faucon rode on.

Kicking up a dense russet cloud behind him, Jaune Faucon turned his horse across a wide, grassy field, leaped a small stream, and then stepped down onto a sunken cart track that led into the heart of a sizable village ahead.

Another clump of buildings was burning on the near bank of a twisted black river beyond. He heard windows breaking. People screaming. To his right, a dozen peasant foot soldiers, torches held high, scurried like rats across an adjacent field anxious to destroy a large stone-walled church crowning the hill above. Clambering over its high outer wall, they trampled underfoot a single cross-bearing priest tearfully invoking the claim of sanctuary for the many Jews sheltered within before breaking down its large wooden door with pickaxes and spade-shovels. Flames rising. Children crying. The bloodthirsty mob killing anything that moved.

Facing down the demons he'd never before confronted, Jaune Faucon could feel his anger rising, spurring him to action. Then—from somewhere behind him—an apocalyptic shout of "God's kingdom has arrived!" accompanied by the sudden sound of a hundred hooves pounding on the blood-stained ground.

Mounted on large Norman *destriers*, a wild-eyed Count Emicho with a contingent of perhaps thirty men in short white tunics and burnished metal breastplates suddenly swept past Jaune Faucon on both sides. Armed with short, double-edged thrusting swords, bearded axes, hammers, and spears, when they were a hundred ells distant—a hundred-fifty feet—they suddenly veered off the road, crashed their horses through a crude timber fence, and charged across a wide, shimmering swath of dew-heavy clover draping the grassy slope. Clinging to a thin dirt spine snaking through the rolling hills ahead of them, the soldiers—once out in the open fields along the river—beat a straight line toward a small group of women and children fleeing out of a clump of rough, wood-planked cottages into the forest beyond. Cut down in less than a minute in a storm of slashing steel, their bloodied bodies scattered the ground like the felled beasts of a hunt.

Whooping, hollering, and riding tight circles around the dead Jews, Emicho and his men suddenly spied another group huddled under a large willow tree overhanging the river's edge. Another minute, another slaughter. Another victory for the Lord.

Rejoicing in the utter massacre, Count Emicho then pointed to the sky and shouted out that he could see with his own eyes—the same as the great Constantine before him—the truly magnificent image of the Holy Cross burning in the light of the setting sun. "It is destiny," he proclaimed upon withdrawing his shimmering victory-sword from a small, bloodied hump on the ground, "that Christianity shall be recognized as the supreme religion of the world just as the Lord God of Heaven will crush all pretenders to His throne."

Staring over the macabre landscape before him, Jaune Faucon hardly noticed when a dark little man suddenly appeared at his side, tugging on his sleeve. His face hairy as a gopher and looking as if he had just crawled out of a hole in the ground, the man pointed a short, gangrenous forefinger toward a pile of dead Jews heaped on the roadside ahead and said, "Two more over there. Old women." Proudly showing Jaune Faucon their fresh red blood glistening on the tines of his rusty pitchfork, he then added in a low, dastardly voice, "Fought like Hellcats, they did. Had to keep at it awhile to kill them."

With his long, greasy hair slicked back on his head and his sore-festered skin showing through the many tears in his thin, sackcloth tunic, the peasant then pointed at the horsemen in the valley below and said, "Sure are pretty them fellows in all their fancy clothes and plumage. But, sure as a little chunk of coal is worth so much more than a fistful of diamonds on a cold winter night, I will take the measure of any one of those big, shining knights—long swords, leather boots, feathery hats, and all."

The little man's gaze slowly climbed to the very tip of the tall red plume sticking up from Jaune Faucon's hat—the hat his father Alain used to wear; the smirk on the peasant's pocked, dirty face a poor disguise of his outright ridicule.

"I will take the measure of you, even," the peasant further stated without a hint of fear. "For, uncorrupted by wealth or power, I am a true soldier of the Lord. A lowly man of the fields, I cannot buy my place in Heaven; I must fight for it. Fraught with hardship, disease, pain, and hunger, my life has been a struggle that nothing a silvertooth like you could ever hope to survive. I can see the disgust in your eyes. The flare of your nose. Indignant. Like smelling a dead rat rotting on a hot rock. Yet, I take no offense. For, just as sure as the Lord will soon return among us in a final judgment of our souls, the only differentiation He will make between you and me is the purity of our faith. Endowed with neither riches, wisdom, or commanding stature, I do not pretend to radiate the splendor of the sun. I cannot boast of a multitude of gifts I have laid at His feet. But neither do I make a mockery of His divine goodness by begging a gold crown to wear on my head in recognition of my service. I doubt you or any of those dandies down there in the valley can say the same. No matter: at our deaths, any earthly distinction between us will be obliterated ... your riches cast into the fiery abyss ... fancy hats and all."

Delighting in cutting down Jaune Faucon to his own pathetically small size, the peasant continued with his smoldering rant, his words wielded like a keen-edged sword: "The preachers say, 'The blessed meek are destined to inherit the earth.' And as sure as the only begotten word of the God above is a promise made to all His children, I have rightly earned what I am about to receive." The peasant glared at a group of old men, women, and children silently huddled at the edge of a small green pond in a grassy glade beyond, Count Emicho's spearmen pressing them all around. "Those people you see over there are neither blessed nor meek," the peasant said. "Of all races, they are the worst enemies of God. Murderers of our good and gentle Jesus. Only to complete my holy mission—convert them or kill them—God's grace will at last shine down on me. This hard life will end. And I will be richer in Heaven than any king of this world has ever imagined."

Slipping a short, sharpened stick from inside the rope at his waist, he then put its point in his mouth and began picking the crud from his teeth. Watching the Jews with an expression of cold indifference, the man suddenly stopped and—with the same sparkle in his eye as a mischievous child—exploded into laughter.

In the glade, prodded with the ragged end of a long, broken tree branch, a pretty, young woman was suddenly stripped of her thin linen gown and dragged to the edge of the slimy green pond. Condemned to suffer the consequences of having a body men lusted for, she swung a fist at a man trying to force her down onto her hands and knees before two spearmen seized her, rammed her face into the mud, and held her in a position in which their silver-helmeted leader—a fat Angevin nobleman—could easily enjoy her.

With his mouth twisted into a rabid snarl, the man unbuckled his sword and, pulling up his sweat-soiled tunic, threatened to rut every hole in her body. Crushing his big hands on the woman's hip-bones and lifting her off the ground, he punctuated his every savage thrust into her with a loud, almost demonic, "I hate Jews!" The venom in his veins surging even as the vigor of his attack waned with his sudden expulsion, he then flipped the sobbing woman onto her back and offered his men to have whatever was left of her.

So did they all have their turn ... until she breathed no more. Tying a rope around her heels, the men then dragged the woman off behind a fast horse, her dead body bouncing over jutting crags of stone with pieces of her breaking off all across the field. Throwing her bloody carcass down the side of a steep, rocky ridge, the men then stood laughing, mocking her—"Not such a pretty thing anymore, is she?"—like it was the most fun they'd ever had.

Horrified by their evil act, such anguished sounds that escaped Jaune Faucon's mouth he could barely believe were his own.

Indeed, he was witnessing madness. God-driven savagery. Devils on Earth.

In the glade, the Angevin nobleman pointed to another woman he wanted pulled out of the line. Admitting that he'd need a little time to regrow "this good hard oak between my legs," he ordered the men to baptize her, instead. Dragged into the pond's waist-deep water and thrashing wildly, she dared the men to dunk her beneath its slimy green surface. Stunned by her fierce fight as she slammed her elbow into the mouth of one man and then bit the nose of another, two more spearmen waded into the green sludge and, after a long moment of hesitation, joined the others in trying to force the woman's head under the water. Hands at her throat. Punching her. Pulling her hair. Twisting her nipples. Tearing her breasts. Still, she fought on.

Thrashing like a bear in a trap whilst smashing her fists against red snarling faces all around, the young woman suddenly cried out to Jehovah that she would "sooner be sent into the Great Light beyond than besmirched by the heresy of this risen man-god! This Jesus! This fraud! I will not swear for any false prophet! I will not! I will not! I will not!"

So did the furry little hate-mongering rodent of a man at Jaune Faucon's side laugh harder still when the soldiers at last banged her head down into the rippling red water, then smeared the sign of the Christian cross on her forehead. Because he knew there wasn't a damned thing the god of the Israelites could do about it.

Jaune Faucon went numb. Sickened by the woman's screams and with bile surging in his throat, the fiercest fighting man Normandy ever knew stood there in his ridiculous red-feathered hat, just staring—not doing a damned thing to help her, either.

The sun went down on over a thousand corpses strewn along the banks of the River Rhine at Mainz that fine spring day in the year 1096. Yet Jaune Faucon's terrible swift sword claimed not one of them. No longer able to fabricate enough hatred of the Jews nor enough love for his God to keep up his lifelong charade of being a heartless killer, he tore that red, viscera-stained Christian *croise* from his chest, and stomped it into the muck. Suffering the crude jeers of the rag-tag throng, he then slowly pulled his sword from its sheath ... and laid it on the ground ... turned his back on that long, bloody river ... and headed for home.

Count Emicho threatened to ruin him.

In the eyes of the Church, he was an outlaw. A crime against God. Punishable by death. Jaune Faucon didn't care.

Killing was not so easy anymore. And never would be again.

# THE FATHER

*Dawn*

## 10 SEPTEMBER 1100

Judith was much relieved by the general peace in the realm. Jaune Faucon had not been in a battle for months. Not since his return from the Rhineland. Yet, her son seemed anything but peaceful. His face etched in hard lines. Muttering to himself. His eyes, once a brilliant green, dimmed to gray; no spark. His hands, clenched into fists and pressed viselike to the sides of his head, rubbed raw from scrubbing stains only he could see.

Finding no spiritual haven within his tortured mind—no place to hide from the many atrocities he had committed against hundreds of defenseless innocents—Jaune Faucon's conscience shouted at him that he was as godless a man as ever created. Even in his sleep he was unable to escape the agony of every scream he wrought; his reliving of each and every killing was to witness cold-blooded, indiscriminate murder.

His name once shouted, now whispered, but still feared in Normandy— nigh a year would pass before Jaune Faucon again took up his sword. Yet, nevermore did he exhibit the pure warrior spirit of his younger day. The *berserker* rage coursing his pagan blood was no longer in him.

The *Christian* rage was no longer in him.

So strange was the feeling that had come upon him that day at Mainz. Thunderous—yet completely from within. As if the murderous beast long living inside him was suddenly struck down and died on the terrible terrain of his troubled mind.

So, too, the quashing of his characteristic rage was not an act of his own doing, but as if by another—better—soul. Of him, yet separate. Embracing the best of him, but destroying the rest. As if inhabited by a twin spirit, sharing his tolerance and compassion. Tempering him much the same as the carbon melded with the iron in his German-steel sword blade, resulting in an alloy hard and strong on the outside while softer and more flexible on the inside. Forging Jaune Faucon to his full strength. Making him a better human.

Nor was it the first time Jaune Faucon had felt the embrace of his twin. Even had he feared him. Struggled against him. Wanting no part of the journey upon which this phantom of his better self would lead him into the deepest abyss of his consciousness and demand Jaune Faucon slay the beasts that had been eating him heart and soul from the very day he was born.

But then Mainz. Standing with his shadowy twin amidst the death, decay, and dusty pall that ruled that bloody day, Jaune Faucon finally fought back and defeated the furies of his mind.

*With your help, gentle brother, at last I might break free of my lust for destroying men and start saving them—beholden to nothing but my own conscience all the remaining days of my life.*

Judith had been wary of the year 1100 AD. Having discovered Jaune Faucon under the great Saint's Tree on this very day in 1067, her son was thirty-three years old now. And while Jaune Faucon attributed no great significance to the number, his mother surely did, for it was the same age at which the gentle Jesus of Nazareth was crucified, died, and was buried. Only, that Jesus had risen from the dead—an immortal—a god—resurrected and taken into Heaven in whole-body perfection and now seated at the right hand of His Father—her son was just a man. As merciless a killer as there ever was, Jaune Faucon could not rightly think to be seated even at the *left* hand of the

Father. Or in any other seat otherwise available. Jesus would soon return in judgment of every man, woman, and child of the Earth; the faithful would be taken into God's kingdom of eternal light while all others would be cast into the fiery abyss of Hell. So, yes, as a mother who dearly loved Jaune Faucon, Judith had a reason to be worried. That he married another of pagan blood— and a whore, at that—caused her even more fright.

Of a most cheerful disposition away from the battlefield in his younger day, Jaune Faucon enjoyed his drink and was given to have in his retinue all sorts of jugglers, harpers, fiddlers, midgets, and magicians. He loved to laugh. To have a good time. To experience the best of everything life had to offer. So, his chance meeting with a lithe, dark-eyed dancer named Germini.

Upon entering into a crowded tavern one sweltering summer night, his first look at the savagely erotic beauty was like lightning through his loins. Dancing on a large table cluttered with ale horns with her gauzy white tunic hiked up high on her thighs, the girl's movements were slow and sinuous, like smoke swirling above an unseen fire, teasing the surrounding pack of drooling drunkards with glimpses of that dark, silky triangle they all so desired to enter.

Showing no fear as the men pressed her all around, howling like dogs, pawing at her, trying to tear off her flimsy garment, the girl seemed but a man-eating vixen. Ready to devour every inch of whoever paid her the most.

Bewitched by her almost feral allure, Jaune Faucon couldn't take his eyes off her.

Skillful at flirtation and calculated sexual charm, all was at her command. The panting dogs. The swilling pigs. Even the music followed her salacious rhythms.

Only, Jaune Faucon wanted Germini to himself. Shoving every other man aside without a challenge because, even drunk, no one was brave or stupid enough to stand in his way, figuring the girl would be good for the night—and maybe once-twice more in the morn—he paid her price to do what whores do.

Sweeping her off the table, carrying her down a few steps, and out the back door, the look on the girl's face betrayed nothing to Jaune Faucon. Staring through the trees at the small stable beyond, she'd been down this path before. The same smells as last night. Horse shit. And lust.

Why it was that he didn't just get up and leave when he was done, Germini was not quite sure. But, strangely, the longer he laid beside her, the more she wanted him to stay.

By the light of a flickering oil lamp, Germini's eyes roved over Jaune Faucon's naked body. Battle-tested and grown to full manhood, he had been vigorous in the act while she'd had no chastity to protect. Now he was sleeping. Much about him screamed *barbarian*—virile and in command. Yet, somehow, he had been gentle, too. A trait women often wish for but seldom find.

Normandy was overrun by all these puffed-up soldier-farmers strutting around like the cock in the barn. Reeking of fish and ale with their dicks in their hands, their little man-boy minds were ruled by three things: drinking, fighting, and fucking. And, while hardly a choir boy, this Jaune Faucon seemed different somehow. Something intangible yet undeniable. Like finding a gold coin lying in a gutter.

Lying slack and still under the lamp's dusky pall, Germini had nearly fallen back to sleep when she felt a hand lightly brush the side of her bare breast. She turned her head. Jaune Faucon was awake. Staring at her with half-eyed sleepiness. And seemingly surprised to see her, too.

Almost like in explanation, Germini gestured toward the stable's wood plank ceiling, the sound of rain on the roof, and told Jaune Faucon she was waiting for it to stop. Then she would go. Jaune Faucon nodded his head and laid back on the thin quilted blanket covering the now flattened pile of straw. Casting a sidelong glance at Germini, his eyes began to wander—face to breasts, belly to thigh—before he forced them back to a long, vacant look at the ceiling. With a sudden thumping in his chest and an unconscious stirring in his loins, he then turned back to her and whispered, "You're very pretty."

With a growing blush on her cheeks, Germini remained quiet; her countenance composed. Opening her mouth to speak, Germini hesitated a moment as if rethinking her words. Her eyelashes dipped and her lips quivered with a faint smile.

Jaune Faucon mumbled some little unmeaning talk.

Germini said something about the rain. Hoping it would stop soon.

Speaking Norse with an unmistakably Danish accent, there was a distinct melancholy, even a sadness in her voice. Jaune Faucon had learned Norse from his mother, Judith—also of Danish blood—and when Germini finally allowed a couple grudging glimpses of things that troubled her much more than the weather, he began to understand her well beyond her words.

Lying abed, side-by-side, staring into Germini's hard, cobalt-blue eyes, Jaune Faucon slowly reached an arm around her slender shoulders and pulled her close—the feelings she stirred in him suddenly so much more profound than the animal desire that first drew him to her. Running his fingers through her soft, sable hair, at last, he coaxed her head down onto his chest and, little by little, she began offering him scraps of her past. The hard road she had traveled to arrive in this place; what made her cry and what made her laugh; what she hated about herself and what she hoped her life still might be. And, slowly, surely, like the sun-sparkle riding a river of dirty water, Jaune Faucon discovered Germini's true nature. Loving. Caring. And deeply scarred.

Six years younger than Germini, Jaune Faucon had been married to her for nearly ten years now. They had four children—two girls and two boys. The oldest was his nine-year-old son Sihtric, named in honor of Germini's father, a fiercely proud man who had reddened the waters of his Danish homeland with his blood when he was felled by no less a sword-warrior than the fierce marshal of King Harald Hardrada's all-conquering army—Styrkar

Kvendulfsson, a voracious killing machine known throughout the Northland as The Wolf. Huddled with her cousin Lisbeth on Fyn Island's rocky shore, a five-year-old Germini watched in horror as the inhumanly large Harald Hardrada himself then cut off her father's head, watching it drop onto a gut-slickened ship deck before the Norwegian warrior-king kicked it into the gray, churning sea. Muffling her shrieks against her cousin Lisbeth's heaving belly, Germini could not bear to watch as her mother, her aunts, and forty others of her *aett*—her family clan—were then herded like swine aboard the triumphant raider's bloodstained longship and rowed off toward a distant northern shore, never to be seen again.

That very night, amidst her young cousin's wild shrieks of pain and despair, the sixteen-year-old Lisbeth—the same as she had done to herself—burned the symbolic rune symbols of Germini's *aett* onto her forearm with a hot iron trenail she'd picked up beside the hulk of a Danish warship smoldering on the shore. With every inch of their Fyn Island home laid to waste by Hardrada and his rampaging host, the two girls then set off walking in the night along its ice-cragged coast toward they knew not where.

Everything hurt.

Thus it was, many years later, unable to heal her scars inside or out and baring her wounds for all to see, Germini began drunk-dancing night after night in taverns all over Normandy to dull the savaging pain. A modern-day Salome, breasts high and legs wide, she hated all pagans and wanted to love them to death. Practiced and perfect, so much more than the whore they paid for, there were times—often at the exact moment of one these beast's loud, conquering grunts—when she would plunge a crude steel shank into their hard-arching backs and then watch them crawl off with their little pink peckers dragging in the sand.

But then, this one—this Jaune Faucon—was different. As if he had a god in his heart. Laying her bare that first night and gently slipping within, softly kissing her breasts, her neck, and her hate-hardened face, slowly, slowly, he probed her deepest depth and rescued her soul. Germini wanted to hate Jaune Faucon like all the others, but she could not. God and Fate had tied their threads together. In the early morning light, whispering his delight at having finally found the woman of his dreams, holding her tight, and she him, never did Jaune Faucon even know of the dagger Germini at last let fall from her hand. Never to be used again.

A good and gentle boy, young Sihtric would never be the warrior his father was. Nor did he want to be. It just wasn't in him to kill. Not a rabbit, not a bird, let alone another human being. Never without a roll of thin yellow parchment tucked under his arm, Sihtric would draw his aim with an artist's eye instead.

Jaune Faucon took pride in being quite an artist himself—supremely proficient at the art of war, the art of love, and the art of the hunt. But he had nowhere near the capability of what his son could do with a goose-quill pen and ink. He considered the nicknames of some of the other young boys of the realm as defined by their manly callings: Jehan "Blow the Death." Philip-pot "Eat the Heart." Gace "the Forester's Knave." Then that of his son: Sihtric "Illustrator of the Hounds."

Still, to whatever end all his son's feminine talents and emotions may lead, Sihtric needed to be readied to live the life of a consummate man. A lion. The defender of his pride. The provider of its daily sustenance. Thus it was that the father and son were out walking through the Talou Forest the morning after the great storm over the Channel even before the first beams of silvering sun streaked through the tall, wet blades of their home-field grass.

In times of peace, Jaune Faucon was first and foremost a huntsman. He was born with the spirit of the huntsman in his heart, and the strength of Judith's resolve to keep it burning brightly throughout her son's formative years only further steeled his steadfast character. In a land studded with the castles and forts of highly armed and avaricious warlords rife with envy and distrust, she was determined that Jaune Faucon would not follow the same path as her brash, sinful, and long-dead husband, Alain.

Judith's father had been a master huntsman for Duke William and, in her younger day, he had often expounded on the innumerable joys of the hunt. How the "successful tracking and harboring of the beast, the inherent understanding between a man and his hounds, the delight in deciphering the clues of the changing seasons, and the keening of mind, eye, and muscle, is to experience the glory of God in all His power." With eyes glistening, he further told his young daughter, "It is a lightness of spirit God instills in the huntsman, an inner joy which cannot be diminished by hunger or thirst, weariness or pain. Such a feeling as to make a man rise at the dawn of a new day full of vigor and purpose, free from all idleness, anxiety, and anger, and, at the end of the day allow him a peaceful sleep only to set out again in the morning with his happily baying hounds until the sun goes down."

It was the life Judith wanted for her son. And Jaune Faucon, in turn, for his son.

Sihtric had been taking care of the dogs for almost two years now. Up before the sun, cleaning the kennels, filling the food and water troughs, replacing the straw, trimming claws, picking burrs, running them by day, and sleeping with them at night. In a few more years, he would be ready to take them on a hunt. Their leash-master. A full-fledged *varlet des chiens*.

But, mostly, Sihtric's early training was meant to prepare him to be a man of war. Despite Germini's protestations and Sihtric's utter disinterest, Jaune Faucon was adamant that his firstborn son develop a wide range of skills, both mental and physical, so that he might defend himself if faced with a sudden battle.

True to his sobriquet, the hunting prowess of the Yellow Falcon of the Forest was unparalleled. From his earliest days, Jaune Faucon had honed his body for war by hunting wild beasts—the powerful hart, the ferocious boar, and the prowling wolf—as his meticulously practiced maneuvers often replicated those necessary for him to emerge victorious in a life-or-death hand-to-hand combat with an equally skilled foe. Training Sihtric in the management of sword and spear—"No, son, not like that. Take your time and pick your strokes carefully, so that they might be few, but terrible"—if he had to bloody his son to show him what he was doing wrong, so be it. But more painful, sometimes even cruel, were the hours Jaune Faucon spent strengthening Sihtric's mind against the hardships of bad food, foul drink, a poor bed, heat, cold, and bone-quivering fear, as he knew that his ability to overcome such debilitating discomforts was far more integral to making a thorough man of him.

Jaune Faucon glanced over at his son sitting on a nearby rock and felt a stab of worry and frustration.

Sihtric was drawing a tree.

# THE SON

*Dawn*

## 10 SEPTEMBER 1100

The hunt was likely the last of the hart season, as the wild boars were now high in flesh and getting ready to mate. Huntsmen throughout the Norman realm would start tracking the great black beasts just a few days forward, on 14 September, the day of the Feast of the Holy Cross.

Carrying no spear, Jaune Faucon turned to his son and declared, "God be thanked if we don't see a boar today, Sihtric. Because with a boar, there's a good chance he will see you first. And a better chance he kills you, your horse, and your dogs instead!"

Still busy with making his little drawing, Sihtric didn't hear a word his father said. The veining of a beech tree leaf is quite intricate, and he was studying one up close.

The sun wasn't up yet and so hadn't started burning off the dark gray clouds still lingering in the sky after last night's thunderstorm. Deep in the Talou Forest, walking along a line of tall plane trees, there was no path to follow. Nor would Jaune Faucon have walked on it even if there was one. He blazed paths, not followed them.

Tracking with his favorite running-hound, Bia, and employing every bit of his extensive knowledge of the land, Jaune Faucon told Sihtric to put away his pen and parchment, take up his bow and quiver, and fall in behind him. His voice even, but with hints of frustration, he told his son that he needed to rein in his fascination with the details of every little leaf in his path and instead focus his eyes on the greater forest about him. Further stating that they were seeking out the finest hart in the area, he explained to Sihtric that the purpose of their morning trek was to gather evidence as to the location of not just one, but several stags, as a larger *par force* chase involving many other men and hounds was planned for later in the day.

Kneeling beside Bia and giving the dog a big hug, Sihtric responded with a most disinterested "Oh."

Black and fat, Bia was old, and no longer truly a "running" hound—the prized *chien baut* she once was—but she could still hunt all day. Always true to Jaune Faucon—strong, obedient, wise of mind, and with a great nose—she would be dead before ever her worth ran out. Of a perfect temperament— sweet, willing, and gracious in carrying out Jaune Faucon's every command— Bia's unabated savagery in engaging the wild beasts of the forest had long ago stamped her reputation as a fearless hunter. Driven by a deep hatred of the animal she pursued, Bia would not let up the chase even when night turned dark as her coat. She would fall for no ruses: no hare's sideways leap, no hart turning back on its trail, or a stag masking its scent in a stream. Rushing this way then that, searching around every log, stone, and tree until she again hit its scent, with a joyous cry, she'd then run straight on, nose pressed to the ground until the prize was taken. Bia was old, yes. A "lick-ladle" now, always hanging around the kitchen, sleeping by the fire. But, still, a fine black bitch. And it was going to be hard to bury her someday.

If only Jaune Faucon's young son—now fanning his face with a large fern frond—had even a glimmer of the dog's warrior spirit.

The hart was the largest animal in the province and the noblest in appearance. A beast to be reckoned with. Sihtric had never killed a hart, and he told his father that he never would. It was his favorite animal, believing it to embody the spirit of Jesus Christ, as the characteristic white mark his mother had pointed out between its antlers was clearly the image of the Holy Cross.

As good and gentle a boy as he'd ever known, Jaune Faucon could easily identify Sihtric's innocent, guileless spirit with that of the beast; but, so too, he hoped that God had put into his son's chest that same fearless heart that so strengthened the animal. That the hart bore in its blood chambers a bone—a piece of gristle, really—which alone prevented it from dying of fear, Jaune Faucon had placed a hart-bone amulet around Sihtric's neck the day he was born. As Germini told Sihtric to never take it off, he believed that his Lord and Savior Jesus Christ was always with him, and it was the source of his tremendous devotion to the Scriptures, the ideals of the saints, and godly art. Saying that he would be no different than the Devil himself if he killed a hart, worse even than Satan's hounds—the Jews, and their cross-building Roman overlords of pure evil—Sihtric told his father that he would never do it—"sooner to bathe the great animal in that crystal clear pool of holy water at the Saint-Aubin church and wash the mud from its feet."

With his son's passionate little speech ended, Jaune Faucon knelt down beside Sihtric, hung an arm over his shoulder, and said, "Okay. Now, pick up that bow and let's go."

Obediently trailing behind Bia and his father, Sihtric walked on—bow in hand.

The well-trained hound barely raised her nose off the ground as a big-eared hare suddenly flashed across their path. Bia had little interest in pursuing the spindly rabbit, as the reward was hardly worth the time to catch this side-jumping, crooked, straight, forward-flashing, fiddle-footed cat-of-the-wood. Other than the head, there was just no good eating on it. Bia pressed on.

When Jaune Faucon judged by the dog's reaction that they were close to something, he quickly stooped and put down a *brisee*—a small branch broken from a tree—as a marker. Suddenly alert to the possibilities of other evidence, or "tokens"—which might include tracks, the hart's bed, frayings of bark where it had rubbed the velvet from its antlers as it went through the wood, and even the flattened grass where its feet had rested—he motioned to Sihtric to continue on down the hill and take cover in the brush ahead. Picking up a handful of droppings to see that they were sufficiently fat and black with rounded ends to indicate a "hart of ten"—that is, ten tines on his antlers, making him eligible to be hunted—Jaune Faucon quickly rose and walked on behind Bia in steps as quiet as the hush of the forest.

Tracking across the rain-soaked ground, the old black hound showed sudden excitement at a flattened bed of sedge grass just above a small stream. Jaune Faucon pressed his hand to the ground; the blades were warm. The hart had only recently left.

A little farther down the slope, Jaune Faucon finally spied it, standing in the shadow of a low-branched, leafy oak. Only, it was not a hart, but a good-sized roebuck. A fine specimen. Flattened in the tall grass with her eyes locked on the beast, Bia waited for Jaune Faucon's command. Jaune Faucon motioned for Sihtric to move down the slope ahead of him. They would take the buck now if they could.

With an occasional click of his tongue, Jaune Faucon edged closer to the buck, nudging it through the thick green wood toward where Sihtric stood hidden with an arrow notched and his bowstring pulled tight. Virtually invisible in his hooded green tunic, Sihtric stared wide-eyed as the buck slowly approached. Walking in the shadows of the oaks—stopping—looking back—and then moving again at another click of Jaune Faucon's tongue, it crossed into a small, grassy glade not twenty ells from Sihtric. When the buck then turned his look straight at him, as if to have discovered his hiding place, a whisper-storm in Sihtric's head tried to convince him to let the quivering arrow fly. With the sinewy string whitening his fingers and his heart pounding in his chest, he closed his eyes and, finally, let it fly.

Out of the sun-dappled boughs, Jaune Faucon saw a sudden, flickering blur, and then heard a loud clattering against the side of a rock. Sihtric had missed. Badly. And, oh, how happy the boy was.

Bounding down the gully's steep side into a little stream rippling along its rutted floor after last night's great storm, Bia sprinted off in full cry after the fast-fleeing buck. Watching her until she disappeared far down the gully, Jaune Faucon knew the old hound would do her best to re-harbor the beast—and he would have to live up to her effort.

Skidding down on the seat of his coarse green tunic into the gully, with two quick tweets on his ruet—a small wooden whistle—he signaled to Sihtric to come down and join him.

Impatient, but infinitely amused, Jaune Faucon stood watching as his son then struggled down the gully's steep, rocky side with a small scabbard filled with the special cutlery necessary for unmaking a killed beast in one hand and his tall, green bow in the other. Seeing every arrow spill from the quiver on Sihtric's back as his son landed hard and then fell flat on his face, Jaune Faucon shook his head and tried not to laugh.

Sihtric had much to learn, and Jaune Faucon would take this opportunity to show his son how to use the gully's deep cleave to force the fleeing roebuck to a point of no escape. Splitting the face of a high, white-chalk cliff where the land meets the sea, the gully's mouth was a little more than a bowshot ahead. Taking a couple of swigs from his water-skin as he waited for Sihtric to catch up, Jaune Faucon joked that he was glad it was not an ibex they were hunting this day. "Bad food, and hard to kill besides. Why, not even the mighty Hercules smashing his broadsword across one's back can bring it to its knees. But this roe, Sihtric—it will be on the table tonight! Just a little farther down, at the end of the gully—we'll trap him on the ledge below the Dead Woodcutter's Hut.

# THE SINNERS

## *Dawn*

---

## 10 SEPTEMBER 1100

There was no ledge. There was no hut. The old woman was gone.

The roebuck could be seen running far up the beach with Bia in flagging pursuit. Fleeing at breakneck speed, the stag turned under the west headland toward God's great sanctuary at Fecamp and then disappeared from sight. An exhausted Bia stopped and put her nose in the air a moment. Hanging her head, she glanced back toward her master and then began a long, limping walk back over the sharp beach stones.

Arrived at the end of the gully, Jaune Faucon stood above the vast waters of the Channel with his mouth opened nearly as wide as the newly eroded chasm in the cliff. But for the rippling sea, nothing of the scene was as he remembered it—the cliff's new face was bright and smooth—its old one now a steep, sloping pile of rubble spilled out of the gully's gaping mouth.

Jaune Faucon thought of the strange, old woman who had long lived atop the cliff. The dead woodcutter's widow. He never knew her name. Turning his look down the steep, rubbly slope and searching for anything that was not white chalk rock or marl, at last, he spied a remnant of the woman's demolished shack near the water's edge. A piece here, another piece there. And then—something entirely different.

Jaune Faucon looked away in horror.

An oblivious Sihtric, on his knees and gathering up the arrows he'd carelessly spilled out of his quiver when he dropped it on the rocky ground before him, was still staring far up the beach in misty-eyed approval of the majestic roebuck's successful flight.

Picking their way over and around the enormous piles of fallen rock littering the much-deepened declivity in the cliff's face, Jaune Faucon and Sihtric, at last, stepped down onto the debris-covered beach. Unaware of the terrible scene he'd entered upon, Sihtric's first look upon the havoc wreaked by the storm roiled his stomach and his face took on a jaundiced pallor. For there was nothing subtle about the night of terror the macabre scene described.

Sorry to have walked his young son into a blind encounter with death at its worst, Jaune Faucon hugged Sihtric hard across his shoulders while steeling his own pulse to the sudden penetrating horror of seeing the old woman broken and bloodied and sprawled flat on her back on a small section of the shack's north wall. Wiggling free of his father's grip, Sihtric quickly dropped to a knee and puked.

With the shack's shattered walls shunted to one side of that massive black boulder long-known as God's Rock, the woman laid on a raft of loosely connected boards with her arms bent at gruesome angles above her head and one foot wrenched up nigh to touching her hip. She had a long crimson gash between her flat, shriveled breasts, which Jaune Faucon judged to be a purposeful cleave straight through her heart into the very depth of her chest. A bright red swath stained her thin cotton shift where a river of blood had poured from the wound and pooled in the open space between her legs. Strangely, the old woman's lips were smiling. Her countenance deadly pale, but unblemished by fear.

At first look, Jaune Faucon had not noticed the decrepit old man curled against the woman's side. Naked, the man's skin was as white as the chalk-rock rubble heaped around him with a ragged red rip across his stomach standing out in a stark contrast. With one arm cradling the woman's head and his lips pressed against her cheek, his eyes were closed like sleeping.

Or dead.

The storm had raged deep into the night. And that longest, nerviest hour before the sun first peeked down onto the beach had its murderous tale to tell. People died. Others lived. Some were still between.

It was so dark, Odo was not even sure his eyes were open. Still, he could see them. Death-walkers. Six of them. Pressing him all around. Massive and ugly with their flesh decayed off their cracked yellow skulls and their mouths bristling with sharp, wolfish teeth—a jeering riot of spears and swords thrusting at his head, belly, and flanks as if in the celebratory torture of a long-hunted quarry—the big Ponthievin guard was their pig, and they intended on making him squeal until his last breath.

Just so, the biggest, ugliest of the dead men suddenly leaped forward with his jaws snapping like to bite off Odo's head. His empty eye holes flashing like blue crystals out of the conical steel helm closed round his ghastly face, he shouted, "Your corpse will soon be colder than we that have been dead all these thirty-four years!" Erupting in a burst of shrilling laughter, the dead warrior then pressed a short steel shank under Odo's left ear and ripped it across his gurgling throat. The first in a whirring, unrelenting storm of cuts, thrusts, and chops that tore away great chunks of Odo's flesh, staggering over his feet, with his guts squirming out of his belly and his severed sword-arm lying on the ground beside him, the big guardsman suddenly fell flat on his back, flopped to one side, and tried to fake being dead.

His cowardly ruse only heightened the death-walkers' rage. Attacking him in a rush, kicking and punching his body with their unfleshed feet and fists—dealing a most brutal death to a most brutal man—Odo's blood was soon running onto the beach as if from a cheap leather wine sack punched full of holes.

After a time, with his unfleshed rib cage heaving within his chainmail sheath, the biggest and fiercest of the dead warriors stood back, bloody broadsword in hand, and commanded the others to stop. Another punch. Another kick. Again the leader's command, louder still. "Stop, I say! All of you! Away! He is not ours to kill. It is Styrkar, our heroic marshal, who has earned the right to finish this man." Then, kneeling on Odo's bloodied chest with a glowering sneer, the ghostly warrior shoved a little iron key into his gaping mouth and made him swallow it. Turning on his heel, he then joined the other dead Norsemen as they stomped down the beach. Laughing, joking, and kicking the sand, pointing their swords to the heaven and exhorting mighty Thor to stir Styrkar from his death-spiraling sleep, they demanded the gods put the *berserker* rage in the old warrior's heart and a jag of murderous steel in his hand. Kalf, Thjodulf, Ivar, Thormod, Asmund, and Finn—brothers-in-arms in this world and the next—they shouted in unison: "Fight! And die! Then fight again!"

With the voices screaming both in and out of his head finally fading, Odo cracked open his blood-crusted eyes and peered into the enveloping darkness. As bewildered as a fair-hearted boy surveying the wreckage in the aftermath of his first battle, he could still see the death-walkers skeletal faces, feel their heavy metal blades breaking his bones, even smell the ferric odor of his open flesh. Daring not move but for the dread of another attack, at long length, Odo put a hard-trembling hand down into what he feared was a pool of his own cold, syrupy blood only to realize that it was but the thinnest layer of fine-grained silt and seawater; to his relief, his mauling by the jaws of the Viking beast was revealed as but a figment of his over-weary mind during the briefest interlude of sleep. Vacillating between a state of faint awareness and pure hallucination, Odo did not know what it all meant. But, in this, his last hour before being rowed off in shackles aboard a boat crossing that fiery river in Hell with a huge three-headed dog snarling in the bow—unless truly stupid—he would figure it out.

Lying flat on his back on the sharp beach stones in the pre-dawn light, Odo began mumbling, as if scolding himself. "I have been lucky. Undone by wicked waves of water, crushing rocks, and cutting steel, I should be among the foul-smelling dead by now. But I am not. And if that decrepit old man still lives, he will surely suffer for my good fortune."

Of course, Odo considered it ridiculous that that wrinkled little ball sack could have survived such a powerful storm. Nevertheless, with the darkness still reigning around him, he would not be a fool. The Norseman had proven to be as tough as a forest boar; his mind bold and crafty; his courage and sagacity second to none. That he possessed many feral traits inherited from a long line of forebears who often stalked their enemies by night and struck before the sun's first glow, Odo could not dismiss the possibility of the man falling on him out of the ever-shifting shadows. He would finish the man if he was still alive; drag him off by his feet and fling him into the sea if he was already dead. His search for the shackled wretch would start at first light. That would be another hour. Maybe more.

Hunched in the space between two large, tent-like rocks where the sea-water had dumped him during the storm, Odo peered into the darkness, his mouth slack and drooling, and his skin stinking of warm piss. With anger twisting his face to a look much as puss-filled sore, his endless cursing of the Ponthievin guardsmen that had abandoned him in the night occupied every minute of his tedious wait. "Filthy, bleeding bungholes! *Poltroons! Couards!* By thunder, I will have them gibbeted like common brigands! With their peckers tethered to the wharf and an oar jammed up every ass, they will rue the day they ever thought to leave Odo of Montreuil on this—"

Odo's rant was cut short by a sudden rattle of wind-borne sand against the enveloping rocks. Whipping his head left then right and throwing up a hand to protect his eyes, Odo could hardly believe his luck as he watched a large, leafy clump of yellow-brown kelp flip wildly past him and then disappear like a rabbit down its hole. As if the All-Powerful Destroyer Himself were out there offering him a charitable clue as to why he was still stuck on this "goddamned beach in the middle of goddamned nowhere," Odo saw just a stone's throw to his right what appeared to be a large pit gutted out on the seaward side of a massive black boulder that laid half-buried under the rubble of the fallen cliff. Indeed, it was in the shadow of this same big black rock that he'd gotten a brief respite from the sun during the hottest hour of the previous afternoon.

Odo glanced at the cliff rising behind him. Backlit by the early glow of the eastern sky, he could see that the storm-ravaged gully was now considerably wider and deeper than it had been the day before. Gouged out, gorge-like, nearly to the mid-point of the cliff-face, an immense pile of fallen chalk and marl made its ragged end. That the rubble only covered the back half of the boulder spoke of its enormous size.

Again looking up and running his eyes along the cliff top, Odo strained through the blackness to identify the outline of the little wooden shack that was there the day before. Finding no hint of it—or even the white-chalk precipice it so precariously sat upon—at length, he dropped his look back to the beach, shook his head ever so slightly, and mumbled, "Gone." The old woman, Odo thought—the one who had waved at his prisoner the previous day—was probably buried in the pile. A horrible thing to have happened to the woman. But he certainly wasn't going to waste any time looking for her.

Stripped naked by the storm and struggling to gather his wits in the half-light, Styrkar tried to make sense of all that had happened during the night. As he lay at the foot of a pile of broken rock and debris, something like fire burned from the gaping wound in his gut. Neither angry nor anxious as he pressed a hand to the gash in an attempt to staunch the bleeding, he knew what was and what would be. The injury was fatal, and today he would die.

With his ribs being painfully twisted one on another as a low, grinding wave slapped hard against his chest, Styrkar bent his head backward and looked for a glow in the eastern sky. *One more sunrise*, he thought, *and then all will be done.* Only, Styrkar saw not the faintest hint of the climbing orb. Not the massive cliff. Not his hand in front of his face, even. All was shadows—fog—the seawater's wash up the beach but a field of grainy white; his stone-gray eyes now turned black, nearly blinded by onrushing death.

Yet, it hardly mattered to Styrkar if he was blind or could see—his eyes no more to reveal the tragedy wrought by the night's fierce storm than the little drops of blood that kept drip, drip, dripping on the top of his balding head. That he hesitated to twist around and identify the source was not due to a lack of courage, but more the dread of knowing. For, when finally he did look back, such was the blow to his faintly beating heart that he thought it had stopped in his chest.

Shocked by the gory minutiae spattering his death-black eyes, in that very moment, Styrkar knew, beyond all doubt, that there was nothing left in this world to make him want to live a moment more. For, just above him, sprawled on a small, splintered section of wall from her fallen shack, her arms and legs bent at grotesque angles and her dead husband's wood-ax impaled in her chest, his dearest Adelvia—the woman he had held so close in his dreams all these tortuous years he'd spent in prison—laid like garbage on a heap. Choking on a scream gurgling in the back of his throat as he pulled on her foot, trying to drag her closer to him, such was the river of blood running down onto his head and his shoulders that in no battlefield memory did the carnage compare.

Spurred by his anguish, Styrkar suddenly leaped up lion-like beside Adelvia's storm-ravaged body, reached an arm across her hard-twisted waist, and pulled her toward him. His open wounds pulsing with pain as he struggled to slip his arms under her sodden remains, to lift her, to carry her far from this place, he was resolved to allow no further gratuitous display of Adelvia's naked flesh by whatever god had perpetrated this heinous crime upon her. Only, try as he might, Styrkar could not lift her—the once indomitable warrior having not the strength to raise her even an inch. Windmilling his fists at the imagined faces all around, mocking him as a useless old man for his inability to do anything to dignify her horrible death, Styrkar's heart was a dead, empty lake in his chest. Collapsing at Adelvia's side and his eyes melting tears onto her bloody face, with a gentle brush of his trembling hand he calmed her terrified expression. Smothering a sob in the crook of Adelvia's neck, Styrkar then began to weep.

With long rills of chilling seawater streaming down his body, Odo scrambled out from between the two large tented rocks and crept up on the front side of the massive black boulder. Dropping to his knees and bending hard at the waist, he then peered into the big, ragged hole blown out beside it. Only, the light was weak; his eyes nearly useless. Digging his hands into the sharp beach stones in an attempt to clear the area in front of him, he then flattened onto his belly and hung his head inside. Black, black, and more black. "Goddammit!" Odo said, sitting back on his haunches and growling into the hole. "As sure as I saw two shooting stars collide above this very spot and rain down glitter from the sky last night, there is something buried in this ground that reeks of sudden death, destruction. Of someone's loss ... and someone's gain."

Again, Odo flopped his huge torso over the rough, shingled edge of the hole and hung his head within. Staring, staring, staring. Stretching his arms downward. Feeling with his hands: rock, shell, sticks, sand. His breathing was heavy and his face turned beet red as nigh every ounce of his blood sloshed around inside his big, bald head. But then—just beneath the thick, swarming shadow—just out of reach—something began to show its shape. Sucking in big gulps of air, suddenly Odo's lower jaw dropped down, snakelike, and an uncharacteristic gleam of joy splashed across his face. Odo could hardly believe what he was seeing.

His arms milling madly and his legs flailing behind him, pounding the hardened clods of sand into a billion little grains, tossing aside rocks and shells and heavy rags of kelp, Odo began clearing the dark hole as with the tentacles of an octopus. At last, with the faintest hint of morning light in the sky, there came into view what appeared to be a giant dragon's head jutting up from the sand on one side of the hole. Carved and colorful as the mythic beast itself, Odo immediately seized hold of it with both of his hands as if fearing it would suddenly rise, take flight, and be lost to him forever. A few moments more, and all doubt that he had uncovered the rudder of the Norseman's wrecked warship disappeared like mist under a hot morning sun. Dropping his head back down into the hole—laughing and singing in nigh senseless delight— he shouted out that he would dig all day for the treasure if he had to, "Even all the way to Hell!"

Far gone with fever and quietly weeping at Adelvia's side, Styrkar raised his head at the sudden—and most unexpected sound—of uproarious joy coloring the darkness. Carrying on the air much the same as a young boy's gleeful squeal, it had no place in this somber scene. Only, as he darted his eyes up, down and around, at the cliff, at the beach, and then into the sea, Styrkar resolved that there was not a child anywhere to be found. *A trick of my fever,* he thought. *A bird. A ghost. A devil in the wind.*

But, there, again. A burst of laughter. Louder still. And not far away.

Again, Styrkar picked his head up off Adelvia's bloody shoulder and stared at the water. Nothing.

*Much is imagined by a muddled mind,* Styrkar thought as his head began nodding down in his leaden confusion. *So long has it been since I last heard laughter, it is likely any such joyful sound is more an illusion of my memory than the here and now.*

Only, just as Styrkar again closed his eyes and laid his head on Adelvia's shoulder—as if welled up out of the very ground around him—a full-throated eruption of "Good morning, world! All you highborn shits! Now, on your knees and kiss my ass!" emphatically ended the intense back and forth tug between his mind's wonder and doubt.

Heaving himself up on an elbow and again slashing his eyes into the darkness, in the next instant, out of the corner of his eye, Styrkar saw something move. Wriggling on the ground on the seaward side of God's Rock. Sticking out past the boulder's high, smooth face and kicking up a time or two. After some study, Styrkar realized that he was looking at a man's legs, booted to the

172

knees and with his toes ground down hard on the beach shingle. An other-worldly cold crawled on the Norseman's skin as another shout of "Kiss my ass!" filled his ears.

"The great Ponthievin beast still lives," Styrkar whispered to the six dead warriors buried beneath the huge rock. "And he has discovered our king's ship."

"A good day to be alive!" Odo crowed. "A damned good day to be alive!"

"So, too," whispered Styrkar as he fixed a terrible look on the unsuspecting guardsman, "it's a good day to make a bad man dead."

Turning his look back toward his beloved Adelvia, so monstrous was the anguish burdening Styrkar's heart that he could hardly breathe. At length, from his tight, trembling lips broke a low sort of malignant growl. A fist thumped against his chest. Then a sneering resolve. Rousing himself from his debilitating grief, Styrkar then turned to Adelvia and declared, "An evil lurks in the yonder black. A man as vile as the Devil's serpent. And so it is by my hand, my swan, my queen, I will cast him back into that hissing, squirming tangle in the ground from which he came." Pressing his face close to hers as he placed a hand over the crimsoned blade buried in her breast, he whispered, "I will raise my eyes upward to the heavens, and then let this murderous steel bear down. And I will leave it there, buried in the devil's rotting heart, banished to the blackness, so nevermore may it ravage the soul of the fairest woman the world has ever known." Struggling to stifle his hard, sobbing breaths, with his thin arms trembling Styrkar then pressed a hand down on Adelvia's shoulder and, with his other hand, gently pulled the woodsman's ax from her cold, bloody chest. Telling Adelvia, "You and I are twin spirits, destined to leave behind all our pain and our sorrow on the same dark spot on this earth," Styrkar then told her he loved her—and that he would be back.

Wraithlike in the faint light, Styrkar crept along the side of God's Rock and drew up behind the oblivious guardsman, still flopping around in the hole below. Brandishing the woodsman's old ax like ready to chop through a thick, fallen tree limb, the fiery-eyed Norseman was a bit perplexed, even silently regretting Odo's awkward position. Ass up, flat on his belly, half in the hole with his head hung low—a strike at his back was not how Styrkar wanted to do it. *This man must die in the manner in which he lived,* he told himself. *Nothing less than this murderous blade buried in his beastly head straight through his brain.*

Agitated but undaunted, Styrkar marked time by the dimming of each star in the sky as Odo persisted in his machinations deep in the hole. Poised to strike, the same as a spear-tipped tree branch tied back upon itself and only needing the clumsy bear to trip its spring-cord, Styrkar had not killed for many years. No matter, he thought. There was no special skill needed to reduce a man to a dark red stain on the earth. A quick strike. The bleed-out. The devil's flesh and bone carried off by the carrion bird and the wolf. And the dirt never long to drink in every last drop of that warm raven's wine.

Hanging upside down, a huffing and puffing red-faced Odo struggled to keep a hand on the crumbling edge of the pit as he furiously raked aside the thick accretions of sand and shell with his free hand. Not to be thwarted by his flint-slashed fingers or any amount of blood sloshing around in his down-turned head, at a sudden gleaming within the hole, so immense was the joy that filled Odo's shriveled heart, he could not hold it all inside. Grabbing up handful after handful of Greek *nomismata* coins pouring out the broken side of a large wooden chest beneath him, so utterly delirious was Odo in the imagining of all the fun and finery they would buy him it hardly mattered whether all those little princes in their fairy garb and curly-toed slippers were imprinted on silver or gold. "They'll pay the price of a whore," he shouted out through a boisterous smile. "And open the legs of those swan-throated, honey-lipped noblemen's daughters just the same."

Absorbing the grating joy of Odo's long-sought discovery of King Harald's treasure like a dagger through his heart, Styrkar's mind began wandering over the long-forgotten faces of the many men he had sent to their doom of far-greater worth. That this man should so ignobly perish—unnamed and unknown—troubled him not. The beast himself could expect no other end. *A man rises and falls on an accumulation of his deeds in this world. There is no special indulgence granted for the plaint of a hard life. You get what you deserve. And, from the very day the Devil crawled inside this godless savage, his destiny was to die like a pig on a spit overhanging the fires of Hell.*

That his own words suddenly triggered the painful image of his young sons' faces melting in a cauldron of fire that once was the warship now buried below him, Styrkar would not allow even the slightest comparison of this thug's imminent death to profane the memory of their glorious lives. Kalf and Thjodulf. Brave like no others, warriors to the end, his sons had done their duty. Suffered Death's hard fall. Then perished without a trace. But, unlike this man—now virtually dancing in the hole below as he flipped up coin after coin into a growing pile at Styrkar's feet—a man with no allegiance to anything but the obscene ambitions in his heart and the pecker in his pants—his sons' lives mattered.

*They were loved. They are missed. And their names will be remembered!*

Soon standing ankle-deep in a glimmering mix of Greek, Rus, and Roman coins, Styrkar had trodden enough gold underfoot during his long career as a raider to pave the byways of his Norwegian homeland ten times over. Only never had that soft yellow metal felt as good against his big, muddy feet as when he began methodically sweeping all those little kings, khans, sultans, and emperors back into the pit as fast as the giddy Ponthievin guard could toss them out.

Scooping up riches upon riches as he dove down hard and ripped off the splintered top of another wooden chest, at the happiest moment of his short, sad life, Odo again shouted out with maniacal joy. "Ah, but to be swimming in this wine-bowl of riches, drinking in this sweet golden nectar until I can no longer see straight, I suddenly feel so much more than mortal. So much more powerful than any man has ever been! Finally, undeniably, I will be looked at with all the ground-quivering awe and prestige such ungodly wealth commands. Nevermore to be harrowed by my lowborn birth—ugly, unwanted, mocked as a beast—standing on the threshold of my glory, at last I will get what I deserve!"

Styrkar calmly waited until Odo's outburst ended. His face bloodless and serene, turning the ax in his hand, adjusting his grip until it felt just right, he widened his feet to make a sturdy base, stared down at the man for a moment, and then hefted the old woodcutter's blade up high over his head. Steadying over his mark, poised to strike, Styrkar shouted out, "For humanity!" and then brought the blade down with such force as to cleave straight through the Ponthievin's back, his chest, and the ship's thick, straked hull, besides.

So it was, at that very moment, an eerie tranquility settled upon the world—the only sound heard over the gentle wash of the sea being the rhythmic clinking of gold piling on gold as Styrkar finished sweeping the coins, one by one, back into the huge, storm-gouged pit with the side of his foot.

With the big guard rammed down face-first into all the riches he'd ever dreamed of, Styrkar then paid Normandy's newest lord extraordinaire his most heartfelt respect—pissing into the slow, rolling water of a silty gray wave as it filled the Ponthievin's self-dug grave to preserve the happiest moment of Odo's life for all time.

Begging that she forgive him for the time taken to silence the man's rude interruption, Styrkar then slowly made his way back to Adelvia and, again, laid at her side.

So then did the sun suddenly peek over the cliff, bright and shining out of a flawless blue sky. Birds sang. Flowers opened. Mother was dead. It was a great day to be alive.

Slowed by the storm-tossed debris, it had taken Wido to nearly sunup to ride his old mule down off the huge chalk wall. On top of the cliff, the mule plodded along a well-worn forest path far to the east so that he might descend a more navigable gully onto a rough stone beach near the small fishing village of Dieppe. Hot and sweaty, and with a bitterness now eating at his heart, Wido declared to absolutely no one that it was an irksome waste of his time to then have to make a long westward ride down the beach only to stand on a spot straight below that which he had begun his ride two hours earlier.

*But, then too,* Wido thought, *for what reason should I hurry? Mother is dead. And that is that. Nothing is changed. Not for her. Not for me. Cursed here or cursed there. All is as before.*

Staring at his mother's lifeless body, Wido told himself that she got what she deserved—then turned away and covered his face ... not knowing why he was crying.

The scene was grotesque. But fascinating, too. Fighting the urge to grant his mother the forgiveness he had so long denied her, Wido's indifference to watching the shack crash down on the beach during the previous night's storm with her still inside was yet to feel wrong; burning in his heart like a wild flame, the venomous anger he held for his mother was undiminished no matter how many times she apologized to him.

Crimsoned chest to crux as if torn apart by the jaws of a wolf, there was a long gash between her flattened breasts that spoke of a deliberate act of violence executed by an unseen hand. Seemingly much too precise in its place-ment, the ridge of thick, pulpy red flesh fringing his mother's wound bore an eerie similarity to when Wido's father, the woodcutter, would pull his cold steel ax-blade from a dark heart of oak. Considering the possibility—as farfetched as it seemed—that his father's ax, grabbed up by the sheer power of the storm and flung end over end over the edge of the cliff, had struck one devastating blow deep into the heart of his unfaithful wife, Wido judged the act a spiteful thing for a dead man to do—but, in a way, ingenious too.

Wido had only the barest memory of his father. A woodcutter for the duke, he had heard it said that he was the fastest log-splitter the Talou Wood ever knew. So too, a man who took no slight in stride, nor allowed any seizure of what was rightfully his to go unpunished—food, mule, wife, or otherwise. Thus, did Wido look upon his mother's slaughtered body and feel a certain pride in the confirmation of her oft-repeated, eye-rolling claim that he was, indeed, his father's son.

Only his father's ax was nowhere to be found in the widely scattered debris. In fact, Wido saw nothing of his mother's household items worth salvaging. *And what of this pile of human excrement sloughed on top of her?* Wido thought, with the sudden notice at a bloodied old man curled against her side, his skin so white as to be almost hidden from view amidst the fallen chalk. Spurring his little mule closer, Wido was particularly curious about the man's broken wrist-shackles. *A brigand? An escaped convict? A prisoner pitched off a ship during last night's storm?* Wido stared at the man's bloodless face, his mind working convulsively. Barely at first, then slowly growing, Wido's eyes shot wide at his sudden, shocking recognition of the wretch. Boldly marked by that long, red scar slashed down onto his shoulder and the thick mud caked between his toes—it was hard to fathom such a possibility—but it could be no other man.

"Like two slimy white splats of raven's shit dropped from the sky—" Wido spit in disgust—"the barbarian and his whore together again. Oh, how you deserve each other."

Turning his attention back to the scattered remnants of his mother's shack and meager possessions, picking at broken pieces of this and that, there was nothing recognizable, save a chair back, a couple splintered planks from the door, a table leg, and that devil-stick she'd so enjoyed beating him with day after day. Seeing nothing of worth, after a time Wido narrowed his focus on finding the only thing that could inspire any real emotion in him as his eyes wandered over the storm-strewn mess: that little silver crucifix his mother had so cherished all the years of her miserable life. Praying and praying and praying, but never getting an answer—it had made her crazy.

Whispering into the air as if scheming with a dead man, "I, too, have an ax to grind, Father," Wido then returned his sneering look to the thrashed, bloodied woman who had so selfishly betrayed them both. "Jesus Christ the Savior," Wido said to her with a wry grin. "Was it really so surprising that He wasn't around when you needed Him, Mother? Or is this the fool's end you spent all your life praying for?"

Wido stared at his mother long and hard before slowly dropping his head. Tears were again welling in his eyes. Only, this time, he would not let them fall.

The little silver Jesus was, in fact, nearby, but easy to miss. Standing no taller than the tip of Wido's middle finger to the heel of his hand, he finally spied the figurine peeking out between the old man and his mother like a sprite in a winnock. Broken off His wooden cross during the storm, the crucified Lord stood with His arms outstretched as if He was drawing the two dead lovers together to celebrate some kind of eternal union.

Drying his tears and scowling at the little Lord Savior, Wido's mind was a torrent of accusations. He wanted answers; he wanted revenge; the crippled six-year-old boy screaming inside him almost too much to bear. *But that I have suffered so much agony in my life, it would have been a far better end had I been left buried in rock that fateful day than to witness this devious stranger's cruel ruse to bed my mother. That she could have been so stupid to believe the man cared about her. Cared about me. The pagan beast mounting her like a stray hound a barnyard bitch! Planting his evil seed. And then she has the gall to blame me for all that was sorrow in her life. Scheming with the black-robes to rid me from her life. Snatching me up off my bedstraw as if a scurvied old rat and flinging me out the door! Throwing me, bound and screaming, on the back of an old cart only to watch the black-robes carry me off through the forest and imprison me in a stone-cold cell! Day after day, force-fed God, Jesus, Mary, and the Saints until I puked! Whom dares belittle my hatred having suffered such wrongs?*

A sinner from the day he was born, Wido never had the fortitude of mind to believe that the very same God who branded Adam's original sin on his unborn soul could possibly love him. Never seeing past his useless legs, twisted like ropes beneath him, he had prayed to be healed, confessed all his sins, knelt at all the shrines, kissed all the bones, beseeched God for a miracle. But, nothing. Only the fist of the phantom Creator, in the guise of a big black rock, falling on his head every day of his life.

Hence, Wido's terrible anger. Hating his life. Hating the world.

*My mother. Evreux. Jesus. All of them, liars! And God! Floating across the sky in His magical ship, caring only of piling gold into His hold and gathering up sham praises from all these self-righteous "Alleluia" peddlers of the Holy Catholic Church! Miscreants masquerading as reincarnated apostles, but no closer to God's chosen few than the bugs skimming the waters of a scum-covered pond! Parading about in their holier-than-thou vestments, preaching hypocrisy and cynicism to the dimwitted masses, all the while selling eternal salvation as if just another commodity, the same as fish, figs, olives, and eggs. Vain, arrogant megalomaniacs pouring forth such a diaspora of corruption and sleaze through the soaring stained-glass windows of their grand cathedrals as to leave a stink on the Earth as never before. No matter a pope or village priest, all of them possessed of the same gutter-morals as the painted whores of pagan Babylon. Nakedly opportunistic. Deviantly lustful. Wildly paranoid. Mad. Murderous. Repressive. Pathological liars. Trailing their fingers over strings of Rosary beads in one hand, while shamelessly tickling the testicles of young boys with the other. The "all-embracing" Catholic Church! More myth than mortar. A trivial Jewish cult brought forth as a great world religion because one dusky evening some pagan emperor—the famed Constantine I— paying homage to the "Unconquerable Sun," sees a big red cross burning in the fires of the falling orb, wins a battle the next day, and then proclaims Jesus Christ of Nazareth—a Man nigh forgotten for almost three hundred years—divine. A pretender to holiness from its earliest days, it is no wonder that such a sham of a church was raised over the mysteriously missing bones of the greatest charlatan of them all!*

Wido's eyes again flashed with ungovernable ferocity upon the little Lord Jesus peering out from between his mangled mother and the old man. *After but a few hours hanging on a cross—a fate suffered by thousands of nameless, faceless others before and after You—You know not a thing about the agony of an earthbound man's inescapable life of mockery and pain! "Oh, please, Father God, take this cup of suffering from My hands …"*

"You want suffering, Jesus?" Wido shouted. "Ceaseless suffering? My suffering!"

With venom boiling in his throat, Wido cracked his whip-stick against his mule's flank and growled at him to move closer to where his mother and the old pagan laid side by side. Tipped nearly sideways in his saddle and stretching his arms out so far as to nigh fall off the beast, he snatched up the little Lord Redeemer from between their bloody heads, forced himself back upright in the saddle, then—screaming, "Suffer as I have!"—bending, twisting, and viciously snapping off Jesus's head —he threw the crucified Lord's cheap silver body into the dark, swirling sea.

Never did Wido feel so alive!

Again striking his mule's flank to turn him about, Wido the Lame, the unrepentant sinner with the useless legs, then began riding a slow half-circle around the huge black boulder that still mocked him to this very day. Glaring at God's Rock every inch as he turned along its broad seaward face through the skirting sea-foam, the mule's forward foot suddenly sunk down hard in a shallow depression and—nearly falling as he stumbled over what appeared to be the upturned sole of a man's boot sticking up at its center—struggled to pull himself free from the deep, sucking sand. While considering that the hole may have been much deeper just a short while ago, once Wido had turned upon the rock's half-buried western side, the irrefutable evidence of the power of the previous night's storm was, indeed, revealed as the raging sea had also blown out a huge, cave-like void that extended far under God's Rock.

Finding the hole to be dark as a dungeon in the early light, Wido inched his mule closer to its crumbling edge, bent low, and peered inside. With his eyes struggling through the shadows, all he could see was thick, sodden rags of yellow-brown sea-kelp humped over chunks of rock, pebble, and shell.

Only, just as Wido was twisting the mule around for a return to his mother and the old man, something flashed in the corner of his eye. Glittery. Gold.

Again dropping his head low and staring into the hole, all was black and more black. Only, just then, with the sun inching up a little higher in the sky and its first beams of light striking down from the cliff, a sudden and glorious golden shine, pure and diaphanous, lit up Wido's colorless face. He stared into it until nearly blind.

With his curiosity getting the best of him, Wido tapped his whip-stick on the mule's backside in a command to make him sit back on his haunches. Excited just the same as if he was standing on the spot marked by a big red X on a treasure map, Wido then slowly slipped down the mule's spine and flopped onto the beach. Wriggling his belly over the ragged edge of the pit, he then reached down with both hands and started to dig.

With his mind racing through the possibilities of what he might find, Wido pawed aside rock and shell and clumps of sand as if a dog digging for a hidden bone. So intense was the light shining into his eyes that he considered it wholly possible that he had uncovered another sun buried in the Earth's core. What with the brightening light seemingly beckoning him to slip farther and farther into the hole and bathe in its luxuriant gold, he paid no heed to his brain's whispered warning that the Devil's hidden hook was surely trolling the deep, shadowy lake below him. Wido would have none of it. As he was already living a life of eternal damnation, some fictitious creature of the netherworld worried him not a whit. So it was, utterly unencumbered by good sense, Wido descended deeper and deeper into he knew not what. A struggling, flailing, little man. Completely fearless. And without the semblance of a plan.

"I will be all right," Wido assured his dumbstruck mule. "I'm not stupid."

But as this was Wido—his entire life a disaster in progress—as if on cue, the ragged edge of the storm-gutted pit suddenly gave way under his all his wriggling and the earthbound imp dropped wholly within. If Wido the Lame's longtime nickname hurt him, the six-foot fall on his face hurt even more.

With his bloodied nose driven into the gritty sand, *a la folletoere*—that is, "like the woodcock" in search of worms—and his worthless legs twisted one over the other and bent up the side of the pit, Wido could not turn his head in the slightest, lift his face, see, or even breathe. Squirming across the bottom of the pit with the point of a rock gouging his gut, Wido twisted a look up to the little mule staring down at him so dark and anguished that it was as if the last flicker of light he had in him had gone out.

Distorted by his dirt-filled eyes, Wido's frenetic glances here, there, and all around gathered in nothing but rubble and wreckage at every turn of his head. Chunks of rock, charred timbers, splintered benches, snapped ... oars. An anchor? Wido's roving search of his cave-like surround was suddenly halted by a long, head-spinning moment of confusion. Then his terrifying recognition: he had fallen into the burned-out hulk of a long-buried ship. With no way out.

Scowling in disbelief of his self-induced imprisonment in the dark, oak-ribbed hull of the shattered vessel, Wido couldn't help but wonder if he was, in fact, lying in his grave.

Nothing like the broad-beamed, high-sided cogs he had often seen at Saint-Valery in the Somme River estuary, it hardly seemed to be much of a ship, its wrecked remains suggesting it was more of a mid-sized fishing boat fitted out for excursions along coasts and up rivers; not so different from those low, sleek raiding ships used by those yellow-haired demons from the north.

So then it was, a lightning bolt exploded inside Wido's head.

*Yellow-haired demons!*

It all came rushing back to Wido.

For while many of the happenings during his forty seemingly interminable years lived upon this godawful earth had slipped into the deepest recesses of Wido's brain, the moment the world fell away under his feet when he was six years old was not one of them.

Nor had Wido forgotten that crude little canvas cloth his mother had stitched every inch with depictions of that fugitive Norseman's far-flung adventures. Of battlefield mayhem, storm-ravaged sea crossings, fiery pursuits ... and shipwrecks. Always had Wido scoffed at the man's fabulous tales as wild exaggerations, if not outright fabrications. Only, now, glancing about the brutalized remains of the ship into which he had fallen, Wido could not deny the possibility that he was wrong about the man. Fixing his look on a shackled foot and ankle bone dangling from the broken end of an oar jutting up out of the hard-packed sand covering the bottom of the ship, and then at the shattered bones piled like pig parts in a heap just below it, he thought, *That mud-foot Norseman was many bad things ... but maybe not as big a liar as I thought.*

With the same clarity as if that night's brutal wind had returned to sweep away the fog of time, the fractured images in Wido's mind finally began to make sense. Standing on God's Rock. His arms thrown wide. Tempting God's wrath. Wind. Rain. Lightning tearing across the sky. Thunder shaking the ground underfoot. Storm-water roaring through the gully on both sides of him before spilling off the cliff and pounding down on the beach below. He remembered dropping to his knees, then flattening on his belly; inching over the rock's broad, rounded top; staring straight down the cliff face at the roiling water below. Something strange catching his eye: a whale-sized island of fire being swept toward the shore. The flames dancing in the wind, savage and wild; the closer it got, looking more like a flailing dragon. Swept shoreward by a huge wave, crashing upon the steep shingle beach directly under the roaring whitewater fall. A loud crackling sound in the sky. A bolt of lightning striking the cliff just below him. A long, jagged, fast-widening fissure suddenly ripping across the full breadth of its crumbling face. In a flash, the fire-breathing dragon disappearing under the ferocious waterfall. Massive chunks of the great white chalk wall shearing off beneath his feet, falling, burying the tortured beast. God's Rock shunting forward. Hanging over the cliff edge. Then falling, falling, falling. Crashing onto the beach. A mountain of rubble beating down on him. Screaming. Screaming. Screaming. No one hearing. Slowly dying. God not caring.

Wido stared through the hate-darkened shadows of his mind. *A storm not so different from that earth-shaking squall last night,* he thought. Only this time, Wido's boyhood home was demolished ... and his mother killed.

Buried in a deep rut gouged into the beach by the storm-water pounding down from the cliff that long-ago night, if not for the ship being filled in the blink of an eye with falling rubble it would have been crushed beyond all recognition when that massive, otherworldly rock crashed down on it a moment later. A crypt-like hulk reeking of death, all which remained of the ship spoke in no uncertain terms of the sudden, grisly destruction of its crew. *They were the lucky ones,* Wido thought. *Spared the pain and ridicule of living life as half a man—their God loved them.*

Wido didn't know much about ships as in his crippled state he rarely ventured far from hard-packed dirt but—staring about the charred hulk littered with ropes, buckets, rigging blocks, bailers, and pole-hooks—there was much evidence that that yellow-haired mud-foot and his pagan mob had been on a long-range voyage. That it had been attacked. Burned down to the waterline. And could not have stayed afloat a moment more. Wido shook his head in surprise, for it was just as Styrkar had described to him and his mother with his little pictures drawn in the dirt. The story was real.

Considering together the placement of the rowing-benches with the number of oar-holes still visible in the remnants of the gunwales, Wido figured no more than eight to ten men could have manned the ship. Now pressed into the subterranean bed of coarse glacial sand and marl by the weight of the rock, the ship's oak-framed hull showed great torment. Thick as a tree and riddled with iron arrowheads sheared from their feathered spines, a ragged remnant of the mast timber jutted up from the middle of the ship's shallow storage hold. It appeared to be the only timber of any strength keeping God's Rock from crushing Wido alive.

Below the burn-line, the sheerstrakes—the hull's upper planks—had large holes blown out where the iron rivets had been. The twisted strips of tarred sheep's wool used to seal the gaps between the overlapping boards were now shredded and hanging down like the cobwebs in an old barn. On the top-strake, a shaft of sunlight revealed a simple carving of a single acanthus tendril trailing myriad rune symbols. Expertly executed but poorly preserved, Wido recognized the plant immediately, as more than once he'd seen it drawn in the sand by the Norseman's artful hand.

The ship's floor was crowded with wooden chests stacked up to the bottom of the splintered oak crossbeams spanning the mid-ship. Tossing aside what appeared to be the lesser half of a broken sun-shadow board—a crude navigational tool used by sailors to set a ship's course by the position of the stars—Wido then turned his look onto two large oak-plank chests lying half-buried in the debris littering the ship's rearward section. Seemingly positioned to act as makeshift rowing-seats between benches made unusable by the over-piling of the ship's cargo area, they were similar to many wagon seats with a thin strip of wood tacked down the middle to prevent a man from sliding forward when pulling back on his oar. Wido judged this slight ridge to have served its purpose particularly well as an unfortunate seaman's shattered bones laid in a heap on the very spot upon which he rowed his last stroke.

Unclear in the shadows, just ahead of Wido, sitting between two iron-bound chests, was a simple stone box. At least it looked like stone. Slightly wider than deep with its lid slightly askew, the hard-packed accretions of frag-mented pebble, shell, and sand clinging to its chiseled sides made it hard to tell. The front of the box, however, was clearly visible—all debris having been swept away by the gutting storm-water. Digging his elbows into the sand and wriggling closer to the box, Wido then reached out a hand and ran it down its cold, rough face. *Sure enough, it is stone,* he thought. *Hardly common. Not in these parts, anyway.* He stared at the box a moment more. *Still … Some-where before.*

Inching even closer, Wido again reached a hand toward the box, this time flattening his palm against its face and sweeping it side to side. On his second pass, the little finger on his right hand snagged in a large crack; illuminated by the few rays of sunlight shining down into the hole, a closer inspection of the box's front face revealed two long fissures that formed an inverted "V" with its point stopping a thumb's length shy of its thickened top edge. Much smaller than the two traditional wooden storage chests flanking it, the box appeared to have been hewn from a single chunk of limestone or marl.

*Somewhere* … Wido thought, closing his eyes, the better to dig into his mind.

Then he remembered where he'd seen such a box: *The church at Saint-Riquier!*

*But, no.* For while this box was made of stone and similar in size to the reliquary of some saint or other Wido had often walked past in the church, the two boxes in no way compared. Set on a raised altar in Saint-Riquier's south transept, the reliquary had been displayed with prominence in a place where the nobles of the realm prayed to their favorite saints. The abbot Evreux told Wido that it had been brought to Saint-Riquier in a grand *translatio* from the Holy Land many years ago. Said to contain a leg bone of a great prophet interred during the reign of Herod the Great, such was the rich ornamentation covering the box as to make its simple stone core unrecognizable. Gold-plated, bejeweled, and carved with rosettes, it was a work of art like nothing Wido had ever seen.

But this little stone box in the boat had none of that. Not even the faintest inscription. Not an *Abba* for "Father" or an *Emma* for "Mother." And it likely cost less than a *drachma*—a coin worth less than a few arrowheads—to make. Nothing about the box commanded any interest at all. That is, until the moment when the morning sun began to shine down into the blowout under God's Rock a little brighter. Reflecting the early morning sun into Wido's gritty eyes, he saw what first appeared as but dull yellow pebbles visible through the fissure in the front of the box. Only, as he pressed his face closer, his eyes suddenly widened to a much sharper focus. With his body starting to quiver and his blood jumping in his veins, he slipped a shaky index finger inside the point of the inverted "V" and whispered to his mule, "If this is the Devil's hidden hook," my little friend, "I am just the fish to bite."

With Wido's lips turned up at the corners and the lines of doubt smoothing on his brow, his flat, inquisitive eyes traced every inch of the fissure, now standing in sharp contrast to the dull gray sheen of the pitted stone box.

Stunned and staring in amazement, Wido slowly began to grasp that there was enough silver and gold piled inside this box to build himself a home just like the nobles—bigger, even—and a small city, besides.

Wido, angry and hate-filled for much of his life, had lived as a tree covered in brown, withered leaves, with nothing but rotted fruit scattering the ground under his gnarled, broken branches. All that would change now.

One especially large gold coin wedged into the narrower left-side crack was just begging to be freed. Wido reasoned that it was as good a place as any to start gathering his wealth. As it presented just enough of its thick, ribbed edge for him to extract it from the box, Wido pinched the coin between his short, larvae-like thumb and a forefinger and, with the slightest pull, attempted to draw it out. It moved not a bit. Wido pulled harder. Nothing. He was incredulous: *A most-adroit cutpurse in my younger day, now, in my middle age, I cannot even pilfer a coin from a broken box?* Another pull, harder still. Much harder. A cracking sound. The fissure suddenly widening. The top edge splitting fully apart at the juncture of the inverted "V." Another cracking sound. The entire front face of the box crumbling to pieces. So it was, in the next instant—with his eyes nigh falling out of his head—Wido beheld the glorious sight of hundreds of gold and silver coins and loose jewels tumbling toward him like a rockslide down the side of a high mountain gorge.

Wido opened his mouth like to shriek; only nothing came out. Throwing his hands forward and clawing through the sudden wellspring of riches— imagining himself feasting all the rest of his days on every lusty, fleeting, forbidden delight the Earth had to offer—so utterly overwhelmed was he by his sudden rise to great wealth as to fill him with the powerful sense of a dive-bombing young goshawk at the instant of his first kill.

Alas—just as sure as somewhere a woodcock was singing his sad song— Wido's open pleasure turned into big, blearing tears when a great yellow-brown cloud of sulfurous dust suddenly exploded in his face and began burning his eyes. Gouging his fingers at the pain and screaming as if he was lying in a field of fire, he then buried his hot yellow face deep in the coarse, cutting sand—*a la folletoere*—just like the woodcock—the stupidest bird alive.

Long moments passed before, finally, the sulfurous cloud began to clear. Wary of he knew not what, it was only when Wido slowly lifted his dust-covered head and opened his eyes that he saw them: three cracked, hollow-eyed skulls glaring at him through a thin curtain of copper-colored mist.

Recoiling in horror, Wido jerked a hand to his forehead and quickly crossed himself—"The Father, the Son, the Holy Spirit!"—the first time he had done that of his own, unforced act in his entire life.

There was much evidence of dead men in the crushed ship. Their bones, all broken and strewn about, sanctifying not a soul. *These Norsemen were no noble warriors who fought in the name of justice, the widow, the orphan, and the poor,* Wido thought. *Led by their murderous one-eyed god Odin, they were as a pack of ravenous wolves. That the shards of their shattered skulls were scattered like loose turds on a dung heap was a befitting end for such thieving heathens.*

Then again, Wido thought, there was nothing about these long-buried skulls staring out at him from within the shattered bone box to suggest their ever having worn a Viking helm. Decayed of their flesh and their mouths bristling with cracked yellow teeth, they were no different from all human skulls. But the box—that very plain stone box—was the giveaway: *They were Jews.*

Wido's mind wandered the likely path these old bones had traveled to this remote, rocky shore. Dug up from their native ground, carried off, passed along, hidden, stolen, sailed up rivers and over oceans, they had been inexplicably included with the vast treasure piled aboard this doomed Viking ship. Reburied in this place. But not *of* this place. Wido wondered of their worth. Had their grim remains still had tongues, what stories would they tell? Prophets? Priests? Kings? Or were they criminals of the vilest sort—their skulls once filled with fire and hung on wooden posts to light some riverside wharf when the daylight expired?

Seeming to speak of a long-ago time and faraway place where it rested upon the shoulders of a man of some importance, the skull in the center—

raised highest on the riches still contained within the unbroken sides of the stone box—had a small, sheer, golden-white cloth draped upon it from crown to lower jaw. Delicate, exotic, it was a material Wido had never seen. Stained red in the undeniable image of a face, as of a man badly beaten yet enduring his great suffering without fear, even grace, there was a haunting, dark burn over the hollows of his eyes that spoke of an unquenchable fire within. Studying the faint outline of what appeared to be a beard and a mustache framing the half-open mouth, it was the face of a man Wido had seen many times before. A tableaux. A tapestry. A painting. In a church. On his mother's wall. The most famous face ever. *But that is not possible.* Wido reached a wary hand toward the skull, wanting to remove the covering cloth, only to quickly withdraw it as the unfleshed face began to drip blood. Seeping out of several small punctures ringing the top of the skull before spreading across the broad broken brow, Wido watched wide-eyed as the blood then slowly streaked down the center of the gold-shimmered cloth to complete a bold red cross.

Stunned, Wido shifted his uneasy look to the skull sitting to the right; brittle and black with its jaws opened wide, it seemed to be screaming in pain like once engulfed by fire. With a blade-thin slot cleaved in the bone above his vacant left eye, it had the look of a man once proud and perilous. And not afraid to die. Turning an eye on the skull to the left, with its lower jaw gone and red-orange flames flickering in the web-like cracks of the fractured cheek-bones, it had an overhanging brow that said he was quite capable of anger. Of vengeance. And making men die. Death masks more frightful than any Wido had ever seen.

Yet, steeled by his hard-rooted disbelief in the mystic power of old bones, his eyes never quailed. "Relics!" Wido literally spit the word as he glared at the skulls perched on their pedestal of ill-gotten riches. "Dead bodies working miracles. If only I could send you back a thousand years to when you were buried in Jewish dirt, I would. That you might rot in that big gopher patch they call Sheol once and for all … put an end to the great Christian farce of claiming you otherworldly saints … find peace for your souls and some worth for your dust."

Wido was never a man to applaud the miraculous, and he was not going to start now.

Forced to be a man of the Church, but never a man of God, Wido knew too well the Catholic mind to be a believer in relics. Adamant in his belief that they fostered nothing but hypocrisy and superstition, he would take his chances that there was nothing magic about bones at all. Feeling wholly vindicated for the integrity with which he clung to his belief that any god that relies on working miracles through dead men to heal and protect is a fraud, Wido loudly proclaimed to the blatantly accusatory skulls, "Yes, I am a sinner! Guilty! I make no bones about it, venerated or otherwise. What can I say? The logic of my doubt greatly exceeds my ability to fabricate faith."

Whether he wanted to be or not, Wido was well versed in the Scriptures and the histories of the saints. As such, he could not imagine anyone who claimed a sane mind to believe even half of what they read. "There are no miracles to make blind men see or cripples walk," he said to the cloth-covered skull in the center. "They were but fabulous storytellers, those biblical scribes. Jokers, all of them: Matthew, Mark, Luke, and John. No less than a hundred of their bones collected from all over the Holy Land, yet not an ounce of integrity among them. Divine intervention. Magic bones. What tripe! The Church's money-grubbing hands disguised as poor boxes. Drops of blood; Virgin milk; arms, legs, and heads; larger-than-life statues of dead men. Saints made into slaves. All the while, the hoodwinked masses worshipping them like gods!"

Sinister and accusing, Wido's eyes remained fastened on the skull boldly marked with the blood-red cross. "Walking so close to the boundary between Heaven and Earth, maybe it is true that certain people can have otherworldly powers while here on Earth, in the flesh. So much so that even a carpenter's son from a small village on the fringe of the Roman Empire could sell His daily miracles to thousands of the beaten-down and oppressed in the hope that He truly was the Son of God.

"But what of the hypocrisy of the apostles and holy men who had imitated His virtues in life being transformed in death to these ridiculously idolized characters without regard for any credible proof? Their fanatical admirers licking and kissing and moistening with their tears any spot these purported angels of God ever sat or ate or prayed or took a shit. As if being dug up out of the ground then chopped into pieces is some kind of heroic endeavor!

"How absurd! The blessed apostle Paul—pure in heart, walking in the light of Lord—preaching among the sinners, saving souls, only to end up with his head on a marble slab beside a basketful of coins. Shilling for God! The Church bastardizing an offering of gifts to the Almighty Creator into a ham-fisted demand to pay a ransom for His love and buy forgiveness for their sins! Emptying the pockets of the poor, the sick, and wretched of mind so only to raise grand cathedrals to the sky in glorification of His precious name!

"And what of you!" Wido said, suddenly grabbing up a jagged piece of marl and throwing it at the skull hiding behind the bloody cross. "In all these years lying under this rock, not a single miracle has there ever been on this beach. Only pain and suffering, sorrow and death. Betrayal! Who are you? Tell me! How did you die? Where are your bones? And who dropped your head in this box?"

Tinged red, like burning, the skulls left and right suddenly flared like lanterns kicked over in the night. A fire fueled by righteous indignation, a hunger for vengeance. With anger burning in their empty eye sockets, their silent threat was that Wido would soon pay the full price for his irreverence toward the one true God and true Man who died to redeem his blackened soul.

"And what of you two, with so much anger yet staining your wounds?" Wido shouted amidst the skulls' murderous flare. "No matter holy men, prophets, or crucified saints; John the Baptist, Jeremiah, or Moses himself. In whose name do you dare demand such reverence and respect?" Then, raising a hand, and knocking the right-side skull into the back corner of the box, he laughed long and ridiculing. "What makes you burn with such pride?" Wido demanded. "Would you have me believe that you were once attached to that headless holy man who is said to have been carried off in a boat without sailors or rudder and then encased in a rock on some faraway coast? That this is the boat, and your head finally found?" Wido flicked a large gold coin at the skull, and then another and another at the one on the opposite side. "Or you!" he shouted at the glaring skull on the left. "I suppose you would claim to be the decrepit bone that shined up through the dirt at Compostela in Galicia the day Saint James was pulled from the ground?" Again, Wido laughed, toothy and vulgar. "Even that I should be so lucky to discover somewhere in this rubble the long lost Holy Grail—the great chalice used to catch the blood of Jesus as He hung on the cross—I suppose one of you will then jump up and claim to be the head of the man who held the sacred vessel, Joseph of Arimathea. Well—too late for you—because there are no less than five heads claiming such distinction in France alone!"

Wido waited for a response—anything—and then laughed at the skulls again.

Only then, all of a sudden, the blood-crossed skull in the center began glowing hot from within, its rich, golden aura billowing onto the charred walls of the oak-ribbed crypt like a ship's sail filled by a hard-blowing wind. Overawed, even fearful, Wido at once ceased his laughter, his ridiculing japes and jokes, dropped his head to his chest, and put up a hand to shield his eyes from the now blinding light. Trying to deny his fear, in his mind Wido had questions, pointed like arrows. He had the gall to ask them … yet not quite the courage to stand the reply.

When, at last, the frenzied light dimmed to a smoldering glow, Wido lifted his head and uncovered his eyes. Struck dumb by what he had just seen, he half-expected a flight of demons to storm out of the darkness and carry off his wicked soul. Instead, as he stared into the hot, hollow eyes peering through the sheer cloth draping the skull, he felt a sudden, inexplicable feeling of peace enter him as if through the very air he breathed. At a loss to understand the strange sensation—a lightness inside him he had never felt before—Wido began to doubt his better sense and wonder if the yellowed old skull—this relic—was, indeed, worthy of worship. For, despite having no covering flesh to crease into lines of joy or despair or any other living emotion, its big empty eyes exuded a feeling of more woe and compassion for Wido's lifelong plight than any purple-robed purveyor of God's forgiving grace ever could.

Hesitant to do so, but determined that he would, Wido again stretched forth a slow, trembling hand and gently slipped the covering cloth off the softly glowing skull. "The Veil of Veronica," he said. "The 'True Image.' The one believed to be of Christ's face. Imprinted on the cloth when the woman wiped away His sweat and blood as He carried His cross to His place of execution. I have seen it: an artist's rendering. Yet, never have I believed it to be anything more than another fabulous creation to help sell the Christian tale." Wido then gently stretched the cloth between his hands and smoothed out the folds, his eyes narrowing in a close study of the bloody image of the face it had captured. After a time, he returned his increasingly dark, anxious look upon the skull, and with a chill in his spine and a fumbling of his words, asked, "Are you ... Jesus of Nazareth? ... And how can that be?"

It was one of the few things written in the Bible that Wido struggled to dismiss as outright storytelling: Born of a virgin, Jesus had lived and suffered, then died on a cross for the glory of God's name. Raised from the grave, He then ascended into Heaven in full-body perfection. And never would a trace of His body—not a bone, not a drop of His blood, not a single hair of His head—be found anywhere on Earth ever again. So it was written. So it was done.

With anger again beginning to boil in his gut—feeling mocked, made a fool, duped in his one true belief that Jesus was a Man like no other, a singular creation both human and divine—Wido then shouted: "But all that is as written in a book. The word of God. As written by man. You cannot exist! For, if Jesus was not raised from the dead, the entire Christian faith is in vain."

With the hairs on the back of his neck raised like a distempered dog ready to bite, Wido again riveted his eyes on the nameless, faceless, blood-dripping skull and said, "Charlatan, sage, or god incarnate, it matters not whose shoulders you sat upon in life. You are nothing now. For, as rock is just rock, so bone is just bone. That you should have the temerity to suppose yourself anything more than a prop used to trick the poor into handing over their meager offerings, to make them believe they can buy their way into Heaven, is no different than the farce perpetrated by the God for which you so foolishly chose to die.

"I have suffered much in my life," Wido further spoke with his dirty, contemptible eyes fixed squarely on the skull, now haloed by a brightening light. "A life buried in the rubble of hatred and scorn, abandonment and deceit. I am just as much a martyr as you are. Only I do not believe in the apocalyptic rhapsody of resurrection. Of life ever after. Unlike the eternal thrones promised to those twelve men you favored most—even he who betrayed you with a kiss on your cheek—I have no tomorrow. No heavenly riches floating around on some cloud in the sky. So, if it's no matter to you, Brother Jesus, I'll just take my due right here, right now." Wido reached out to take up a handful of coins. Glancing at his useless legs twisted up the side of the ship behind him, he then turned his icy look back to the skull and said, "Maybe if you had given me a reason to believe."

Again, the skull's hollow eyes flared.

Wido sneered.

Only—with his hands poised in that narrow space between Heaven and Hell, and about to seize all the riches a motherless, fatherless, godforsaken man needed to buy love and respect—Wido hesitated at feeling a subtle quiver deep in the ground beneath him. Long and soundless, a stillness ensued. Again, Wido reached for the gold. Another quiver. A quake. A cold, howling wind now sweeping into the pit from above. The wrecked ship starting to pitch and to roll on its thick oak keel. Its ribs creaking, its strakes cracking. A fantastic breaching din sounding in Wido's ears. Deafening, like thunder. The charred hull suddenly splitting in half. Water rushing in. Waves of coarse gray silt pouring down the crumbling sides of the pit, filling the ship. God's Rock slowly sinking ... sinking. Splintering the ship's upper strakes. The rock's full weight bearing down on the top of Wido's tonsured head. A tremendous sundering sound. The ship's mainmast timber, like a huge spike driven through soft flesh, suddenly breaking through the ship's thick oak-wood bottom and piercing the seabed.

And the water kept pouring in.

Increasingly cold and airless, moments away from being just another sinner crushed under God's Rock, Wido knew he was a dead man. Yet, he showed no fear of God's final judgement of him. With the wind-shivered water swirling about his neck, swallowing mouthfuls of silt and gasping for air, the black-hearted monk suddenly raised up a fistful of coins and, in an outright challenge to this supposed Son of God who had died on the Golgotha hill to prove his otherworldly might, yelled out, "Save this sinner if You can, Lord Jesus! Prove that You have as much power to renew as to destroy! The same as You did for that crazed, chained, disbelieving lout who accosted You in the Biblical land of the Gergesenes, make this unclean spirit come out of me! Drown the hateful beast in this cold, rushing water the same as those demon-infested pigs You made dead in the Sea of Galilee! Make the magic! Be the omnipotent miracle-maker the Bible says You are! Heal me so that I might walk on these cold, dead legs straight to the Gate of Heaven! For the first time in my life, make me believe God knows who I am!"

Carried lightly on the surf over the rough pebble beach, a little silver Man without a head, unburdened of His cross, returned to stand upon the precipice of the gaping, water-filled pit with His arms thrown wide like leading a gathering in prayer. A massive black cloud suddenly swept down the cliff face like a veil of storm-driven smoke, blotting out the early morning sun as fast as its fall off the heavens' rim at the end of the day. Far below God's Rock, an angry shout: God's name taken in vain. A loud, plaintive groan from the tortured warship as, one by one, its thick oak strakes snapped like twigs. God's Rock crunching down. A sudden, desperate cry: "Please, God! No! Forgive me! I am a sinner! But I do believe! I have always believed!"

A bloodcurdling scream. The seawater turning red.

Hanging on the edge of the pit, the headless little Jesus then dropped into the water.

A man and his young son approaching near on the beach above heard not a thing.

# THE SAINTS

*Sunrise*

---

## 10 SEPTEMBER 1100

Jaune Faucon De La Foret, born in the exact image of the baby a young Wido slew on the limestone slab underlying his boyhood home on the cliff, stood with his son Sihtric patting the muzzle of a trembling old mule they had found standing at the edge of a huge blowout on the west side of God's Rock. Knowing nothing about the crippled Brother Wido from the monastery at Saint-Riquier or hearing a word of his terrible tale, Jaune Faucon didn't know to whom the little beast belonged or why he should be there alone on this storm-torn beach.

Nor did Jaune Faucon know that when the monk was but seven summers grown, riding this very same mule during his meandering return to his mother's cliff-top shack late in the afternoon of that murderous day, the young cripple found a rag-swaddled baby in the deepest depths of the Talou Forest. Didn't know that, confused and fearful of the yellow-haired child staring up at him in wide-eyed silence, as if a dramatic, blood-embellished sculpture of the baby he had just killed had been placed in his path to haunt him, the boy rode off with every intention of letting the infant die where he laid. Didn't know that, succumbing to a relentless attack of his mind's screamed accusations, he suddenly turned back through the forest, bundled the newborn in his arms, then carried him off into a dark green glade of creeping myrtle and placed him at the base of the majestic Saint's Tree.

Without looking back, the boy again rode off toward the cliff.

Only, the guilt hammering inside his skull would not stop.

So did the boy again double back on the path and return to the forest glade. Slipping off the mule's back and withdrawing a coil of braided leather attached to a small silver Hammer of Thor amulet he'd long hidden in an open hem of his tunic, the boy then put it around the baby's neck in hopes that whatever god made him might find him in his hour of need. Watch over him. Or, at the very least, take him up into whatever place in the sky he reigned over upon the baby's last breath.

Jaune Faucon didn't know that the boy had remained with him under the huge Saint's Tree, lying at his side until well past the sun's fall from the sky. Didn't know that the boy had snugged that blood-soaked little picture-cloth about him to keep him warm when the north wind began to blow; then, with the night's shadows drawing in about him, slowly rode off with tears burning on his cheeks, bawling like a baby, burdened by a guilt he had never known. "Nameless, faceless, blue-headed baby!" the tormented boy cried to the sky. "The child is innocent! The demon is in me! And its name is Jealousy!"

Neither did Jaune Faucon know that the crippled little boy was soon taken away to a faraway monastery in the north and locked in a cold stone cell, never to see the baby again. Didn't know that the brutalized woman at whose side he now knelt had carried them both in her womb. That he had another brother. A twin. Murdered by the outraged boy in the moments before Jaune Faucon was born. That the boy—now a crippled monk named Wido—was covered over by a pool of blood-red seawater just six feet below where he and his son stood. Falling headfirst into Hell.

Calling on the Virgin Mary to bless the souls of these poor dead people, this man and this woman so brutally destroyed by the indiscriminate wrath wrought by the Lord of the Storm, Jaune Faucon bowed his head and prayed with all the vehement piety he could summon. He knew that the Mother of

God was easily insulted by anything less than enacting the proper Catholic ritual in a legitimate act of devotion by Her supplicants, and—fearing that She would withhold Her holy graces—was careful not to offend Her with a mumbling of meaningless words. He had visited many of Her shrines. He knew that any show of improper reverence to Her many locks of hair, shifts, veils, slippers, or drops of breast milk only angered Her, and Her heart would grow so hard in Her chiseled marble chest you might as well be praying to any old rock in a field. Jaune Faucon had never had much success in getting his prayers answered. As such, he was thunderstruck when the old man curled against the woman's side suddenly lifted his head off her shoulder and peeked up at him through the slits of his blood-crusted eyes.

So it was on the beach, in the aftermath of the murderous storm, that Styrkar—The Wolf, son of Kvendulf Skullsplitter, father of the great warriors Kalf and Thjodulf, slayer of the Nord Wood ogre—first laid eyes on his Christian son. Tall, strong, and golden-haired, the man he saw kneeling beside him was but the water's reflection of himself at the height of his warrior might. Nay, the same man who had clambered out of a hundred dragon-prowed warships, sword in hand, onto every beach from Byzantium to Palestine to Afrikka and back now staring down at him like a ghost of his distant past. So also, Styrkar saw six of the bravest warriors he'd ever known standing around the golden-haired apparition with a fierce hunger to resume their long-ago fight burning in every eye. Unseen by the man who looked so like him in his youth—spirits risen from the world of the dead—the warriors declared that they had remained on the beach all these years waiting to accompany Styrkar on his voyage into the sky, to Valhalla, to take his rightful place in the great heroes Hall of the Slain. Faint at first, but now growing in Styrkar's ears, even could he hear the harsh shouts and barbarous singing of that same warmongering, guttural voice that had once been his own calling out to him to fight … to die … then fight again!

In fact, Jaune Faucon was speaking to the dying man in the softest tones his voice was capable of. He had no idea who the brutalized wretch was, but when the old man suddenly reached up and took hold of the Hammer of Thor amulet at his throat and jerked his face down close to his own, Jaune Faucon saw in his fiery eyes a warrior who had given much of his flesh and blood to a noble cause, yet retained enough of his fighting spirit to reclaim what was rightfully his own.

Hot-tempered and spitting blood out of the vengeful heart of a true Norseman, in his grunting speech Styrkar was relentless in his demand to know how it was that Jaune Faucon, this mirror image of the man he once was, came to possess his sacred totem.

"By the hand of Harald, son of Sigurd Syr of Nitharos, the future king of Norway, this amulet was placed about my neck when I was but fifteen years grown. Whereas Harald's noble brother Olaf, the reigning king of Norway, had been struck dead by a rebel sword during the battle of Stiklestad, a wounded Harald, of the same fifteen years on this earth, was forced to take cover in the forest near my childhood home while being hunted by a hundred men intent on killing the boy who would now be king. Sent off by my father, I guided the young prince Harald through the endless eastern forest only steps ahead of the murderous horde. Tracked like animals through the dead of winter over mountain, field, and lake, we arrived in Novgorod where we were taken in by King Olaf's trusted friend Jaroslav, the great king of the Rus himself. Bonded for life—The Wolf and The Raven—Harald had this amulet made for me as a symbol of our eternal alliance. And, oh, how inseparable we were! The sons of Sigurd Syr and the Skullsplitter—two of the boldest men under arms the world has ever seen!"

Closing his fist on the amulet and tearing it from around Jaune Faucon's neck, Styrkar then thumped it against his heaving chest and, with a feral growl, reclaimed it as his own.

All spit and drivel, Jaune Faucon understood nothing of the man's excitable speech. Nor his anger. But that was hardly the matter. The man had taken from him his most precious possession, and he meant to take it back. Glaring down at the bloody wretch with his fist crushed around the amulet, Jaune Faucon yelled out that he would tolerate none of the man's audacity and then grabbed him by the throat.

Not a moment in his life had that talisman been off his person, and so did Jaune Faucon have a horrible, empty feeling that the very core in which was born the seed of his greatness had been ripped out through a gaping hole in his throat. A gift from the gods, it had ensured that Jaune Faucon could not be bent to another man's will. Not now. Not ever.

Standing at the apex of his power, Jaune Faucon was about to smash a tight, white-knuckled fist into the man's scarred, bony face when a small, trembling hand suddenly slipped atop his own and pushed it down. At a glance upon Sihtric's gentle face, Jaune Faucon's rage burned a few moments more before waning, smoldering under his skin just the same as a fire's last pulsing embers. In time, unclenching his fists, Jaune Faucon let his anger carry off on the breeze as if a butterfly in flight.

Looking down at the beaten old man, his face white as a cadaver and his eyes turned almost completely black by onrushing death, Jaune Faucon slowly pointed to the sky, then to the amulet the old man held in his balled, bony fist and said, "The gods gave me that amulet on the day I was born." Then, raising his hands to his neck and touching his thumbs and forefingers tip to tip around his throat, he said, "That Hammer of Thor was put around my neck so that I might know of the Norse blood that ran in my veins. I have worn it with pride every day since. Thirty-three years ago today." He pointed to his chest. "It is my heart that has given me my humanity, but it is that amulet that has given me my soul."

Styrkar suddenly rolled his head back on the piled rubble and, with a gaping, gap-toothed smile, nodded his head in full understanding. His reddened teeth biting down hard on his tongue as a mouthful of blood dribbled over his chin, he said nothing, but only pointed to the sun-silvered sea before drawing in the sand with an artist's deft hand a beautiful dragon-prowed longship and a large royal crown. Then, pointing to the sky, Styrkar indicated that he, too, was gifted the amulet by a king of heaven.

With his visage suddenly turned dark as nightfall, Styrkar once again put his finger in the sand and, raking it back and forth, scribbled a wicked wall of flame across the dragon-ship. Then, taking up a large black beach pebble in his hand and raising it high over his head, he pounded it down on the ship as if a hammer on an anvil, crushing the rock half into the sand.

Jaune Faucon could scarcely conceal his astonishment when the old man—spitting a mouthful of thick, rimy blood into his hand and violently smearing it on the stone—suddenly untangled his tongue and boomed out in a voice as deep and powerful as his own.

"Aye, these men gathered around you now—my brothers Ivar, Thormod, Asmund, and Finn—lo!—my firstborn son Kalf and second son Thjodulf— six of the bravest warriors upon which the sun ever shined—died on this very spot thirty-four years ago. I alone survived—which was a fate far worse than Death. Chained to a wall. Tortured. Beaten for entertainment. Ridiculed by lords, priests, and drunkards alike. Yet, then and now, my warrior-brothers did not abandon me. Neither have I ever questioned the gods' decree of the punishment I earned, these ten thousand days driven under the head of Thor's giant hammer. Only now, after all these many years of gray and murk, the hour is upon us that the brutal storm will finally end. Today the glorious day when, sailing on a bearing straight and true through a swath of stars marked by the brightest light in the northern sky, we shall return our noble king's hard-won treasure to his beloved Norway and, at last, lay our bones to rest upon the long-sought shore of the fairest land any of us have ever known. I am Styrkar

Kvendulfsson. Son of the Skullsplitter. Slayer of the Nord Wood ogre. I am their captain, and they are waiting for me to board."

Amidst a sudden cold wind swirling around Jaune Faucon, the six ghost warriors—as if at Styrkar's command—then dragged the splintered remnant of the shack on which the old man and woman laid off the piled rubble and began pushing it through the crashing surf. What with the rolling waves shunting Styrkar's and Adelvia's shattered bodies back and forth on the make-shift raft nigh to dumping them into the sea, Jaune Faucon ran out into the water and grabbed a hold of it with both hands to steady it. Looking down at the woman—her face streaked with filth and viscera, a gaping gash between her exposed breasts, and her belly smeared with blood—she was hardly distinguishable from many of the men he'd slaughtered in battle. Only, unlike a warrior, in which it was an honor to die a violent death, Jaune Faucon could not allow the woman to leave the Earth in this most pitiable way. He would see to it that she got a proper burial. A stone for her grave. With a space for her name.

Spinning the raft broadside against the pounding waves and lifting the dead woman in his arms, Jaune Faucon had hardly turned to carry her back to the shore when the sudden, contemptible sound of the old man's voice broke like a storm cloud over a high mountain peak. Snatching up the small wooden cross he spied in the blood pooled in the spot where Adelvia had laid on the raft, Styrkar demanded that Jaune Faucon immediately return her to his side.

"The little silver man is off his cross now," Styrkar bellowed. "So, too, is she!"

With a murderous glint in his eyes and the unbearable grief of Adelvia's death preying on his heart, Styrkar thrust his words at Jaune Faucon like blades of fire: "Your god made a mockery of her. Sitting on his high seat, judging her worth, ignoring her prayers, denying her forgiveness, and doing nothing to soothe her aching heart! Taking from her whatever love and happiness she had in her life, crushing her under the guilt of a natural longing to fill that raw, hollowing hole in her soul, this blackhearted God of yours made her feel like a whore, but only for wanting to give freely of her wellspring of compassion for another dispirited human. What kind of god does that to his own child?" With tears now rolling unheeded down his cheeks, Styrkar waited for no reply, but simply stated that there was no argument to be made: "Your god does not deserve her," he told Jaune Faucon. "She is going with me. Now set her down—or be prepared to die!"

Banging his hand down emphatically on the wave-tossed remnant of the shattered shack, the ferocity did not fade from Styrkar's eyes until Adelvia was again lying at his side.

Rendered mute by the old man's earnest emotion and blinking back tears of his own, Jaune Faucon watched in stunned amazement of what was nothing short of a miracle now taking place.

With the foaming waves of seawater gently washing over Adelvia's body, cleansing her wounds and whitening her skin, Styrkar watched as her face gradually took on what he remembered to be the pearl-like perfection of her younger day. She was as a rose unfolding its new petals in spring, her skin soon as soft and unfurrowed as when he first laid eyes on her. Styrkar's eyes danced in adoration. The same as an alabaster statue freed from the filth of time, Adelvia was beautiful again—as beautiful as any woman has ever been. As he stared into her face, whose god restored her mattered nothing to Styrkar, for Adelvia was one of those precious souls that every man's heaven holds as sacred. A being of such love and compassion as to make a merciless god feel the shame of his deeds.

Unable to take his eyes off Adelvia's peaceful face, Styrkar then took her small, delicate hand in his and kissed her cheek. He whispered in her ear that he loved her. And a sudden gleam of joy shot across his face when he heard her answer back. Rolling onto his back and pointing up to the sky, Styrkar then began speaking to her excitedly, his voice rising like pleasurable singing.

Stunned by the woman's transformation, neither Jaune Faucon nor Sihtric understood a word of what the old man was saying to her. Yet, as his boundless love for her was etched in bold lines on his face, both were helpless to choke back the emotions surging inside them as they knew well he was describing the immense joy he felt at spending all eternity walking the open air amidst the soft mists of cloud with the love of his life in Valhalla above.

With a subtle, sweet fragrance wafting off the dark, rolling water, as if they were passing through a field of large, open flowers, Styrkar then gently laid his head upon Adelvia's breast, closed his eyes, and died.

With the wind now blowing from the land toward the sea, Jaune Faucon and the six unseen ghost warriors began pushing Styrkar's makeshift raft through the Channel's heavy chop. Tall and proud, and striding in hard, purposeful steps, all hands on the raft and propelling it out to sea, every eye was fixed forward as if the world-orb had no end. Shooing away the Valkyries swooping down from the sky as if pestering gulls, the ghost warriors cared nothing about their promises of fine wine, food, rewards, and glory. The Norsemen had waited thirty-four years to return to the service of their god. They were ready to fight. To die. Then fight again.

With Sihtric studying the unfamiliar expression on his father's face, trying to read his hidden emotion, Jaune Faucon again gazed down at the woman on the raft. Astounded by her transformation, as an apple suddenly ridded of its rot, flawless beyond all belief, he couldn't help but wonder about the god that possessed such power to make a perfect end of such an ugly life.

Studying the woman's serene face, trying to fathom all the pain and anguish she had endured in her life, Jaune Faucon remembered meeting her once—only it was so many years ago that little of the encounter remained in his memory. Knowing her only as the "dead woodcutter's widow," he was along on a ride with his father, Alain—supposedly on a hunt. Which, even then, Jaune Faucon found strange as his father had not the competence to track a pig to a sty.

The only thing that stood out about the woman that day was that she was old. Her skin was spotted and brown and heavily creased, as if always out in the sun. Her face gaunt. Almost mean. But with very pretty green eyes. She seemed very sad. Not even the slightest smile. Slump-shouldered and stooped at the waist, she seemed beaten by life. Like always crying. Even so, he remembered that when the woman first laid eyes on him standing in her doorway, she suddenly grabbed hold of her face and burst into tears.

It was around the same time of the year as now, Jaune Faucon recalled. Michaelmas. 29 September. The Feast of Saint Michael. The time of year when accounts were balanced up, as well as the collection of rents and quotas for products owed to the lord-owner of the land. The woman explained to Alain that her husband, the woodcutter, had been killed while off fighting in one of Duke William's wars. Only, Alain waved a hand at her and told her to be quiet. He told her that death was hardly an excuse for her husband shorting his contractual responsibility. Much wood was owed to Duke William. And the time to deliver was at hand.

Pushing in the door of her little shack, Alain had demanded food and drink from Adelvia. Bread for his hounds, and wine for himself. He was master of her land—and a huntsman, besides. By law, Adelvia could not refuse him her hospitality. And Alain had further bad news for her. Withdrawing a small piece of folded parchment from the hem of his tunic, he explained to Adelvia how most peasants held their land from a master and possessed their plots on a hereditary basis in return for service, money, or kind payable to the master. "However," Alain put the little paper up close to Adelvia's face and pointed out that, "I clearly specified that the land you live on is to revert to me in the event of your husband's death." Alain then showed Adelvia where he'd forced the woodcutter to put his X upon it.

Slipping the document back within the hem at his knees, Alain then threatened a trembling Adelvia with a purple-faced fury: "So be it! Your husband died in William's little war! That's hardly a matter to me. The land is mine now. The only bit of this God's good earth you'll ever call your own is what they pile on you in that six-foot hole when you die. And make no mistake about it: every cord of wood you owe me better be hacked, stacked, and delivered in the next three days or you're going to be looking for another rock to shit on!"

Jaune Faucon remembered recounting his father's aggressive treatment of the woman to his mother upon his return to their little fortress. And, although Judith did not know the woman, she seemed to care deeply about her. Sending out many large men with sharp, glistening axes into the forest that very afternoon, she paid out of her own purse to ensure the full quota of cut, split, and neatly stacked wood was carted into the court square at Rouen with a full day to spare.

Alain De La Foret had not a clue how that was possible. Nor did he care. Perched on his high seat in the isolation of his dark, dank hall, he only puffed out his little peacock chest and told a young Jaune Faucon how much he enjoyed being one of the *gens de proie*, the "people of prey before whom all lesser people tremble in fear." He was the falcon; they were the hares. Scaring the shit out of them made life fun. "And I can see it in you already, my boy: you're just like me."

As he shoved the raft through the waves, the realization that he had lived much of his life looking down on those less fortunate than him turned Jaune Faucon's face brilliant with a gnawing and profound sense of shame. A shame on his family name. A shame on himself. Alain De La Foret had been right: despite not sharing one drop of his blood, he, Jaune Faucon—baptized Alain II—shared the same haughty feelings of superiority over the poor, the weak, the small, and the meek as his notorious namesake. Never showing an ounce of sympathy for these lowliest creatures of God's Earth, crushing them underfoot the same as bugs on the road, their meaningless little lives and deaths he'd viewed with utter indifference. Appalled that such people even existed, subhuman beasts so infinitely alien and inferior, it hardly occurred to him that just because a person is obscure does not mean they do not have real significance.

Only now, staring down at this woman so obviously cherished by the gods, Jaune Faucon found himself walking into the light of a new day, with new eyes. She had been poor, to be sure, but so much richer than he in ways he could never comprehend. And already that made him want to be a better father, a better son, than he had ever been. More tolerant of other people, other creeds. A man beholden to nothing but his own conscience, his own heart, not the attitudes of others.

With hard whips of seawater striking across the entwined couple as he and Sihtric propelled the raft through the foaming swells, Jaune Faucon turned his mind upon a recollection he considered much more than coincidence. Stealing sidelong glances at the woman, he was trying to recall where before he had seen all those bright green, blue, red, and yellow threads used to sew the many rips in her dingy white gown. Feeling it was quite indecent for him to stare overlong at the thin, wet cotton that left her nearly nude, with one last, hasty look, Jaune Faucon suddenly realized the colorful threads were, indeed, the very same as those he had seen so skillfully woven throughout the soiled tapestry in which he was wrapped the day he was found at the base of the great Saint's Tree.

Years ago, one of the dog-handlers that was out in the forest that day with Judith told Jaune Faucon the story of the falcon's stunning discovery. How the falcon, named Hardrada, had attacked him—drawn by the bright red of a bloody picture-cloth that covered all but Jaune Faucon's head. Always did Judith deny that any such embroidery existed. "A tattered piece of canvas, was all," she'd say. "Pictures of dragons and ships? No. Just some patchwork mending of the thing. Nothing more. And disposed of that very day."

Only, little did Judith know that Jaune Faucon had, in fact, discovered the picture-cloth even as she still denied it. The truth was, she did not throw it away, but had tried to hide it. Possibly holding onto it for its sentimental value, long had she tried to make sense of the images.

Finding the cloth stuffed into the bottom of an old larder tucked into a far corner of the feed barn while he waited to ambush an unsuspecting friend, Jaune Faucon hardly knew what he was looking at that day: men on horses;

ships on fire; oceans; forests; rocks falling from the sky. The events it depicted meant nothing to him. Roving his eyes over the colorful embroidery for a few moments before stuffing it back into the larder, no matter whether he'd been wrapped in that old canvas or not—Jaune Faucon couldn't have cared less of the story it told. Never did he even tell his mother he had found it. Nor think about it again.

Until today.

Studying every feature of the heavily scarred old man sprawled across the makeshift raft, with his face frozen as if by a sudden chill, Jaune Faucon slowly began to unravel the tale the tapestry told. Unrolling the canvas in his mind and imagining the great warrior rowing into shore aboard his dragon-ship under a pounding waterfall that fateful night, so vivid were the details the expertly embroidered scenes captured that the massive rock's subsequent fall from the cliff and cataclysmic crash upon the man's ship and crew was almost audible. Amazed that any man could have such strength and fortitude not only to survive such an apocalyptic event, but then find happiness during his succeeding days, was unfathomable. Yet, as he gazed down upon the two people tenderly entwined on the raft before him, their story became very clear. Jaune Faucon had not a doubt in his mind: this man and this woman had given him life.

"My mother and my father," he said softly to Sihtric.

Jaune Faucon then turned his tear-glimmered gaze straight out to the sea and, with his incomparable strength, began driving the raft through the Channel's pounding surf.

Running around and quickly grabbing a hold of the raft opposite his father amidst all the increasingly loud bellowing and fist-waving of the dead Viking horde, with immense wonder in his look, Sihtric then fixed a long, wistful look on his heretofore unknown grandparents. That they had died before he ever knew them was both shocking and emotional. That his father cried was even more shocking. More emotional. And, somehow ... wonderful.

Digging his feet in hard against the fast-sinking seabed, with a last powerful push Jaune Faucon launched the raft through one final high-walled wave before arresting his forward charge. Pulling Sihtric up high on his hip, he gave his son a big kiss on his forehead and then watched as those six proud ghost-warriors propelled the raft infinitely on.

With the heavy waves breaking on his chest, Jaune Faucon's mind was racing, sparing no superlatives in recreating the great man his father must have been when his feet were still nimble and his sword-arm strong. Unbending of will and pathologically stoic. Suppressing the fear of fatigue, pain, and even death in the most extreme crisis. A man capable of such rage in battle that, in the moment of his ultimate fury, he would want to cut the heart out of the man he had just killed. Yet, too, a man capable of showing such compassion for the most timid, delicate creatures of the Earth that he ultimately elevated himself to the highest realm of human goodness.

Jaune Faucon believed such a man should be emulated. Be remembered. Be known.

So it was, after many months sailing in and out of every port along the endless shores of the North and Atlantic seas—Norway, Sweden, Finland, Denmark, the Baltic, and beyond—Jaune Faucon De La Foret—The Yellow Falcon of the Forest—returned to his Norman home and proudly declared to his wife and children that he was the son of Styrkar Kvendulfsson. Son of the Skullsplitter. Slayer of the Nord Wood ogre. Odin's last warrior.

Yggdrasill's last leaf.

Once back on the beach, Jaune Faucon abruptly turned back toward the sea and pulled from his quiver a long, black-feathered arrow. Wrapping its point in the dried bark frays he'd gathered while he and Sihtric were tracking the roebuck and smearing them with pitch, he next slipped one of the smoldering embers from the little earthenware fire-box he wore on his hip and pressed it into the mix. Notching the arrow to the string and raising his bow, he stood poised in perfect stillness as he waited for it to burst into flame. Remarkably, Sihtric, standing stock-still at Jaune Faucon's side with his bowstring tensed, had done the same. Launched with a simultaneous whir, flying side by side with points ablaze, the two arrows arced far out to sea before diving down to set his parents' funerary raft on fire when they perfectly struck their mark.

Standing, watching, as the raft burst into a conflagration of wildly leaping flames, Jaune Faucon and Sihtric then witnessed the god-crossed lovers begin their slow ascent into one-and-the-same heaven on a coiling tower of smoke. Drifting across the cerulean sky with six white wraithlike wisps trailing, the smoke moved over the water as a great-ship with its sail billowed full of wind. Northward. Toward the horizon. Vanishing without a trace. Without a sound.

His gray-green eyes sparkling with emotion as he stared at the funerary fire raging far out at sea, Jaune Faucon reflected on how death, the great beyond, not the short here and now, is at the very core of all being and creation. How true belief is resurrection. And the heavens' faint song not about lives lost, but God's children going home.

Walking back into the shadow of the cliff amidst the storm-strewn pieces of his mother's demolished shack, Jaune Faucon scooped up a tired, limping Bia and carried the dog up the beach. Licking her master's salty cheeks and nuzzling his neck as they approached the old mule still standing beside God's Rock, Bia had the pride but not the strength to fight Jaune Faucon as he loaded her on the beast's back. Jaune Faucon would not be leaving the little mule on the beach alone, and told Bia that he would be going home with them. "So be nice."

Sad-eyed and confused, trying to make sense of the man, the boy, and the dog on his back, the trembling old mule then sat back on his haunches, causing Bia to slide belly-first onto the beach. Ignoring the dog, the mule then turned his head toward God's Rock and stubbornly waited for the dirty little black-robe to emerge from the ground. Tugging on his lead, Sihtric—having a special way with animals—dropped the rope and, kneeling beside the mule, began running a hand down his flank while softly coaxing him: "Come on, you old shaggy, you're going with us." Another rub on the mule's muzzle and a little scratch of his ear. "Come on, Shaggy—it's time to go home."

As if in understanding, an instant later the old mule struggled to his feet, fixed a long look on Sihtric, and then swung his head back toward God's Rock. His coat patchy with age and his mind set in its ways, hanging his head, the mule pawed a hoof at the edge of the water pooled beside the rock before again looking up at the young boy gently tugging on his lead. "C'mon, Shaggy," Sihtric said. With a sudden spark coming into eyes as big and placid as mountain ponds, in that moment, the mule knew that things were going to be different now—somehow better—as for the first time in his life he had his own name. "Ready, Shaggy?" Sihtric smiled. With his little tail now ticking at his backside and his eyes glistening with the excitement of walking a new path, the only friend Wido ever knew then turned up the storm-ravaged gully and headed for home.

The old mule would live only two more years. Showered with love and the favorite ride of countless adoring children, they would be the best years of his life. He was buried beside the ever-faithful Bia in a small forest glade beneath the biggest tree in all of Normandy. A large white stone was placed over the beloved pet's grave. Etched by Sihtric's artful hand, the name "Shaggy" was easy to read for years to come.

Slowed by a whir of emotions, Jaune Faucon remained on the beach watching the old mule and his young son climb the cliff. With a last look at the pyre burning on the far-off horizon, he then picked up his quiver, slung his bow over his shoulder, and started after Sihtric and Shaggy.

He would not get far.

For, when only a few steps removed from God's Rock, Jaune Faucon was stopped in his track by a sudden commotion behind him. A loud splash. A yell. Turning quickly, he was struck dumb by the sight he beheld: a black-robed monk flailing wildly in the silty gray seawater pooled in the shadow of God's Rock. Seemingly appeared out of nowhere—thrashing, sinking, gasping, pounding his fists—yelling for help and then disappearing under the water's churned surface—Jaune Faucon ran back to the rock, grabbed hold of the monk's sodden wool habit, and dragged him onto the beach.

Staring at the pale-faced monk in wonder, the man's sudden appearance made no sense to Jaune Faucon. *Did he roll in on a wave? Drop out of the sky? Had he been under the water all along? An hour? More? Impossible!* Jaune Faucon shook his head in disbelief. *It's a miracle he's still alive.*

As he laid flat on his back with his chest heaving and speaking not a word, such was the astonishment in the monk's wide-eyed gaze into the heavens that, after a time, Jaune Faucon looked up, too. Clear. Blue. Beautiful. The sky was the same as ever.

Jaune Faucon returned his look to the shivering monk. When, at last, the man's breathing began to slow, he knelt beside him, took hold of his hand, and then gently helped him to his feet. Wrapping an arm across his shoulders to steady him as he wavered like a newborn colt on untried legs, without a word between them, Jaune Faucon and Wido—brothers with a bloody past and an improbable future—then walked off down the beach, out of the shadow of the cliff, and into the light of a bright new day.

# IV

## THE REFORMER
### ROUEN, 24 AUGUST 1126

Sitting the cart's high-board behind a stout brown plow horse borrowed from a local farmer, Brother Sihtric of Saint-Riquier was at the reins with his aged Uncle Wido at his side. They had started out at daybreak from the monastery in Abbeville and were now far to the south on the long, dusty road to Rouen. The historic seat of Norman royalty and one of the most prosperous cities in all of Christendom, Rouen would be the scene of a grand *translatio* ceremony today to celebrate the relocation of the hallowed remains of a beloved saint from a nearby cemetery to a magnificent cathedral recently completed in his honor.

The heat of the midsummer's day was suffocating, and Sihtric had been squirming on the rough wooden seat for an hour now. His neck and face running with sweat and itching under his collar, he was openly contemplating tearing off his prickly wool habit and jumping into the creek bordering the road. Nudging his dozing uncle, he jokingly asked him if he thought that was an acceptable thing for a Benedictine monk to do.

Wido—red-faced and as sweaty as his nephew—rubbed his hands over his bald, glistening head and told Sihtric, "Naked, you say? It's fine. Do it."

But Sihtric knew better. His sixty-six-year old uncle was not a patient man, and known to turn surly during even the slightest delay. Start here, end there—no stopping in between. That's the way Wido liked it. So the little cart creaked on.

Already, they had been forced off the fastest road to Rouen upon discovering that the rickety little bridge that had once spanned a low, muddy creek was gone, its splintered boards sunken in the muck of a recent storm. Straight south and no great distance away, they would have been rolling into Rouen within the hour. Forced to backtrack on to a small farm road which led far to the west towards Saint Germaine, eventually they would intersect a road along the snaking bends of the Siene River in a roundabout eastward approach to Rouen. Sihtric was relieved that Wido had remained surprising placid over the course of the long detour. Pleasant, even. "The world is a beautiful place, Sihtric," Wido said as he stared out over the endless rolling fields of oats streaked with bright bursts of red-orange poppies, oxeye daisies, and giant yellow buttercups. "Everything seems so much prettier now than in my younger day. The sky bluer; the grass greener. And a lot more flowers."

Sihtric loved his Uncle Wido. He was the most worldly-wise person he'd ever met and he could talk to him about anything. Intelligent beyond belief— the way Wido's mind worked fascinated Sihtric. And he was never boring. The fiery old man had an opinion about everything.

Only, today, Sihtric was unsure of how to broach a subject that had been causing him increasing worry. Stewing over it for a few days now, he'd decided there was no good way to say it. So, he took a deep breath and just blurted it out: "Dear Uncle ... If it's not too forward of me, there are some important matters I wish to discuss with you. In confidence. And with all honesty."

"Of course, Sihtric," Wido replied. "I would have it no other way."

"Well, first off," Sihtric started, "I'm curious—the way you think: How did such beliefs as yours about God, religion, and the world get into your head? Have they always been there? Were they taught? And by who? Your mother? Old man Evreux at Saint-Riquier? ... God rest his grumpy soul."

"No, Sihtric. Amusing. But, no. A much higher power than the Abbot Evreux."

Sihtric suspected as much. Licking his salty lips, he hesitated a moment, wary of pressing Wido too hard. "Was it when you were young, Uncle? Or was it spurred by something that happened later? That day when I first met you on the beach below the cliff ... Trapped under that rock ... When you emerged from the water ... What I saw in your eyes ... Staring up at the sky ... You seemed so—"

"I don't talk about that day, Sihtric. Under that rock—that's between God and me."

Quickly turning his head away, Wido offered not another word on the subject.

Riding over the vast, wheat-covered Norman landscape, the two men sat in silence for a long spell. Rounding a high hill covered with heavily-laden apple trees, at last, they turned back eastward and rejoined the main road to Rouen. At seeing Mount Riboudet—a familiar landmark—humped up in the distance, Wido finally broke the increasingly uncomfortable silence and declared, "God be good. Not much longer."

Again falling quiet, Wido took in a sparkling view of a big bend in the Siene through gaps in the scrub willows scattering the river's north bank. With a slight narrowing of his eyes, he maintained a particular focus on the many sweat-dripping peasants seen poling their small skiffs against the current towards the great city, not yet in view.

In a quick, side-eyed glance at his uncle, Sihtric again attempted to broach the subject that was troubling him. With many questions on the tip of his tongue, he opened his mouth to speak. Only, just then, with steam rising off of his uncle's mostly bald, tonsured head, as if full-boiling with thoughts, Sihtric was surprised when Wido suddenly turned to him and blurted with all the willingness of a man with his arm bent up his back, "Plain and simple, Sihtric: I believe what I believe—however it got in my head. The same as you, my beliefs have been shaped by the unique composite of the people I've met, the places I've been, and experiences I've had in my life. Good and bad. And while your life experience may dictate otherwise, I've long believed that Christians living in these modern times are being burdened with thoughts about God and religion that are not truly their own. Helpless to prevent such thoughts from being beaten into their brains by educators, priests, and parents from their first born day, one's true beliefs are often overruled by the jaded views of others. Freethought—the idea of free will—is discouraged by the Catholic Church, even punished. I don't believe that is what God intended. So be it if that makes me a heretic."

So there it was: *Heretic*. The word Sihtric dared not speak to his uncle but hitting at the heart of what was worrying him. That Wido should say the word with such pride was madness.

Over the many years they'd spent together in the monastery at Abbeville, Sihtric had often witnessed Wido's spirited debates with his brother monks over his belief in free will and the detrimental effects of force-feeding faith to the masses. Challenging the Church's obsession with rote rituals and smash-mouth doctrine, Wido argued that what mattered most was the cultivation of a personal relationship with Christ. "One-on-one, talking to God."

While affirming his deep respect for the traditional faith upon which the Church was founded, Wido was adamant that it needed to be achieved in accordance with the truths revealed by one's own unfettered thought. "Christ's teachings are not so much a set of intractable dogmas," Wido loudly proclaimed despite the other monks' fear of a higher power listening outside the cloister door, "but are meant to inspire us to live in a manner consistent with His foremost principles of care and compassion for others."

So also, Sihtric had witnessed a fire-eyed Wido alienate many priests and clerics by speaking his mind about the rampant abuses of the Catholic Church—and of organized religions, in general: Judaism, Islam, Hinduism, Norse-Germanic—none were spared. But Wido's most trenchant criticism was directed at the hierarchy of the Holy Roman Catholic Church. Asserting that their leaders were becoming morally and spiritually bankrupt, Wido did not believe the Church could achieve a clear moral conscience in its present form. "Our riches are rotting our soul!" he railed. Stating that the disillusioned souls at the lowest levels of society were becoming increasingly distrustful of the "haughty, lying, cheating, oversexed hypocrites who claim to be their spiritual guides," Wido warned that an uprising was imminent. Waving a hand in indication of the many bedraggled supplicants floating on the river ahead, he said, "These peasants are neither blind nor stupid," he said. "The inconsistency between what these professional theologians say and do is undermining the Church's credibility. Struggling to keep the faith in a time of Jesus's prophesized return upon the Earth and fearing for their immortal souls, the Church might as well be slipping communion wafers laced with hemlock into their mouths for all the spiritual killing they're doing."

A shiver went up Sihtric's spine at reliving his uncle's latest tirade. *Madness.*

Warned by his brother monks that God was listening and that the fires of Hell awaited him for his constant blasphemy did nothing to deter Wido's outbursts. So even today, he turned to Sihtric sitting quietly beside him on the cart and asked: "Honestly, Sihtric: What do you think Jesus would think of His Church today? Would He think the Catholic Church has been a good shepherd? Feeding His sheep? Or would He see it for what it has become—a self-serving power-monger taking the side of wealth and rank at the expense of His flock?"

As always, Sihtric thought for a moment before responding to Wido's barbed prompt. Reflecting on the Catholic Church from its origins as a small Jewish sect being persecuted for their belief in the One True Lord through its next three hundred years as no more than a minority cult worshiping in the catacombs of Imperial Rome to it becoming the dominant religion in the world, Sihtric could not dismiss the brutality and violence that spearheaded a faith born of the peace and love of the Gentle Jesus of Nazareth. *It is indisputable that the Church has a dark history populated with many bad people,* Sihtric thought as if crafting his opening statement to Wido. *But, still, it is more a matter of opposing points of view: whether the focus should be on the unflattering excesses and manipulation of "fundamental truths" by the Catholic hierarchy, or on the heroic efforts of so many unrecognized priests, nuns, and members of the laity throughout the centuries to put non-believers on the road to eternal salvation.*

Strong in his beliefs, Sihtric was not a man to swat a wasp and invite its sting, but neither would he flee from its angry buzz. For Sihtric was his father's son, and Jaune Faucon had taught him to always think for himself. He would not be spoon-fed "truths" by the pope, Wido, or anyone.

"What say you, holy man?" Wido pressed Sihtric for an answer to his question.

Opening his mouth yet saying nothing as he gave his thoughts a final semblance of order, Sihtric fastened his steely gray-green eyes on his red-faced uncle and, at last, entered into the fray. "Much of what you say, Uncle, cannot be argued. Through the years, the Church has shown itself to be very much human—flawed and susceptible to Satan's influence. But—regardless of whatever deep and dark vales of sin it is occasionally mired in—the truly transcendent, heavenly aspect of the Church must also be acknowledged. The good that the thousands of its faithful servants have done throughout the centuries cannot be denied. Men such as yourself, Uncle Wido—ministering to the poor, the sick, and those who have lost their way. And while perfection cannot be achieved by anyone of the human tribe, I believe that most people are good and strive to live according to the Word of God every day."

Slapping a hand on Sihtric's knee and smiling, Wido wholeheartedly agreed. "You're right, Sihtric. By my harsh criticism of an institution that presumes to judge people without holding itself to the same standard, I do not mean to besmirch the reputation of those who daily toil under a cloud of exploitation by the Church hierarchy."

Raising his voice to a level that made Sihtric cringe in worry of anyone listening to his rant, Wido then stated: "Preying on the fears of the poor and superstitious, these self-proclaimed holiest of the holies will all rot in Hell, as an absolution of their sins can only be achieved through true faith. A faith they do not possess."

Committed to God's work at a young age and choosing to travel the difficult path to priesthood, Sihtric had spent much time contemplating his faith over the years. God's humble servant, in many ways he held a much opposite view from his Uncle Wido. Often hearing Wido refer to the Church as the "Painted Whore of Babylon," he felt his uncle's distrust of the Church hierarchy to be visceral, hostile. And Sihtric wanted to know why. Where did it come from?

"While I cannot agree with your view of the 'irreversible degeneracy of priests and prelates who, while claiming to be cut of the same cloth as Jesus's apostles, are being exposed as impudent, arrogant vagabonds,' Sihtric said, "you are right in saying that the Catholic Church has no business making itself rich and working in concert with secular governments to subjugate the masses. So also, Uncle, I agree that the whole elaborate hierarchy of the Church needs to be scaled down and stop making so much of itself. Crushed under the weight of money and power, the morality of our leaders is failing badly. Still, Uncle Wido, it is not by chance that Catholicism is the foremost creed in the history of humankind. And I am firm in my belief that the Church can overcome its temporal temptations and return to doing God's work. For, even as the institution is human, the faith is divine."

Despite having much more to say on the subject, Wido did not respond, falling strangely silent for a time. Deep in thought. Brooding. And, knowing his uncle as he did, that worried Sihtric just the same as if he was still spouting for all to hear.

Finally, after hours on the road, through the haze of a hot day, Wido and Sihtric could see the tall spires of Rouen's many churches looming ahead. An awe-inspiring sight to see, the many stained glass windows adorning the soaring front facade of the magnificent Rouen Cathedral reflected colors as bright as a rainbow. As the two road-worn monks entered the city from the west side, the newly rebuilt Abbey Church of Saint-Ouen stood in all her majesty about six stades distant. Saint Ouen, a long-ago beloved archbishop of Rouen whose relics were well proven for their healing powers, would have his deserved feast this day; his venerated bones to be celebrated with all the pomp and praise a miracle-worker deserves.

Built near the Seine River, Saint-Ouen was one of the most influential Benedictine monasteries in Normandy, and the saint's remains had been buried on the site of the original church in 864 AD. Only, the same as all over Europe, the church was later sacked by a Viking horde and stripped of all its wealth. In the aftermath of the attack, the saint's bones were rescued from the rubble and reburied nearby. At the behest of the Holy Abbot Nicholas of Normandy, another sanctuary began construction in 1062—sixty-four years ago today. And now, with the work finally completed earlier this year, Saint Ouen's relics would be moved to their new place of worship—inside one of the largest and most beautiful churches in all of Christendom.

Sihtric had never attended a translation ceremony and was excited for the day.

Wido was here because he was a Benedictine monk and ... well ... he had no choice.

Saint Ouen's feast-day, August 24, only grew hotter as the sun climbed to its apex. The air was dry and still. Shouts of frustration ruled the Rouen Road as the long line of horses, carts, and litters arriving for the celebration had ground to a halt almost an hour ago. Much to his credit, Wido had remained calm for a time; but that was over now. "We'll be here all day!"

Sihtric thought to distract Wido with polite conversation.

It wasn't long before he wished he hadn't.

Hardly did Sihtric realize that his rather generic commenting on the beauty of Rouen's churches would invite such vitriol from Wido.

"As splendid as the architecture and décor of these grand cathedrals may be, Sihtric, such opulence has no place in any Church of Christ. Have you forgotten our origins? The poor fishermen of Galilee? To see our venerated leaders weighed down by gold-embroidered palliums, bejeweled diadems, and thick silver crosses around their necks in a decadent celebration of the miraculous healing powers of the scraps of bone to be paraded before us today is maddening.

"Shysters and charlatans, sexually deviant, immoral, piratical popes and priests seizing upon every opportunity to sell eternal salvation to the legions of pious pilgrims. Day and night raking up the coins piled around the thousands of bejeweled reliquaries required to be displayed in every church in the Empire. The Holy Roman lords feeding the voracious beast they created with manna pilfered from the pockets of the poor.

"Today is no different, Sihtric: ruthless greed is the order of the day. True piety is not born of such outrageous shows as you are about to witness, but of an inward belief in God's singular powers to heal both our bodies and souls. Relics are but foolish trifles of the damned. Their worship is idolatry. Their miracles are fake. Perpetrated by money-grubbing shovel-men digging up every inch of the Holy Land, the Catholic Church is a wolf in sheep's clothing. A business like any other. And the middlemen in Rome are getting fatter and fatter and fatter."

Throwing anxious glances all around him, Sihtric's first, last, and best hope was that no one was listening to Wido's blasphemous tirade. His uncle had a dangerous mouth, and he wanted nothing to do with this conversation. While he judged that the three Benedictine monks riding on the cart nearest to him were unwilling to acknowledge that they'd heard Wido, neither could Sihtric ignore their collective gasp at the instant they turned their heads away from him.

Neither was Wido finished with his harangue.

"My beliefs, Sihtric? Do you want to know where my beliefs come from? They come from my heart; my brain; my gut. My conscience. My God. He was there with me under the rock that day. Not a sham relic, but the living God! His presence, His power was overwhelming—getting right up in my face and shining a light on everything that was bad about me—the hate-filled wretch I had become. Pointing His finger down into the Pit of Hell yawned open beneath me, God told me that He takes no pleasure in damning the wicked to eternal pain and suffering. Rather, He wants them to change the way they think and act, turn from their evil ways, break free of their sinful urges, and live in peace.

"With the barbed tentacles of Death wrapped around me, trapped and drowning under that massive rock, I was gasping for air ... only there was none. It was as if I'd been stripped of my flesh and my blackened soul exposed. Begging His forgiveness, God then told me that there was no salvation in simply confessing my sins. That my expressions of sorrow were trite and empty without the conviction to become a better person. That I must live my words. It was brutal. Unsparing. Terrifying. God then said that He loved me. Had always loved me. And if only I would finally take Him into my heart and truly believe in His good and merciful nature, I would be healed of my afflictions. I would inherit eternal life.

"Crushed under God's Rock. Broken. A sinner. I stared into the glorious face of my Lord Savior Jesus Christ and offered up my profound sorrow for the many devilish acts, words, and thoughts that had marred my life, meaning it in my heart like never before. Desperate for another chance to serve Him, to do His will, to lead his many lost children back onto the path of the righteous, such was the otherworldly power that suddenly surged through my body when I, at last, burst through that cold, gray water's surface, I felt born anew. God's love and true remorse: that's what it took for me to stop crawling around in the dark, stand to my feet, and walk into the light. I continue to talk to God every day. Let Him guide me. Carry my burden. All else is just noise."

Listening to his uncle spill his most precious memory as if a diamond from a dirt-filled chest, Wido's desire to bring about a positive change in the world and not just a hope for happiness in the next realm struck Sihtric in such a way as to make him fear for his uncle. *Many men over the years have challenged the Church to purge itself of its evils. Some have been put to death for their audacity. Would his Uncle Wido soon be counted among them?*

Breathless and parched, Wido could feel the mid-day sun burning on his tonsured head as he stared at the Abbey Church in the distance. Complaining that it was "The same distance as an hour ago!" he suddenly stepped down from the cart and, blowing out a hot breath, told Sihtric that he would walk the rest of the way. Cheerfully proclaiming that he loved walking as he hadn't had a chance to do it much in his life, Wido then indicated his rather paunchy mid-section. "The exercise will do me good. Saint-Ouen's is not that far." Grabbing a water-skin off the back of the cart, he added, "We'll meet up in the churchyard. Enjoy your ride." And then he was gone.

When the long line of wagons, carts, and carriages backed up on the Rouen Road finally began moving again, Sihtric smiled, his heart beating in time to his cantering horse with the excitement of soon immersing himself in the sea of good will overflowing the feast-day.

Rumbling past an uncountable number of small tents and lean-tos raised along the sides of the road as local peasants called out everything from fish to fowl to wine to souvenirs of the saints for sale, never in Sihtric's thirty-five years of life had he witnessed such a splendid scene. Invigorated by the raucous activity, his chest swelled with the pride of being a man of the Catholic Church and was humbled to participate in honoring one of the many righteous men and women who'd given their lives to raise the Christian religion to such lofty heights.

Teeming with people of every sort, Sihtric had never seen such a crowd. Handing off his horse and cart to a young boy who pointed out where he could reclaim them later in an adjacent field, Sihtric paid what the boy said was a "transit fee" before joining the flow of pilgrims southward.

When, at last, Sihtric entered into Saint-Ouen's vast front courtyard, being knocked this way and that, he felt as if to be trapped on a field of battle between two clashing armies—one streaming through the north gate, the other through the south.

*It's a good thing it's a saint's day,* Sihtric thought, *because finding Wido amidst this swarm of priests, pilgrims, penitents, and peasants will be a miracle in itself.* Roving his eyes over the crowd for some time, just when Sihtric had resigned himself to the fact that Wido was not in the courtyard at all—his uncle being hardly enthused about the ceremony and probably walked off into some dark shadow to ponder the sins of the Church—Sihtric saw him. Standing with a large group of monks huddled in the shade of the south entry portal surrounded by life-sized statues of the Twelve Apostles but talking to no one, Wido might as well have been alone.

No longer the boy on whose cheeks not a single whisker grew the first time he'd visited Rouen, Sihtric was a full-grown man now—big like his father—and began shouldering his way through the chittering throng with ease. Arriving at Wido's side and clapping a hand on his shoulder, with a short musing look over the bustling courtyard, Sihtric asked, "So, who's that man getting out of that fancy carriage near the main entrance, Uncle Wido? The Pope? The King?"

Wido was not tall like his brother Jaune Faucon or nephew Sihtric, and so couldn't even see the gold-trimmed carriage over the courtyard wall. "What color is his robe?" Wido asked.

"Scarlet with a tall four-cornered hat to match."

"A good bet that's the Cardinal-Bishop sent up from Rome to represent Pope Honorius II. His name is Aymeric de Bourgogne, and he holds the official title of Papal Chancellor."

Aymeric was among the most senior prelates in the Roman Catholic Church, and Wido was forced to reach far back into his memory to conjure a vision of the one time he'd met the man when he was just an ordinary bishop. Forced by Abbot Evreux to follow behind the Frenchman like a handmaiden as they toured the Saint-Riquier monastery grounds many years earlier, what remained most vivid in Wido's memory of the Frenchman was that he was filled with such arrogance as to simultaneously fart it out both his ass and face in great malodorous gusts. Following in the man's foul wake for three long hours lived on in Wido's nose to this day.

Sihtric saw two more men step out of the carriage. One had a quite regal bearing; the other not so much. Greeting Aymeric and roundly embracing each other outside the courtyard's entrance, the men—like the three kings of the Magi—stood talking among themselves in complete ignorance of the adoring throng. Laughing like long-lost brothers as they strolled shoulder-to-shoulder through the garden's ornate entry gates, neither were they quiet in voicing their agitation over so many peasants being let into the courtyard ahead of them. Admonishing the captain of the Church Guard for the travesty—"Move these ragamuffins away from the entrance!"—the Cardinal-Bishop—the so-called "Prince of the Church"—then turned back to his fellow dignitaries with an entirely genuine—and quite practiced—smile etched on his face.

The guards began quickly rounding up the massed peasants and forcing them far back from the church, shoving most of them into the in-pressing crowd bunched outside the courtyard walls. Dragging the stragglers across the cobbled stone courtyard, many of the peasants were rib-bare, ravaged by starvation and sickness. Others had faces festering with bloody pustules. A few had no arms, no legs. Some, barely able to walk, clutched small wooden crosses in mangled, gangrened hands.

Gaining a clear line of site with the peasants now out of his way, Wido tugged on Sihtric's sleeve and informed him that "The tall one in the purple pallium standing next to Aymeric is King Henry I. The second son of William the Conqueror and the ruler of all England and Normandy."

Never before having laid eyes on Henry I, Sihtric was impressed by the new king. Wide at the shoulders and narrow at the waist with a scar slashed across his left cheek, he seemed to be a soldier of the Lord in every way. He had a good feeling about the man. And, what with kings being deposed all over Europe, Sihtric hoped that he might prove to be what he seemed and stay in power long enough to restore the Norman province to its former glory.

"And the other man, Uncle Wido? The pale and unsteady one in the black vestments?"

"That would be our illustrious Archbishop of Rouen, Geoffrey Brito," Wido answered with disgust. "I'm surprised he's even here. I heard he almost drowned in an ocean of blackberry wine last night."

Observing the smiling, if slightly wavering archbishop, Sihtric said, "He seems nice."

"He's a prig," barked Wido. "A self-righteous sodomite. A peddler of flesh and bones. A man who'd collect a coin for every thorn he claims Nicodemas pulled from Jesus's head the day he took Him down from the cross."

Grinding his jaw bones together, Sihtric silently asked God to help Wido keep his mouth shut. This was not the time, not the place.

Slowly progressing toward the south end of Saint-Ouen's transept amidst the new church bell's vibrant ringing, the Cardinal-Bishop's entourage included a flutter of monsignors, priests, prelates, bodyguards and, inexplicably, some cat-eyed young "lady-in-waiting" who was at this very moment pressing her ample bosom to his flowing vestments and whispering in his ear. Stopped often by this old friend, then that, Aymeric was forced to engage in chatty conversations with what seemed like every knight, nobleman, magistrate, prior, baron, and count in Normandy. Fingering the silver and pearl Rosary around his waist as he moved one magnate to the next, he seemed as if to be counting off his dwindling patience one bead at a time.

Anxious that he might miss an opportunity to meet the revered man, Sihtric kept the Cardinal in the corner of his eye as he approached near. Taller than most men, Sihtric stretched himself up to his full height so as to take in the broader view of the thirty thousand people or more descended upon Rouen to witness the carefully choreographed spectacle of the translation ceremony. *What with so many priests and primitives jammed into the same small space*, he thought, *the biggest miracle would be if everyone observed Christ's teachings and got along today.*

*So far, so good*, thought Sihtric, as everyone seemed to be in good humor and excited for the start of the day's blessed event. That is, until he turned his head toward his scowling uncle.

Wido's gritted teeth said it all: he'd had enough of this old monsignor at his elbow trying to make polite conversation with him and wanted the man to move on and bother somebody else. Gleaning a hint of Wido's annoyance from the glare in his eye, the chatty monsignor abruptly stopped talking about the prodigious number of eggs being produced by the chickens at his monastery in Avignon and turned to Sihtric with more than a hint of sarcasm in his voice: "Well, Brother Sihtric—being mentored by Brother Wido, I hear. What good hands you're in." Nodding his head at Wido with a tight-lipped smile, the monsignor then moved on to bore another dim acquaintance with his incredible egg story.

"Who lets such morons into the Church?" Wido growled.

Sihtric shook his head. And then he panicked. For Aymeric, Rome's Chosen One—the scarlet-robed "Prince of the Church"—had somehow snuck up on him and was now standing three feet away. Listening as the Cardinal was finishing his conversation with another starry-eyed servant of the Lord—"Serve fearlessly, acting with courage and a generosity of the heart, even to giving your last breath for the increase of the Christian faith ... and the eternal glory of the Holy Roman Catholic Church." Blessing the young monk, Aymeric de Bourgogne then turned his attention on Sihtric.

And on Wido.

Suffering another loquacious priest's long, boring monologue, Wido was none aware that the be-caped, brocaded Cardinal-Bishop was waiting for him to acknowledge his holy presence and observe the protocols his high office demanded. Tapped hard on his shoulder by Sihtric, a surprised Wido stood unblinking for long moments trying to remember what he was supposed to say to a man elevated to such heights as to touch the face of God. Bowing deeply, almost like a little girl's curtsy, Wido then looked into the Cardinal's dark, burning eyes and, as if forced from his mouth by a brainwashed sense of Catholic etiquette, croaked, "Your Eminence." Again bowing his head, he hung it there for an overlong moment in wonder of how much of this obligatory ass-kissing he could tolerate.

Stone-faced in his obvious disdain for mingling with lowly monks, Aymeric nonetheless extended to Wido his big ruby ring to kiss. In a flash, that same little egg-crazed monsignor Wido had recently rid himself of appeared at the Cardinal's side, leaned in close, and whispered something in the holy man's ear.

Despite Aymeric's best efforts to betray nothing amiss, his already withering look upon Wido turned to outright disgust. Withdrawing his ring from Wido's pursed lips, the Cardinal then nodded his head at the monsignor in an indication that he had, indeed, heard something of this rebellious Brother Wido of Saint-Riquier.

Staring into Wido's face, culling his memories, Aymeric was not long to remember meeting the monk while visiting his now dearly departed friend Evreux at the Abbeville monastery many years ago. Quite a handful, he remembered Evreux telling him. So often speaking in open defiance of Church doctrines as put forth by the Holy Father in Rome, Brother Wido was a blasphemous rogue that Evreux had assured the Cardinal, if given time, could be saved.

Forcing a smile on Sihtric as if he was his best friend in the world, Aymeric then walked off and, with a flick of his hand, indicated that his entourage should follow him into the church. Whispering his intolerance of the concentrated odor wrought by so many filthy pilgrims standing near him, he then said to no one in particular, "It's time."

At a sudden blast of horns from outside the courtyard wall, Wido grabbed hold of Sihtric's arm and started steering him toward the church door. He'd learned his lesson over the years and wasn't going to be caught lagging behind this big, mooing herd and not get a seat.

With some blessed banner or other leading the procession, the Church Guards quickly cleared a lane on the wide, cobbled walkway so that the holiest of the holies might enter the church first. Doing their best to follow behind the Three Wise Men, pushing and shoving their way through the in-pressing crowd, when at last Wido and Sihtric were inside the church—in a quick separation from God's Chosen—a stern-faced prelate directed them to take their places on the monks' benches in the choir area near the crossing of the nave and transept.

Close enough to see the Cardinal-Bishop now standing in the full splendor of his arrogance behind the newly consecrated altar before which Saint Ouen's reliquary would be placed for the ceremony, with all the gaudiness of his brocaded vestments and a golden chalice in his hand, Aymeric proved himself a sight eminently worthy of Wido's undisguised smirk. *Why*, Wido thought, *not even Babylon the Great—the Mother of All Prostitutes and Abominations in the Book of Revelation—could hold a candle to Aymeric this day!*

Sitting beside Wido on the crowded bench, Sihtric easily interpreted the look on his uncle's face. And it made him nervous.

What with hundreds of Rouen's parishioners working for weeks to prepare for the thousands of pilgrims descending on their fair city to celebrate the translation of Saint Ouen's earthly remains to their new resting place, Wido did not doubt that the Herculean effort was worth it to the Church. There was a lot of money to be made. That such megalomaniacal pomp as that about to be witnessed was meant to play on the plight of the poor and sick seeking divine healing and redemption only to be tricked into paying for the privilege of kissing what were often nothing more than cat and cow bones masquerading as holy relics, it was no wonder that Aymeric—having proven himself so adept at fleecing Christ's suppliants the Empire over—was hailed a hero in Rome.

After a long wait for the ceremony to begin, a hush swept through the church as six white-robed priests suddenly appeared in the large arched doorway at the nave's west end, three to each side of a large reliquary they carried in the space between them. Walking in slow, solemn steps down the nave's long, colonnaded center aisle behind a tall, red-robed priest holding forth a large jewel-encrusted crucifix, Wido shuddered as if the church floor was crawling with rats. Passing through the intersection with the north-south transept, the priests then carefully set the reliquary down on the raised white marble floor of the sanctuary before a beaming Aymeric.

Following behind the reliquary, the Saint-Ouen Church abbot accompanied by six black-robed monks pulled a large, gilded pedestal on a small wheeled cart upon which was set a life-sized statue of the saint. Commissioned by the king—and with a prominent plaque attached attesting to the generosity of his gift—after playing its part in the ceremony, the statue would be installed in its permanent place in the ornate, semi-hemispherical apse constructed at the north end of the transept.

With daylight flooding through the uncountable number of clerestory windows set in three tiers along the entire length of the high, vaulted nave, Aymeric watched as the priests positioned the statue on the right side of the sanctuary, bowed before it, and then stepped away.

Flanked by twelve lesser bishops, Aymeric paused as two long files of white-clad oblates carrying white candles then took their places beside each thick, marble column along the nave. Stepping down from behind the high-altar as if floating on air, the Cardinal-Bishop then turned to the congregation and held up the large jewel-studded crucifix that had preceded the reliquary down the aisle. With his voice raised, expectant of the glorious event, Aymeric joyously proclaimed, "By the power of the Living God, Saint Ouen is with us today!"

Glancing back toward the main entrance, Wido was surprised that the midgets, mimes, acrobats, and animals had yet to appear as he knew that the magic act was about to start for real.

Leaning forward on the backless bench, Wido watched as Aymeric, predictably, implored Saint Ouen's powerful intercession to heal the gathered faithful just as he had for more than four hundred years now. Standing over the reliquary with outstretched arms, the Cardinal then made the sign of the cross, knelt beside it, and bowed his head in prayer.

The Church fell stone silent.

Constructed in the popular French *chasse*, or church-shaped, form, the reliquary was larger than most others Wido had seen as it needed to accommodate the great saint's complete skeletal remains; a rarity, as somehow Saint Ouen had avoided the indignity of being pieced out over the years. Saint Stephen, for one—seemingly scattered all over Europe—was not as fortunate. Wido's mind began wandering over the Catholic landscape trying to recall all the places the famously stoned-to-death martyr now resided as he cast a vacant eye on Ouen's coffin-like box. Oblong with straight sides and two sloping roof-like panels meeting at an intricately carved central ridge, the reliquary was covered in pure white ivory enamel in an indication of the sacredness of its contents. Inlaid with extraordinary mosaic images of the saint made of tiny tesserae of gold, white, blue, and red glass set against a vermiculated background, it had a hinged front panel which allowed the reliquary to be opened for public display and worship of the holy bones.

Before proceeding with the ceremony, the Cardinal-Bishop reminded the supplicants that they were expected to offer as much money or valuables as they could afford. Even did he issue a strong warning: "A worsening of your afflictions is within Saint Ouen's power if you are not appropriately generous."

Lifting his head at hearing Aymeric's novel addition to the usual relic rigmarole, Wido stared at the saint's statue and wondered what Saint Ouen would think of Aymeric making such threats in his name. Artfully sculpted, the statue was made to look like living flesh with eyes so astonishingly real as to spark to life at any moment, and the longer Wido studied the saint's face, the more distraught the holy man looked; angry, even, that he should be starring in this sham ceremony that honored little more than his cold, dead bones.

Indeed, God's commandment against worshipping false idols was of little concern to the Catholic Church from the time of its inception. "A holy memento that invites pious devotion and strengthens our wish for the powerful intercession of a venerated saint is not in conflict with the Lord's intent," the Pope once said with a straight face. *So let it be written, so let it be done ...* Wido thought ... *Or not.*

While waiting in the courtyard earlier, Wido had read a detailed account of the saint's many selfless acts and years of dedicated service to God and the Church prepared for his feast-day. *This Saint Ouen seems to have been a very good man,* Wido thought, and so held him blameless for the unfolding farce. *Even in death the man was prodigious: Fifty-three miracles! And most of them cures, at that. Such a man deserves to be celebrated—but not this.*

Incense. Candles. Chanting. Prayer-songs—soft, lyrical, poetic. The Cardinal-Bishop singing the *Te Deum* from the depth of his soul. So selling the illusion of the relic's exceeding holiness, Aymeric had the Catholic tribe on the edge of its collective seat waiting to witness the supernatural power of the dead saint.

Lowering his head and pressing an ear on the reliquary's front panel, after a time, Aymeric declared that he could hear the voice of Jesus Christ Himself communicating through the relic lying within. Many in the congregation began to weep. To wail. To beg the Lord Savior to heal them. And so, at the very moment Aymeric lifted the reliquary's large, enameled lid, the bones of Saint Ouen began to glow for all to see. Faint, at first. Soft. Celestial. But then like on fire.

Astonished at what he was seeing, Sihtric quickly crossed himself as a single white-gold flash suddenly leaped from the bone-box and quickly spread an ethereal light into every corner of the church. In the next moment, Aymeric again raised the crucifix over the relic; a pure blue smoke began wafting up out of the open reliquary, bathing the air with a sweet-smelling fragrance. Indeed, all present took that as a sign that Saint Ouen approved of his translation to this new place and that his miraculous healing spirit was alive and well.

Drowned out by the fanatical moans and cries of the supplicant horde, not another word Aymeric spoke was heard. No matter; Wido knew the spiel and so recited it in his head: *We beseech you, oh benevolent saint, give succor to the sick and oppressed ... Blah, blah, blah. Rhetoric, rhetoric, rhetoric.*

Amidst endless, unbridled shouts of "Hallelujah!" resounding throughout the church, Wido took a quick look around to see what crippled man was now walking and blind woman seeing. Actors all, there were usually at least three or four of them, and they played their parts well. He spied one and smiled, silently mocking those who were so easily duped by such chicanery. "The human mind is a strange and simple thing," he whispered to Sihtric, who had fallen on his knees and was now deep in prayer—doing his best to ignore his uncle. Still, Wido persisted: "Rumor has it, if you need a miracle, John the Baptist's head works much better."

Holding his arms out Christ-like, Aymeric sought to restore the solemnity of the ceremony. So done with the help of the scattered guards, he then genuflected and began casting incense over the saint's flaring remains. "Recalling the

Feast of the Baptism of Our Lord, which follows the Epiphany—by today's sacred happening does God make His mystery clearer to the human mind."

Every head was bowed. Save one.

Sitting as quietly as a June-bug in May, Wido just stared at the relic, but a boxful of bones shrouded in a cloud of blue smoke, trying to figure out how these Catholic wizards worked their magic on them this time. *A good trick, to be sure*, he thought. *But, the same as all the others, a fake.* Diabolical and genius. Contrived by the very hands of Satan; executed by his scarlet-robed hellhounds on Earth to swindle the sick and the superstitious. Manipulating the minds of uneducated innocents while stealing the life-giving manna from their pockets.

The Holy Roman Catholic Church.

Making a mockery of the only relic on this Earth imbued with the divine powers of Jesus.

A relic as precious and immutable as God Himself.

And which can—by its very existence—reduce the Christian empire to dust.

Suffused with such grace as to heal the blind, the deaf, and the crippled.

A relic the world will never see, hold, or disgrace.

Never to be just another skull on a pedestal in the pope's throne room.

Wido would take the knowledge of the relic's deep, dark resting place to his grave.

The Lord God to raise it into the light of day at a time of His own choosing.

Blessing this and kissing that, at last, Aymeric brought the curtain down on his grand performance. With the practiced precision of all great actors, he slowly unrolled a long, browned piece of tattered parchment, and then proceeded to quote from Victricius, a bishop of Rouen seven hundred years ago: "I affirm that in these relics perfect grace and perfect virtue are contained. He who cures lives. He who lives is present in his relics. There is nothing fragile in them. Nothing that decreases. Nothing which can feel the passage of time. They are extraordinary signs of eternity." Pausing for effect before rerolling the scroll and setting it down on the altar, Aymeric then made the sign of the cross in the air and closed with a quote from Saint Augustine's *City of God*: "That we all may testify to faith in which the resurrection to eternal life is proclaimed."

Another solemn pause.

"The peace of the Lord be with you all on this sacred day."

A broad smile.

"Now, let the Feast begin!"

With his eyes bulging out of his head, Wido lifted his look to the cloudless sky through the clerestory windows above. His anger was immense. At length, forcing himself to an outward calm lest his unholy attitude should betray him, bowing his head and closing his eyes, Wido then let the brilliance of the miracle that saved him from the fires of Hell that long-ago day fill his mind.

*At the penultimate moment of my death.*

*The darkness bloomed into pure light. A holy ghost. God.*

*Hollow inside, as a weed withered to its roots, no more to be cured of my affliction than a man can be raised from the dead, I told God that I did not believe He was good.*

*Accused Him of caring nothing about human pain and suffering.*

*And so it was, at that very instant, the ground began to tremble. The Earth broke open beneath me, and I began sinking farther and farther into the pit of the damned. Sore afraid and gasping my last breaths, I then felt someone lifting me from the place I had fallen. Pouring over me an abundance of water from above, covering my body, my head even to my feet, as if washing me, a voice then said to me, "Wido, fear not; but open thine eyes, and see who it is that speaks to thee." And looking, I saw the Lord Jesus. Only, being terrified, I thought it was a phantom. He spoke to me: "I am Jesus, the Son of God. And I love you." Then taking hold of me with His hand—His touch mild and cathartic, easing the torment of my strangled soul—He kissed me, and said: "Peace to thee, Wido." Then raised me up.*

# THE HERETIC
## ROUEN, 24-25 AUGUST 1126

Amidst a gathering of nearly two hundred people in the monastery's vast interior courtyard, a phantom voice suddenly boomed: *"In gaudio prandete, Domini!* In the name of God, eat, enjoy!" So did the service of the food and wine that put the feast in Feast-Day commence.

Fat and slothful, the Archbishop of Rouen, Geoffrey Brito, passably recovered from the wine attack of the previous evening, rubbed his belly with a raucous laugh. "What with that little swim I took in a bottle or three last night, I've hardly had the time to indulge my true passion: eating copious amounts of food. I'm famished!"

Wido, sitting in his assigned seat adjacent to the long "Lord's Table" reserved for the important people—its entire length covered with gold plates, gold goblets, and gold candelabras—again wondered what Jesus would think of His Church today. Swindling the faithful with the promise of miracles, then stuffing their faces with food and swilling wine while the hooded craftsmen are out back secretly gilding another altarpiece for the next money-making show, even more Wido wondered: *What does the Devil think?*

Again, the Latin phantom boomed: *"Ut Sant Audoeni—bibe!* To Saint Ouen—drink!"

And so Wido got his answer.

Cringing through another spontaneous chorus of Hallelujahs filling the air, out of respect for the genuinely good man being honored Wido meant to make no trouble this day. The same as the archbishop, mostly he was here for the food. And it was outstanding in every way: one large silver platter after another filled with the delicacies of the rich being set on the table before him.

Pork, venison, lamb; fish and fowl of every kind; plums, apples, grapes, berries, figs, and nuts; breads and cheeses of all colors and textures—some brought all the way from Rome. Black caviar. And olives. Wido loved olives! Sumptuous almost to the point of being sinful. Wido gorged himself until he thought he would fall over. And—as he was prone to do—washing it down with one too many goblets of wine, his tongue grew loose, and a torrent of words began spilling out of his mouth.

Seated next to him, an alarmed Sihtric grabbed his uncle's arm, only to have Wido shrug him off. It was too late. Sitting within earshot of Wido at the head of the adjacent Lord's Table, the Cardinal-Bishop Aymeric looked up from his gleaming gold plate and, peering over a tall wine ewer, said, "No, please, Brother Sihtric, let your dear uncle speak." Taking another long sip of Burgundy wine from a filigreed gold goblet worthy of comparison to the Holy Grail, the Cardinal was genuinely interested to hear what the notoriously contrary Brother Wido of Saint-Riquier had to say.

While he was badly out of step with the Catholic doctrine of the times, Wido had no intention of confronting the powers of Rome this day. Had no plan to make his argument that salvation was God's alone to grant. That the saints were only human, subject to error and ignorance like the rest of us. That the Church hierarchy was falling badly short of the moral standards expected of them by the faithful. That they were too busy sanctifying saints' remains to notice that Judgement Day was coming. Too busy building grand basilicas to the sky to realize all the good they could do in the world if only they stopped stealing from the poor and started healing their souls.

Wido had no intention of saying any of that; only, he could not stop himself—his words slashing at the stunned holy men like a heathen's sword. Punctuating his rant with an ultimately damning statement that the Roman Catholic Church was a scourge on the world, Wido then stood up from his seat to ensure that all could hear, and said, "True faith is not instilled by any such carnival act as that performed today. This pagan-inspired ruse. Nor by any other mumbo-jumbo devised to manipulate the masses. Demi-gods masquerading as divine messengers and jangling the keys to Heaven's gates so to keep them under the thrall of the Catholic Church. Demanding that the faithful deceive themselves, act contrary to their beliefs, and make them doubt what they know to be true. Distorting what their conscience tells them is right and what is wrong."

Wido's angry voice boomed against the monastery walls.

"True faith is lived in one's heart and soul. Those who listen to us must see in our actions what they hear from our mouths. And, oh, the uncountable number of liars there are among us!"

Turning a cold eye on the stunned Cardinal, neither waiting for his response or hesitating to strike a final blow, Wido said, "Rife with power-mongering and greed, the future of the Church as it stands today is bleak. The Church should be a leader in making the world a better place, not be dragged kicking and screaming behind a fellowship of outcasts such as myself who strive to improve its morality despite the efforts of the Catholic hierarchy to debase it.

"The faithful are suffering. The Church must purge itself of its evils ... or surely perish."

When Wido finished, Aymeric leaned back in his gilded chair and with a look at once ominous and calm addressed the flabbergasted others seated along both sides of the impossibly long Lord's Table: "So ... what else might we talk about? Has anybody been to a good burning lately?" The nervous laughter elicited by the inquiry was welcomed by the stone-faced priests, but not nearly enough to quash the tension now permeating the feast-ground.

Wido looked about the courtyard, only dimly aware of the ashen faces staring at him. He had no illusions that he would not be punished, yet would betray no fear of whatever form it may take. He said what he said, and he meant it. He was in God's hands now.

Settling back onto the bench-seat, Wido reached into the waist-fold of his habit and squeezed his hand around the headless little Jesus he always carried with him. Steeling himself to the repercussions of his blasphemous rant, he was well aware that not a man present—even if he believed Wido spoke the truth, which many secretly did—would be foolish enough to support his view publicly. Even Sihtric—sitting at his side with tears brimming in his eyes—a good and gentle man who believed the Church was corrupt in its ways and had lost sight of the central truths of Jesus's teaching—remained silent.

Pushing his throne-like chair back and standing to the full height of his Gallic ancestors, Aymeric then demanded that Wido rise so that all may gaze upon him in his shame. Despite his restrained tone, the Cardinal's words were charged with an inward, seething anger that pounded in Wido's ears like hammer strikes against his head. "Fancying yourself some kind of iconoclast or revolutionary with your forceful rejection of established Church doctrines, be warned, Brother Wido, any further attempts to promulgate your heretical beliefs will carry grave consequences. God has the power to save the damned if he finds them sufficiently contrite; but, so also, He lets the Devil destroy those accused of the most heinous crimes."

Wido was not by nature such a fool as to offer himself to this red-robed wolf as if just another slab of meat on one of the many silver platters scattering the table before him; but there was a much higher authority than the Cardinal demanding he not be swayed from his struggle to change the course of a Church that had lost its way. So did Wido's voice again boom out over the feast-ground, "For unto the world did God say, 'I am the Lord your God ... and you shall have no other gods before Me. You should not make yourself a graven image'"—Wido pointed a finger at the elaborate statue of Saint Ouen now prominently displayed on its gilt pedestal in the center of the fountain-studded courtyard—"'or any likeness of anything. You shall not bow down to them or serve them.'"

Wido's glare was like an all-out attack on the uneasy crowd. "So too, today—the lot of you—parading through the city just another dust-to-dust relic of no more spiritual worth than a carved image of Fricco, the Norse god of peace and pleasure thus depicted with his huge erect phallus. Oh, how we Christians have far surpassed those heathens praying to their engorged god! Worshipping no different than the pagans we seek to destroy!"

His eyes liquid with fright, Sihtric attempted to drag Wido back down onto the bench amidst a stuttering apology to all those his uncle had offended. "He knows not what—"

Wido drowned him out.

"Relics have no sacred powers and diminish the true Christian faith. So does God demand that this religious fiction—this worship of Saint Silver and Saint Gold—stop lest He casts us all into the fiery lake of Hell!"

Unquailed by the ferocity flashing in Aymeric's eyes, with a look equally venomous, Wido said through his gnashed teeth, "Do as Church laws require, Your Eminence." He spit out the ungodly word as if it burned on his tongue. "But do not expect me to prostrate myself before you and burst into howls for forgiveness. I will be judged by God, not you."

His icy eyes filled with contempt, Aymeric pounded his fist on the table and said, "You will be judged according to the Holy Commandments by which all our souls will be judged. And not only is your eagerness to stand before the heavenly tribunal surprising, it is foolish."

Wido returned Aymeric's penetrating look, cutting him to the bone. "Foolish? Maybe. But it will hasten the day when you must face the same ... A day I suspect will not go well."

Aymeric's smile was dismissive, his words taunting. "Buried headfirst in a hole with only your feet sticking up above the Devil's fiery ground, I assure you, Brother Wido, for delivering sinners like you into God's grateful hands I have no fear of my eternal fate."

"So let it be written," said Wido.

"So let it be done," said Aymeric.

The Cardinal's jaw jutted up in a wide sneer as he prepared to announce the decision of the quickly assembled council of high priests and ecclesiastical authorities gathered in King Henry's centuries-old palace on the hill. Signaling to the guards to bring the blasphemous monk forward, Wido was then dragged across the floor in chains and pushed down on his knees before Aymeric. Now wearing a dirty black sackcloth in place of his monk's habit, he was hushed when he attempted to speak, kicked when he tried it again, and then informed that he had been found guilty of being a "crowd-inciting nuisance." Glaring down at Wido as if from a throne on a mountaintop, Aymeric further stated that the most serious of the twelve articles of accusation brought against him was his rejection of Church authority in favor of direct inspiration from God. Warned that he had cast himself as an enemy of the Pope and faced excommunication or worse, Wido only growled when given a last chance to recant his outrageous beliefs and was summarily convicted of being a heretic.

Jerked to his feet, Wido was then returned under guard to the dungeon far beneath the King's palace.

Over the course of the next hour, Wido's fate was determined according to the laws decreed by the Papal Council in Rome. Although his punishment was much discussed, even argued by a few, the solemn judgment of the pious assemblage was unanimous: Wido would be burned at the stake.

For the desecration of Saint Ouen's memory and the profaning of his feast-day, Aymeric and the assembled holy men assured themselves that Brother Wido's execution was just. Even did the Archbishop of Rouen imagine the saint's hearty endorsement of the punishment: "From his high seat in Heaven, Saint Ouen will enjoy the full benefit of his beatitude with an unobstructed view of the sinner's fiery end."

Wido's execution fell to the secular authority in Normandy, King Henry I—like his father William, a good Christian man. Upon Sihtric's impassioned plea, the nonplussed Henry had even visited Wido in his cell, again strongly urging him to recant his heretical words. So did Wido answer the king in an unwavering voice: "I cannot and will not recant a word of it, for it is all true. I cannot go against my conscience. The Church must change, Your Grace. The perpetration of these egregious acts in the name of Jesus is rampant, and I fear Satan is reaping the benefit of our sins. Victory is within his grasp; Hell on Earth is real—for his minions are all here with us today."

Unlike his Uncle Wido, Sihtric believed that all worldly events were brought into being by God's explicit will and that He had foreknowledge of all activity within the mortal realm. Predestination. The Church preached it; so Sihtric believed it.

Wido, however, argued that foreknowledge did not equal predestination and that God allowed each of us to choose our path as determined by our own conscious decisions about right and wrong. That he had in the aftermath of his miraculous healing abandoned any notion of a jealous, judgmental, vindictive God that only exists to be worshipped, Wido came to believe that God granted us the ability to think and act freely during our short time on Earth. That He has a plan for each of us but does not determine how we ultimately fulfill our purpose in life.

So also, Wido argued that it was sinful not to challenge contradictory pronouncements and acts declared in the name of God that in no way reflect the teachings of Jesus, and further believed that the blind acceptance of others' beliefs was impossible for a fully functioning brain. "God wants us to listen to Him; to learn; and then think for ourselves."

While never revealing to Sihtric the most life-altering details of his face-to-face encounter with the living Christ during his miraculous rebirth under God's Rock, Wido claimed to be an eyewitness to the immense power of God and was, in fact, living proof that God had endowed humanity with free will and would reward or punish them according to their choice of good or evil.

"What is it the Bible says, Sihtric—the Book of James?" Wido then quoted: "'You don't know what will happen tomorrow. You are mist that is seen for a moment then disappears. This is not a threat against non-believers. But a warning.' I don't know what tomorrow holds, Sihtric; nor does it matter. For, I have found my reason for living and will do as I must."

Sihtric, in fact, agreed with many of his uncle's "outrageous beliefs," and considered it not so farfetched that men such as Wido in their struggle might lead us out of the growing darkness and make the world a better place for the human tribe. Indeed, Sihtric believed that Wido was one of God's Chosen—only he had not the courage to say so.

Slumped on the cold stone floor outside Wido's iron-barred cell, King Henry had allowed Sihtric to remain with Wido during his last hour on Earth. It passed much too fast.

With a sudden jangle of keys, the dungeon's heavy outer door flew open, and four heavily armed guards entered the dark space. Shoving Sihtric aside, one of them smashed a large wooden mallet on the door's big iron latch and then pushed the door open. Amidst the resounding clang of its iron bars against the cell's stone wall, two guards then seized Wido by the back of his tattered sackcloth and jerked him onto his shackled feet. Staring into his uncle's expressionless face with tears in his eyes as the guards dragged Wido past him, Sihtric said in a voice much weakened by the violent emotions wracking his body, "God be with you, Uncle."

With his eyes radiating the glow of an extraordinary love of his nephew and the hope of his glorious future as a leader of men, Wido responded softly, "And with you, Sihtric."

Prodded by the impatient Cardinal Aymeric, a young Benedictine priest stepped out of the murmuring crowd and walked toward Wido with an open Bible in his hand.

Tied to a tall wood post in a field adjacent to the Abbey Church of Saint-Ouen with a tangled mass of branches and twigs piled around him, Wido growled at the trembling man, "Come no closer. Have you not been listening?" Wido fastened his look on Aymeric, standing front and center of the anxious crowd. "I need no priest to absolve me of my sins. God is here with me. I need not beg His mercy."

Unsure of what to do, dreading the rough edge of a dead man's tongue, with a glance back at the grim-faced Cardinal, the priest quickly made the sign of the cross, and then backed away from Wido.

Regarding the tightly bound heretic with a bitter eye, Aymeric then signaled for the torches to be brought forward. Staring into Wido's impossibly serene face, Aymeric would allow no feelings of admiration to crease his momently more thoughtful and grave countenance, and at an emphatic drop of his hand the pyre was lit.

Standing at the front of the now silent crowd, a colorless smear of stunned monks was soon turned bright orange by the burgeoning flames. Some seemed confused, others anguished, while all feared what this senseless execution of one of their brothers would lead to in the future.

Sihtric, tucked into the second rank of monks arced about the burning pyre, could watch no longer. With the fire's heat blurring his eyes and hot tears rolling down his cheeks, grabbing his face, he then dropped his head on his chest with the shame of swallowing his tongue this day.

Drawing strength from the headless little Jesus he held in his hand as the wood shifted and crackled and the flames exploded around him, with a bath of sweat dripping from his face and limbs, Wido called out to Sihtric in a voice strong and steady, "God has put the strength in you to do His work, Sihtric. To lead his people. To change the world. The warriors' blood of your father and grandfather is in your veins and the unshakeable faith of your mother and grandmother is in your heart. Have no fear of pursuing what is right and good. For the Kingdom of Heaven awaits you." With the lines on his face unchanged as the fire climbed on his flesh—his legs, arms, and chest—denying his excruciating pain, Wido locked his eyes on Sihtric's now upturned face and spoke his last words: "The battle will be fierce, Sihtric. But only to stay strong in your faith, you will be victorious ... and then be raised by the powerful hand of God to your hard-earned place in Paradise."

Turning his gaze upward, a single, white-gold ray of sunshine streaked through a fast-darkening sky to brighten Wido's face. Clutching the crucified

Jesus in his hand, his lips were moving even as his eyes slowly closed. Mouthing a prayer. Talking to God.

*Late have I loved Thee, O, Lord;*
*And behold,*
*Thou didst gleam and glow, and dispel my blindness.*
*Thou didst touch me and heal me with Thy merciful grace.*
*Late have I loved Thee, O, Lord;*
*Thy beauty is ever old and ever new.*
*Take me into Thy kingdom, Lord. Take me home.*

A low, deep rumble was heard in the sky. The air turned cold and a heavy wind swept across the ground. The pyre's blue-bronze flames then flashed high into the overarching heaven, consuming Wido head to toe. A slow, spiraling wreath of bright white vapor rose on the air.

And Wido was gone.

When the fire finally died down, Wido's burned remains were shoveled into a bucket, carried across the field, and unceremoniously dumped into the nearby Seine River. Sihtric—hollow-eyed and his face raked in hard lines of sorrow—then collected the rest of Wido's ashes and a few small pieces of charred bone from the foot of the smoldering pyre. With a steadiness of purpose, careful and reverent, Sihtric then placed his uncle's mortal remains in an unadorned apothecary jar and, after scratching Wido's name on it with a sharp stone, carried his uncle's remains back to his boyhood home.

Buried on the white-chalk cliff overlooking God's Rock—the place where Wido was born, played, and dreamed of a joyous life—where he first talked to God and felt His loving embrace—a place he never wanted to leave—and never would again—returned to the dirt—no tomb, nor a cross to mark the spot—a relic more sacred to Sihtric than any saint or Biblical martyr would ever be—Wido was at peace. At last.

The headless little Jesus Sihtric kept for himself, determined to keep the spirit of a truly remarkable man alive. Deformed by the heat of the fire, Sihtric would take the crucified Lord into his hand every morning and pray over it, drawing from it the same strength and courage to drive forth the reforms his Uncle Wido fought and died for. To lead a wayward Church back onto a path of righteousness. Rediscover its faith. Its morality. And make the world a better place.

# THE HOLY SPIRIT

## *Sunset*

And so it was, even in his old age, Monseigneur Sihtric—the beloved Abbot of the monastery at Saint Riquier—would sit on top of the cliff and think about all the wonderful people who had helped raise his spirit to such heights of love and compassion that he might live his life as lightly as a feather held aloft by a warm summer breeze. He would think about his mother and his father. His grandmother and grandfather—people he barely knew but talked to every day. But, most of all, he would think of his Uncle Wido—about their long, inspiring walks on the beach together; their spirited debates about human nature, free will, morality, and truth versus illusion.

A man unbounded in his joyful glorying of God for His unconditional love and forgiveness of even the most wretched sinner, Brother Wido—formerly known as "The Lame"—was entirely reborn at the moment God restored his legs and helped him to save himself from the very Pit of Hell. The Lord-Savior's faithful servant for all the rest of his days, Wido died with no doubt that his soul would be ascending into the kingdom of a God unique unto Himself. And that the mother he longed to see again, to love again, to forgive, would be there.

As he sat atop the cliff drawing pictures of the sea, a smiling Sihtric would often imagine seeing the old monk standing knee-deep in the Channel water, staring up at the sky. The towering chalk wall hard-cleaved. God's Rock now far off, lapped by the surf, ringed by a halo of light on even the darkest of nights. The Earth in all its magnificence. Blue sky. Gilt-clouds. The horizon veiled in soft mauve. A place of immortals. A cathedral without walls. Paradise. A prayer-house for all.

# END

# HISTORICAL FIGURES

(In order of mention)

Styrkar (Kvendulfsson is a fictitious surname as real surname is unknown)
Norwegian King Harald Sigurdsson's marshal at the Battle of Stamford Bridge.

Only known historical reference is included in Snorre Sturlason's *Heimskringla Vol. III*

Harald Sigurdsson (better known as Harald Hardrada or "hard ruler").
King of Norway from 1046 until his death at Stamford Bridge on 25 September 1066.

Often referred to as the last great Viking king.

In his earlier years, he was a mercenary fighter for King Jaroslav of Kiev, before arriving in Constantinople in 1034, where he rose to become commander of the Varangian Guard.

Count Guy of Ponthieu (corresponds to an area within modern-day Picardy region of France)
Succeeded his brother Enguerrand as Count of Ponthieu, a Norman vassal state, in 1053.

The Ponthievin-Norman alliance had been earlier secured by Enguerrand's marriage to Duke William's sister, Adelaide. Guy died in 1101.

William the Conqueror (formerly known as William the Bastard; Duke William of Normandy)

A descendent of the Norseman Rollo, the first ruler of Normandy, he was the illegitimate son of Duke Robert I of Normandy, and inherited his father's title upon his death in 1035.

Crowned King of England after his victory at the Battle of Hastings in 1066; died 1089.

Harold Godwinson

Earl of Wessex, he was named heir to the English throne by King Edward the Confessor on his deathbed in 1065 despite an earlier promise of the same to William of Normandy.

The last Anglo-Saxon king of England; killed at the Battle of Hastings, 14 October 1066.

Emperor Michael IV (the Paphlagonian—a Roman province on the south coast of the Black Sea)

Byzantine Emperor from 1034 until his death in 1041.

Rumored to have assisted the Empress Zoe, his lover, in poisoning her husband, the reigning Emperor Romanos III in 1034 before immediately marrying her and being named joint ruler of the empire. Believed to have been poisoned to death by Zoe in 1041.

Empress Zoe (Porphyrogenita—Greek: "Born in the purple"—signifying her inherited royalty)

Byzantine Empress from 1028 until her death in 1050 at age 72.

Ruled alongside four emperors and is rumored to have poisoned to death the first two: Romanos III in 1034 and Michael IV in 1041; she also ordered the blinding and exile of Michael V after he attempted to depose her in 1042. Married Constantine IX in 1042.

Halldor Snorrason (an ancestor of Snorre Sturlason, poet and author of *The Heimskringla* sagas)

An Icelander, he served in Constantinople's Varangian Guard with Harald Sigurdsson; he was named Harald's Naval Commander after he became the King of Norway in 1046.

Over the years, his friendship with Harald deteriorated, culminating in his threat to kill the king over money owed; he was paid, returned to Iceland, and they never met again.

Emperor Michael V (Calaphates—Greek: "the Caulker", which was his father's occupation)

The eighteen-year-old nephew of Emperor Michael IV and adopted son of Empress Zoe, he was named co-ruler of the Byzantine Empire upon his uncle's death in 1041. Four months later, he exiled Zoe to a convent; a popular uprising ensued and she was quickly restored to the throne. Publicly blinded and castrated, Michael V died in exile in 1042.

William d'Arques

Count of Talou and Arques (near present day Dieppe, France); Duke William's uncle

Challenged young William's right to assume his father's ducal seat due to his illegitimate birth, believing he had the foremost claim to the title. He denounced all oaths of allegiance in 1049, rebelled in 1053, was defeated, and forever banished from Normandy.

Richard de Heugleville (formerly known as St. Valery-en-Caux; located on the Normandy coast)

Established a borough on the Scie River, which he named Auffay. In 1053, he and many members of his family helped defeat Duke William's rebellious uncle, William d'Arques.

Geoffrey and Hugh de Morimont

Sons of Turketil de Neuf-Marche, who was murdered while protecting the child Duke William in 1042. The brothers were killed in a battle against soldiers fighting for the rebellious William d'Arques near Morimont in 1047.

Pope Urban II (original name Odo of Châtillon-sur Marne)
Head of the Roman Catholic Church in Rome from 1088 until his death in 1099.

In 1095, at the Council of Clermont (France), he gave a speech that launched the Crusades, calling on all Christians in Europe to reclaim the Holy Land from the Muslims.

Count Emicho of Leiningen
The leader of the 1096 Rhineland massacres (also referred to as the "Peasant Crusade")

Just prior to the First Crusade, driven by a belief that both Jews and Muslims were agents of the devil and had to be destroyed or converted to Christianity for the earth to reach the prophesized end of days, he spearheaded a series of attacks and mass murders of Jews.

Saint Ouen (Canonized upon his death around 684 AD)
Archbishop of Rouen, elected in 639 AD

As paganism was still prevalent in many barbarian districts of the Diocese of Rouen, he caused the worship of false gods to cease and founded numerous monasteries. Despite his views, he collected many relics for display in Rouen during a pilgrimage to Rome in 675.

Aymeric de Bourgogne (Roman Catholic Cardinal-Bishop)
As Papal Chancellor he ensured (through many bribes and promises) that his preferred candidate would be installed as the new pope after Pope Callixtus II died in 1124. In a struggle between two powerful political factions in Rome, the unanimously elected Pierleoni family's candidate, was wounded in an attack arranged by Aymeric, forced to abdicate, and the Frangipani candidate was proclaimed Pope Honorius II.

King Henry I (byname Henry Beauclerc—French: "Good Scholar")

King of England (enthroned 1100) and Ruler of Normandy (1106) until his death in 1135.

Assumed the English throne after his brother, King William II, died in a hunting accident.

A harsh yet fair ruler, his preference for diplomacy over the risks of the battlefield was belied by his ardent defense of his Anglo-Norman state against rebellion and invasion.

Geoffrey Brito

Archbishop of Rouen from 1111 until his death in 1128.

Selected by King Henry I to succeed William Bonne-Ame and was instrumental in arranging the marriage of Henry's daughter and heiress Matilda to Geoffrey of Anjou.

# GLOSSARY

*A la folletoere*—(French) scatterbrained

*Aett*—(Norse) extended family, clan

*Amulet*—an object worn to ward off evil and harm

*Anthropomorphic*—non-human with human traits

*Apse*—a semicircular, often vaulted recess in a church

*Arm-rings*—an upper arm bangle often worn by men

*Berserker*—a warrior of unnatural strength and fury

*Bnefatafl*—(Norse) board game similar to chess

*Bowshot*—distance traversed by a bow-shot arrow

*Brisee*—(French) a tracking marker used when hunting

*Brocade*—a rich silk fabric woven with raised patterns

*Bulgar*—S. Balkan ancestors of modern Bulgarians

*Byrnie*—a typically sleeveless coat of chainmail

*Capon*—slang for a castrated young male servant

*Chainmail*—metal rings linked to form armored mesh

*Chalk*—limestone formed from pulverized sea life

*Chamberlain*—manages affairs of a royal household

*Chasse*—(French) a reliquary box with "gable" sides

*Chien baut*—(French) lead hunting dog

*Clinker-built*—ship hull featuring overlapping planks

*Cog*—Clinker-built cargo ship with a single square sail

*Comital*—of or relating to a count or earl

*Conrois*—(French) a fighting unit of 10-20 horsemen

*Cooper*—maker of wooden casks, barrels, and buckets

*Coxcomb*—a vain, pretentious, and foolish man; a fop

*Croise*—(French) the sign or form of the Christian cross

*Dervish*—one that exhibits abundant, frenzied energy

*Destrier*—(French) a powerful medieval era warhorse

*Diaphanous*—having a delicate, translucent quality

*Dinar*—Islamic gold coin of the medieval era

*Drachma*—a silver coin in ancient Greece

*Dromon*—a galley-type Byzantine warship

*Ell*—about the length of the elbow to fingertips

*Eunuch*—a castrated man; often a chamberlain

*Farrier*—a specialist in equine hoof care

*Fates*—3 goddesses who decide one's destiny

*Fealty*—a vassal's sworn loyalty to a lord

*Filigree*—intricate raised gold and silver tracery

*Folleis*—silver-coated bronze coin of little value

*Fortnight*—a fourteen-day period of time

*Gauntlets*—armored gloves; also protect wrists

*Greaves*—felt-padded, strap-on lower-leg armor

*Gunwale*—the topmost plank of a ship's hull

*Gyrouagi*—(French) an itinerant, beggar monk

*Halyard*—rope for raising/lowering a ship's sail

*Hauberk*—a long-sleeved chainmail mesh shirt

*Headland*—a high, often steep coastal landform

*Hide*—plot of land sufficient to support a family

*Hilt*—a sword handle, incl. guard and pommel

*Hogging*—boat keel bending upward amidships

*Housecarle*—a member of the king's bodyguard

*Iconoclast*—a person who attacks sacred beliefs

*Immutable*—cannot be changed

*Jongleur*—(French) an itinerant entertainer

*Kersche*—(German) a cloth head covering

*Kortinarioi*—tent guards for Byzantine royalty

*Magnate*—a man of great wealth and power

*Marl*—a carbonate-rich, fresh-water mudstone

*Masthead*—the uppermost part of a ship's mast

*Mead*—a wine made from fermented honey

*Megalomaniacal*—obsessed with one's own power mesh

*Miliaresia*—(Greek) a common Byzantine silver coin

*Monsignor*—an honorific Roman Catholic title

*Motte*—(French) a mound serving as a site for a castle

*Nave*—the large, central congregant part of a church

*Nomismata*—(Greek) Byzantine word for "money"

*Norns*—three virgin goddesses who care for Yggdrasil

*Oblate*—a layperson dedicated to religious life

*Par force*—(French) horsemen hunting with hounds

*Pecheneg*—semi-nomadic Turkic tribe in Central Asia

*Pike*—a long thrusting spear used for close-in fighting

*Pommel*—the nob on the hilt of a sword or dagger

*Prelate*—a high-ranking member of the clergy

*Quillons*—the transverse cross-guard on a sword

*Ragnarok*—(Norse) "Doom of the Gods"; world's end

*Rascal*—young, hungry, often destructive animals

*Reliquary*—a container which contains holy relics

*Rood*—a large crucifix displayed in medieval churches

*Rowing-spell*—distance covered before pausing to rest

*Ruet*—small wind instrument akin to a modern kazoo

*Runic Symbols*—Used to communicate with the gods

*Samite*—a heavy silk fabric with twill-type weaving

*Saracen*—referred to any person of the Islamic religion

*Saxons*—Germanic settlers of ancient England

*Scimitar*—a curved, single-edge saber used by Turks

*Scythian*—a nomadic people originally of Iranian stock

*Seljuk Turks*—ruled the ancient Middle East

*Shade*—an evanescent, disembodied spirit

*Sheerstrake*—the topmost plank of a ship's hull

*Shingle*—a mass of small rounded pebbles

*Shoat*—a young, newly weaned pig

*Skald*—singers and tellers of ancient Norse tales

*Slag*—glass-like by-product of raw, smelted ore

*Sprite*—an elfish person, pixie, or fairy

*Strake*—a hull plank running from stem to stern

*Te Deum*—Latin hymn ascribed to St. Ambrose

*Tesserae*—one of many small tiles in a mosaic

*Transept*—the area crosswise to a church nave

*Translatio*—a ceremony to relocate holy relics

*Tunic*—a loose thigh- or knee-length garment

*Tzakones*—(Greek) Byzantine border guards

*Valhalla*—Odin's grand heroes' hall in Asgard

*Valkyries*—carry the Chosen Slain to Valhalla

*Varangian*—Norse (Rus) mercenary fighters

*Varlet des chiens*—(French) servant to the dogs

*Vassal*—a person who is subordinate to another

*Venerated*—to regard with reverential respect

*Vermiculated*—carved with sinuous, wavy lines

*Vestments*—liturgical garments worn by priests

*Vicomte*—a local administrator of ducal affairs

*Vigrid*—the mythical battlefield of Ragnarok

*Villein*—a peasant legally tied to a landed lord

Wall-*eyed*—an eye with a streaked white iris

*Wattle & Daub*—woven twigs covered in mud

*Winnock*—a Scots word for "window"